RAINBOWS

Katherine Stone

RAINBOWS

WHEELER
PUBLISHING, INC.
ROCKLAND, MA

★ AN AMERICAN COMPANY ★

Published in Large Print by arrangement with
Kensington Publishing Corp. in the United States and Canada.

Wheeler Large Print Book Series.

Set in 16 pt. Plantin.

Library of Congress Cataloging-in-Publication Data

Stone, Katherine, 1949–
    Rainbows / Katherine Stone.
       p. (large print) cm.—(Wheeler large print book series)
    ISBN 1-56895-469-7 (hardcover)
    1. Large type books.
  I. Title. II. Series.
  [PS3569.T64134.R33 1997]
  813'.54—dc21
                                 97-023390
                                       CIP

Prologue

The reporters clustered outside the main entrance of Memorial Hospital were an unusual blend—political commentators from Washington's elite press corps and entertainment editors from the major networks. Politically speaking, it was a "quiet" time in the nation's capital. The House, the Senate, and the Court were in recess for the holidays, and the President and First Lady were engaged in the charity galas of the Christmas season. But it wasn't the seasonal slowdown in political news that lured the suddenly-not-busy political reporters into a domain that should rightfully have fallen to their show business colleagues. They came because the story was Alexandra Taylor, and in this town of power, influence, and celebrity, Alexa was celebrated.

Alexa was an actress, not a Senator or Congresswoman. She held no elected political office in a city where politics was all. And yet, in a way, Alexa *had* been chosen by the people— by the millions of viewers whose love affair with her had made *Pennsylvania Avenue* the top-rated dramatic series for the past five years. Although some of Washington's political journalists felt obligated to make the occasional derisive remark about the sizzling prime-time drama of passion, power, and destiny in the nation's capital, none found fault with the show's talented and enchanting star. The press liked Alexa, just as her public did, and the somber faces of the reporters assembled in front of Memorial Hospital reflected genuine unscripted concern.

"We've been here all night, Joan, *hoping* for good news." Good Morning America's entertainment correspondent's wind-chilled and fatigued face provided vivid testimony to the all-night vigil, and her grim expression gave advance warning that the news wasn't good. "A hospital spokesperson met with us ten minutes ago and simply reiterated what we have known since shortly after midnight. Alexa Taylor is in critical condition. She survived last evening's emergency surgery for internal bleeding but she remains in a coma."

"Have you learned any details of the accident?" the show's hostess, Joan Lunden, queried from the studio in New York.

"The police have not yet issued an official statement, but we do have a few facts. Late yesterday afternoon, moments after receiving a mysterious phone call, Alexa left her secluded cottage overlooking Chesapeake Bay and began the drive down the winding road from the cottage to the Interstate. The road is a tortuous series of hairpin turns—a treacherous stretch that is, of course, very familiar to Alexa—and, although it is snowing now, at the time of her accident the roads were clear and dry. Despite her familiarity with the road and the safe driving conditions, however, for some reason Alexa failed to make one of the turns and her car plummeted over the cliff and exploded into flames on the beach below. Miraculously, she was thrown, or managed to jump, before the car became airborne."

"You said 'For some reason.' Do you have any idea what the reason was?"

"At this point there is only speculation. Judging from the distance travelled in air before landing on the beach below, the car must have been going very fast as it left the cliff. And yet, there were no skid marks, nothing to indicate that the brakes had been applied at all."

"Which means?"

"Which *seems* to mean that the brakes failed. An accidental mechanical failure . . . or an intentional one."

"The police suspect foul play?"

"As I said, the police have made no official statement. It is generally believed that the car has been so badly damaged that evidence of tampering would be impossible to detect."

"And what about the phone call?"

"Again, there is no information except that apparently it was immediately after receiving the call that Alexa began her ill-fated drive."

"So it is possible that she was upset—or distracted—by the call and as a result was driving too fast and lost control of the car?"

"Very possible. In fact, most likely. But, Joan, as you know in this town rumors travel faster than facts and a simple yet tragic accident can quickly become steeped in mystery and intrigue."

"Yes. Well. Thank you for this update. We'll be checking back with you later in the show, hoping for some positive word about Alexa's condition."

"I hope so. Oh! Wait a minute. I think I see Alexa's sister Catherine. The world-renowned concert pianist has been inside the hospital throughout the night, but now . . . Yes, this definitely is Catherine. And, oh, this is interesting, she is with Senator Robert McAllister. I wasn't aware of a connection between either Taylor sister and the dashing Senator from Virginia, but, like many Senators, he has probably served as a consultant for *Pennsylvania Avenue*. I don't know if Catherine will speak to the press, but perhaps the Senator will."

As Catherine grasped the sleeve of his overcoat, Robert instinctively placed his strong hand over her delicate and trembling one. He squinted beyond the bright glare of the television cameras to the limousine that was waiting in the distance to take them to the airport to meet her parents' plane. Between the hospital steps and the sanctuary of the limousine stood a wall of reporters. The wall parted, a narrow tunnel to enable Robert and Catherine to pass, but from both sides, in strident stereo, came the painful, unanswerable questions . . .

"Catherine, how is Alexa? Senator, can you tell us?"

"How significant are the injuries? Is she still in a coma? Do the doctors think she'll recover?"

"Ms. Taylor! We understand that you were in the cottage with your sister when the phone call came. Who called? What was the message? Is that the reason Alexa rushed out? Do the police suspect foul play?"

"The word from the doctors is that Alexa had internal bleeding and suffered traumatic shock to her kidneys. Have you donated blood for Alexa, Catherine? Would you be willing to donate a kidney if your sister's kidneys don't recover from the shock?"

Robert had warned Catherine that there would be a barrage of questions and had advised her to offer no answers during their journey to the limousine. Catherine knew what questions the reporters would ask—the same unanswerable questions that had tormented her all night. The same questions, except for that last one.

Would you be willing to donate?

Catherine's heart had a swift and confident answer to that question, "Yes, of course!" But with that answer came a silent anguished scream of pain. If Alexa needed my blood, my kidney, my heart, I would so willingly give it, but . . .

But what I could give would be no better than the gift of a stranger. Because Alexa, whom I love as my own sister, is not really my sister at all . . .

RAINBOWS

Part One

Chapter I

Kansas City, Kansas . . . May 1968

"My husband will be here soon," Jane Taylor told the pink-coated volunteer who had escorted her from her hospital room to the lobby. "I'll wait right here, in this unnecessary-but-hospital-policy wheelchair until he arrives. You needn't wait with me, really, I'll be perfectly fine."

The truth was that Alexander would *not* be arriving any moment. Jane hadn't even called to tell him that she had been discharged. And the truth was, too, that as soon as the volunteer disappeared Jane *was* going to get out of the wheelchair.

Jane didn't feel too guilty about lying. They— the doctors, nurses, and psychologists—had, after all, been lying to her. Their lies, like Jane's, were well-intentioned: what was best for her.

"We're going to transfer you to the General Medical Ward," the doctors had told her when she was well enough to leave the ICU.

The General Medical Ward—not Obstetrics— very far away from the new molters whose babies had survived. As if seeing *their* joy would make *her* grief even greater! Jane knew that wouldn't happen, of course; her grief could not be greater than it already was. How astonishing to

3

remember that only seven days ago her life had been pure joy.

Only seven days ago, on a glorious spring morning, Jane and Alexa and Alexander had driven from their home in rural Topeka to Kansas City, where Jane's exquisite pottery was to be displayed and sold at the prestigious Art Fair. It was their final adventure as a family of just three. Soon, very soon, they would joyfully welcome a new life into their circle of love. How excitedly six-year-old Alexa had chattered about *her* new baby, predicting, with her golden confidence, "A baby sister!"

The weeks of preparation for the fair had been easy for Jane, a creative pleasure not a stress; and Alexander, with Alexa's help, had loaded the van as a very healthy seven-months-pregnant Jane simply watched, laughing lovingly at the unnecessary pampering from her husband and daughter. There had been no stress, only joy and laughter, but still, inexplicably and horribly, just as they reached the outskirts of Kansas City, Jane went into labor. It began as a tearing pain and was followed quickly by a hot gush of blood.

Alexander sped to the nearest Emergency Room, and the doctors swiftly separated Jane from the baby that had been so safe inside her. Then there was an even greater separation, a permanent one, as Jane was taken by ambulance to the Intensive Care Unit at the Medical Center and her infant daughter was rushed, sirens blaring, to the Neonatal ICU at the Children's Hospital ten miles away.

Mother and infant received the best that

4

medical science had to offer, but only Jane benefited. The daughter she was never to see died after five valiant days, and after Jane survived her own precarious battle with death she was transferred from the ICU to the General Medical Ward. The General Medical Ward, not Obstetrics, not Postpartum, just a somber place of sickness many slick linoleum corridors away from joyous new mothers and their babies.

This is best, Jane was told by the doctors, nurses, and staff psychologists. She was never told for whom it was best. For her? Or for the other mothers who might be made uncomfortable by her presence?

But the medical professionals were wrong! She should have been with the other mothers. She was a mother after all, Alexa's mother and the mother of the baby girl who had died. She should have been among the mothers, and she should have been allowed to visit the newborn nursery.

That was where Jane was going now, to see the babies in the nursery. She believed that seeing the babies would somehow give her the strength she needed to tell her golden-haired daughter about the baby sister who had died. Today, gently and together, Jane and Alexander would tell their precious Alexa the truth. And tomorrow, they would return to Topeka and tell the friends— who expected triumphant news of talented Jane's success at the Art Fair—the sad reality of their week in Kansas City.

When Jane reached the newborn nursery and gazed through the plate glass window at the infants cradled in pink and blue bassinets, she

5

knew instantly that she had been right to come here. It helped to see the babies. Even though she had lost her baby and could have no more, seeing these tiny new lives filled Jane with hope.

A smile crossed Jane's lovely face, the first smile in a week, the gentle loving smile of a mother . . .

As Isabelle tenderly kissed the silky black hair of her infant daughter, her blue eyes swept down the corridor. Ahead lay the newborn nursery and behind, as always, lurked one of the men sent by Jean-Luc to follow her. Jean-Luc's men had been with her, constant menacing shadows, for over five months, throughout her pregnancy and still. They were less hidden now, and even more watchful, because now her baby had been born.

Isabelle lived in constant fear that the men would receive a lethal instruction from the madman who had hired them, an order to simply put an end to the innocent little life that threatened him so. That order would come one day, but for now Jean-Luc seemed content to torment her, a beast playing with its prey, confident of his complete control. She was trapped, he was telling her. There was no escape. Did she not understand?

Of course Isabelle understood. But she knew, too, that if she kept moving, as if ever hopeful that one day she would escape the men who shadowed her, Jean-Luc would keep his henchmen at a distance. As long as Jean-Luc believed it was Isabelle's naive and desperate hope for escape that compelled her restless journey, he would

6

enjoy this tortured game of hide-and-seek. And that would give her more time . . .

Time to find the woman to whom she could entrust her precious daughter. In her months of searching, before the baby's birth and after, Isabelle had spoken to so many women—brief conversations under the watchful eyes of Jean-Luc's sinister shadows—and still her search continued. The woman existed, *she had to,* and when Isabelle found her she would know by a knowledge of the heart that was as deep and compelling and confident as the instinct that gave her the tireless energy to search until she found a safe and loving home for her baby.

For months Isabelle had roamed from city to city, always moving, always searching. And now her random yet purposeful wandering had brought her here, at this precise moment, to the nursery where a blond-haired woman with tear-damp emerald eyes gazed with such wistful gentleness at the newborn infants.

As she drew near, her heart began to quicken.

"Hello." Although French was her native language, Isabelle spoke so many languages flawlessly that her French accent was lost in the refined elegance of her speech.

"Hello." Jane smiled warmly at the beautiful woman with the soft regal voice. After a moment, her gaze fell on the baby girl wrapped in a plush blanket of pink cashmere. The woman's hair was blonde, and the infant's was lustrous black velvet, but the brilliant blue eyes left no doubt that they were mother and daughter. "What a beautiful little girl."

"Thank you. Is your baby here?"

"No." Jane gave a soft apologetic smile, remembering that she wasn't supposed to be here, among the happy new mothers and babies. But there was something in this mother's lovely blue eyes that made it seem all right for her to reveal her own sad truth. "I recently lost my baby girl. She was born prematurely and there were complications."

"I am so sorry. Surely you will have other babies."

"No. But I am already very blessed. I have a lovely six-year-old daughter. I had hoped to give her a baby sister, but . . ."

"Yes. I see," Isabelle murmured distractedly as she felt the intense gaze of the menacing figure twenty feet away, too far away to hear the words but staring at her with watchful eyes. The eyes would become more watchful, more interested, with each passing moment. "There is something I would like to discuss with you."

"Oh?" Jane asked, surprised at the suddenness of the request. She saw the soft plea in the brilliant blue eyes, a silent yet almost desperate cry for help, and added gently, "Yes. Of course."

"We can't talk here. Will you go to the Ladies Room in the main lobby and wait for me there? It will be at least thirty minutes before I can join you."

Jane noticed the man hovering in the distance and guessed that he was the reason for the clandestine meeting. Jane's mind sent firm warnings to politely extricate herself from the situation, but all the warnings were quickly overridden by her kind and generous heart. She would help if she could.

"I'll wait for you."

"Thank you. Now will you please say good-bye, as if our conversation has ended and we have no plans to meet again?"

"Yes." Jane smiled, then glanced at her watch and exclaimed, raising her voice slightly, "Oh dear, look at the time! I'd better go. It was very nice talking to you. Good-bye."

After Jane left, Isabelle spoke unhurriedly to several other new mothers who arrived to gaze at their infants. After thirty minutes, she returned to the lobby, and, just as she was about to walk outside, as if the thought was sudden, she turned and asked the volunteer at the Information Desk for directions to the Ladies Room.

Thank God Jean-Luc had sent only men to trail her like bloodhounds! He would not have considered sending women to shadow her, of course, because he placed no value on women whatsoever—except when he wanted them for his pleasure. How ironic to find a silver lining to Jean-Luc's contempt for women! But there it was: Jean-Luc had sent no women to follow her, and that meant that she and her baby were safe, for a little while, in the Ladies Room.

"Thank you so much for agreeing to meet me," Isabelle murmured softly when she saw Jane.

"You're welcome."

"Are we alone?"

"Yes."

"Good." Isabelle looked from Jane to the small

beloved face tenderly bundled in pink cashmere. Tears filled her eyes and her voice trembled as she asked, "Will you take her?"

"Of course." Jane saw the tears and heard the emotion, but nonetheless interpreted the question to be a simple request to hold the baby. A simple request . . . but it wasn't so simple for Jane. As she cradled the little girl in her arms, rushes of pain swept through her.

"I mean," Isabelle whispered softly but confidently as she saw the gentle loving way Jane held her baby, "will you take her and raise her as your own daughter?"

"Will I do what?" Jane asked, a whisper of hope and disbelief.

"She is not safe with me. I love her with all my heart—she *is* my heart—but . . ." Isabelle was swept by a sudden rush of rebellious emotions, voices from the heart that urged her to pretend that Jean-Luc and his men didn't exist. Fantasy! she reminded the defiant voices. Forcing herself to remember the reality, she continued with quiet calm, "You have lost your baby . . ."

"Yes, but you shouldn't lose yours," Jane answered softly as she waged her own private battle against emotions. *Yes, I will take her,* her heart had swiftly and joyfully answered Isabelle's stunning question. But Jane knew the pain of her own loss and believed, truly believed, that this mother and daughter should not be separated. She forced that belief, that island of rationality in the swirling sea of her own emotions, to speak, suggesting gently, "Maybe if you told me why it is you believe you can't keep her, together we

10

could find a way that you could. Surely there is a way. Please, let me help you find it."

"I cannot tell you, and there is no other way." Her quiet, resigned voice and anguished blue eyes eloquently conveyed the truth of her words. She had searched tirelessly for other solutions and had found none. After a moment, she gave a trembling smile, and the anguished sapphire flickered with hope as she continued, "But you can help. All that I have prayed for from the moment I knew I could not keep her was that I would find a mother who would love her as I would have. I believe you are that mother."

It was a long moment before Jane could speak, a moment in which their glistening eyes met and held, and silent promises were made from the heart.

"I will love her," Jane whispered finally, unnecessarily, because her eyes had already made that promise.

"Yes. I know that you will." Isabelle's eyes held Jane's for a few moments longer, then she forced herself to turn away and focus on the other things that needed to be done before she left to begin the rest of her life without her daughter. She removed the large purse from her shoulder and withdrew a satchel made of plush blue velvet and bound by drawstrings of gold. Her delicate fingers opened the satchel and removed several of the many neatly folded pieces of tissue paper which, when unwrapped, revealed glittering diamonds, rubies, sapphires, and emeralds.

"She would have had great wealth," Isabelle explained. *She would have been a princess.* "I have converted some of her inheritance into precious gems. All are flawless and of the finest cut and color. The current wholesale value of the stones in this satchel is about twenty million dollars. I would suggest that you only sell the gems as you need them, because their value will surely increase over the coming years."

"I can't take these."

"I assure you they aren't stolen. They are rightfully hers."

"My husband and I aren't rich, and never will be, but our life is comfortable. We have worked very hard to save enough money to afford two children." Jane shrugged, not certain why she was refusing to take the gems, yet quite confident of the decision. Their life was modest, but so very happy. Jane had no wish to change it.

Jane's refusal to accept the life-changing fortune was more proof to Isabelle that she had found the woman with whom she could entrust her precious daughter. Isabelle had been very poor and then very rich, and she knew quite well that the only real treasure was love. This woman with the glistening emerald eyes knew that, too.

"Shall I tell you about myself and my husband?" Jane offered quietly.

"No, please don't. It is best if I know nothing about you and you know nothing about me . . . except this: she is my daughter, and she was conceived in the greatest of love. It is not safe for her to be with me, and it never will be." Isabelle's eyes filled with fresh tears as she heard the finality of her words. She thought she had prepared herself for this, steeled her heart, but now her

12

breaking heart made a soft impulsive request, "Will you tell her, please, on her twenty-first birthday, about today? Will you tell her that I loved her, but that I had no choice?"

"Yes. Of course. What day was she born?" Jane asked, knowing that on that distant day, twenty-one years in the future, this mother, wherever she was, would send silent messages of love to the daughter who would just be learning the ancient truth.

"A week ago today. May twentieth."

"The twentieth," Jane echoed softly, as if memorizing the date. But that date was already etched in her heart—it was on that day that her own infant daughter had been born. "I will tell her then. Is there anything else I should tell her?"

"Please tell her not to try to find me. It would be impossible anyway, but there might be danger in the search." Isabelle frowned as another impulsive wish swept from her heart to her lips. "Her name is your decision, of course, and I wouldn't want it to be her first name, but . . ."

"Yes?"

"If one of her names, perhaps her middle name, could be Alexandra . . . ?"

Alexandra. After her father, Jane guessed, hearing the love in her voice as she asked the question. The baby girl's father's name was Alexander, and it was another astonishing coincidence, but she concealed her surprise, because the woman had said it was best if she knew nothing about them. So, Jane did not say, "My husband's name is Alexander," nor did she say, "My other daughter is Alexandra." She didn't speak that thought, but she heard her own unspoken words, My *other* daughter.

"Her middle name will be Alexandra."

"Thank you."

Isabelle forced herself to focus again on the important final details. After returning the blue velvet satchel to the large purse, she removed a small cloth diaper bag for Jane, a doll with dark black hair, and a blue-and-white checked cashmere blanket. Wordlessly and together, they removed the pink cashmere blanket from the baby. Then, as Isabelle tenderly wrapped her beloved infant in the blue-and-white checks, Jane clothed the doll in pink.

And then there was nothing left for Isabelle to do but say good-bye to her baby girl. Cradling her gently, she withdrew to a corner of the room, and as her lips caressed the soft cheeks and their sapphire eyes met, she whispered words of love, in French, as all the precious private words spoken to her daughter had always been.

"*Je t'aime, je t'aime, je t'aime,*" she whispered, over and over, as she had done so often. And then, kissing the small lovely face for the last time, she changed the tense from the present to the future—a future they would not share but in which her daughter would live in her heart always. "*Je t'aimerai toujours.*"

Then she turned, walked swiftly back to Jane, and gave her the beloved bundle. She slung the large purse over her shoulder, but before reaching for the doll, the decoy she would carry to lead Jean-Luc's men far away, and before leaving forever, she made a final impulsive decision. With trembling fingers, she unfastened the solid gold clasp of the necklace that had been, until then, hidden beneath her silk blouse.

The necklace was a strand of bright blue gems, from which was suspended a heart-shaped pendant made of more of the same brilliant blue stones. Jane saw at once that the brilliant blue precisely matched the remarkable eyes of the mother and daughter, but she had no idea that the glittering jewels were sapphires, or that that bright blue was for sapphires the most rare and precious color, or that the necklace was worth a fortune. She saw a different value for the magnificent necklace—a much greater one—in the emotion and love in Isabelle's eyes.

"Give this to her, please, on her twenty-first birthday. It was a gift from her father to me. We had one heart, her father and I, and now we give that heart to her." Isabelle frowned briefly, testing her own judgment in giving her baby the necklace, and then, confident that it was safe, she reassured Jane. "The necklace is lovely, breathtaking, but the design is quite traditional. It will not lead her to me."

Jane nodded as she took the stunning piece of jewelry.

"Well," Isabelle whispered as she felt the beginning of fresh tears in her eyes. She blocked the tears and the emotion in her throat with the vivid memory of the men who waited for her in the lobby. She spoke calmly, her voice strengthened by that ominous memory and the knowledge of what she must now do to insure her daughter's safety *forever*. "I must go. Please remain here

15

another thirty minutes, or even longer if you can."

"I will love her," Jane whispered.

"Yes. I know that you will. Thank you. God bless you."

Then Isabelle was gone, to continue the journey that would lead Jean-Luc's men far away from Kansas City, and Jane was left to absorb the enormity of what had happened. It had taken place so quickly, and she had accepted it all so calmly, and now . . . now she knew that she had just lived through a miracle.

"Hello, precious little one," Jane whispered softly to the brilliant blue eyes that now looked to her for love, for answers, for the promise of a safe and happy life. "Hello, Catherine Alexandra. Do you like that name, my little love? I think it's perfect for you. And your sister will be so pleased, because it will make you two even closer. She is Alexandra Catherine, you see. Oh, little Catherine, how loved you will be, by me and your Daddy and your big sister. How very loved."

As you have been so very loved for the first week of your life, she thought, her joyful heart aching for the mother who had just given her this greatest of all gifts. She made a silent promise to the sapphire eyes: And, precious Catherine, if someday your mother returns, because it is safe for her to have you with her, then, somehow, we will make that right, too.

But, Jane realized with a mixture of sadness and relief, Catherine's mother would never be able to find them. They lived in Topeka, not Kansas City, and even though she had said that she'd recently lost her baby, she hadn't said when or where the baby had died. Her baby girl had died in a hospital across town, and in this hospital, where she herself had survived, Jane had been a patient on Medicine not OB. Unless Catherine's mother returned now, she would never be able to find them.

Please remain here for another thirty minutes, or longer if you can, Catherine's mother had asked. Jane remained for a full hour, ample time for Catherine's mother to get safely away—or to change her mind and return. Jane's heart stopped each time the door opened and then raced again when it was not the lovely woman with the sapphire eyes.

The baby girl born to her had died, but still Jane's breasts defiantly filled with rich nourishing milk. Even in the days in the ICU when she had needed all her strength just to survive herself, the milk was there, a painful symbol of her loss. And now, as the tiny hungry lips pulled eagerly at her welcoming nipples, Jane was surprised that she could feel even greater joy and love, but she could, and she did.

And later, when she removed a diaper from the bag Isabelle had left, there was another surprise: one hundred thousand dollars in large bills. Money to invest and give to Catherine on her twenty-first birthday, Jane decided. She and Alexander made enough money for the modest life they lived. But, Jane thought, perhaps we can use a little of this money, just a little, so that Alexander will need to give fewer music lessons at night and on weekends, and he can spend even more precious time with his daughters. His *daughters . . .*

"Alexander."

"Hello, darling," Alexander whispered with relief. He knew Jane had been discharged—*hours ago*—but he knew, too, that his wife might need a little private time. He imagined she might wander first to the newborn nursery, and then, perhaps, across the street to the park, to feel the warm May sun and see the flowers and try one more time to make sense of what had happened. It was an impossible task, he knew, because he had been trying, too. Alexander knew that his wife would need some private time, but as the minutes had turned to hours, he had become very worried. He asked gently, "Are you ready? Shall Alexa and I come get you?"

Jane's eyes misted at the tenderness in her husband's voice. How difficult this past week had been for Alexander, more difficult for him even than for her. He had spent sleepless days and nights commuting between the crosstown ICUs, believing for the first four days that he was about to lose both his wife and his baby, but lovingly concealing his heart-stopping fear. Alexander had been strong for all of them: for Jane, for the baby girl who had died, and for the golden-haired daughter who still did not know the truth about her baby sister.

And now would never need to know.

"Is Alexa right there?"

"She's in the other room, playing dolls with yet another new friend," Alexander's voice softened

18

lovingly, ever-amazed, as Jane was, by their charming and extroverted daughter. Alexa had made lots of new friends this week, in hospital playrooms and at the motel. Alexa made friends easily, and that was wonderful, especially now, since she would never have a little sister. "Janie? Is there something—"

"Oh, Alexander . . . a miracle has happened."

As she sat in a phone booth in the park and cradled a contentedly sleeping Catherine, Jane told him about the miracle. She couldn't see the face of her beloved Alexander, the talented musician with the gentle soul of a poet, but she could imagine the sensitive eyes she knew so well and the range of emotions flickering through them— hope, fear, joy, disbelief . . . and worry.

"I haven't gone crazy, my love," Jane reassured him softly during a long silence. She knew Alexander's unspoken worry, and that he wouldn't utter it until he could hold her in his arms and protect her from the postpartum grief which had apparently become a psychosis and caused her to kidnap a baby.

"But Janie, it's just too . . . Why are you laughing?" he asked, his voice filling with even deeper concern as he heard her soft laugh.

"Because I forgot to tell you about the money and the jewels and the necklace."

She had told him the story, *three times,* but until that moment she had forgotten to tell him about either the fortune in jewels she had declined or the fortune in cash she had been given. The money and necklace were tangible proof that the miracle was true, but she had forgotten about them, because the only treasure that really mattered was sleeping happily in her arms.

"The money and jewels and necklace?"

Jane told him the story again, every detail, and she heard his soft worried protests fade into joyous disbelief until finally he whispered hoarsely, "We'll come get you now, darling. Alexa and I will come get you and Catherine."

"She's not my sister," Alexa announced with familiar Alexa confidence moments after first seeing the tiny infant cradled in her mother's arms.

"Yes, darling, she is your sister," Jane whispered softly after a stunned and worried moment. She reached for Alexa and as she lovingly stroked her daughter's silky blonde hair she explained gently, "Catherine's hair is dark, like Daddy's, not golden like yours and mine, and her eyes are blue, but she is your sister."

"*No.*"

"Alexa?"

"I don't want her to be my sister, Daddy. I don't like her."

"Alexa!"

"She's not my sister! I don't want her! Take her back to the hospital, *please*. Mommy! Daddy?"

For three weeks after whispering farewell to her beloved daughter, Isabelle tenderly cradled the doll and continued her restless journey. Somehow, she made her search appear as compelling as before, even though she was a mortally wounded creature, astonishingly still alive, roaming the earth without her heart.

She led Jean-Luc's men from Kansas City to New York, where, moments before boarding her flight to Nice, she approached one of the menacing shadows and handed him the pink cashmere bundle.

"I'm on my way to see Jean-Luc," she hissed softly in French. "I'll tell him you did your best but that he hired fools."

Isabelle had believed she would never return to L'île. But she was returning now, to confront the man who had so cruelly taken from her the immeasurable joy of living her life with her daughter. In Nice, she chartered a small plane to L'île des Arcs-en-ciel, and during the short flight from Nice to the Mediterranean island kingdom, her mind travelled to the time that had been the beginning of her loathing for Jean-Luc and the beginning of her love for Alexandre . . .

The year was 1948. The war that had claimed her entire family was over, but not—*never*—forgotten. Seventeen-year-old Isabelle had learned that in war no horror was beyond belief; and now, as hope began to find fragile footing in the remnants of despair, she chose to believe that in peace all dreams were possible. During the war, she had served the resistance in her native Paris with unwavering bravery. Now, in peace, as she pursued a dream, she wrote a bold letter to a Prince.

I have made a careful study of the designs of the jewelers in the Place Vendôme, Isabelle explained in her letter to Prince Alexandre

Castille. She did not reveal that her "careful study" was simply made by peering into the glass showcases in the glittering boutiques of Cartier, Van Cleef and Arpels, and Castille. Of all the *joailliers*, it was Castille, she decided, that needed her creativity the most. The Castille designs were too baroque and not nearly *romantic* enough, she wrote bravely. She included sketches of her own innovative romantic designs and offered to journey to L'île to meet with the Prince, if that was his royal pleasure.

Alexandre laughed softly when he read Isabelle's letter, and then grew thoughtful. She was right, of course, this woman whose talents were so obvious from the sketches and whose boldness intrigued and enchanted him. Since the war, Alexandre had devoted himself to restoring the beauty of L'île, leaving his younger brother Jean-Luc to manage Castille Jewels. Jean-Luc had shrewdly handled the business end of their profitable, *if baroque*, jewelry empire, but there had been no innovations, no new art in their designs, for a very long time.

Alexandre made arrangements to travel to Paris to meet Isabelle. But on the eve of his departure, during his daily ride to watch the splendor of the rainbows for which his island kingdom was named, he was thrown from his horse and his leg was broken. Thus, it was Jean-Luc who journeyed to Paris to meet the young designer. And when he saw beautiful Isabelle, her golden hair and sapphire eyes and provocative lips, he knew that he must have her for himself.

Isabelle's years as an orphan of war had made

her fearless. She taunted the evil men who had descended on Paris, insulting them and then fleeing to safety. She was street tough and courageous, because she had to be; but in her heart lived the delicate hope of an artist and the lovely visions of a romantic girl.

A romantic *girl*, a virgin until Jean-Luc raped her, his need for her an obsession, her desperate pleas only fueling his madness. As he brutally raped her, Jean-Luc whispered his love for her, and when it was over, he promised more: she would become his bride, his *princess*. Isabelle heard Jean-Luc's astonishing words, gazed bravely into his cruel eyes, and quietly whispered a solemn vow of eternal hatred.

On his return to L'île, Jean-Luc told his older brother that the girl had merely been toying with them. Her plan from the outset had been to work for Cartier. The news surprised and disappointed Alexandre. Six weeks later, when his leg had healed and he was in Paris, he himself paid an impulsive visit to the talented young designer.

Alexandre saw such terror in the beautiful blue eyes when she opened the door to him! The terror faded to confusion when Isabelle realized she was not looking at Jean-Luc. This man shared Jean-Luc's handsomeness, but he was older, and his expression was concerned and gentle, and there were no flickers of madness in his dark brown eyes.

Seventeen-year-old Isabelle and forty-year-old Alexandre fell in love, despite her hidden hatred for Jean-Luc, and despite the fact that the horror of Jean-Luc's brutal act lived within her still, a growing seed of evil that tainted her with sickness and unspeakable dread. She did not want to give birth to Jean-Luc's baby; but she could not bring herself to have an abortion. She simply, desperately, wished that the pregnancy would miscarry of its own accord. Then she fell in love with Alexandre, and her wishes became less desperate and more confident; surely the goodness that lived inside her now, because of Alexandre's love, would vanquish the growing evil.

Isabelle's wish came true at the beginning of the fourth month. Alexandre found her, unconscious from blood loss, and rushed her to a hospital. When she was well enough to speak again, Alexandre cradled her tenderly as she told him the truth about Jean-Luc.

Alexandre banished Jean-Luc, and married Isabelle, and they lived their wonderful love in the enchanted island kingdom in the sea. Jean-Luc was gone, but not forgotten. Alexandre and Isabelle wanted children, but in twenty years of loving it was not to be. The damage to her womb from the miscarriage had made it impossible, they decided sadly.

Alexandre and Isabelle wanted children as treasures of love, not as heirs to the kingdom, but there was that sadness, too. By the rules of royal succession that had governed L'île centuries, the reigning monarch was always the firstborn of the firstborn. But if Alexandre had no children, then on his death Jean-Luc would inherit the throne, and thereafter it would be Jean-Luc's descendants who would become the rulers of L'île.

In September of 1967, Alexandre was diagnosed to have a rare and rapidly fatal form of leukemia. Isabelle and Alexandre spent very little time in the precious months they had left together discussing what would happen when he died. There was nothing to discuss. They both knew that Jean-Luc would make a swift and triumphant return to L'île. The only plans to be made were for Isabelle.

Alexandre moved his vast personal fortune in gems and money off L'île and placed it, in Isabelle's name, in bank vaults in New York, London, Paris, and Zurich. Then, in the time they had left together on earth, Alexandre and Isabelle simply loved each other, as they always had. And sometime in those tender nights of loving sixty-year-old Alexandre and thirty-seven-year-old Isabelle conceived a child. It was a joy Isabelle never shared with Alexandre. She knew it would not bring him happiness or peace, only fear at what might happen and rage at his own helplessness. Jean-Luc was too close to having the kingdom he so desperately wanted, just a dying heartbeat away. No matter what proclamations Alexandre made before his death about his unborn child, or how carefully he planned protection for Isabelle and the baby, the reality was that Jean-Luc would never allow Alexandre's baby to take L'île away from him.

Not that Isabelle wanted the island for their child of love! All she wanted, after she said farewell to her beloved Alexandre, was to spend the rest of her life loving their baby. Jean-Luc could have everything.

When Isabelle left L'île, shortly after Alexandre's funeral, Jean-Luc's men were already following her. Her pregnancy was still hidden then, but Jean-Luc's intentions were painfully, terrifyingly obvious: his evil obsession for her was alive, evergreen, still. Isabelle tried to escape Jean-Luc's men, but it was useless, and in time her pregnancy became apparent and their ominous vigilance only intensified.

All Isabelle wanted was freedom to spend her life loving her baby. But Jean-Luc intended no freedom for either mother or child, and only through her own cleverness was Isabelle able to trick him and find freedom for her precious little love.

And now, three weeks after saying farewell forever to her tiny infant, Isabelle was returning to L'île to tell the man who had taken her daughter from her how much she hated him . . .

The palace during Alexandre's reign had been like the entire island, a welcoming place of beauty, open to all who wished to view its graceful grandeur. But the palace gates were closed now, forbidding not welcoming, and heavily armed guards sent a solemn silent signal that Prince Jean-Luc was in residence. Despite the fortune he had taken with him when Alexandre banished him from L'île, during his years in exile Jean-Luc had discovered new ways, sinister ways, to amass even greater wealth and an even more intoxicating treasure—power. By the time of Alexandre's death, Jean-Luc was known throughout the world as a merchant of guns and drugs and terror.

L'île's new monarch was in residence now, and the elegant white marble palace had become a fortress, and a pall had fallen over the once joyful paradise. Even the birds are still, Isabelle thought sadly. And the warm air that had once been filled with the delicate perfume of a thousand flowers felt cold and stale. She wondered about the magnificent rainbows that filled the sky every evening after the nourishing tropical rain. Had they vanished, too, their dazzling brilliance faded to gray, an illusory memory of what had been and now was gone forever?

"Isabelle," Jean-Luc whispered when he saw her, his breath halted as always by the sight of her. His dark eyes were unrevealing and cold, even though his entire being filled with a powerful emotion that was beyond desire, a desperate need to possess her.

"You bastard."

"Isabelle . . ."

"How I hate you!"

"Don't hate me, *chérie*. A father does what he must for his children."

"You did it for yourself! You wanted L'île, and already you have contaminated it with your poison."

"Such anger, Isabelle. You are far too beautiful for anger."

As Jean-Luc spoke his eyes left hers and drifted to the wall behind her. Isabelle followed his gaze to a magnificent oil painting—of *her*. Before Alexandre's death, she had sent letters, diaries, portraits, and photographs—*all* the tangible symbols of their love—to her château in the Loire Valley.

But the portrait in oil that hung in Jean-Luc's private library in the palace was not a painting that had been left behind in error. It was a portrait he had commissioned himself, painted from the famous photograph of her taken twelve years before in the palace gardens at Monaco. She and Alexandre had been there, of course, to attend the wedding of their dear friends Rainier and Grace, the other Prince and Princess of an enchanted Mediterranean kingdom. The breath-taking photograph had appeared in *Life* magazine, a full page and in color, even though Princess Isabelle Castille was only a guest, not the fairytale bride. She looked like a bride, though, standing amidst the white gardenias, her lovely expression matching the romantic hopefulness of the day. And there was more romance in the photograph, private romance, because Isabelle had chosen on that romantic day to wear the sapphire necklace her beloved Alexandre had given her.

Over the years there had been hundreds of photographs of Isabelle and Alexandre, she so delicate and beautiful, he so strong and hand-some. And in those photographs she had worn millions of dollars of jewelry designed by Castille—and yet it was *this* photograph, in which she had worn her most treasured jewels, from which Jean-Luc had commissioned a portrait for his own private viewing!

It angered Isabelle that Jean-Luc had the portrait, and it terrified her that in it she wore the necklace she had given her baby. Even if, twenty-one years from now, her daughter chose to search for her, it was beyond imagination that the sapphire necklace could lead to her. But Jean-Luc, using photographs of the necklace and beginning now *might* find the missing princess. What if he placed photographs of the necklace in American newspapers, captioned with an impassioned plea, ostensibly from her, searching for her daughter? What if the lovely woman with the emerald eyes read the plea and was tricked into coming forward?

What if? The unanswerable question came with such terror, until she remembered . . .

Jean-Luc doesn't know I gave her the necklace! He doesn't know, and it will be twenty-one years before my precious daughter even sees it. By then, if there is a God, Jean-Luc will be in hell. Before returning her gaze to Jean-Luc, Isabelle silently reminded herself, a calming mantra, She is safe. My baby girl is safe.

"How *dare* you have a portrait of me!" Isabelle accused when she turned, funneling all her emotions into anger, hiding her terror beneath layers of rage.

"I want far more than a portrait. I want *you*. I love you, Isabelle."

"You're mad."

"Mad with love. If we were together, your daughter could be with us."

Isabelle's heart missed a beat, a suspended moment of hope, but it was a cruel treachery. Jean-Luc might allow the little girl to live for a

29

while, but one day there would be a tragic accident . . .

"I don't know where she is, Jean-Luc. She is hidden forever, even from me." Isabelle emphasized her words by issuing a challenge and a wish of hatred. "I hope you try to find her, Jean-Luc. I hope you squander your entire fortune in the search and spend the rest of your nights on earth tormented by the fear that she will appear. I hope it is that torment that kills you."

"Isabelle, Isabelle." Jean-Luc's soft mocking laugh could have been a loving tease in a normal man, but in him it was merely further evidence of his madness. Her hatred titillated him. "We are meant for each other, can you not see that? Marry me, my love. Be my Princess. I will show you love and passion that my older brother never could. It disgusts me when I imagine him making love to you in those months when his body was dying."

"It is you who are disgusting, Jean-Luc. You who are beneath contempt."

"You will learn to love me."

"You have a wife, Jean-Luc." Isabelle paused a beat, and even though her mind sent a warning, she whispered the taunt, "Or would you murder her as you murdered Geneviève?"

Geneviève was the lovely innocent girl who had fallen prey to Jean-Luc's wicked charms and married him. Isabelle would never have met her, because Jean-Luc had long since been banished from L'île; but one day, because L'île was the only place on earth that her monster husband could not follow, a desperate and frightened

Geneviève appeared at the palace seeking sanctuary. Isabelle and Alexandre welcomed Geneviève, *and should never have allowed her to return to Jean-Luc,* but she was pregnant with the heir he wanted so much. She decided to return to him, to give him his child in exchange for her freedom. Geneviève gave Jean-Luc his son, but she was never free. A month after her son's birth, she was killed.

And now, even though her mind had sent a warning not to taunt him, Isabelle was accusing Jean-Luc of Geneviève's death. Surely this king of terrorists, this amoral madman, would not take offense at the accusation. But as she saw the sudden murderous rage in his dark eyes, she realized she had pushed too far, and the fearlessness she had always felt with Jean-Luc, her own immunity to harm because of his obsession for her, gave way to immobilizing fear. She was frozen, unable to flee. But then, as his powerful hands closed around her delicate neck, and she understood that she was going to die, the fear melted into an almost peaceful relief. She would die. The pain of her loss, her losses, would be over. She would be with Alexandre.

"Papa?"

At the sound of the young voice, the fingers that had been seconds away from crushing her slender throat released their grip. Jean-Luc's dark eyes flickered for a moment with bewildered horror at what he had almost done to the woman he loved. Then, as if nothing had happened, he smiled and turned in the direction of his ten-year-old son.

"Alain. Please come in and meet your Aunt Isabelle."

Alain. Somehow the realization settled in her swirling mind. *Geneviève's son.* But there was nothing in the serious yet calm young face to suggest that Alain had overheard her accusation about Geneviève, or even to indicate that he was aware of the violence his "Papa?" had interrupted.

"Bonjour, Tante Isabelle," Alain greeted her politely.

"Bonjour, Alain." Isabelle found a wobbly smile for the boy who would one day rule the island. In a different world, a world without Jean-Luc, would he and her daughter have been loving cousins? Or would Alain have resented being second in line to the throne *behind* his younger female cousin? Alain's genetic inheritance appeared to be all Castille, the dark handsomeness of Jean-Luc and Alexandre with none of Geneviève's fairness. Had this little boy inherited anything from his mother? Was there goodness in his veins, or was he pure evil like his father? The face was sweet now, a boy's face, and the dark eyes *seemed* sensitive. But the apparent sensitivity could be merely an illusion, she knew, like Jean-Luc's charm, a weapon to be used when it was expedient to do so. It didn't matter what kind of man this boy was to become. Whether it was his destiny to be good or evil, on this day Alain Castille had unwittingly saved her life.

"Well," she murmured after a moment, using Alain's appearance as a chance to make her escape. "I must go. Adieu, Alain."

Jean-Luc didn't try to stop her. He would have her followed, of course, perhaps forever. She didn't care. *Her* freedom, *her* safety, didn't matter any longer.

Her swift journey toward the palace gates halted in the midst of a marble courtyard. There, splashing her small fingers in a pond that swirled with colorful koi, was a beautiful little girl. She was Natalie, Isabelle assumed, Jean-Luc's four-year-old daughter and Alain's half sister. Isabelle's heart filled with more warmth for Natalie than it had for Alain, because she was a daughter, a princess, and because she smiled a lovely innocent smile at her aunt.

What kind of life could there be for children who lived in a world shadowed by Jean-Luc? Isabelle wondered as she left the palace forever. An unhappy life, she decided sadly. A life tainted by treachery and fear, not love and joy. For the first time in the weeks since she had been forced to give her daughter away, Isabelle felt a sense of peace. Her little girl was safe, and she would be loved.

Be happy, my precious little love, her heart whispered to her beloved baby in faraway Kansas.

Kansas . . . the home of the little girl who dreamed of enchanted places over the rainbow. Isabelle wondered if her daughter, like Dorothy, would dream such magical dreams. Of course she would—all little girls did. She would dream of enchanted magical places, but not even in her wildest dreams would she ever imagine the truth: that she was, and always would be, the Princess

of the enchanted and magical L'île des Arcs-en-
ciel . . . the Island of the Rainbows.

Chapter 2

Manhattan . . . April 1989

Summoned by engraved gilt-edged invitation,
New York's literati and glitterati assembled in the
Plaza's Grand Ballroom for the annual Academy
Award gala. Held on the Saturday evening
following the presentation of the Oscars in Hollywood, the star-studded event was Manhattan's
answer to superagent Swifty Lazar's after Oscar-
party at Spago. The guest list for both parties
was similar—only the very rich, very famous, and
very influential—but the sheer size of the Grand
Ballroom permitted even greater lavishness. The
pièce de résistance this year was a twelve-foot-tall
ice sculpture of the famous Oscar. The glistening
statue towered-above a pond of vintage champagne, its icy surface tinted gold by the reflection
of the expensive liquid that swirled at its feet.

Alexandra Taylor wove slowly through the
bejeweled, couturied, and tuxedoed guests. She
whispered gracious thank-yous to those who
spoke their congratulations and smiled beautiful
replies to those who simply raised crystal champagne flutes in silent toast. To the many
appreciative and admiring eyes that watched her
throughout the evening, Alexa seemed remark-

ably calm about her stunning triumph, greeting her victory with a regal dignity appropriate to the role for which she had just won the Oscar for Best Actress—Elizabeth I in *Majesty*, Lawrence Carlyle's stunning portrait of the magnificent queen.

Alexa's apparent calm was merely another demonstration of her remarkable talent. Beneath the tranquil facade her heart raced, *still*, even after six nights, a fluttering symbol of her immense joy. The joy was quite private, although she'd had very little privacy since the moment she had received the small golden statue. Very little privacy, and that was what was needed now, she decided, as she felt the invisible tug of the secluded moonlit terrace beyond the French doors. It was almost midnight, almost time to go home, but she needed a few moments of solitude in the shadows before beginning her smiling gracious journey back through the sea of rich and famous.

She would be alone on the terrace, she thought, a rare celebrity who preferred shadows to lime-light. But she was not alone. Her immediate disappointment vanished quickly as she recognized the elegant tuxedoed silhouette and the midnight-black hair that shined in the moonlight.

"Bond," she purred softly as she approached him. "James Bond."

"I beg your pardon?"

"Oh! I beg *your* pardon," Alexa exclaimed when he turned to face her. "I thought you were Timothy."

"Timothy?"

"Dalton." As Alexa clarified she realized that her words did not enlighten the very dark, very seductive blue eyes. Whoever he was—*not* Timothy Dalton but certainly an acceptable Bond by any measure of elegant sensuality—he apparently was far enough removed from show business he knew neither Timothy nor his role as the master spy. "You're not Timothy Dalton."

"No. I'm James Sterling."

"Oh. Hello," Alexa breathed softly.

She had heard of James Sterling, of course. *Who hadn't?* The stunningly successful attorney was at once phantom and legend in New York. *Phantom,* because although he donated generously to charities and the arts, he rarely bothered to appear at the galas; and *legend,* because although only thirty-four his skill as a negotiator made him the man chosen by the most powerful industrialists in the world to orchestrate their billion-dollar mergers, takeovers, and real estate deals.

The world's wealthiest chose James Sterling for their most important negotiations, although in truth it was James who did the choosing. From the moment of his birth, James had more than enough wealth to never need to work at all. But he had chosen to become an attorney, and a negotiator, and now he selected from the many projects offered to him only the ones that appealed, challenged, or intrigued.

The blood that flowed in James Sterling's veins was quite blue, quite patrician, and, his admirers embellished, it was as calm and cool as ice. It was the iciness, the unshakable cool under pres-

36

sure, that made James the best at what he did. It was that same iciness, his detractors noted, that resulted in his notoriously short-lived liaisons with some of the world's most glamorous women.

Alexa was quite untroubled by James Sterling's reputation with women. He was a man, after all, completely within her control. A very handsome, very sexy man, Alexa realized as the seductive blue eyes met hers and she felt a wonderful rush of heat, like the tingling, giddy warmth of too hastily swallowed champagne. She acknowledged the moment with a demure smile. Then, because he seemed to be awaiting a follow-up to her obvious surprise in response to his name, she gave a beautiful provocative frown, as if his name triggered a distant but uncertain memory, and asked, "James Sterling, the attorney?"

"Yes." After a patient moment he asked, "So, who are you?"

Alexa blushed slightly at her own presumptuousness. She had assumed he would know her. She was practically the guest of honor at the gala. Did he really not recognize her? Or was he feigning uncertainty, *playing* as she had been?

"I'm Alexandra Taylor."

"Oh. Hello," James murmured softly, as surprised by her name as she had been by his. "Alexandra Taylor, the actress?"

"Yes. Alexa."

"Well, Alexa, you're the reason I'm here tonight. I wanted to tell you how magnificent I thought you were in *Majesty*."

"Thank you," she replied calmly, even though her mind swirled. James Sterling, the phantom whose everyday life was so dazzling that he rarely bothered with the glittering galas had come tonight *to meet her?* The revelation was astonishing and intriguing . . . until she detected something more than surprise on his handsome face. What was it? Alexa couldn't be sure, but she feared that it was the one thing she dreaded most—*disappointment.* She offered quietly, "I guess you expected someone a little more Elizabethan?"

"I guess so," James admitted.

It had only been four nights since he had seen *Majesty* on a rainy evening in Hong Kong, but in that time he had formed a clear image of the extraordinary actress. She would be British, of course, and although she had convincingly portrayed Elizabeth from seventeen to seventy, James guessed she would be about his age. He had envisioned a solemn and dedicated veteran of the London stage who had been lured to the silver screen by the gifted director Lawrence Carlyle. Her beauty would be sublime, as Elizabeth's had been, a magnificent richness of character. Her remarkable green eyes would be thoughtful, reflective, quite uncomfortable with the glitter of the party; and her red-gold hair, unattended by the stylists who were constant fixtures on the movie set, would be an unruly mane, a curly tangle unceremoniously snared with barrettes at the last minute, a small concession to fashion by a sensible woman who usually couldn't care less.

James had such complete confidence in his image of Alexandra Taylor that, as he had searched for her in the crowded ballroom, it had not occurred to him to ask someone to point her out. His eyes *had* lingered on the breathtakingly beautiful woman with the long golden hair and the sparkling emerald eyes, wondering who she was and if they should meet, but . . .

But now that dazzling and glamorous woman was here—claiming to be Alexandra Taylor. Was this really the woman who had so compellingly portrayed the many layers of the complicated and extraordinary queen that he had left the theater wishing he had known Elizabeth?

Yes, James realized as he saw the surprising flickers of uncertainty, clues to Alexa's own complexity, rippling through the remarkable emerald.

"The day after I won the award, I got a call asking if I would wear one of the Oscar-winning costumes and a red-gold wig for the party tonight," she murmured with a shrug, a soft apology to the man who had come tonight hoping to meet Elizabeth . . . and had found only Alexa.

"But you said no."

"It seemed a bit much."

"Because there are actresses here who didn't win?" James guessed quietly, hoping that was the reason, seeing at once in her surprised eyes that it was.

"I'm sort of an impostor."

"I see." He teased lightly, "Never done much acting?"

Only almost all of my life, Alexa mused. She never thought of her acting as a talent. It was and always had been simply survival.

"I've been a professional actress for the past eight years. Most of my work has been in television, although I have done a little theater. *Majesty* was my first feature film."

"Quite a debut."

"Quite a role."

But it wasn't just the role, James knew. Not many actresses, no matter how talented, could have portrayed Elizabeth as Alexa had. It hadn't *felt* like performance, and that had been the magic. There had been no distinction between the extraordinary queen and the extraordinary actress who had brought her to life. Alexa's Elizabeth was very personal and very intimate. As if Elizabeth was who Alexa was . . . or who Alexa wished to be.

"Tell me about Elizabeth," James urged quietly. Tell me about Alexa.

"Elizabeth was magnificent. I hadn't really known that before. I realized how terribly superficial my knowledge was when I began to research the role. In grade school, I remember learning about Sir Francis Drake gallantly throwing his cape across a mud puddle. I remember that mostly because it precipitated a flurry of similar gallantry among the boys in my class."

"Lots of muddy raincoats?"

"Lots. And then in high school . . . well, the issue of the Virgin Queen prompted quite a bit of extracurricular discussion as I recall."

"And remains unresolved in *Majesty*," James observed. Alexa's portrayal of Elizabeth had been of a sensual, passionate, bewitching woman, however the specific issue of the famous queen's virginity, or not, had not been addressed. "What did you decide from your reading?"

"I decided that Elizabeth had intimate relationships with men. Whether the relationships were sexual or not is trivial because the intimacy was so much deeper than that. I am very sure that Elizabeth was loved passionately for who she was, for her heart and spirit and soul."

"Which is what really matters? To be loved for who you are?"

"Yes. I guess," Alexa admitted softly, frowning slightly as she realized how personal the admission was and wondering why she had made it. "Weren't we talking about Elizabeth?"

"We were, but now we've shifted to you. We've already established that you consider sexual relationships—at least some sexual relationships—to be quite trivial."

"Yes," she agreed with a soft laugh. Then, with emerald eyes sparkling, she said firmly, "So, that's all we need to know about me. Let's shift to you. I wonder . . ."

"Yes?"

"Well," Alexa purred as her mind searched for clever, provocative questions to ask James Sterling. Her search was intercepted by a serious question, one for which she legitimately needed an answer. The question was serious, and important, but her tone remained soft, teasing. "I'm desperately seeking an attorney. Perhaps you could make a referral?"

"Of course. You'll need to tell me a little about the case."

"All right. Did you really not recognize me?"

41

"I really did not."

"Then you're probably not familiar with *Pennsylvania Avenue,* the television show, not the address."

James smiled. He had dined, more than once, at the address. And as for the show?

"I've heard about the show, but I've never seen it. That's not a value judgment by the way," he added swiftly. "I just don't watch much television. I never have. I do know, however, that it's the top-rated prime-time dramatic series. Are you the star?"

"It's an ensemble cast, but the character I play, Stephanie Winslow, is fairly high profile. She's a reporter—sexy, savvy, and intensely dedicated—and somehow she manages to be woven into almost all the major story lines."

Which means you *are* the star, he thought, realizing that, as with Elizabeth, Alexa somehow diminished her own talent by giving credit to the role. And, as with Elizabeth, James heard admiration in her voice as she spoke of Stephanie, as if she had nothing at all to do with Alexa.

"Why do you need an attorney?"

"Because it's contract time and I'm between agents."

"Why?"

"Why what?"

"Why are you between agents?"

"Why do you keep asking all these questions? The James Sterling that I've heard of does corporate work—you know, mergers and takeovers? But I feel like I'm on the witness stand!" Alexa's sparkling eyes narrowed as she added knowingly,

"You're really another James Sterling, aren't you? James Sterling, the brilliant trial attorney."

"No. I really do my work in boardrooms, not courtrooms. But all attorneys, all good ones, ask the key questions."

"It's key to find out why I'm between agents?"

"Apparently. You seem to be resisting giving me an answer."

Alexa sighed, amazed that the conversation had become so personal, so quickly, *again*. She glowered at him, and he answered the glower with a laugh that was so soft, so gentle, so surprised that she gave a bewildered shake of her golden head and quietly told him something she had never told anyone ever before.

"I guess that my agent and I parted company because of artistic differences. When Lawrence Carlyle approached him to see if I would be interested in playing Elizabeth, he said no without even checking with me. That's part of an agent's job, of course, to screen projects. But he was supposed to turn down projects because they weren't worthy of me, *not* because he thought I wasn't worthy of them."

"But you were most worthy of playing Elizabeth," James reminded her. "Fortunately, somehow you and Lawrence Carlyle did get together."

"Yes. One day Lawrence simply appeared on the set of *P.A.* to talk to me directly. He had seen the series—it's very popular in England—and decided that Stephanie was a modern day Elizabeth."

"I see," James said, realizing that once again

43

she had excluded herself from the equation. "So, not surprisingly, you and your agent parted company. You need a new agent."

"Yes, I do. But because of my success with *Majesty*, any agent worth his or her salt would be signing me to more movies."

"And that doesn't appeal?"

"Not until at least two years from now. *Pennsylvania Avenue* is in production from July through January, and so far I've filled every production hiatus with a major project. Next year, no matter what, I've promised myself the entire five months will be vacation."

"What are you doing now?"

"*Romeo and Juliet*—Juliet—on Broadway. I had promised myself this spring off, but . . ." But every time I remember the reason for the promise, that I need time away from the heroines I admire so much to be with myself—whom I don't admire?—I seem to find ways of breaking it. Alexa dismissed the disquieting thought with a soft shrug and continued, "Anyway, that's why I'm not looking for an agent. The only commitment I want to make now is to *Pennsylvania Avenue*. I already have a contract, of course, so all that needs to be negotiated is the new salary. I know exactly what I want, but I would prefer to have someone else do the talking. It would probably just be one simple call to Los Angeles. Is there someone you would recommend?"

"Sure. I'd recommend myself."

"No. I know a little about your reputation, James. This would be much too small for you."

"Really? Like you, Alexa, I have the wonderful

luxury of being able to choose projects. I only choose ones that interest me—which this does. Besides, by remarkable coincidence, I'm flying to Chicago tomorrow, for two days, and then will be in Los Angeles until Friday. The meetings in L.A. are inconveniently spaced over several days. If I can fill the spaces by making phone calls for you I'll feel my time has been better spent."

"It would only be one phone call."

"No, it wouldn't. After I've read your existing contract and discussed with you what you want, I would need to do some research to see if your demands are reasonable." James saw the sudden flickers of worry in her beautiful eyes and guessed softly, "You were planning to have me make some unreasonable demands?"

"Can't I just tell you what I want and ask you to make the phone call?"

"You can, but I won't do it. I can promise you that I'll do my homework and get you a very fair deal." He smiled and added quietly, "And Alexa, I don't make promises I can't keep."

"I really just expected you to give me the name of someone else."

"I know. But in good conscience I have to recommend myself."

"Because you're the best at what you do."

"Just like you."

"Oh! Thank you. Well, if you really want . . ."

"I really want. So, let's see. Why don't you messenger a copy of your contract to my office Monday morning? They'll fax it to me and I'll review it and call you Monday night."

"All right." Alexa frowned as she thought

45

about her already impossible Monday morning. But the contract negotiation was a top priority—which made getting the contract to James of utmost importance. She would simply have to shuffle her other commitments, unless . . . "My apartment is on Riverside Drive. I have a limousine outside and could go to my apartment, get a copy of the contract, and be back here in fifteen or twenty minutes. If you wouldn't mind waiting."

"I wouldn't mind. I would also be very happy to accompany you."

"Oh! Well, I . . ."

"Or would that put me in great danger of being challenged to a duel by the Earl of Leicester or some other suitor?"

"Jeremy—the good Earl—is quite married."

"And therefore off-limits?"

"Absolutely."

"And all the other suitors?"

"I'm here alone, James. But surely there's a lady-in-waiting nearby who would not be terribly pleased."

"I'm here alone, too," James said quietly. He added, even more quietly, "I told you, Alexandra Taylor. I only came tonight to meet you."

Chapter 3

Alexa's apartment was on the third floor of a red-brick building on Riverside Drive. The building was old but solidly built, and the apartment had the kind of detailing that revealed the meticulous craftsmanship often missing in newer construction—vaulted ceilings, carved wainscoting, charming alcoves, and luxurious spaciousness. As James followed her from the foyer to the living room, he silently admired the floral wall coverings and soft pastel accents. He had been in many designer apartments, his own penthouse on Fifth Avenue included, and this felt quite different . . . homemade, comfortable, uncluttered.

There *was* clutter in the living room, he discovered, fragrant clutter from Alexa's recent triumph—hundreds of long-stemmed roses artfully arranged in an array of vases. James recognized some of the vases, the elegant carved crystal designs of Lalique and the delicate spring flowers of Limoges; but many of the vases were not china or crystal, but pottery, made by a talented artist whose work he had never seen. The same artist, he decided, who had crafted the beautiful hand-painted lamps that adorned the room.

"This is very nice, very homey. Are you the designer?"

"Yes. Thank you. It does feel like home."

"Which is where?"

"A farmhouse outside of Topeka. My father is a music teacher." Alexa gently touched one of the hand-painted vases and added, "And my mother is a potter."

"Talented family."

"Thank you," she murmured softly as she thought, And you haven't even heard about the most talented Taylor of all. The thought came

47

with memories, bittersweet and unsettling. After a moment, Alexa shook the thought and looked up from the delicate hand-painted vase to him— only to be unsettled anew. Here he was, this devastatingly handsome, compellingly sensual stranger; and here they were, alone at midnight in her romantic rose-fragrant apartment. As his seductive dark blue eyes studied her, appraising and obviously approving, she felt once again the lovely rushes of delicious warmth; but she felt, too, tremors of uncertainty. When she'd told him that she was looking for an attorney it had been the truth, important, serious, and quite innocent. What if he thought it had all been merely a provocative ploy to lure him to her apartment?

James felt unsettled, too, struck anew by how beautiful, how alluring she was. She was even more appealing here than she'd been in moon-light; because here, in this charming place decorated by her, proudly and lovingly accented with homemade pottery, he saw even more enchanting glimpses of the lovely woman beneath the gold and emerald dazzle.

James knew very well that their chance encounter on the moonlit terrace might have led them here. They might have danced on the terrace, learning more about each other, leisurely affirming the attraction that had been so obvious from the first. They might have danced and smiled and sipped champagne, and eventually, the glowing emerald eyes might have invited him here. But, even though they both knew that might well have happened, that wasn't why he was here now. And he knew, and perhaps the uncertainty he saw in her eyes now meant that she *didn't* know, that the moment he had offered to represent her everything had changed.

Alexa was his client now. Which meant that for now, and for as long as she was, their relationship would be purely professional. James took his obligations to his career and to his personal code of ethics very seriously; just as, he knew, she did, too. He told her that now with his dark blue eyes. The eloquent blue told her everything: that his attraction to her hadn't vanished with the moonlight, *not at all;* and that he knew she took her career very seriously, as he did his; and that he was here, now, to help her with this contract that was obviously so important to her; and that, some other time, when she was no longer his client, he would very much like to be invited back to this romantic place.

His dark blue eyes sent all those messages with such clarity that the emerald ones understood perfectly and were both flattered and relieved; and they sent a clear and eloquent message in return, a sparkling promise that yes, if he wanted, there would be another time.

"Contract?" he asked finally, with a soft laugh.

"Contract," she echoed. "It's in the other room."

"Shall I follow you?"

Alexa smiled. "Sure."

She led the way to one of the apartment's two large bedroom suites. The two rooms, located at opposite extremes of the spacious apartment, were mirror images of each other, although for the moment only hers looked like a bedroom at

49

all. The other, to which she led James, looked like the dance studio it once had been.

"As you can probably tell, the previous owner was a ballerina," Alexa explained. "I've been using this room as a combination gym, study, and storage room."

"But it looks as if it's about to be transformed," James observed as his gaze fell on the rolls of wallpaper, cans of paint, and drop cloths lying on the hardwood floor.

"Yes. The mirrors and ballet bar come out on Monday. After a little replastering and installation of chair rails, it will hopefully become a bedroom again. My little sister Cat is moving to New York in June. As you can see, I'm keeping with the Laura-Ashley-does-Kansas theme, although I've decided lilacs, not roses, for Cat." As she looked at the beautiful wallpaper, clusters of lilacs on ivory, Alexa's eyes filled with new uncertainty. She wanted the room to be like a bouquet, fresh and cheerful and romantic, and she had spent hours carefully selecting the floral wallcovering, and the perfect pastel green accent for the woodwork, and the matching fabric for the curtains and bedspread. But still she worried. After a reflective moment, she added quietly, "I hope she'll like it."

"Why wouldn't she?"

"Oh, I don't know," she answered with a soft shrug. It wasn't the bedroom she hoped Cat would like, of course, it was something so very much more important: I hope Cat will like *me*.

James watched as her lovely eyes became more thoughtful, and, just for a flicker, terribly sad.

50

The moment passed quickly, but he was left with an indelible impression: there was something very important—and yet very troubling—about her little sister. And even though they were in this room to get the contract, and tonight was professional, not personal, he couldn't resist learning just a little more. "Her name is Cat?"

"Yes. Short for Catherine. She's a gifted musician, a pianist. Even though she'll only be twenty-one next month, she's already won both the Tchaikovsky and Van Cliburn competitions. Her professional career as a concert pianist could have started years ago, but she decided to go to college first. She's in her junior year at Oberlin now, although she's enough ahead on credits that she can graduate in December if she takes full course loads this summer and fall."

"So she's coming to New York to finish college?"

"Yes. At Juilliard. They're obviously quite happy to have her, if only for two terms. She needs to be here because the promoter wants an album to be released in time for her first professional concert tour, which debuts at the Opera House in San Francisco on New Year's Eve and then continues through North America and on to Europe."

"So she'll be going to school, learning new pieces for her concert tour, and recording an album? That seems like too much."

"Not for Cat. She'll handle it with ease."

"I guess so, if she's anything like her older sister."

"Like me?"

"Your nonstop award-winning career hasn't happened by accident. There must be a little discipline and drive sprinkled in with all that Taylor sister talent." James thought the observation was quite obvious, but it seemed to confuse her. Why? She had already admitted that she kept promising herself a little much needed time off, so she couldn't deny that she was driven. Was it possible that she doubted her own talent? "No? Not true?"

"I guess it's true. I just never think of Cat and me being at all alike." She frowned briefly, then shrugged. "Well. Let me get the contract, then we can go to the kitchen. There's a table there, paper and pencils if you need them, and good light. And I could make you some coffee or maybe something to drink?"

"Coffee would be fine." I have a contract to read, he thought. Tonight, we'll sit in the kitchen and drink coffee and talk about your contract. And next time, we'll sit in the rose-fragrant living room, and drink champagne, and, maybe, just maybe, you'll tell me why there is such lovely uncertainty in your emerald eyes when you speak of your talented little sister.

Alexa watched as James read the contract, his intelligent dark blue eyes focused, his handsome aristocratic features set in neutral and totally inscrutable. The master negotiator was at work now, and as she unabashedly studied him, she began to appreciate the reasons for his extraordinary success. There was the obvious—intelligence combined with the perfectionism of

52

all successful people; and the subtle—his stunning sensuality. She imagined him at the negotiating table, disarming his opponents with his aristocratic elegance, his inscrutable calm, and the sensuous eyes that could appraise so intently, searching for truths, but which, unless he chose, would reveal nothing of the thoughts that lay in the dark blue depths. Women, if James Sterling ever even negotiated with women, would be distracted, unwittingly seduced by his compelling sexuality; and men would be distracted, too, envious perhaps, certainly admiring.

"OK," James said when he had finished his thorough reading of her contract. "Let's go point by point and you tell me what you had in mind."

"There really wasn't anything other than salary, assuming they don't want to undo other previous agreements."

"What about the residuals and royalties you get for reruns, syndication, and sales ex-U.S.?"

"I think the amounts in the existing contract are very standard."

James nodded, but then, as if "standard" was an unacceptable concept to the master negotiator, he pencilled question marks next to the pertinent paragraphs.

"OK. So, what salary figure did you have in mind?"

"One million." Alexa had been silently rehearsing how to utter the large sum—twice what she had been paid last season—and rehearsing, too, the reasons she had used to convince herself that the amount was fair. High but fair.

If James had an objection, or even a reaction, he didn't show it. He simply jotted the numeral "1" above the five hundred thousand. Just a "1," without six zeroes, without any embellishment at all.

Just a "1," Alexa thought uneasily. It was probably the smallest number he ever wrote—just a million. Just a million was probably far less than his usual fee for any one of the many important deals he negotiated.

"Do you have a feeling for how that salary compares to other prime-time stars?" he asked.

"Just a feeling. Rumors, actually."

"I'll need to check. Could you give me some names?"

"Sure. Let's see, there's Joan Van Ark, and Susan Dey, and Dana Delany, and . . ." Alexa gave him the names of a number of actresses, as well as the series in which each appeared.

"There are no male stars on these shows?" James asked after he had recorded the names of the principal heroines and villainesses of *Dallas, L.A. Law, Knot's Landing,* and *China Beach.* "Ms. Taylor, don't you believe in comparable worth?"

"Yes, I do. Do you?"

"Of course. Does Hollywood?"

"I'm not sure."

"We'll find out. Give me some male names."

"OK. There's Larry Hagman—that's *Dallas*—and . . ."

James recorded the additional names, and the name and phone number of the executive producer in Hollywood with whom the negotiations would occur, and the numbers where he could reach Alexa both at her apartment and the theater where she was starring in *Romeo and Juliet.*

"I'll call you in a day or two, once I've had a chance to get what I need to determine what salary request we can reasonably make."

"Do you think you'll be able to learn about these other salaries?"

"Yes." James had no experience with negotiating individual contracts in Hollywood, but he had had business dealings—multibillion dollar takeovers—with a number of top industry executives. He had no doubt that he could very easily get what he needed. "That information will be of interest, of course, but most important will be gauging your value to *Pennsylvania Avenue* and *Pennsylvania Avenue's* value to the network."

"How will you do that?"

"Through a combination of informal conversations as well as getting specific data on advertising revenues generated by the show."

"This is going to be a lot of work, isn't it?"

"I don't think so. I'll call you when I have everything I need, and before I make the call to the executive producer. In the meantime, you should think about the deal breaker."

"Deal breaker?"

"The point at which we walk away." James saw her sudden confusion and clarified, "The salary amount that is so unacceptably low that there can never be a deal. Alexa?"

"There's no deal breaker, James. We don't ever walk away." She added quietly, "I would play

Stephanie for free. No, I would *pay* for the privilege of playing her."

"You know the cardinal rule of successful negotiating?" he asked with a soft laugh. "You have to make the other guy believe you don't give a damn."

"But I do give a damn," Alexa countered swiftly. Earlier she had cast James Sterling as James Bond. Now as he was smiling his devastating smile and telling her that you have to not give a damn, her mind cast him in another famous role: Rhett leaving Scarlett. Frankly my dear . . .

Did she really want this man who didn't give a damn to negotiate this important contract for her?

"OK. No deal breakers, I promise. And I told you, I don't make promises I can't keep. Would you rather I didn't do this? Alexa? You've spent enough time in Washington to know how to extricate yourself from any situation."

"I have?"

"Sure. If you don't want me to represent you in this, Alexa, just say no."

During the silence that followed James had two distinct and opposite wishes. Just say no, Alexa, and I will give you the name of another good attorney, and you will no longer be my client, and we will abandon coffee for champagne, and dance amidst the roses, and begin to learn more about each other. That was one wish, undeniably selfish.. But his other wish was even more selfish.. Just say yes, Alexa. Trust me with this thing that is clearly so important to you. And then after, when you are no longer my client, we will begin . . .

"I would like you to represent me, James. You don't even need to check back with me once you've gathered the data. Just go for whatever amount you think is reasonable."

"You're sure?"

"Yes. I guess we should sign something. Most agents get fifteen percent."

"Agents get a percentage because they take an active part in managing your career. This is a straightforward contract negotiation. I will send you a bill for my time."

"The full usual amount."

"Absolutely," James promised as he stood to leave. "I'd better be going. I'll give you a call."

Then he was gone, and Alexa paced restlessly among the roses in her living room. Why hadn't she decided to forget about the contract and simply let him seduce her? Allowing him to negotiate his way into her bed would have been pure pleasure, and so very safe. In bed, she was in no danger from this man who made deals and broke hearts with equal icy ease. Her heart *could not* be broken, not even by the famous James Sterling, because a heart not given could not break.

Alexa never placed her heart in jeopardy, but still, somehow she had permitted him to wander off into the midnight darkness with something that was of immense value to her—the great joy of playing Stephanie Winslow, whom she admired. How could she have entrusted that very important part of herself to a man whose approach to negotiating was to not give a damn? Billionaires trusted James Sterling with their billion-dollar companies, but maybe to the billionaires, it was all a thrilling high-stakes game.

But this wasn't a game! At least not to her.

Alexa desperately hoped that it was not a game to James.

She should have remained in the rose-fragrant living room, or perhaps gone to her own bedroom to touch the small golden statue that was glittering proof of her success and worth. But, instead, compelled by some deep, self-destructive impulse she could not control, she walked to the bedroom that would be Cat's. As she frowned at the so carefully selected lilac wallpaper, she knew that even the enormous doubts she had about entrusting her career to James were quite trivial compared to the great doubts she had about her little sister.

The same April moon that had smiled a golden smile on the secluded terrace where Alexa and James had met now softly illuminated Catherine's path as she made her way across the Oberlin campus from Bailey House, the residence hall where she lived, to the practice rooms in the Conservatory's Robertson Hall. The beam of golden moonlight was lovely, but quite unnecessary. Even on a moonless night in the darkest of Ohio winters she would have found her way along the so familiar path; and even had she never traveled the path before, and even in a darkness darker than a moonless midnight, a deep instinct would have unerringly guided Catherine to a place where there was a piano.

It was midnight. The festive Saturday night noises of campus parties were beginning to fade, the raucous laughter softening as groups became couples and the large parties became private and intimate ones. Lost in thought, Catherine was oblivious to the sounds of love and gaiety around her; but had she heard them, she would have smiled an untroubled smile at the happiness of her classmates, quite unconcerned that she herself was alone on this Saturday night. She was, after all, precisely where she wanted to be, walking happily toward the piano she would joyfully play until dawn.

Catherine didn't hear the noises of parties, nor was she aware either of the chill of the brisk night wind. She felt very warm, warmed from within by the anticipated joy of playing soon and by the remembered joy of the day. It had been quite glorious; fresh and sunny and filled with all the hopeful promises of spring. She had spent the afternoon sitting cross-legged on a warm patch of grass in Tappan Square, reading *La Cousine Bette* by Balzac. She read the classic novel in its original French, and later, after the sun had fallen, taking its gentle warmth with it, she had returned to her room, and, also in French, she had carefully recorded impressions of what she'd read onto the colorful notecards she was compiling for the term paper she had to write.

She spent the evening with Balzac and just before midnight began the familiar walk to the Conservatory. She had been walking briskly, eagerly, but now as she neared Wilder Hall, the student union building, her footsteps slowed, and, on impulse, she veered from her path to the Conservatory to that building where the student mailboxes were housed. Why? she wondered as she tried to analyze the sudden and surprising impulse. Surely there would be no mail for her. It had only been two days since she'd received a letter from Topeka, and even though the long, happy, loving letters from her parents arrived frequently, just as her long, happy, loving ones to them arrived frequently in Topeka, there would not be another one from them so soon.

But something compelled her to check anyway, and as she neared her small mailbox and saw that it wasn't empty her heart fluttered with loving wonder at the remarkable telepathy between herself and her beloved parents. It had always been there, a wonderful, astonishing understanding that required no words. As her delicate virtuoso fingers spun the combination, Catherine noticed through the window that the letter was quite thin. It would be a brief newsy item that her mother had forgotten to include in her recent letter—good news about a neighbor, or about a pottery sale she'd made, or about her father's music. More than once, Catherine had done the same thing, remembering a detail she'd somehow forgotten and jotting it down on one of the beautiful postcards she had of Tappan Square in fall, ablaze with the magnificent colors of the turning leaves.

This was a postcard, Catherine discovered as she removed it. But it wasn't from Topeka. The pale blue card, on which was embossed an elegant white swan, was from Los Angeles, from the Hotel Bel-Air, from Alexa. And it read, in Alexa's sophisticated script: Cat, In all the excitement, I forgot to tell you how glad I am that you're moving to New York. Thank you again for the beautiful roses. A.

"All the excitement" had been the breathless conversation between the sisters on the morning after the Academy Awards. Alexa had called to thank Catherine for the lovely bouquet of Lady Di roses that had greeted her in her suite at the Hotel Bel-Air when, near dawn, she'd finally returned from the last Oscar party. Alexa had raved about the perfect, pale peach roses, how fragrant they were, how delicate and beautiful, how they were her favorite of all roses; and, at the same time, quietly, but like her older sister breathlessly, too, Catherine had told Alexa over and over how happy she was that she'd won. It had been a short conversation, because after the breathless gushes there had been awkward silence, and quickly, awkwardly, they'd said good-bye.

But, after the call ended, Alexa had obviously remembered other important words and had written the note. Catherine had had other important words to say, too; but she hadn't had the courage to say them, nor had she even bravely written them in a note. But she should have! She should have told Alexa how many times she'd seen *Majesty*, and how much she deserved to win the Oscar, and how proud she was of her, *always*, Oscar or no Oscar. And she should have told her

61

older sister, too, how very excited she was about moving to New York. She should have said, or at least written, all those important things; but she hadn't; she had never had Alexa's effortless confidence.

After carefully putting the postcard in her coat pocket, Catherine returned to the moonlit midnight and very chilly night air. But she felt even warmer now than before, and her luminous sapphire eyes glowed from an inner joy. *I forgot to tell you how glad I am that you're moving to New York*, Alexa had written. Oh, how she hoped that was true! She loved and admired her older sister so much, and was so eager to be near her, and so hopeful that the delicate beginning friendship of the past eight years would take brave, firm roots, and then blossom and grow.

Now she hoped Alexa would like her.

Without warning, the wonderful warmth vanished and an icy chill swept through her. It wasn't the brisk night wind, Catherine knew. It was instead the frigid shiver of an ancient ghost, a reminder that even though the recent memories were warm and hopeful, there had been a time—*most of her life*—when there had not been friendship between them. That painful time had been when they had lived together, under the same roof; a time when Alexa had had a chance to really know her little sister.

And she didn't like me then, Catherine reminded herself. *What if, as she gets to know me now, she doesn't like me still?*

All the warmth was gone, and she trembled with a deep, icy fear. And she began to walk even more briskly along the moonlit path to the place she now needed so desperately to be . . . to the piano . . . to her music . . . to that magnificent escape into peace.

Chapter 4

"The network has picked up *Pennsylvania Avenue* for two seasons," James told Alexa when he telephoned Tuesday evening.

"Two seasons? That's very unusual." She had been in show business long enough to know its whimsical nature. Commitments were always short-term—a season, *part* of a season—and cancellations could occur without warning.

"Yes, but it's happened. Obviously the network knows that after three seasons in the top slot *Pennsylvania Avenue* isn't about to lose its audience. The upshot is that they want to sign you to a two-year contract."

"That sounds encouraging, doesn't it?"

"You mean, evidence that they want you? I guess I should have begun with that—they want you, Alexa. Your role in the immense success of the show is critical. They're prepared to pay a substantial bonus, an incentive if you will, for signing the two-year deal."

"So you think we should go for it?"

"It's not 'we,' Alexa, it's you. There'll be plenty of money either way, so the issue should be what

63

you want to do with your time and your career. You'd mentioned wanting to take some time off."

"Yes, but not time away from *Pennsylvania Avenue*. I'm very willing to make a two-year commitment, James."

"OK. I'll let you know when I think we're close to reasonable numbers. Did the mirrors come down all right?"

"What? Oh yes."

"The offer on the table, awaiting your approval, is six million for two years with an increase in your percentage for syndication and ex-U.S. sales to—"

"Six million?" Her voice came finally, interrupting him with a whispered gasp. He said the amount so casually—to him six million was probably just a "6"—but to her . . . "That's so much more than we talked about."

"The value of getting the facts, Alexa."

"They're comfortable paying me this amount?"

"Absolutely. The negotiations were very pleasant." He had been tough, of course, and he'd worn his elegant don't-give-a-damn demeanor to the negotiating table; but because as always he had armed himself with the necessary data, he was negotiating from a secure position of strength. His initial counter offer—ten million— had been purposefully high, just as the producer's initial proposal had been intentionally low. James fully expected to settle at five, and was surprised and delighted with six, although his dark blue eyes had greeted the amount with only calm approval. "I take it you're tempted to accept the offer?"

"Yes." Alexa laughed softly.

"All right. I think the paperwork on this will all happen very quickly. They want to get you signed, sealed, and delivered before someone tries to lure you back to the silver screen. I'll review the contract first, of course, and then forward it to you."

"Did I thank you?"

"No thanks are necessary, Alexa. This is what I do, what I *enjoy* doing." James paused. When he spoke again there was a softening of his voice, a shift from business to personal, as he quietly issued the one-word invitation. "So."

"So?" she echoed, welcomingly.

"So . . . would you like to have dinner with me?"

"Yes. But I should be inviting you to dinner."

"If that means a homecooked meal at your apartment sometime I accept. Are you a country cook?"

"Of course not!" Alexa answered swiftly. That's the other Taylor sister, she thought. With the thought came a wave of sadness as she remembered the joyful laughter that had come from the farmhouse's small kitchen as her mother had taught her little sister how to cook. She could have joined them, of course; but she had spent her girlhood as far away from Cat as possible, demeaning everything that was important to her by her own resolute unwillingness to participate. Alexa vanquished the unwelcome sadness by replacing it with the recent, hopeful memories of

Cat. Then she was back to the present, to the incredible six-million-dollar contract and the incredibly attractive man who wanted to have dinner with her. "I don't cook, but I imagine I could get something from Le Cirque."

"You're proposing gourmet take-out?"

"Why not? Don't you think I could negotiate that?"

"I'm very sure you could. But, let me take you somewhere this time. How is this weekend for you?" When Alexa didn't answer right away, James assumed she was silently visualizing a combination of her performance schedule for *Romeo and Juliet* and her doubtless very full social calendar. He finally guessed, "Completely star-crossed?"

"No. In fact, the teenaged lovers have a Friday night appearance and then are off until Monday. The Shakespeare On Broadway company is presenting four plays this spring. *Richard III*, *Hamlet*, and *The Tempest* are holding down the fort for the weekend."

"But?"

"But I was planning to spend the weekend in Maryland."

"Where in Maryland?"

"About thirty miles due east of Washington. Until last November I lived in a townhouse in Georgetown while *Pennsylvania Avenue* was in production, but now I have a tiny secluded cottage perched on a cliff overlooking Chesapeake Bay. The cottage is wonderful, but it needs a little work."

"Along the Laura Ashley lines?"

"It did need work inside, but I was able to get that done over the winter. The inside rooms are in full bloom, but it's the outside flowers in the long-neglected garden that need attention. A team of gardeners from a local nursery has already done the hardest part, preparing the beds. All that's left is planting the roses that will be delivered on Friday."

"Which is what you're going to do this weekend?"

"Yes. It's my first garden. I like the idea of planting the flowers myself."

James heard the soft shrug in her voice and smiled. After a moment he said, "If your cottage is thirty miles due east of the capital and overlooks the bay, it must be near the Marlboro Marina."

"It is. Very near. You're familiar with the area?"

"My home—my parents' home is five miles north of the Marina."

"Oh."

"My parents' home, and my sailboat. So . . ."

"So?"

"So, if I didn't have a date for dinner with you this weekend in New York, I would spend the weekend sailing in Maryland. If you like, we could drive down together, and I could sail while you plant, and then, if you're not too exhausted to move, we could have dinner at the Marlboro Hunt Club. Alexa, just say—"

"Yes."

"Good morning."

"Hi." She had decided, as she felt her heart

67

quicken in anticipation of seeing him again, that her imagination had surely embellished the reality. He had been wearing a silk tuxedo that night, after all, and there had been moonlight and roses and . . .

But when James arrived Saturday morning, Alexa realized her mind had not been playing tricks. Even in the bright morning sun his eyes were as intensely dark blue as they had been in the moonlight, his smile as seductive, his hair as black and shining; and, in the case of James Sterling, the clothes did not make the man. Quite the opposite. In faded blue jeans, he was elegant still, his lean strength at once graceful and powerful.

"All set?" James asked after a moment. He, too, had needed a little time to adjust to seeing her again. He had almost convinced himself that the lovely vulnerability beneath the dazzling facade must have been an illusion. But no, it was there still, a soft whisper of turbulence beneath the sparkling emerald calm, beckoning and intriguing.

"All set."

"Is this all?" he asked as he reached for the small suitcase.

"Yes, just Cassini sequins for dinner tonight and a few how-to-plant rose books. I have extra jeans at the cottage."

"And a shovel?"

"The Marlboro Nursery has supposedly delivered everything I will need, including *their* planting and pruning instructions. I'm hoping that what Marlboro suggests will agree with at least one of the other books I've read."

"Which don't agree?"

"No!" Alexa laughed. "Minor discrepancies, admittedly, but apparently planting roses isn't an exact science. I hope that means, within limits, that it doesn't really matter."

"That's probably what it means. I think that roses tend to be very hardy. However, if you'd like yet another expert opinion we can stop at Inverness on the way to your cottage and examine the roses there."

"Inverness?"

"My parents' home. They have quite a few roses. I imagine the gardeners have done the spring pruning already, so it might be helpful."

"OK. Sure. Let's stop at Inverness."

"Choose a tape, if you like," James suggested once they were out of Manhattan and on the Interstate. "They're in the glove compartment."

Alexa examined James's tapes—Vivaldi, Mozart, Bach, Beethoven, Chopin—the most beautiful, most eyocative works of the great composers, all so familiar to her, because of Cat; and, because of Cat all so able to stir memories and emotions . . . pride and guilt, hope and pain, hatred and love.

"No Prince? No Madonna? Not even Beatles or Beach Boys?" Alexa narrowed her sparkling emerald eyes and whispered with mock horror, "You're hopelessly classical, aren't you?"

"Not hopelessly." James smiled as he turned on the radio and pressed a button preset to a popular "soft rock" station. "I am, however, as of Thursday night, hopelessly addicted to *Pennsylvania Avenue.*"

"Thursday night's episode was the season-ending cliff-hanger," Alexa murmured softly, very flattered that he had made a point of watching. "The spring and summer reruns begin next week."

"Meaning I'll have to wait until mid-September to find out if Stephanie Winslow escapes the blaze?"

"Yes. Although you happen to have about six million clues that she does," she said, smiling, thanking him again. After a moment she teased, "Of course, if you were to be my agent, you would be allowed sneak previews of scripts and free access to even the closed sets as of July."

"I'm not going to be your agent. I'm quite happy to simply admire your work with the rest of the world. Besides," he added softly, "I don't want to run the risk of encountering artistic differences with you."

"Oh."

She smiled, and he smiled, and after a few moments of silence, he asked, "So, how is *Romeo and Juliet?*"

"The critics and audiences seem happy, but I keep wondering what could have possessed me to agree to play Juliet. I feel like such a fraud."

"Why?"

"*Why?* A love to die for? *Moi?*"

"Alexandra, do I detect a little cynicism about love?"

"Of course you do! More than a little. But

don't tell me you're an incurable romantic, James," she said teasingly to the man who made deals and broke hearts with equal icy ease. She was quite confident that James Sterling did not believe in romantic notions such as falling in love.

"I admit to being skeptical, but not cynical."

"Meaning?"

James hesitated, wondering how much to reveal, reminding himself that he wanted *her* to reveal to *him* the truths that lay beneath the dazzling facade. Wasn't it fair for her to expect the same honesty from him? Yes even though this truth sounded more like good-bye than hello. It was, in fact, what he told his lovers, gently, apologetically, when he said good-bye.

"Meaning that I'm probably not destined to have a consuming love. My life is already more than consumed by my two compelling passions— work and sailing—and I'm quite happy." James saw solemn comprehension, not disappointment, on her beautiful face, and realized that her admission that playing Juliet was a stretch had obviously been quite honest, not a flirtatious ploy designed to uncover his views on the subject. "Unlike cynical you, however, I do believe a *Romeo and Juliet* love is possible. I'm just skeptical that such a love will happen to me."

"You have a reputation as a breaker of hearts, you know," Alexa said quietly, thoughtfully, and without incrimination.

"Never on purpose, Alexa."

"No," she agreed softly. "They just expect too much. They expect more than you can give."

No, James thought. My lovers never expect

more than *I can* give, only more than I *want* to give. For him it was simply a matter of choice. He was happy with his life—his privacy and his independence—and he had not yet met someone for whom he was willing to devote the time, energy, and emotion demanded by a consuming love. But it wasn't a choice for Alexa, he decided as he heard the softness of her words. Her lovers *had* expected more than she could give. But what did that mean? Why in the world would she believe that there was something about her, some essential ingredient, that limited her ability to love?

INVERNESS was chiseled in old English lettering into one of the two stone pillars at the entrance of the eighteen-acre estate. James turned onto the gravel drive, leaving the bright country road for the shadows of pines, but after a quarter of a mile the forest that provided a lush green wall of privacy from passersby opened to acres of mani-cured lawn and bountiful gardens. In the distance, on the bluff overlooking Chesapeake Bay, stood the mansion.

"Will your parents be here?"

"No. They're in Paris. My father is the Ambas-sador to France."

"Ah." Alexa gave her head a slight amazed shake. "And your mother?"

"She's a doctor, an obstetrician-gynecologist."

"Does she practice in Paris?"

"No. She stopped practicing even before my father accepted the ambassadorship, four years ago, on her seventieth birthday."

"She was forty when you were born?"

"Yes. I think she was a forerunner of the career women of the eighties. She was the only woman in her medical school class at Johns Hopkins and was one of the first to make full professor rank in the department. She and my father were thirty-nine when they met. Both had been intensely dedicated to their careers, with no plans of marriage, but . . ."

"Two skeptics taken by surprise?"

"Maybe." James smiled. "Anyway, they married and about a year later I came along."

"Another surprise?"

"I don't think so. If I was, I was a welcome one."

Alexa tilted her head thoughtfully at the sudden softness in his voice, a softness that revealed his gentle and genuine love for his parents.

"Do you see them much?"

"Often. My work takes me to Europe quite frequently, and, like all good Parisiens, my mother and father abandon Paris in August. However, instead of escaping to the Côte d'Azur, they come here."

James gave Alexa a tour of the mansion, finishing in the great room that overlooked a garden of recently pruned roses. After he led the way outside through the immense French doors, she knelt on the warm grass beside the beds intently studying the handiwork of Inverness's expert gardeners.

"This really was helpful," she said finally, standing, after she had fixed firmly in her mind the lengths and diameters of the remaining stems, and the angles and locations of the fresh cuts above the delicate new buds.

"I'm glad. So, are you desperate to start planting?"

"Don't I get to see your sailboat?"

"Of course. You have the choice of a bird's-eye view from the bluff or a close enough to touch view from the dock. The drawback of the close-up view is that the bay—and therefore the boat—is three steep flights of stairs down the bluff. Going down is easy, but coming back up is—"

"I want to touch it!" Alexa interjected swiftly. Three steep flights of stairs were not the slightest deterrent to her. She was healthy, fit, energetic. Besides, as James would discover soon, it was precisely three flights of carved granite stairs from where one parked the car to her cliff-top cottage.

"It's beautiful," Alexa whispered as she delicately touched the shiny teal blue hull of *Night Wind,* James's sleek, flawlessly maintained twelve-meter yawl.

"Thank you. Have you ever sailed?"

"A few times."

"And for some reason sailing doesn't appeal."

"I like to be able to leave when I've decided the party's over."

"Ah. Some heretic has lured you onto a sailboat in hopes of seducing you."

"Heretic?"

"I'm a sailing purist. Sailing is for sailing." James smiled. "There are other times for seduction."

"So I would be quite safe from seduction on *Night Wind?*"

"Absolutely."

But would I be safe from seduction at other times? Alexa wondered. She met his smiling sensual dark blue eyes and saw their eloquent answer, an answer she had very much hoped to see.

No, Alexa, you would not—*will not*—be safe at other times.

They climbed back up the three flights of red-brick steps from the bay to the mansion without breathlessness, and twenty minutes later, as they ascended the three flights of granite to her cottage, Alexa chattered effortlessly.

"Do you know, James," she began, the seriousness of her expression betrayed by her sparkling eyes, "is there a minimum size a place has to be before it can be named?"

"What are you talking about?"

"I think my little tiny cottage needs a grand name. Inverness Minor, or something."

"I see." He laughed, and would have started the search for whimsical suggestions, but they had reached the summit of their climb and all attention was necessarily focused on the *dozens and dozens* of pots filled with roses. "Alexa . . ."

"There's plenty of room for all of them!"

"Yes," James agreed as he gazed at the many freshly tilled beds. "And it's going to be spectacular, like living in the midst of a bouquet when they bloom, but, Alexa, I think I'd better help you with the planting."

"Oh, no, thank you. I can manage."

"Are you sure?"

"Oh, yes." Alexa turned from his smiling blue eyes and surveyed her tiny estate cluttered with potted roses. It was hopeless, of course, far beyond what she could accomplish by herself, but this was her first garden and she had been looking forward to carefully planning the design and puttering around in the warm, rich soil. When she turned back to him, she lifted her chin defiantly and affirmed with a soft laugh and bright eyes, "Quite sure!"

"OK."

"This does, of course, solve the mystery of why the owner of the nursery has suggested about a hundred times that I just put the roses exactly where I want them and let his crew plant them for me. I'd been wondering why he was so persistent about that."

"Do you think, many hours from now, that you might take him up on the suggestion?"

"Many hours and many sore muscles from now, yes, I think I just might."

"Well, I'll leave you then." His dark blue eyes studied her for a moment and then he added very softly. "There is, however, something about which I have been wondering."

"Oh?" she asked, her shining green eyes telling him that she knew what it was, and that she had been wondering, too.

"This," he whispered as his lips met hers.

"This," she echoed as she welcomed him.

They both had been wondering, and they both had been luxuriating in the gentle seduction, the

76

playful teasing, the tingling anticipation. Both had imagined a warm, wonderful pleasure. *But neither had foreseen the fire.*

The kiss began with soft whispers, but very quickly no more words were possible. The powerful hot rushes of desire were all-consuming . . . demanding, consuming, demanding so very much more than a gently whispered hello.

It was James who stopped the kiss, finally and with great effort. As he pulled away his dark blue eyes met her suddenly surprised emerald ones, and he saw a magnificent desire that eloquently mirrored his own.

"Our dinner reservations are for eight-thirty, so I'll be back to get you at eight."

"You're leaving?"

"Yes. I'm going sailing, and you're planting your garden."

"You're playing with me."

"Oh no, Alexa," James said quietly. "I'm not playing with you."

Had he been playing, had she been any other woman, he would have taken her into her romantic bedroom in the charming cottage and made love to her right then, abandoning his own plans and vanquishing hers. The beautiful eyes that glistened with desire urged him so powerfully to do just that. But James had other memories of her eyes, sparkling with eagerness to create her garden of roses, and he knew how very important those plans were to her.

This afternoon they would pursue their private passions. And tonight, when they both chose, because they both chose, they would make leisurely discoveries about the astonishing passion that was theirs to share.

They dined by candlelight at the Hunt Club and danced on the terrace beneath the moon, seducing each other, savoring the seduction until finally it was she who whispered with a soft trembling laugh that they had to return to her cottage *now*.

The moonlight filtering through the lacy curtains cast her romantic bedroom in pale, misty gold. With another man, Alexa would have pulled the opaque layer of drapes and enveloped the room in protective darkness. But James's kiss and the talented hands that undressed her so gently swept away all thought, and she forgot to hide herself in the familiar shadows she preferred when making love. She was unashamed of her flawless body, of course. She knew well the silky, provocative perfection of her full breasts, her softly curving hips, her sleek flat stomach, and her long tapered legs.

The shadows weren't for her perfect body— they were for her eyes. Unshadowed, her eyes might reveal what she so often felt: *annoyance,* because she saw conquest blended with desire; *disappointment,* because the tingling sensations that quivered within her—soft, delicate whispers that teased and beckoned—were lost in the roaring thunder of her lover's passion; and finally *anger,* because her lovers, who knew nothing of her—and wouldn't love her if they did!—made breathless, impassioned confessions of love.

The whispers of desire awakened by James's

tender touch made Alexa forget entirely about closing the drapes. He undressed her, lingering over each new discovery, kissing a tender hello to each new place until her soft laughter urged him to continue his sensual exploration and make even more intimate discoveries. James undressed Alexa, and then she undressed him, lingeringly and tenderly, too, until his soft sighs became as urgent for more intimacy as hers had been.

Then they were together, amidst a cool soft cotton rose garden designed by Laura Ashley, and . . .

"I need you."

"Yes," she whispered with quiet joy, needing him, wanting him, too.

James held her moonlit gaze as she welcomed him, and in the dark blue eyes she saw only desire, not conquest. And she heard, in his soft urgent whispers, only astonished truths about their passion not false promises of love. And she felt at last the magnificence of her own quivering desires, because they were not lost now, as they had always been lost before, but found, discovered, and nurtured so gently, so patiently by him.

"Alexa," he whispered when it was time, for both of them. *"Alexandra."*

"Hi." The moonlit tangle of silky gold was a wonderful symbol of their loving, but James gently parted it now because he wanted to see her eyes again.

"Hi."

"That was very nice," he whispered softly.

"Yes."

"Not trivial."

"No," Alexa agreed softly. Not trivial at all. "Very nice."

Nice, she mused, suddenly liking a word which had always before felt a little bland. If you can't say something nice, don't say anything, wise adults had always admonished; and since then pronouncing something "nice" had always seemed like damning with the faintest of praise. But "nice" sounded neither bland nor damning when whispered softly by James's talented lips. It sounded gentle and tender and special, and so much better than the falsehoods of love usually spoken to her in the awkward and disappointing moments after making love. Now, with James, those moments felt wonderful, so comfortable, so honest, so *nice* . . . until his handsome face became very serious.

Oh, James, don't trivialize this by telling me lies of love! Especially since we both know you don't even *believe* in it.

"What?" she demanded, surprising him with the sudden sharpness of her tone.

"You know the trouble with being seduced in your own bed, don't you?"

"No."

"It's the same as your problem with sailing. You can't leave when you decide the party's over."

"Oh," she whispered quietly as grateful relief swept through her. He wasn't going to tell her lies of love. He was simply, once again, giving her choices and placing value on what was important to her. He had been right to leave her

80

to her garden this afternoon. And now . . . did James know that she always wanted her lovers to leave, preferring solitude to the paradoxical loneliness she felt when they stayed? Yes, he obviously knew that. Because he usually preferred solitude, too? Yes, she realized, but tonight was different . . . for both of them. Tonight he wasn't choosing to leave. He was asking to stay—if she wanted him to.

"I'm beginning to think that you're a very nice man," she said softly. Very nice, she thought, very gentle, very tender, very special.

"Just beginning? I decided that about you the moment we met."

Oh, no, James, I'm not nice! The thought came swiftly, by ancient reflex, an irrefutable truth. Should she share that truth with him? Should she warn him away? As she looked at the dark blue eyes that wanted to know why his words had caused her to frown, she realized that James Sterling needed no warning. He was in complete control, quite capable of making his own decisions, quite immune to love, and quite safe from being hurt, especially by her. James was in no danger. But she was in danger from him, from the compelling demands of their passion, and from the compelling demands of the blue eyes that somehow seduced her into telling truths about herself.

"Alexa?"

"I'd like you to stay."

"Good. I'd like to. Did you make a decision about the party?"

"The party?"

"Is it over?" James saw in her smiling emerald eyes that it wasn't over and gently drew her back to him.

"Not over," she whispered as her lips met his. The magnificent sensations rushed forward boldly now, eager and brave, because now there was a thrilling memory, not simply a trembling hope.

"RoseCliff."

"What did you . . . ?"

"RoseCliff."

"Oh," she breathed with sudden comprehension. "The name for my tiny little estate. I like it."

"Just a suggestion. Something to think about," he murmured between hungry kisses, "some other time."

"Some other time, yes, but I like it," she murmured back. Then, just before her mouth acceded to the wonderful sensations that commanded her to stop speaking and just kiss him, she embellished softly, "It's very nice."

Chapter 5

Manhattan . . . May 1989

Alexa's heart quickened in delicious anticipation as the elevator carried her in swift silence from the building's marble lobby to the Madison Avenue penthouse offices of James Sterling, Attorney at

Law. He had been in Tokyo for the past twelve days, and the separation had been much more than just the disruption of their magnificent passion. The combination of their busy schedules and the time zone change conspired to prevent the luxury of the wonderful late-night phone calls that had become an important part of their relationship whenever he was away; the long, honest conversations that made them feel as if they had known and cared about each other forever . . . instead of for only seven weeks.

James had been back since noon, and now it was after six, but she had stayed away until now, knowing he needed time to work his way through the most important calls of the past twelve days, and wanting, when at last she saw him, to have him all to herself, his attention wholly concentrated on her.

She was so greedy for him! She wanted all of him, all at once, his eyes, his smile, his voice, his touch. She wanted to hear all the details of his successful negotiations in Japan, and she wanted to tell him, because he would want to know, the details of the last twelve days of her life, too. She wanted to laugh and talk and share . . .

But, she admitted to herself as she left the elevator and walked along the plush carpet toward his private office, right now what she wanted most was to see dark blue eyes that were happy to see her . . . and to feel talented fingers gently caress her skin . . . and to hear soft sighs of pleasure as he undressed her and discovered anew the silkiness of her perfect body.

The door to his office was ajar, for her. Without

needing to open it further, she could see him seated at his desk. James sensed her presence immediately and rose to greet her.

"Hello there," he said softly, his voice full of welcome and promise.

"Hello." She leaned provocatively against the door jamb and whispered seductively, "Mr. Sterling, if you don't negotiate a swift, satisfying merger with me right now I'll—"

"Alexa," he interjected with a soft laugh. Then he had reached her, and opening the door to reveal more of the spacious office, he said, "I'd like you to meet Robert McAllister."

"Oh!" Had the man who had unwittingly overheard her seductive command been any other man on earth, Alexa could and would have artfully concealed her embarrassed surprise by smiling at him with an expression of pure innocence. But the man was Robert McAllister, and her cheeks flushed pink and her voice bristled instead of purred, "Senator McAllister."

"Ms. Taylor," Robert countered lightly, although he stiffened at her tone and at the magnificent emerald eyes that greeted him as if he had done something quite unforgivable . . . something far more serious than inadvertently preempting her passionate reunion with James.

"Robert tells me that you have never met," James said calmly, his dark blue eyes gazing questioningly at her.

"No. That's right. We haven't," Alexa replied.

Of course we haven't, she thought. Senator and Mrs. Robert McAllister had been conspicuously absent from "When You Wish Upon A Star"—

84

the annual Christmas gala hosted by the producers and cast of *Pennsylvania Avenue*. In only three years, the celebrity gala benefitting children with cancer had become one of Washington's most successful fund-raisers. "When You Wish Upon A Star" received the enthusiastic support of the capital's brightest stars, political and otherwise. *All* the brightest stars, *except* the brightest one of all—Senator Robert McAllister.

The Senator from Virginia had been conspicuously absent from the Christmas gala, and he had been conspicuously absent, too, from the set of *Pennsylvania Avenue*. Virtually every other senator in Washington had dropped by the set at least once—to observe or kibitz or simply meet her—but Robert never had. Alexa believed, of course, that an elected official charged with the solemn task of running the government *should* have better things to do with his time than flirt with her. But that was not, she knew, the reason Robert McAllister had stayed away. No, he had stayed away from the set of *Pennsylvania Avenue* for the same reason he had never attended the celebrity gala—by careful design, to avoid her.

Now, as she felt the not-so-subtle heat of James's stare, she defiantly searched Robert's handsome face for proof that he had been assiduously avoiding her. But the dark brown eyes that met hers were steady, infuriatingly, *arrogantly* unflickering—his contempt for her quite hidden. Of course, she thought, Robert McAllister is a master politician, and therefore, perhaps even better at acting than I.

"Alexa, this is Robert," James spoke quietly,

and for the first time ever she heard a few slivers of the famous Sterling ice.

"I'm delighted to meet you, Robert." She forced a soft purr into her voice and smiled a beautiful smile. "I didn't realize that you and James knew each other."

"We were in law school together."

"Oh, I see." Her beautiful smile held, even though the news was bad. She had assumed Robert had been seeing James on business, or politics. But this was worse. They were friends.

"My wife and I are in town for the weekend. We have a commitment for Saturday evening, but hoped that you and James would be able to join us for dinner tomorrow." Robert expected a swift yes. He had already learned from James that she didn't have a performance scheduled, and that James doubted she had made other plans for them. But Alexa didn't reply with a swift yes. Instead, she seemed at a loss, a little confused, as if searching for an excuse and finding none. As soon as he realized she was struggling, he helped her by offering quietly, "Of course, this is all very last minute. You probably have a conflict."

Just that I have no wish in the world to see your wife, Alexa thought. Was it possible that Robert really didn't know? Was it possible that the reason he never visited the set really was because he did have better things to do? It *was* possible, Alexa supposed, although she found it a bit surprising that Hillary would not have told her husband of their enmity. But, perhaps she hadn't. Perhaps she had simply made certain that she and Robert always had other "A-list" parties to attend on the evening of the Christmas gala.

How Alexa needed a party now, a legitimate excuse, or at least a gracious and convincing lie. But she had become less good at lying since James.

"My sister's twenty-first birthday is this weekend," she murmured finally. It was the truth, of course, but it sounded very feeble nonetheless.

"Let me give you a call later, Robert," James intervened quietly.

"OK. Good. I'd better be going. It was nice meeting you, Alexa."

"It was nice meeting you, too, Robert."

Alexa remained in the office while James walked Robert to the elevator. When he returned, he found her gazing out the window at the tangle of traffic thirty floors below. Her eyes were cast down, fixed on the snarl below, rather than straight ahead at the magnificent twilight. It was unlike Alexa to seek turmoil over beauty; but this time the turmoil had found her, an unwelcome visitor, and she was very far away. James waited for her to become aware that he had returned. When she didn't, he finally spoke, startling her even though his voice was quiet and controlled.

"I didn't realize you were so political, Alexa. And frankly if I'd had to guess about your politics, I would have imagined they would have been quite similar to Robert's."

"It has nothing to do with politics."

"You can't be annoyed that he overheard your remark."

"No," Alexa admitted softly. After a moment she found the courage to turn from the window to him. And when she did she saw what she had always feared the most . . . *disappointment*. She had behaved badly, rudely, to his friend, and James was disappointed in her.

"What then?"

"Robert's wife and I aren't terribly close."

"You've had a run-in with Hillary in Washington?" He could envision it happening, a clash of Hillary's patrician haughtiness and Alexa's intolerance of same, but it surprised him that such an encounter would bother Alexa for long. Wouldn't she simply dismiss it, and Hillary McAllister, with a defiant toss of her shimmering golden mane?

"A run-in, yes, but not in Washington. I haven't even seen Hillary for eight years, not since high school."

"It's hard for me to imagine how you and Hillary were at the same high school."

"We probably *shouldn't* have been—that was certainly Hillary Samantha Ballinger's view. But, for one glorious year, the poor country girl from Kansas and the rich daughter of the Governor of Texas were classmates. It was on her turf, in Dallas, and at Ballinger Academy. You've heard of Ballinger, haven't you? It's the exclusive, private school founded by Hillary's grandfather so that she and the heirs and heiresses of Dallas wouldn't have to mingle with the commoners."

"This is all about some high school rivalry?"

"It was deeper than that."

"But surely something you've long since

outgrown," James offered quietly, although the bitterness in her voice and her lovely troubled eyes told him eloquently that the ancient enmity was far from over. It wasn't over, whatever it was, but it should be. They had been teenaged girls then, after all, and now they were grown women. "Alexa, Robert is a very good friend. I would like to have dinner with him and Hillary and you tomorrow night."

"Couldn't you go by yourself?"

"Not without a good reason."

"I thought I could always just say no."

"Not this time."

Alexa looked into the inscrutable blue eyes of the master negotiator, the man whose great success was in part his willingness to walk away from any deal if it didn't meet his high expectations.

"Is this the deal breaker, James?" she asked softly. If I don't go to dinner tomorrow night with my ancient enemy are we—whatever "we" are—over? Alexa didn't know what "they" were, but she knew she would miss him terribly if he suddenly vanished from her life. Would James miss me, too? she wondered. As she searched for the answer in his unrevealing eyes, and saw only more layers of the famous iciness, she thought sadly, Perhaps he really could simply walk away. Perhaps he could deliver the celebrated line without a flicker of regret, Frankly, my dear, I don't give a damn.

"Alexa," James began gently without answering her question. "Why don't you tell me about you and Hillary?"

About you and Hillary. As the words echoed in Alexa's mind, she realized that the story wasn't really about Hillary at all. It was about *her* . . . her failures, her unworthiness, her cruelty. Hillary had simply been a mirror, reflecting back with vivid clarity Alexa's own terrible flaws. Mirror, Mirror, on the wall, who's the cruelest of them all?

"Alexa?" James repeated softly, suddenly worried by the immense sadness in her eyes. Sadness and such uncertainty, as if she believed that if she allowed him this rare glimpse into a most private place in her heart, he wouldn't like what he saw. Didn't she know? He trusted his instincts about her, but she apparently didn't have the same faith in herself. "I need to speak with a client in San Francisco before I can call it a day. It's not confidential, so you needn't leave. Have a seat on the couch. Then, as soon as I'm done, why don't we go to your apartment and talk?"

It was a question, posed gently, but Alexa had already learned that this time she couldn't just say no. She would have to tell James the dark truths about herself, the "niceness" that wasn't really there at all, the awful emotions that had surfaced from beneath the glittering sunny gold almost twenty-one years ago, the moment she first saw her little sister . . .

"She's not my sister," she announced with familiar Alexa confidence as her eyes fell on the tiny infant so lovingly cradled in her mother's arms.

Her voice was confident, but already her small body trembled with bewildering emotions. The new and powerful emotions had begun the instant she had seen her parents gaze with loving wonder at Catherine, the same loving wonder with which they had only, and always before, gazed at her.

And now, as she made her pronouncement, there was something else in Jane and Alexander's eyes, something for her, something she had never seen before—worry, and then even worse, *disappointment.*

The disappointment lasted only a moment. But to six-year-old Alexa it felt like forever, never to be forgotten—and never, *please,* to be repeated— and in that moment the pure golden joy that had lived within her was irreparably tarnished. In her heart, she was changed forever, so wary, so wise, but the gifted actress she became on that day bravely acted the storm clouds away. She would be sunny and golden and charming again, *always,* because she so desperately needed to have whatever share of her parents' love could be hers. She needed so desperately never again to disappoint.

Alexa shone as brightly as before, but now the brilliance was artificial; and, like the glaring stage lights she would come to know so well, her brilliance was blinding, preventing with its stunning dazzle any glimpse into the darkness that lay beyond. She permitted no glimpses into the dark shadows of her young heart, but she knew very well what lurked there: bewildering monsters over which she had no control—jealousy, cruelty, hatred. The hatred for Catherine began the instant she saw her, and as her baby sister grew so did Alexa's hatred for her. Catherine was perfect, *perfect,* and Alexa knew only too well her own deep and disappointing flaws.

Even as a tiny baby, Catherine never cried; she just smiled an enchanting Mona Lisa smile. And her greatest joy, discovered long before she could walk or talk, was to sit on Alexander's lap as he played the piano, her huge blue eyes gazing intently as her father's talented fingers glided over the keys. She was completely mesmerized by the music her parents loved so much, but which had never held any allure for her older sister. Alexa had always been far too active to simply listen, preferring to dance and twirl and perform instead.

But Catherine, perfect Catherine, could quietly and joyfully listen to music forever.

"I hate you," Alexa whispered to her little sister. Even though Catherine was too young to understand the meaning of the words, a dark monster within Alexa compelled her to hiss them, a sinister mantra, over and over. The cruel words drew no response from Catherine, and Alexa *needed* a response. She needed proof that the baby wasn't perfect. If she could make Catherine cry . . .

Eight-year-old Alexa pinched herself first, finding a pinch that could make *her* cry and would surely bring tears of pain to a two-year-old. But when her fingers dug into Catherine's velvet soft forearm, not a tear welled in the sapphire blue eyes. The innocent eyes only widened, as if bewildered by what her older sister was doing, and then they softened with something that was even worse . . . *forgiveness.*

After that day, Alexa simply ignored Catherine altogether, as if she had no little sister at all.

Catherine Alexandra Taylor was three when she first touched her small fingers to the keys of her father's piano. From the very first moment, she *played;* and, from the very first moment, the complexity of what she played was limited only by the reach of her tiny fingers, not by the breadth of her talent.

Like her older sister, Catherine's talent was extraordinary; but unlike Alexa, who performed and dazzled for approval and admiration, she performed simply to share the gift for which she was as grateful and astonished as those who listened. She performed without nervousness, even in competition, happily lost in the evocative beauty of the music. Catherine performed to share, not to win, but, from the very beginning, she almost always won.

Catherine's extraordinary talent resulted in an extraordinary offer to her and her family when she was twelve. The world-renowned Conservatory in Dallas wanted her as a pupil. All expenses would be covered, including housing for the entire family; and Alexander, who had been Catherine's only music teacher, would be welcome to participate in the continued instruction of his gifted daughter, as well as the other students at the Conservatory; and eighteen-year-old Alexa would attend the prestigious Ballinger Academy for her final year of high school.

Alexa was immediately enthusiastic about the

move. She had no nostalgia for Topeka, and no qualms whatsoever about being separated from her lifelong friends. Her "friends" were, and always had been, simply an entourage of admirers, not confidants. No friendships bound Alexa to Topeka, nor were there challenges still to be conquered. She had already won all there was to win—the admiration of her teachers and classmates . . . any and every boy she ever wanted . . . the leading role in all the school plays.

Alexa's enthusiasm swayed the three less enthusiastic Taylors. It would be good for Catherine to study at the Conservatory, of course, and the move wasn't irreversible. Since the Conservatory was providing housing, they didn't have to sell their small farmhouse in Topeka. They could return to Kansas whenever they chose.

Alexa decided that for her persona at elite Ballinger's she would be a surfer girl from Malibu, the wild daughter of a famous movie mogul who had been banished to the exclusive school for the rich and privileged because of some undisclosed—and deliciously daring—indiscretion. She created the new image because she was an actress—*and because it was better, always, not to be the real Alexa*—not because she was ashamed of her heritage. She was ashamed of herself, but never, ever, was she ashamed of her parents or her modest upbringing. She loved her parents deeply. It was *she* who had disappointed *them*, not the opposite. And who could blame them for cherishing the always perfect Catherine?

Alexa was proud of her musician father and

artist mother, and it had never mattered at all that they weren't rich. She was proud, not ashamed.

Until Hillary Samantha Ballinger tried to make her feel ashamed.

Hillary discovered the truth about Alexa's real identity and promptly exposed her as a wanton liar. "I'm an actress!" Alexa countered defiantly, aching at the implication, so eloquently transmitted by the haughty arch of Hillary's patrician eyebrow, that she was obviously ashamed of her family. Who wouldn't be? Hillary's knowing look implied. Who wouldn't want to hide a past completely devoid of wealth, breeding, and class? Alexandra Taylor was very *very* common, Hillary warned her wellborn friends, and she should, therefore, be totally ignored.

But Hillary's warning to the other heirs and heiresses came too late. Alexa had instantly intrigued the other students, and now her undaunted dazzle in the face of Hillary's viciousness caused new rounds of admiration. Alexa glittered still, her confidence apparently unwavering, even though Hillary's words had wounded deeply.

Perfectly mimicking Hillary's well-bred Southern accent, Alexa artfully turned the tables on her, exposing the pretentious pettiness with wide, innocent, emerald eyes, until even those most loyal to Hillary were enchanted. The girls shifted allegiance cautiously, lured by Alexa's dazzle and courage but worried about betraying the powerful Hillary. The boys—including Hillary's longtime boyfriend—defected far more swiftly and without a flicker of fear. For years,

Hillary had been a distant object of desire, a beautiful statue atop a marble pedestal, perched far above the admiring eyes; for years, her remoteness had given her a magical allure. But now here was Alexa. And, the boys discovered, Alexa wasn't remote at all, and they discovered too, her allure was even more magical. She was warm, not haughty, and she made them feel wonderful, special, *important* with just the caress of her beautiful smile.

Alexa was terribly popular, and terribly lonely. But, at long last, because of Hillary, the monsters that lurked in the shadows of her heart were allowed to come out to play; at long last, because of Hillary, she was finally able to free some of the hatefulness that dwelled within her.

Hillary Samantha Ballinger was a most worthy opponent. She was deserving of Alexa's monsters, of course, and she was well-armed with her own arsenal of unkind and hateful emotions. Hillary began the war, but Alexa promptly replied, and as the school year progressed the war raged on, bitter but fair.

Until, as in all wars, an innocent victim was claimed.

It was late April. Jane and Alexander had returned to Topeka to visit an ill friend, leaving Alexa in charge of her little sister. It was a simple task: twelve-year-old Catherine was entirely self-sufficient. What Catherine did after all—*all that she did*—was sit at her piano from dawn until dusk, happily lost in her magnificent music. Lost, and safe? Yes . . . unless her happy oblivion prevented her from noticing that the house was on fire or that an axe murderer had broken in and was towering over her, ready to strike.

Saturday came, and Jane and Alexander were still away, and Alexa wanted to go to the polo match between Ballinger and Highland Park. She didn't want her little sister to accompany her, but she couldn't leave Catherine alone because her parents had given her a solemn responsibility and *what if?* So, they went together, arriving at the polo field just as Hillary and three still loyal friends emerged from a silver BMW. Alexa sighed when she saw her enemy. In only six weeks, school would be out, the war would be over, and they would never see each other again. She had been hoping to simply avoid Hillary for these final six weeks. But now here they were, and because she knew Hillary wouldn't pass up the opportunity to say something derisive, Alexa began to summon the energy to cheerfully and cleverly counter whatever slur Hillary tossed her way.

"Well, well. If it isn't the white trash whore from Kansas."

For a stunned moment, Alexa simply stared. Hillary's stinging insult had far more venom than usual. She would have to dig very deep to find just the right reply. As she was searching, another voice broke the stunned silence.

"How dare you say that to my sister!" The brave words came from shy and timid Catherine. Catherine . . . who had been so happy to be included in the plans of the older sister she loved and admired *so much,* but to whom she had not found the courage to say one word during the long drive to the polo field.

As Hillary turned in the direction of the new voice, shifting her icy glare from Alexa to Catherine, her iciness melted into pleasure, perverse joy, as she gazed at the impossibly short hair, the impossibly earnest blue eyes, and the trembling young lips. Who was this unstylish little girl who was so obviously terrified of her own bravery? Was this vision in a rumpled sweatshirt and baggy blue jeans the virtuoso? Could this really be the gifted little sister who was the reason the very much hated Alexa Taylor had descended on her life?

"*What*—pardon me, who—is this?" Hillary queried, staring at Catherine and then glancing to her friends as if so bewildered that she was turning to them for enlightenment. Finally, she stared evenly at Alexa and ventured, "Your little brother? How embarrassing for you, Alexa. I honestly see no hope of this ugly duckling ever becoming a swan."

Alexa might have struck Hillary, might have strangled her, but she sensed the tremor of pain beside her as Hillary's cruel words found their mark deep inside her little sister. Alexa felt the pain and saw the tears in the magnificent sapphire eyes. Tears in Catherine's eyes! Catherine who never cried! Catherine who felt no pain! Catherine whom Alexa herself had once wanted to hurt . . .

Now Catherine *was* hurt, and it was Alexa's heart that screamed with pain. How could she have ever wanted to hurt the little sister who had so swiftly and so bravely come to her defense? Please, please, please, never know that I hated

98

you. Please never remember that I tried to hurt you. Please forgive me . . . again.

As Alexa curled her arms around the little sister whom she had not touched for ten years, she felt Catherine's trembling pain and quivering fright. She tightened her grip and whispered softly, "C'mon, Cat, we're leaving. You are far too good to be anywhere near these people."

When they reached the car, they sat inside, facing each other, and talked for the first time in their lives.

"What she said wasn't true, Cat," Alexa said quietly.

"I know, but how could she have said it about you anyway?"

"Oh," Alexa answered with soft surprise. "I meant what she said about you wasn't true. Not a word of it. First of all, I'm very proud that you're my little sister. And second, there's no doubt in the world that you're a girl, not a boy. And third, there's also no doubt that you're very beautiful."

There was no doubt in Alexa's mind that Catherine was very beautiful. True, her hair was quite short, a shiny black velvet cap, but the functional style simply augmented her huge blue eyes. And true, she was a little plump, but, Alexa thought, the soft layer of luxuriant plumpness sent a rich bountiful message of radiant health. Catherine's life was her music. She had probably never even thought about her looks until now, as Hillary's cruel words forced her to. But the truth was that she was a very beautiful little girl. And one day,

Alexa knew, whether Catherine thought about it or not, she would be a very beautiful woman.

"Oh, no, Alexa. You're the beautiful one," Catherine said with quiet pride for her older sister.

"Well, then, we both are. Everything Hillary said about you was a lie, Cat, and so was everything she said about me." Alexa wondered if her innocent little sister even knew the meaning of the word "whore." She hoped not. "White trash" was bad enough. And both, of course, were untrue. True, she hadn't been a virgin since a moonlit summer night in a cornfield in Kansas when she was sixteen; but even though she had enchanted the boys at Ballinger's, she had slept with none of them. She enchanted so artfully that she had yet to be accused even of being a tease, much less a *whore*. "Everything."

"I know," Catherine said. Then she dismissed Hillary Ballinger altogether and summoned the courage to talk to her big sister about something very important. "You called me Cat?"

"That's my nickname for you," Alexa admitted softly. The little sister she had ignored all these years nonetheless had a nickname. There was no affection associated with the name, quite the opposite; the girlhood discovery was a cloying reminder of their destiny. "It's your initials, of course, and mine are ACT. Mom and Dad must have known from the moment they named us that I would be an actress and you would be a kitten on the keys."

Alexa smiled, but her emotions swept her to all the sleepless nights, years before, that she had spent wondering how different her life might have been had she been Catherine Alexandra not Alexandra Catherine. Had she been CAT, would she have possessed the magical gifts of music so important to her parents?

"Cat," Catherine whispered, her sapphire eyes lighting with a deep joy, so happy that Alexa had a private nickname for her, so happy that Alexa had ever even *thought* about her.

"Do you like it?"

"Oh yes!"

Cat wasn't really right for Catherine, Jane and Alexander decided privately. The name would have been far better for sleek Alexa with her magnificent cat-like grace and appraising emerald eyes. But they embraced the nickname joyfully, because Cat did, and because while they had been away something wonderful had happened. How long they had waited, in silent helpless anguish, for their lovely daughters to become sisters.

Only six weeks remained until Alexa moved to New York, and the rest of the Taylor family returned to Topeka, but during those weeks the sisters spent as much time as they could together. It was the most fragile of beginnings, the delicate meeting of strangers who were bonded by little more than a wish from the heart to become friends. Alexa would invite Cat into her bedroom, and Cat would sit on the bed while Alexa roamed around, chattering on and on about nothing, and Cat would listen intently, mesmerized by her older sister's effortless flow of clever, lively, interesting words. Mostly Cat simply listened, but on rare occasions she conquered her shyness; and whenever she did, Alexa discovered, her little sister always spoke with unaffected and uncluttered honesty . . . and remarkable wisdom.

"I think we should forgive Hillary," she suggested quietly a week before school was over.

"You're kidding," Alexa said to the earnest sapphire eyes that never kidded. "No way, Cat. Never!"

"We should feel sorry for her, Alexa."

"Sorry?"

"Yes. Sorry that she needs to be so cruel. She must be very unhappy to be so cruel."

Alexa gazed at Cat, searching her solemn young face for some proof that her little sister was talking about *her*, forgiving *her*, not Hillary. But Alexa saw no hidden messages in the honest blue eyes. She wondered for a moment if she should confess anyway, You're right, Cat. Hillary must be very unhappy to be so cruel. Just as I was so terribly unhappy when I was cruel to you. Hillary and I are alike, you see. We need to be adored and admired. And when our domain is threatened dark monsters lunge up from our hearts to devour those who threaten us.

But Alexa didn't confess to Cat, nor did she ever forgive Hillary. She simply tried to forget all about Hillary Samantha Ballinger . . . because remembering her enemy, her most worthy opponent, was like remembering the ugliest part of herself, the part she wanted so desperately to believe no longer existed.

But now Hillary was married to a man who was James's very good friend. And Alexa realized that her reason for not wanting to see Hillary was simply fear that in seeing her ancient enemy she would see again her own cruel reflection.

Mirror, mirror . . .

But that old Alexa was gone, wasn't she? She hoped so, but she didn't know. She had spent so very little time with the real Alexa, immersing herself instead in roles of women to be admired and avoiding altogether the treacherous search for the monsters that might be lingering still in the shadowy places of her heart. Alexa didn't know if the monsters were gone, but since her friendship with James, she felt so hopeful. He knew her far better than she had ever before allowed herself to be known, and she was almost beginning to believe in the "niceness" he kept insisting she possessed.

James likes you because he doesn't know you! The harsh reminder came from nowhere, a breath of angry fire from a never-to-be-forgotten monster. Alexa sighed softly, a sad acceptance of her fate. She would have to tell him everything, and it might be more truth than he would want to know. But, a whisper of defiant hope argued, if you can confess to James, who is your friend, then maybe one day you can confess what you must—to banish the monsters forever—to your little sister.

James had watched Alexa while he made his business call to San Francisco, and he had seen the panorama of emotions that touched her beautiful face. When the call ended, he watched still, reluctant to interrupt her obviously so important

103

emotional journey. But when she gave a soft resigned sigh, and he saw her lovely face fill with immense sadness and loss, he could bear watching no more. He hated her anguish, but he hated even more that it had been there all along, hidden, lurking, threatening. It would help her to tell him, wouldn't it?

He walked across the plush carpeting, and when she felt his shadow and she looked up into his gentle eyes, he said softly, "Let's go, sweetheart."

Chapter 6

"This is new," James said quietly when he saw the Steinway baby grand piano in the living room of her apartment. His quiet words broke the silence that had travelled with them from his office.

"I thought it would be much safer for Cat to have a piano here. This way she won't have to go to the music rooms at Juilliard every time she wants to play." Alexa could imagine her little sister wandering around Manhattan at all hours, lured to a distant piano by the music she loved, oblivious of the sinister dangers of the city. "I'm assuming this apartment is so solidly built that she can play all night without disturbing anyone, but maybe you could help me test that sometime? If you could play 'Chopsticks' or something while I visit my neighbors?"

"Sure." After a moment, he added softly, "This is very nice of you."

Alexa gave an uncertain shrug and crossed the room to the piano. She ran her long tapered fingers over the polished wood surface and then onto the ivory and ebony keys, touching softly and evoking the rich clear tones.

"I haven't always been very nice to Cat," she confessed to the keyboard.

"But she's very important to you."

"Yes. She is."

"Tell me."

James extended a hand to her, an invitation to be in a safe place while she shared her darkest secrets. But Alexa didn't move to him. Instead, she sat on the piano bench, surprised by the unyielding hardness of the place Cat chose most often to be. Then she told him the story of the Taylor sisters, from the very beginning, the instant she first saw Cat, and with unyielding hardness toward herself, she confessed her flawed emotions and unforgivable crimes.

"Cat was a perfect baby. She was always so calm, so serene, so regal—just like a princess. She never even cried."

"Surely she cried," James countered gently, interrupting for the first time. He had wanted to interrupt Alexa's anguished words before, but he knew she wouldn't listen to his gentle reassurances until she had told him all the truths. He interrupted now because her breathless words of self-recrimination halted for a moment, and because he wanted to impose some reality on the too-perfect-to-be-real portrait she was painting of her baby sister. "All babies cry, Alexa."

"Not Cat. Really, James, she *never* cried." Alexa dug her long tapered fingers into her palms, a physical reminder of the pain she had once inflicted on her baby sister. "Even though I tried to make her cry."

"By telling her you hated her. But, Alexa, she was very young then, far too young to understand or remember."

"Oh, I hope that's true," Alexa whispered softly. How she wished she knew that Cat remembered nothing! Nothing, especially not . . . "I tried to hurt her once, physically, to make her cry. I guess I desperately needed proof that she wasn't perfect."

"How did you try to hurt her?" James asked calmly, even though a sudden worry swept through him as he gazed at her tormented face. Her emerald eyes were dark now, almost black, and the soft, intriguing ripples of vulnerability had become currents, strong, turbulent, disturbing. Until that moment it hadn't occurred to him that she might actually have done something truly unspeakable, a crime to match the grim anguish on her beautiful face. "Tell me, Alexa. How?"

"By pinching her. The pinch wasn't hard enough to leave marks, of course, but it should have made a two-year-old cry. I tested the pinch on myself, and it would have made me cry. But Cat didn't cry. She just stared at me with huge blue eyes, bewildered and yet forgiving."

Alexa stared at the hands knotted in her lap,

unable to look at him, wondering if she would hear his footfalls on the plush carpet as he left. No, she wouldn't, because the thundering of the blood pulsing through her brain was far too loud. She wouldn't hear him leave, but when she found the courage, finally, to look up, he would be gone.

"That's all?" James asked gently, realizing that it was, and realizing, too, that to lovely Alexa it truly felt like a crime of immense proportion.

"*All?*" she echoed, startled into looking up then, and even more startled by what she saw in the dark blue eyes—gentleness, not disappointment. "Isn't that enough? Doesn't that seem unforgivably cruel?"

"It seems like sibling rivalry, probably a fairly mild case. You're going to have to tell me much more, Alexa, if you want to convince me that you were a cruel little girl."

"There isn't more. I simply ignored her after that."

"Did that bother her?"

"Oh, no, I don't think so. Why would it? Her life was bountiful, filled to overflowing with her music and our parents' love."

"So, once upon a time, you were very jealous of your baby sister. You were a little girl then, too, remember? And you had been an adored only child for six years. It makes perfect sense. Besides, Alexa, it feels like very old history to me. I don't hear jealousy or hatred when you talk about Cat now. I just hear pride and love." And such uncertainty.

"I am proud of Cat and I do love her . . . even though we barely know each other."

"Which means that somewhere along the line something changed?"

"Yes." Alexa gave a bewildered shake of her head as she remembered what—who—was responsible for the change.

"What happened?"

"Hillary Samantha Ballinger happened."

"Oh?"

"From the moment I arrived at Ballinger's Hillary made it abundantly clear to everyone that I wasn't good enough for her or her school."

"I see," James answered quietly. As a grown woman, and especially as Robert's wife, Hillary had learned to hide her disdain for those she considered to be beneath her. But he could well imagine the teenaged Hillary's unconcealed contempt for the beautiful and flamboyant country girl from Kansas; just as he could well imagine Alexa's hurt.

"I was definitely not good enough for Hillary, but her friends found me to be quite acceptable—including her boyfriend."

"You stole Hillary's boyfriend from her?"

"It wasn't grand theft, James! He came to me willingly, *enthusiastically.*"

"And after you bewitched him away from Hillary? Was he a prize worth having?"

"Of course not. He had fallen for Hillary, after all, which meant his judgment and values were fatally flawed."

"So, it was just a game."

"No, James, it was just a war."

Alexa told him then about the Saturday afternoon in April at the polo field . . .

"Hillary really called you a 'white trash whore'?" he asked, beginning to truly comprehend the magnitude of the enmity between the heiress and the country girl.

"She really did. I don't know how much of it Cat understood, but she sprung to my defense like a tiny brave terrier against a tigress."

"And what did you do?"

"I put my arms around the little sister I hadn't touched for ten years and we went home."

"Why don't I put my arms around you now?" he suggested gently as he began to walk toward her. Alexa met him halfway, so grateful that he still wanted her in his arms.

"Thank you."

"My pleasure," he murmured into her silky golden hair. After a moment, he guided her to the couch and encouraged her to finish her story of the Taylor sisters. "And after that you and Cat became friends?"

"I don't know, James," she answered softly. "The beginning of friends, I think, at least that's my memory of the six weeks between that April afternoon and when I moved to New York. Since then we've seen very little of each other—brief visits at Christmas and holidays—and each time there have been so many changes in our lives since the last time that we never quite seem to catch up, much less go on. In the past eight years Cat has grown from a little girl to a young woman, and I . . ."

"You've become a superstar. Maybe Cat is a little star-struck."

"Oh, no. Why would she be? Her accomplishments are already so much greater than mine."

"How can you say that?"

"Because it's true! Admittedly, my career's higher profile, my successes more public, but . . . I told you about the competitions she's won, and the concert tour and album, and that she's being managed by Fordyce, the top performing arts agency. Cat's accomplishments *are* greater, James, but it's true, I guess, that it's my celebrity that has gotten in the way. During my trips home to Topeka, friends and neighbors are constantly dropping by and when I've tried to visit Cat at Oberlin, there's always been a steady stream of her classmates wanting to meet me."

"Which is why you're looking forward to her move to New York? Because celebrities are virtually ignored here?"

"Yes. That, and because for the first time in our lives I feel that Cat and I are the same age. During childhood, six years seems like a generation gap, but now we're both grown-up, away from home, pursuing our careers." When she spoke again her voice was filled with hope, "I have this fantasy that even though she'll be here, and I'll be in Washington, we'll make an effort to see each other. You know, I'll fly up for Sunday brunch at the Plaza, or she'll fly down for a weekend at RoseCliff, something like that." She shrugged softly. "Just a sisterly fantasy."

"But something that Cat obviously wants, too."

"No. Cat *needs* to be in New York, and it's logical for her to stay in my otherwise vacant apartment for the six months that she'll be here. That's all."

As James gazed at her hopeful, yet uncertain, emerald eyes, he wished he could reassure her that Cat was as eager to be sisters as she. But because he had no way of knowing, he knew such a reassurance would sound false.

"Is this Saturday really Cat's twenty-first birthday?" he asked finally, remembering Alexa's mumbled excuse to Robert.

"Yes."

"Are you braving the fans and visiting her at Oberlin?"

"No." Alexa frowned. "My parents are going, and although I'm trying not to put too paranoid an interpretation on this, when I suggested to my mother that I let my understudy do Juliet Saturday afternoon and fly to Oberlin to join them for dinner, I got the very distinct impression that I wasn't invited."

"Probably wise not to over interpret. So, why don't we do something special that night? Our own private celebration of Cat's birthday? And," he added tenderly, "why don't I just say no to dinner with Robert and Hillary for tomorrow night?"

"Really?"

"Really." James smiled and found her soft lips. "I've missed you."

"I've missed you, too."

"You mentioned something about a merger? A very friendly takeover maybe?"

As James led her to the bedroom where he would so slowly and expertly undress her, Alexa

111

thought about how much she had missed him . . . and why. Because of their magnificent passion, yes, but because of something that was even more important—their magnificent friendship. That friendship had become even closer, even more important, in the past few hours. He had listened, and he had been so gentle, and he believed in her still; and maybe, someday, she would believe in herself. As Alexa thought about their wonderful friendship, she realized that there was another important friendship that had become quite lost, quite forgotten, because of her selfishness.

When they reached her romantic pink bedroom, James turned to face her. He circled her slender waist with his hands and waited to see the lovely anticipation and desire he knew so well. But when she looked up at him, he saw a frown, and very serious emerald eyes.

"What?" he asked gently.

"Robert is a very good friend, isn't he?"

"Yes."

"Like a brother?"

"I guess so."

"Including sibling rivalry? There wasn't an ugly battle between the two of you over Hillary was there?"

"No." James laughed softly. "No ugly battles about anything. We graduated first and second in our class from Harvard Law School—Robert was first—but even that wasn't the finish line of a three-year competition."

"It sounds strange to hear you being so calm about coming in second."

"Robert deserved to be first," James said quietly. "What do you know about him, Alexa, other than to whom he is married?"

"Not much. He's a major topic of conversation in Washington, of course, but because of Hillary I've usually tuned out whenever his name is mentioned. Despite that, though, I'm aware that virtually everyone—it almost seems to be a bipartisan vision—believes that he will be President."

"Yes."

"Which means, I suppose, that I *should* know about him." Alexa gave a theatrical sigh, and then smiled. "And who better to tell me than you?" With that, and a lingering kiss, she left him. She sat on the edge of her bed, and with the rapt attention of a child awaiting a favorite bedtime story, she said, "I'm listening."

As she waited for James to settle in a nearby chair and collect his thoughts about the story he was about to tell, Alexa began to imagine what the story would be. The tale of the handsome and dashing Senator would be a tale of wealth and privilege, the golden life of the golden boy, a life without struggle or torment. She was quite confident about what she would hear . . . and she could not have been more mistaken.

"Well. Let's see," James began. "He was born in rural Virginia. His father left when Robert was two, six months before his sister Brynne was born. The family was extremely poor, so from the time he was just a child, he worked to help support his mother and little sister. He's very bright—I told you how he did at Harvard Law School—but his grades in high school were just average."

"Because he spent so much time working to support his family?"

"I assume so. Anyway, he didn't qualify for a college scholarship, and he couldn't attend school and work enough hours to earn both his college tuition and help with the expenses at home, so he enlisted in the army."

"Why didn't he just work full-time for a few years and then go to college?"

"Because Robert's thirty-eight—four years older than I—and those were a very critical four years. He graduated from high school in the midst of the Vietnam War. At that time, any able-bodied eighteen-year-old not bound for college was likely to be drafted. He enlisted before being drafted, but it was only a matter of time. Being in the army provided a small but stable income for his mother and Brynne, and there was a little more money—combat pay—when he was sent to Vietnam."

"He went to Vietnam?" Alexa asked softly. She was younger than Vietnam, a different generation entirely, too young to remember the emotions and divisiveness as they actually occurred. Most of what she knew about Vietnam—what she'd seen and heard and read—was a blurry kaleidoscope of images, never in sharp focus, multifaceted and ever-changing still, even after all these years. Hollywood had begun to tell the stories now. But, she thought, it was a vision balanced more by politics than history. Most of what she knew about Vietnam remained a confusing blur, but there was one thing that was crystal clear: for the men who had fought in the war, their lives were irrevocably changed. "He *fought?*"

"He was a soldier, Alexa. He fought." James sighed softly, thinking, as he often did, especially since his friendship with Robert, how easy his own life had been, how privileged, how *lucky.* "Robert went straight from the battles of poverty in rural Virginia to the horror of war in Vietnam. That's entirely my editorializing, by the way. He never talks about either his childhood or Vietnam. What I know about his childhood, I've learned from Brynne, and what I know about his war record, I've learned from what I've read in articles that have been written about him."

"What do the articles say?"

"They mention the medals he received, of course, but most telling are the accounts of his leadership and bravery given by the men with whom he served."

"So he's a war hero."

"Yes, he is, although 'war hero' is not a label you'd ever hear him apply to himself. Anyway, by the time he returned from Vietnam, his mother had died and Brynne was a scholarship student at the University of Virginia. He enrolled at Virginia, too, on the GI bill, graduated from college with highest honors, and went on to a similar academic performance at Harvard. He could have joined any private firm in the country, of course, but even during law school he'd planned a career in public service. So, on gradua- tion, he began with the District Attorney's office in Richmond. He dazzled as a prosecutor, and was clearly on track for election to DA, but the

115

political powers came to him with an alternate plan—to bypass local politics altogether and make a bid for the Senate."

"Which he has done with such success that everyone thinks he'll be President some day," Alexa said quietly.

"That's right," James answered, quietly, too.

After a thoughtful silence, she tilted her golden head, smiled a mysterious smile, and said, "You still haven't told me the worst part."

"I haven't?"

"No. You haven't told me how the loving son and brother, war hero and patriot, brilliant attorney and dedicated public servant met the Wicked Witch of the West."

"Robert met gracious, charming, beautiful Hillary in Dallas while on a trip to discuss his Senate candidacy with her father, Sam Ballinger."

"And the ex-Governor promised to endorse him for the Senate, and eventually the White House, if he would marry his daughter?" Alexa teased softly. Then, forcing seriousness on her beautiful face, she continued analytically, "Sam doubtless knew that no man in his right mind would ever marry Hillary without such an incentive. All the oil money simply wasn't enough. He had to throw in a few votes, something, perhaps, like the entire state of Texas in the Presidential election?"

"Cute, but no. Robert McAllister is very much his own man. He met Hillary and chose to marry her."

"And what about Hillary? She's never been

overly fond of us folk from humble beginnings. I suppose, however, that if marrying a dirt-poor country boy could provide a one-way ticket into Washington's most elite inner circle, not to mention the White House, she would deign to do it."

"Maybe, Alexa, Hillary recognized Robert's greatness."

Alexa drew a soft breath at his words, his tone, and the solemn expression in his dark blue eyes. "You really respect him, don't you?"

"Yes, I really do."

"And Hillary?"

"Hillary is Robert's wife."

Alexa sighed softly. She knew what she had to do, even though it scared her. But she would be with James, and that would make it easier.

"I think we should have dinner with Robert and Hillary tomorrow night."

"You do?"

"Assuming Hillary wants to. James, it's not by accident that I haven't run into the McAllisters in the three years I've been in Washington."

"I'm sure Robert has no idea that you and Hillary knew each other. He would have told me if he did."

"Well, maybe he doesn't know. But Hillary does, and she needs to be given a chance to say no to dinner."

"OK." James walked over to her then, and drew her up to him so that they were standing as they had been before the story began, his arms encircling her waist, her hands resting gently on his shoulders. "Are you sure you want to do this?"

"I'm positive," she replied, her confidence soaring as she saw a wonderful message in his dark blue eyes, something of immense value coming from him: he was proud of her. Feeling tinglingly giddy, and so safe, and knowing that very soon they would be making love, because there was such desire, too, in the seductive blue, she teased, "Of course, I won't be able to vote for Robert for President."

"No?"

"He has that same fatal flaw in judgment—falling for Hillary—that her high school boyfriend did. That kind of judgment problem worries me in a President."

"I see," he murmured, kissing her now, whispering between kisses. "That's why they don't let little children vote, Alexandra. You have to be a grown-up to vote."

"And I'm not?" she asked softly, sighing with pleasure as his talented lips began their journey down her neck and his talented hands found the buttons on her dress.

"Maybe you are," he whispered. "Why don't we see if we can think of something grown-up to do right now . . . ."

Chapter 7

"James will be bringing Alexa Taylor to dinner tonight," Robert told Hillary after speaking to

James the following morning. "Apparently you know her?"

"Yes. James and Alexa?"

James had been vague about why Hillary needed to know, but now as he saw obvious displeasure on his wife's beautiful face, Robert asked, "Is that a problem for you, Hillary?"

"No, of course not," she answered, forcing a smile.

"Good."

As soon as Robert returned to the documents he had been reviewing when James called, Hillary's smile vanished. It was not a problem to see Alexa, she thought, but it was most definitely an annoyance. So far, she had masterfully avoided seeing her old nemesis. But with each passing year, as Alexa's name appeared on more and more of the important guest lists, it became increasingly difficult, and increasingly irritating. Did no one remember that she was merely an actress, playing a role, a faux celebrity with no *legitimate* claim to Washington society whatsoever?

Apparently not, and Hillary knew that it was only a matter of time.

And now the time was here.

As she adjusted to the inevitable, a slight smile touched her lips. They would see each other here, tonight, when Alexa was with James. And when they saw each other the next time, at some charity event in Washington, he would long since have tired of her, and she would delight in Alexa's

119

obvious misery at her inability to hold the interest of rich, elegant, restless James Sterling.

She was perfectly dressed for the role of an adult, her flowing golden hair subdued into a sophisticated knot, her emerald silk sheath simple and elegant, her gold jewelry delicate and demure. And he had made a teasing but solemn promise not to leave her alone with Hillary, and she had made a teasing but solemn promise to be "incredibly nice," but as they neared La Côte Basque, Alexa felt sudden waves of panic. Did she really think she could behave as if nothing had ever happened between them? What if Hillary greeted her with "How very lovely to see you again"? She was just about to confess to James that she'd made a huge mistake, that with his gentle help she had *vastly* overestimated her maturity, when Robert and Hillary appeared from the other direction.

And then they were face to face, and it was Hillary who spoke.

"You probably hoped you'd never see me again, Alexa."

Alexa drew a stunned breath at the bluntness, and at the cool elegance with which Hillary spoke the words. It wasn't an apology, of course, nor was it an invitation for her to apologize, either. It was, simply, a way for them to go on. The *only* way, Alexa realized with a begrudging flicker of admiration.

"You probably felt the same about seeing me."

"Of course I did."

"Ancient history?"
"Ancient history."

Her memories of Hillary were so clear, so vivid, and yet, Alexa realized as she gazed across the candlelight at her old nemesis, the memories were dark amorphous emotions, uglinesses of the heart, not accurate portraits of Hillary herself. The memories were so monstrous and so ugly that Alexa had forgotten entirely how truly beautiful the sable-haired, sable-eyed Southern belle heiress really was.

Hillary was truly beautiful, and Robert was truly handsome, and the McAllisters were truly the perfect modern couple. He listened so attentively to her words, and she listened so attentively to his, and each greeted the other's thoughts with appreciative smiles of respect and approval.

The perfect modern couple, Alexa mused. Indeed, she thought, if Hollywood ever created a show about the First Couple of the Baby-Boomer era—short of casting a woman as President— the President would be a stunningly handsome Vietnam veteran, and the First Lady would be stunningly beautiful, and intelligent, and quite unafraid to express her own views. The President's sensitive eyes would give solemn testimony to the horrors he had seen, but they would smile, too, with proud admiration for the wife whose opinions he obviously valued so greatly.

In short, Hollywood would cast Robert and Hillary McAllister.

But Robert and Hillary weren't actors vying for a role. They were the real thing, the future

121

occupants of the White House, and their act was stunning.

But an act! Alexa decided suddenly, surprised by her observation and certain that it must be wrong. The perfect couple *were* perfect, weren't they? Yes, of course, even though the perfectly scripted smiles of respect and admiration seemed to come more from the mind than the heart or the soul. And there seemed to be no spontaneous affection, no gentle surprised laughter, no swift knowing glances as some casual remark triggered an intimate memory.

Propriety, no doubt, she told herself. Appropriate, dignified, perfect First Couple behavior.

And what about the players themselves? Sincere, sensitive, thoughtful Robert McAllister was simply too good to be true. The Senator was definitely in contention for his own private Oscar, Alexa decided. His performance was quite convincing, of course, and most deserving of a small golden statue, but, unfortunately, the immensely talented actor had been given an impossible script. Whoever had written it— presumably Robert himself—had forgotten to sprinkle in even one tiny flaw, some small proof that the man was real.

Alexa wished she could believe the extraordinary and compelling sensitivity she saw in the sensuous dark eyes, but she couldn't. As the evening wore on, she found herself disliking him very much. How arrogant it was, she thought, to pretend to possess a sincerity and sensitivity that were so obviously contrived.

And what about the future First Lady? At least

there was an honesty about Hillary. Now, just as eight years ago, the beautiful heiress did not even pretend to like Alexa. Of course, now Hillary's contempt was protected by layers and layers of impeccable manners, but even that downy comforter of graciousness was not enough to conceal the fact that she had not really changed at all. She was still very much the cruel little girl Alexa had known in Dallas . . .

"Tell us about your career, Alexa," Hillary suggested politely as they lingered over coffee. The evening had gone surprisingly well, a comfortable flow of neutral topics—until now. "You moved to New York after graduation?"

"That's right." Alexa smiled sweetly, even though she was quite certain that Hillary knew the details of her career and was laying a trap. "I studied at Juilliard for a year and then got my first role on television."

"A soap opera, wasn't it?"

"Yes," Alexa replied smoothly, despite the fact that Hillary had almost choked on the words "soap opera." Daytime soaps were apparently quite beneath her, incomprehensible to a patron of the fine arts such as she, almost as unimaginable as being raised in a farmhouse in Kansas. Alexa smiled beautifully and evoked a wincing smile from James as she calmly dropped a hand under the table and dug her fingernails into his thigh. "I was with *All My Children* until three years ago, when *Pennsylvania Avenue* began."

"Alexa has also worked in the theater, and, of course, has done the one movie," James added quietly, returning her hand to the table top, curled gently but firmly in his. He didn't elaborate on the "one movie," his words more meaningful by the understatement, his dark blue eyes sending an eloquent reminder of her astonishing performance.

"*Majesty* was your first movie?" Hillary asked. "I thought there might have been others along the way."

"You mean 'B' movies?" Alexa countered, realizing then what she should have known: the politely delivered soap opera slur was simply a warm-up. Hillary was cleverly drifting from the clean but not highbrow suds to the seamier and steamier aspects of show business—explicit sex and nudity. Surely the whore from Kansas had had no qualms about baring all along the way to her success. Alexa felt the instinctive rush of adrenaline, a soldier steeling for battle, and fought to keep her promise to be "incredibly nice." She was succeeding, calming herself, until she made the mistake of glancing at Robert.

For a wonderful, grateful moment, Alexa was actually convinced by, *seduced by,* the anguish and apology in the dark brown eyes. But, she reminded herself quickly, the sensitivity is simply pretense. He is neither wounded by, nor apologetic for, Hillary's sudden unkind attack.

If there was an authentic apology at all in the wounded dark eyes, she realized with sudden fury, it was an apology for *her* decadent morals, not for Hillary's assault on same. After all, *he,* the dirt-poor country boy, had managed to overcome all hardships with his integrity and honor completely intact; while *she,* the ill-bred country girl, had not been nearly so strong, succumbing to the most unfortunate compromises in an effort to advance in her déclassée career as an actress.

When she had told James the truth about the year at Ballinger, Alexa had shared the blame equally with Hillary for their war. But had Hillary, when she recounted the same story to Robert, confessed to either her own jealousy or cruelty? Of course not, Alexa thought. She had probably merely conveyed to her husband her lingering bewilderment that the administrators at Ballinger had permitted Alexa to roam its hallowed halls at all. Hillary had surely told Robert only *her* disdainful version of the saga of the white trash whore, and he had been able to add his own fuel to the fire of outrage by recounting Alexa's seductive remark in James's office.

And now Robert was gazing at her not with gentle apology for Hillary's cruelty, but rather with gentle apology for Alexa's own pathetic destiny—her decadent and unprincipled path from whore to actress, by way of nude movies.

How arrogant! How patronizing! How judgmental!

Alexa willed her voice not to reveal her trembling anger as she said very quietly to his arrogant dark eyes, "The wonderful thing about acting as a profession is that one needn't compromise his or her ethical standards. It's simply not required."

She paused, a carefully calculated moment of drama before delivering her next line, but Robert McAllister stole the line and the silence from her.

"Unlike politics?" he suggested softly.

Unlike politics was what Alexa had planned to say, of course, a silly taunt. And now Robert had intercepted the taunt, saving her and perhaps the entire evening, and making her dislike him all the more.

"Oh," she replied, recovering quickly and feigning confusion as she considered his suggestion. Finally, smiling beautifully, she added, "Well, yes, I suppose, now that you mention it, Robert . . . unlike politics."

"Sorry," Alexa whispered softly, an hour later, when she and James were alone in her apartment. As she freed the long golden silk that had been restrained in the sophisticated knot, she added, "So much for being grownup."

"You were fine."

"But I let her get to me and I shouldn't have. Oh! I *really* don't like her."

"That's fair. I don't think she's crazy about you, either. No one is asking you to become best friends. You were fine. The evening was fine." James smiled reassuringly, but the emerald eyes remained troubled. "What, Alexa?"

"I really don't like either of them, James."

"You don't like Robert?" he asked, surprised.

"Not really."

"Because he intercepted your missile in midair?"

"I already didn't like him before that. He's *so* arrogant."

"Arrogant? Robert?"

126

"Yes, James, *arrogant*. You know, as in God's gift to We the People."

"You're wrong, Alexa," he told her with quiet confidence. "Robert McAllister is not arrogant."

"I can't believe you don't see it!"

"I don't see it, and I know Robert far better than you do."

Alexa gazed at his serious dark blue eyes and knew this was an argument she wouldn't win. "And what about Hillary?"

"I admit that Hillary isn't exactly my cup of tea."

"Well, that's at least a step in the right direction. So? Do we have to see them again? Another fun-filled evening?"

"No." James smiled enigmatically. "I had actually hoped that we'd be able to do a fun-filled weekend."

"You're kidding."

"No. Don't worry, there will be other people around."

"When? Where?"

"In August at Inverness. My parents will be home from Paris for a few weeks, for vacation and to host their annual garden party. The party is held on Sunday, and is a fairly major event, but there will be a small house party beginning the day before. Robert and Hillary will be there, and Brynne and her husband Stephen, and possibly Elliot Archer, another close family friend, and my parents and me. Even without Elliot that should provide ample buffer between you and Mrs. McAllister, shouldn't it?"

"You're inviting me to the house party?" Alexa

asked softly. We're making plans for three months from now?

"Yes, and to the garden party, too, of course. You're invited, and, if you like, so is Cat."

"Please explain the point to me, Hillary." Robert's quiet words broke the silence that had travelled with them from the restaurant to their suite at the Plaza.

"The point, Robert?"

"The point of your unkindness to Alexa. You were taunting her, intentionally trying to demean her career. I think you hurt her feelings."

"Really?" Hillary smiled. "Good."

"*Good?*"

"I have known Alexa for a very long time, Robert. She's a tramp."

"I thought she seemed very nice."

"Nice? No, Alexa is not nice. I'm actually quite surprised that James is seeing her. She's really so far beneath him." She frowned briefly, then shrugged dismissively. "Well, she won't last long. None of James's women ever do, of course, and I imagine he'll tire of Alexa far more quickly than most."

Hillary turned, and began to walk to the bedroom, but she was stopped by his voice. It was quiet still, and edged with ice.

"I'm still waiting for you to explain to me, Hillary, the point of your unkindness to Alexa."

"Oh, Robert." Hillary sighed softly as she turned back toward him. "Let's not waste any more time talking about someone like Alexa Taylor. Trust me, she isn't worth it." Smiling

128

seductively, she returned to him, and swaying gently against him, curled her perfectly manicured fingers under the lapel of his jacket, and whispered, "Come to bed."

Robert answered her by wrapping his fingers around her delicate wrists, and, with quiet strength, removing her hands from his chest. His dark, troubled eyes stared at her defiant, furious ones for a long moment, and then he said, "I'm going for a walk."

"A walk? In the middle of the night in Manhattan?"

"That's right."

"Allô Bonjour."

Alexa frowned at greeting, even though she expected it. All calls to the French House on the Oberlin campus were answered in French; but, still, it always seemed a bit much. It was fine, *wonderful,* for the students who lived in the house to speak exclusively French within its walls, but she disliked being made an unwilling participant in the game whenever she called. Not that she participated, of course, never even so much as a *Merci beaucoup.*

Although it seemed a pretension to her for the students to impose their house rules on the outside world by answering the switchboard in French, Alexa didn't consider her little sister's fascination with French pretentious at all. From the first moment Cat had heard the elegant language, she had loved it; and now the melodic language of love flowed as flawlessly and as joyfully from her lips as music flowed from her talented fingers.

"Hello," Alexa replied in resolute but pleasant English. "Will you connect me to Cat Taylor's room, please?"

"Certainement. Un moment, s'il vous plaît."

Catherine answered in English because the distinctive double ring signaled a call from outside.

"Hello?"

"Hi, Cat, it's Alexa. Happy Birthday."

"Alexa. Hi. Thank you."

"So, how does it feel to be twenty-one? Completely grown up?" Alexa frowned at the awkward triteness of her words. It was the kind of unimaginative question a virtual stranger might ask.

"Fine, I guess, not really different," Catherine mumbled, frowning, too, as she searched for words to speak to her older sister. "How is your play?"

"Good. Fun." *Fun?* A fun play about a love crazed teenager who kills herself? Alexa laughed nervously and added, "I mean, it's a fun cast and crew. When do Mom and Dad arrive?"

"They thought by mid-afternoon."

"That should be nice."

"Yes. It's nice of them to make the drive."

Alexa wondered if Cat knew that she had wanted to be there, too, but that their mother had quite firmly discouraged her plans to join them. She shook that memory, and the ancient feelings of rejection it triggered, and moved from the uneasinesses of the past to the hopefulness—hers anyway—for the future.

"Have you decided when you're coming to New York?"

"When would be convenient for you?"

"Any time is fine with me. *Pennsylvania Avenue* begins production bright and early on July third, so I'll need to be in Maryland by then, but I was hoping, depending on your schedule, that we might have a week or so together here at the end of June? I could show you around Manhattan."

"Oh, that would be wonderful."

"Good. So, when can you come?"

"My last exam is at eight A.M. on the twenty-third, and my term paper in French is due that afternoon, so . . .

"So, that night or the next day you can hop a plane-fly into LaGuardia—and I'll be at the airport to meet you. OK?"

"Yes. OK. Thank you."

James appeared in the kitchen just as the conversation was ending. The soft uncertainty in Alexa's voice, and the telephone cord, tangled and twisted by her anxious fingers, told him quite eloquently that she had been speaking to her little sister.

"How's Cat?" he asked when she replaced the receiver and smiled up at him.

"Fine. Twenty-one. School's out on June twenty-third and she's planning to come right here."

"Good," James said, deciding on the spot that the end of June would be an ideal time for the long business trip to California he needed to make before August.

"You look as though you're about to leave."

"Guilty. I have a full day of work ahead of me. I'm not going to be able to make it to the play today."

"That's fine! I can't imagine being able to sit through *Romeo and Juliet* as many times as you have."

"It's not sitting through . . . it's enjoying. But, not today."

"Maybe we should defer our dinner plans," Alexa suggested, sensing his restlessness and knowing that he had not yet fully caught up from all the work that had accumulated during his trip to Tokyo.

"Defer our private celebration of Cat's birthday? Not a chance."

Alexa's graceful gait came to an abrupt halt as she neared the theater. There, in the line of people hoping to get a last-minute ticket to today's long since sold-out performance of *Romeo and Juliet*, was Senator Robert McAllister.

What is he doing here? Alexa wondered, and then, as emotions began to embellish the question, she thought, *How dare he?*

There was no doubt in her mind that Robert considered her acting career a totally useless and trivial pursuit. Fine, he had a right to his opinion. But couldn't he keep himself and his opinion far away from a place that was so important to her? Her career was terribly important to her, and so was this play, and she felt very much as though he was invading her privacy.

It's a free country, she thought wryly. And even though I don't want him here, Robert McAllister, patriot par excellence, is enjoying the hard-fought unalienable rights of free people to assemble where they choose and to appreciate the uncensored words of the world's great and gifted playwrights.

But, still, it felt as if Robert's *freedom* violated her *rights*. Just as Alexa's thoughts were drifting to the ACLU—does he really have the right to sit in arrogant judgment of my work—reality, wonderful reality, quieted her angry emotions and a soft contented smile touched her lips.

Robert McAllister couldn't get in. Even if he were recognized, and by some unwritten rule of Senatorial privilege managed to advance from seventh place in line to first, the performance was sold out; and, if this Saturday matinee was typical of all the others in May, there wouldn't be any "no-shows."

As Alexa looked at the man who stood calmly in seventh place, she detected no impatience, no furtive or hopeful glances that he *would* be recognized, no concern even that his dark brown hair had been unceremoniously tousled by the wind. Robert didn't look arrogant at all. In fact, she conceded begrudingly, in this unguarded wind-tossed moment, the darkly dashing Senator was terribly handsome, terribly sexy indeed.

But it wasn't an unguarded moment at all, Alexa reminded herself. Every stunningly handsome expression and mood was undoubtedly

133

carefully rehearsed. She wondered what would happen when Robert discovered that he would not be able to get a ticket for today's performance. Would there be an unguarded rush of annoyance that he had wasted his precious time standing in line? It was hard to imagine, of course, that he would actually be upset if he didn't see her play. Wouldn't spending an afternoon at the theater be for the important Senator an even greater waste?

Well, no matter. Robert would not be in today's matinee audience. The realization made Alexa feel much better . . . and then a little guilty. She had made a promise to James that she would be nice to his friend. And she would be! She would make no scene whatsoever. She would simply walk on, enter the theater through the side door not the front, and never tell a soul that she had seen him.

But then Robert looked up, right at her, and she saw such uncertainty in his dark eyes. *Practiced* uncertainty, she reminded herself swiftly, the sensitive-man-of-the-eighties look which was carefully calculated, she supposed, to appeal to the female vote. The look did nothing for Alexa, except to annoy, because now she could not escape. She walked over to him so that he wouldn't lose his useless place in line.

"Good afternoon, Robert."

"Good afternoon, Alexa."

"No Hillary?"

"No. She's shopping." Robert gazed at the eyes that from the first moment in James's office—and still—met his with beautiful emerald ice. After a thoughtful silence, he added quietly,

"I wanted to see your play, but I get the impression you'd rather I didn't."

"Oh, no, Robert. I'm very flattered, of course," Alexa lied graciously. "I don't have extra tickets, but I can have a folding chair put in an aisle, or find you a place backstage. Neither is ideal, not terribly comfortable, and it wouldn't offend me in the least if you said no, but I'm quite certain there won't be any last-minute seats for this performance."

"I would really like to see the play—from any vantage point. Are you sure it's all right?"

"Sure."

Alexa had told James truthfully that playing Juliet was a major stretch for someone as cynical about love as she. But, from the very first performance, her Juliet had been convincing and magical. Every audience believed in the love of the star-crossed lovers, wanted it to last forever, and hoped against hope that, with apologies to the Bard, the all too familiar tragic ending would be overthrown for a happily-ever-after one.

The lovers died, as always, on the Saturday afternoon that Robert McAllister watched from a folding chair in the aisle at stage right, but on that day Alexa's Juliet was more unforgettable than ever. There was a new emotion in the romantic heroine—*defiance*. The defiance was Alexa's, of course, as she eloquently showed the arrogant Senator the great value of her art; but the defiance came alive in Juliet, who, on that day, fought more courageously and passionately than ever to proudly defy the contrary stars.

135

Alexa couldn't see beyond the brightly glaring lights to know whether Robert had stood with the rest of the enraptured audience to applaud her remarkable performance, but she wondered vaguely as she took her curtain calls if he would come backstage to tell her what he thought. Not that she had invited him to, but no one would stop him if he tried. But, apparently, he didn't try. Nor was a note, not even a few words of praise hastily scribbled on a torn scrap of playbill, delivered to her. He had to get ready for the politically important black-tie reception followed by the politically important Governor's Ball, she knew, and he had thanked her, more than once, before the show, *but* he still might have found a quick and easy way to simply acknowledge her performance. She had been good today, especially good, but maybe that was too much for him to admit.

Not that it mattered what Robert McAllister thought of her, she repeatedly reminded herself as she sat in her dressing room, winding down from the performance, finding that it took far longer today than ever before. It couldn't, shouldn't, matter less; and yet, inexplicably and annoyingly, it bothered her very much that he had disappeared without a word.

When she left the theater at last, an hour and a half after the enthusiastic applause had finally stopped and the theater had emptied, her mind was still swirling with imaginary conversations with the arrogant Senator.

The arrogant Senator . . . who was waiting

patiently outside the theater for her . . . and who did not look arrogant at all.

"Hi."

"Hi."

"I just wanted to tell you how magnificent you were."

"Oh," she breathed softly, all imaginary tirades suddenly quite lost. "Thank you. I didn't realize you were waiting. You should have come backstage."

"Oh, well, I . . ." Robert shrugged. "I didn't mind waiting."

"I usually leave the theater much sooner than this," she murmured. But, you see, I was so wound up, so angry with you. With *you?* she wondered as she met his gentle and uncertain dark eyes.

"I didn't mind waiting," Robert repeated quietly. And then, with a soft smile added, "But I'd probably better go now. You truly were magnificent, Alexa."

"Thank you, Robert."

And then he was gone, already quite late for his politically important reception, and she was left with the stunning truth. She had been very wrong about Robert McAllister. He wasn't arrogant at all. And there was no pretense.

He was simply, remarkably, the sensitive and thoughtful man that he appeared to be.

Chapter 8

The Loire Valley, France . . . May 1989

Isabelle stood at a window in her seventeenth-century château. Her brilliant blue eyes gazed far beyond the magnificent vista of river and meadow, as if hoping to see the faraway place where, today, her beloved daughter would learn the truth about her birth. How astonishing that twenty-one years had already passed! The memories of the few precious days she had spent with her baby girl were so vivid, a journey traveled so often in the past two decades that, in many ways, those distant days seemed more bright and clear than all the years that had come between. And now, on this day, her little girl, a grown woman, would learn of those faraway days. But would she have any idea about the great love that had filled them?

"Isabelle? I brought you some tea."

Louis-Philippe's voice gently interrupted Isabelle's thoughts. At the sound of his voice, she withdrew her gaze from the panorama of the Loire Valley and turned to the kind man who had been her husband for the past ten years. Louis-Philippe had lost his much-loved wife, as Isabelle had lost her beloved Alexandre. Their relationship had begun with tender under-

138

standing of each other's loss and loneliness, and it had grown into the gentlest of loves.

Louis-Philippe knew Isabelle's secrets, and he had lived with her shadows—the men who had been sent by Jean-Luc to watch her always. At first, he had wanted to rid their life of the ever-watchful eyes, but his annoyance had faded as he came to realize how comforting their presence was to Isabelle. As long as the men were there, watching her and hoping she would lead them to her daughter, it could only mean that Jean-Luc's relentless search continued unrewarded. He had not found the missing princess. *She was safe.*

Then, six years ago, two weeks after the small plane carrying Jean-Luc and his second wife dove into the Mediterranean during the short flight from L'île to Nice, the shadows vanished. The plane crash was no accident, the news reports said, although the identity of the saboteur remained a mystery. Not that it mattered to Isabelle who among Jean-Luc's many enemies had chosen to murder him. What mattered was that the monster was dead . . . and the shadows were gone.

After fifteen years, the sinister watchdogs were gone. But what did their disappearance mean? she asked herself over and over. Why had Alain called them off? Was he, perhaps, unaware of their menacing mission? Or was the new monarch simply more cunning than his father? Had the boy who had unwittingly saved her from the powerful crush of Jean-Luc's hands grown into a man of even greater evil, more dangerous in his subtlety, more cruel in his deceit? Was it Alain Castille's plan to lure her into believing it was now safe to search, in hopes of following her to the princess who was such a threat to his kingdom?

Isabelle was so tempted, so very tempted . . . but she couldn't take the chance. Even when she heard that the new Prince had restored L'île to the magnificence of Alexandre's reign, a paradise of music and art and flowers, she forced herself to wonder if that, too, could be a clever deception. Alain was Jean-Luc's son, after all. He had spent his boyhood in a palace that had become a fortress. The lessons Alain had learned from his father had been lessons of power and greed and guns and terror, not ones of love and joy and music and poetry.

How she wanted to search for her daughter! But she could not take the risk. It would be virtually impossible to find her, of course. And, she told her pleading defiant heart, it wouldn't be fair.

Just as what's going to happen today isn't fair, she thought, as her trembling hands took the cup of tea Louis-Philippe brought for her. The delicate rattling of the Limoges china betrayed the emotions that swirled within her. Not that her husband didn't already know.

"What are you thinking, my love?"

"Just now, I was thinking how wrong it was for me to have asked that she be told the truth. It wasn't what I had planned, but when I gave her away and realized that she would never know of my love . . . such a selfish request, made for me, not for her. I would undo it if I could, but now I can only pray that the truth doesn't hurt

140

her, and that she won't hate me. I have a memory of such love during the short time we had to-gether . . ." Isabelle shrugged softly. Her memo-ries of her daughter were treasures of immeasurable value. How she wanted to believe the memories were shared, mother and daughter, but that was nonsense! Her daughter would have no memory of her. And what would her reaction be when she learned the truth today? Anger? Betrayal? Sadness? Isabelle wanted no unhappi-ness, ever, for the daughter she loved so much; and yet, the realization that the now-grown little girl might well acknowledge the revelation with an indifferent shrug, a past history that was of no consequence, was devastating to her, too. She wished for something—a silent message of love from the faraway heart—but that was only more proof of her own sentimental foolishness.

"You're very confident that she will be told."

"Oh, yes." Isabelle knew the lovely woman with the emerald eyes would keep that promise, just as she had been comforted for the past twenty-one years with the knowledge that the woman would keep all the promises she had made, especially the most important one: *We will love her . . .*

"There's something that Dad and I need to tell you, darling." Jane spoke gently to the trusting and innocent sapphire eyes. It was time. The three of them had spent a lovely spring after-noon wandering around the Oberlin campus, and soon they were to leave for the birthday dinner at a nearby country inn, but they needed to tell

141

her now, in the privacy of their motel room, because lovely, sensitive Catherine had already read the worry in their eyes.

"What is it?" she asked anxiously. The unspoken worry had now been acknowledged, and she was suddenly very fearful of what it could be. A serious illness, perhaps, in one of the parents she loved so much? Or in Alexa?

"It's something that happened a long time ago," Jane began quietly, looking from Catherine, whose lovely worried expression reminded her so vividly of the mother she had met twenty-one years before, to Alexander, who had agreed to help tell the story she had promised to tell on this day.

Jane and Alexander told the story together, one continuing when the other faltered, beginning where it began, on a glorious spring day and a trip to Kansas City. As Catherine heard about the sudden bleeding, the emergency delivery, the mother and daughter in ICUs in separate hospitals, she was amazed and saddened that her birth had been so terribly difficult for her mother— and a source of such worry for her father. It didn't surprise Catherine that her parents had never shared this with her before, but she wondered vaguely why they had chosen to tell her today.

"The baby died on the fifth day." Alexander's voice was gentle, and so quiet, but still the words thundered.

"Died?" Catherine echoed finally, not understanding, *not even beginning to understand.*

She waited, expecting to hear about a miracle. Had she been pronounced dead only to miraculously revive? Or was she a twin, undiscovered until after the sister had died, then suddenly announcing her appearance? A twin, yes, that was it. Catherine had read about twins, separated or lost at birth, and about how each sensed the loss of the missing half. She tried now to sense her distant twin, the baby girl who had died, but there was no sense of loss, *not for that sister.* There was only one sister she had missed, and she had spent her lifetime missing her desperately, but that sister was Alexa.

Alexa, who had sounded so eager to have her come to New York as soon as possible, *hadn't she?* Alexa, with whom, maybe, please, there had been delicate and precious whispers of friendship over the past eight years, *hadn't there?*

"I had a twin sister?"

"No, darling," Jane answered softly. Her emerald eyes brimmed with tears as she looked from Catherine to Alexander. But her husband could not tell this part of the story. Only she knew the words and emotions of the woman who had given them their beloved Catherine. "On the day that I was discharged from the hospital, I decided to go to the newborn nursery to see the babies before I left. I needed courage to face my loss, and courage to help Dad tell Alexa the baby who had died. I went to the nursery looking for courage, Cat, and I found a miracle. I found you."

With loving wonder, Jane recounted the astonishing truths about that day. A distant corner of Catherine's mind heard the words and the emotion, and saved both to be remembered later, but only one truth swirled in her mind now, a thundering anguish, not an astonishing miracle . . .

"I'm not your daughter." It was a whisper, soft, delicate, tentative, like the deceptively gentle first breath of even the most devastating storm. *I'm not your daughter. And I'm not really Alexa's sister, even though I have spent my life missing her.*

"Yes, Cat, you are our daughter!" Alexander interjected, his gentle voice hoarse with emotion. "We aren't your biologic parents, darling, but you *are* our daughter."

Jane and Alexander had spoken the usual words to each other—"biologic," "birth," "natural," "real"—and rejected all but biologic and birth. They *were* Catherine's real parents, and to imply the relationship was anything but natural, *wonderful,* seemed so very wrong.

"You adopted me."

"Yes." Jane frowned and admitted quietly, "It wasn't an official adoption. Your mother didn't give me your birth certificate, and you were born on the same day as the baby who died, so . . ."

"So my birth certificate is hers? Her name was Catherine, too?"

"No, darling. Her name was Mary. She died before the name on the birth certificate was recorded—it just read 'Baby Girl'—so when we provided the correct name to the Bureau of Vital Statistics, we told them Catherine."

The name on the baby's death certificate was Mary, and Jane and Alexander had worried that the change might be discovered, but the registries of birth and death were quite separate, unlinked then by computers, and it had been a matter of simple paperwork. And it was safer than a formal legal adoption, they had decided, because there would be no trail that might lead whoever it was that Catherine's mother feared so much to Catherine.

The room fell silent. In the stillness, Jane and Alexander tried to reach the daughter with whom there was no genetic link, but with whom there had always been such deep and astonishing bonds. They were bonded by their love of music, of course, but bonded, too, by their quiet reserve, their serenity, and the important wordless messages of their hearts. Always before, from the very beginning, they had understood each other's silences. But now, as they tried to penetrate Catherine's silence, Jane and Alexander felt their emotions ricocheting back, blocked by a new invisible wall. And the eyes that had always been the brilliant, hopeful blue of a winter sky after a snowstorm were wintry still, but no longer hopeful, just the cold forboding blue of ice.

"Cat," Alexander whispered helplessly.

"Why are you telling me this now?" she asked, a soft demand and an even softer unspoken plea, Why couldn't you have never told me?

"Because I made a promise to . . . your mother . . . that I would tell you the truth on your twenty-first birthday."

"Why? So that I could know that she didn't want me?"

"Oh, no, darling, she wanted you. You must believe that. She loved you very much."

"But she was very young and very poor?"

"No," Jane admitted softly. "She was neither

145

young nor poor. She told me it would be dangerous for you to be with her. I don't know why, darling, but I do know that she was being followed and that she was very fearful of the men who were watching her . . . and you."

"But what was her name? Who is she?" *Who am I?*

"I don't know her name, Cat. She told me nothing about herself, except that she was your mother and she loved you very much." Jane paused, and then added softly, "I think, although I'm not certain, that your father's name was Alexander. It seemed very important to her that your middle name be Alexandra."

But my middle name is Alexandra because of Dad! The thought came swiftly, a proud familiar truth that had been with her all her life. She had been named for her father, Alexander Taylor, the quiet, talented, wonderful man from whom she had inherited so many things, including her magical gift for music. She was named for him, and she shared that name with her sister, and it was all wonderful comforting proof of who she was—daughter, sister—and that she was where she belonged.

And now?

Now how she wished that this was all just a cruel joke! The incredible wish, because her parents were no more likely to play cruel jokes than was she, was suddenly so appealing. She could live with the discovery that there was a dark side to Jane and Alexander, some sinister twist in their minds that had made them tell her this. She could live with that if only she could have back everything she had believed to be true all her life.

But it wasn't a cruel joke, and as Catherine gazed at the mother and father she loved so much, something terrifying began to happen. She felt herself separating from them . . . drifting far, far away . . . and she couldn't make it stop!

Catherine tried to stop it, but as if she were in quicksand, the harder she struggled, the more quickly she suffocated. She was suffocating now, and she saw Jane and Alexander through a blurry fog, and they looked so different! No longer were they her mother and father, not really. Instead, they were the kind, generous, loving people who had rescued an endangered orphan from some mysterious peril and had so lovingly welcomed that tiny helpless visitor into their lives. They had been so wonderful to their little guest, making her feel as if she truly belonged.

But she didn't belong! She was an impostor! She had been a guest in their home and in their hearts and in their lives, placed there by chance, not by the passionate union of a man and woman who had chosen to create a new life from their loving. Alexa was such a creation of Jane and Alexander's love, and so was Mary, the baby girl who had died, but she . . .

Catherine tried to stop the thoughts, but she was powerless against them. Like a raging river they swept through her, and then, engulfing her, they carried her swiftly away, downstream, so very far away from everything she had ever known. The past, that wonderful place where she had lived in such secure love, was a distant memory, a lovely dream, vanquished forever by the truth.

The truth. She was not their daughter. She was the abandoned baby of a mysterious woman and a man named Alexander. Had she been a creation of love? Or an unfortunate mistake? It hardly mattered, because there was the truth again: whatever she had been to the man and woman who had created her, it wasn't enough. They had been able to give her away.

"They never tried to find me?" she asked softly.

"Not that we know, darling. I believe, although she didn't say this, that your father was no longer alive when you were born. It would have been almost impossible for her to find you, Cat, and there was the danger."

"But what kind of danger? How can it be dangerous for a baby to be with her mother?"

"I don't know, my love," Jane answered gently. "But I truly believe the danger was real. She was very definitely being watched, and she took great care to be certain that the man who was watching her didn't realize what was happening. That's why Dad and I have been so very careful, too, Cat. That's why we have told no one."

"But that's not true! You told Alexa! She has known all along!"

"No, darling, Alexa doesn't know."

Yes she does know! a voice from deep within her screamed. The voice had once been so familiar, a constant companion, but recently its relentless taunts had been silenced by hope. Now the unwelcome voice was back, harsh and clear, bringing with it all the ancient pain. She knows that I'm not really her little sister, and maybe that's why she has never liked me . . .

"Alexa doesn't know," Jane repeated quietly.

"Promise me that you will never tell her."

"I promise," Jane agreed softly, wishing she could add gently that it wouldn't matter to Alexa, but knowing that she couldn't confidently make such a reassurance. Yes, Alexa's voice filled with loving pride when she spoke of Cat now, but Jane would never forget the girls' first twelve years together, nor would she forget the astonishing pronouncement Alexa had made when she first saw Cat—"She is not my sister!"

Somehow Catherine survived the visit, hiding her pain, reassuring them that it was fine, she understood, it didn't matter. And then Jane and Alexander were gone, and she was alone, truly alone, with the truth and its glittering symbols: the magnificent sapphire necklace and the staggering fortune. Alexander had invested the one hundred thousand dollars very cautiously, but in the past twenty-one years even the most conservative investments had grown enormously. The trust he established for her, and which was now in her sole control, was valued at just over one million dollars.

She wanted none of it! She just wanted to go back to the time when she knew who she was and where she belonged.

But that time had vanished. No, worse, it had never even existed. As Catherine thought about who she had always believed herself to be, she realized how simple her identity had been. Cath-

149

erine Alexandra Taylor was, *had been,* three important things: a daughter . . . a sister . . . and a musician. That was all, and it had been enough, *more* than enough. And now she was no longer either the daughter or the sister she had believed herself to be.

But she was still a musician. It was two weeks before Catherine summoned the courage to play again. She was so afraid of losing that final piece of herself, the gossamer thread that kept her tethered so precariously to her vanishing past.

She had always believed that her musical gift was part of her beloved father alive within her. But when she played again, and found that everything that had come before was only a whisper of her astonishing talent, she felt remarkable new relationships, compelling bonds to the great composers whose music she played. Her roots were centuries deep, a dominion beyond life, an inheritance of heart and spirit and soul. She had always marvelled at the genius of Mozart, Bach, and Beethoven; but now she felt their passion and emotion living within her, and now she understood their sadness, their isolation, and their pain. She played the familiar music as she had never played it before. And she played new music, too, breathtakingly poignant compositions that flowed from her own broken and bewildered heart.

Catherine clung ferociously to her music, the only part of her that hadn't vanished with the truth, and she tried desperately to adjust to her losses. She was not Jane and Alexander's daughter, not really, not in the way she had always believed herself to be. That truth was new for her, but it was not new for them. They had known always, and they had welcomed her and loved her *always*. She loved them too, so very much, but she still felt far away, and so awkward and unsure. In time, *please*, she would feel comfortable again with the parents she loved so deeply.

And what about Alexa? What about the much loved sister who was not a sister after all?

You're not her sister, the truth reminded her, an incessant chorus of pain.

But she doesn't know that! her desperate heart pleaded.

No, the truth conceded easily. But she'll find out soon enough, the instant she sees you. You feel so very different on the inside, can you possibly imagine that it doesn't show? It is as if you have a scarlet *A*—for Adopted—emblazoned over your heart! Alexa will know immediately . . . and she will be so relieved. She has never wanted you to be her sister, remember?

But she doesn't know, not yet, and what if I could keep my secret from her until some time when it is safe to tell her, some faraway time when it won't matter to her?

When will that faraway time be? When you and Alexa are good friends? Sheer fantasy!

But what if it isn't fantasy? What if Alexa and I could be friends? I have to find out. Somehow, *somehow*, I have to hide the truth until I know.

But how could she hide a truth that consumed every waking moment and surfaced in gasping nightmares during the rare times when she was able to sleep? Alexa would see the painful truth instantly in her exhausted, honest, troubled eyes.

As Catherine struggled for control over her turbulent emotions, a subconscious part of her found other ways to help her hide. Without making a specific decision, she allowed her always short hair to grow, until her sapphire eyes were veiled by soft, black-velvet curls. And she added a new layer to the plumpness that had always before been simply a rich and luxuriant symbol of her bountiful health. The new heavy shell, designed to protect and conceal her, was sallow and unhealthy, an eloquent symbol only of her immense pain.

How excited she had been about the move to New York, how happy that Alexa had wanted her to come as soon as possible, how hopeful that they could become friends. But now, in the few weeks left before she would see the sister who wasn't her sister after all, Catherine merely struggled to find the courage to make the most important journey of her life.

Chapter 9

Manhattan . . . June 1989

"Hi, Cat."

"Alexa."

"I was just calling to see what time your flight arrives Friday." Alexa spoke cheerfully even though she heard the flatness in Catherine's voice. She had heard the same flatness two weeks before, when she had called to see if her sister had made plane reservations yet, and the flatness was still there now, two days before she was scheduled to move to New York. "Cat?"

"I don't think I'll be able to come on Friday after all."

"Oh. No?"

"No. I haven't finished my French paper yet."

"Oh," Alexa replied calmly, despite her amazement. It was more than just another French paper; it was the major requirement for Cat's degree in French. And now that important paper wasn't finished? What possibly could have distracted her always disciplined little sister so much? "Have you been ill."

"No. I guess I've just been concentrating on my other classes." It was true, although the concentration had only occurred in the past few days, an intense focus so that she could pass her final exams.

"So, when do you think you'll be arriving?"

"I'm not sure."

"Couldn't you finish writing the paper here?"

"Oh. Yes. I guess," Catherine answered hesitantly even though she knew that she would *have* to finish the paper in New York. She had many weeks of work yet to do on it, and her classes at Juilliard began in ten days. New York . . . ten days . . . it still seemed impossible. She spoke aloud something she had been thinking, a sad but sensible idea, and one that she could easily afford now that she was an heiress to a mysterious and unwanted fortune. "I was wondering if I should get my own apartment."

"Oh," Alexa whispered softly, trying to hide her disappointment. "Well, of course, if you want. But, Cat, this place really will be yours. In fact, it already is. I'm virtually all moved to Maryland."

"I just don't want to impose."

"It's no imposition! Really, it's a relief for me to have someone here. Besides . . . there's a piano here that needs to be played."

"A piano?"

"Yes. And the apartment is completely sound proof, so you can play any time you like without worrying about the neighbors—not that they'd mind hearing you. Why don't you stay here, Cat, at least in the beginning? If you don't like the apartment, you and the piano can always move."

"I'm sure I'll like the apartment. I just didn't want to impose."

"You won't be! So, when do you think you will be coming?"

"I really don't know."

"Well, why don't I send you a set of keys? That way you can arrive whenever you want. I'll send the keys by overnight mail, so you'll have them by Friday."

"I'm sure I won't be arriving until next week."

"That's fine. Whenever's convenient for you. I'll be at the cottage in Maryland."

After the conversation ended, Alexa fought her disappointment. How casually the ten days they had planned to spend together had been tossed away! The ten days *they* had planned to spend together? No, she admitted, the ten days *she* had planned. Cat obviously had no great desire to spend the time with her. *Why would she?*

The phone rang as Alexa was beginning to write a note to accompany the set of keys she would send by overnight mail to Oberlin. It was James, who had left yesterday for business in California that would keep him away for the next twelve days; James, who heard immediately the soft sadness in her voice.

"She seems very ambivalent about coming," Alexa told him.

"Maybe she's feeling nostalgic about college, or a little panicky about all the new projects she's undertaking, or a lot panicky about leaving the pastoral tranquillity of Oberlin for the chaotic energy of New York."

"No, it's none of those things. Those aren't the sort of things that would bother Cat."

"She's not bothered by normal human things?" James pressed gently, ever-amazed by the portrait Alexa drew of her perfect little sister.

"I think her ambivalence is about staying in my apartment."

"I think that's nonsense." His voice softened as he added, "I, for one, have no ambivalence about staying in your apartment whatsoever. It sounds to me as if you're now free this weekend?"

"Yes, but after your meeting Saturday morning you're sailing to Catalina."

"Unless I get a better offer." James waited for a moment, then asked lightly, "So, *do* I get a better offer? I can be in either New York or Washington by about nine Saturday night."

"New York, I guess. Cat won't be arriving until next week." Alexa added softly, gratefully, "Did I ever tell you what a nice man you are?"

"I want your honest opinion," Alexa told him solemnly as they walked from the entry hall to the living room at ten P.M. Saturday night.

"Always."

The moment they reached the living room, James saw at once what honest opinion she was seeking. The sleek shiny piano had been adorned with an assortment of pastel satin ribbons, crowned with a colorful satin bow, and draped with a hand-painted sign, lettered in her beautiful script, WELCOME, CAT!

"Since I won't be here when she arrives," Alexa explained haltingly, "I thought . . . it's too much, isn't it? Too silly."

"I think it's very nice," he reassured gently as he smiled at the emerald eyes that were uncertain, as always, about her little sister. The beribboned piano *was* nice, of course, even though a bit young; but that was where the delicate relationship between the sisters had begun, and left off—when Alexa was eighteen and Cat was only twelve.

James looked at the gift-wrapped piano and wondered what Cat would think. Would she appreciate the sentiment, or simply dismiss the effort as silliness? He hoped the little sister who meant so much to Alexa would appreciate the loving welcome. He hoped that she was nice, and

156

that she cared about being a sister to Alexa; but, as he thought about Cat, he realized he had formed no real image of her. How could he? What he knew about her, he had learned from Alexa, whose vision of her little sister was hopelessly blurred by her own complicated emotions—and from which cloudy yet rose-colored vision she had created a fanciful portrait of perfection.

James had heard about the perfect baby, the serene little princess who felt no pain and never cried, and about the extraordinarily gifted musician she had become, but he wondered about the reality of Cat Taylor. She would be beautiful, of course, like her big sister. Would her dazzling confidence be susceptible, as Alexa's was, to lovely vulnerabilities? Or would she be, as he feared, quite self-absorbed, believing herself to be what Alexa described—the *truly* talented sister— and dismissing, as Alexa herself did, her older sister's own immense gifts?

"What are you thinking?" Alexa asked, interrupting his thoughts, wondering at the sudden gentleness on his handsome face.

"I was thinking about your little sister." About how much I hope she doesn't hurt you, he thought, drawing her to him. As he kissed her, he added softly, "Actually, that's not quite true. I was thinking mostly about your little sister's big sister."

It felt like an impulse, at once self-destructive and alluring, and yet she had simply succumbed to the powerful magnet that had tugged at her ever since the conversation with Alexa on

Wednesday evening. She finished her final exams, filled boxes to be shipped with clothes and books, and packed two suitcases with the essentials: her music, her term paper in French—now due in late August—and a few clothes. By Saturday evening, she was at the Cleveland airport waiting for her already much delayed flight to LaGuardia.

The flight was originally scheduled to arrive in New York at nine, but as it became clear that it would be more like midnight, Catherine was glad she hadn't called Alexa to tell her she was coming after all. Had she called, Alexa might have taken a shuttle from National to LaGuardia and would be waiting now, too. Catherine was glad she hadn't called. Tomorrow, when she was settled in the apartment, she would let Alexa know she had arrived.

Take a cab from LaGuardia. Give the driver the address—from memory, as if you've lived there all your life!—and tell him to take the bridge, Alexa had written in the long note that accompanied the keys sent by overnight mail. Have two dollars ready to give him for the toll. The total fare should be no more than twelve dollars. I usually tip fifteen percent.

Catherine knew the instructions in Alexa's letter by heart, but as the plane touched the tarmac fifteen minutes after midnight, she worried that she would have trouble finding a cab so late at night. No, she discovered quickly, her new city was quite awake at midnight on Saturday night. As they crossed the bridge, and she saw the brightly lighted silhouette of

Manhattan, she felt a sudden and surprising eagerness for the life that lay ahead. In the next six months she would explore New York, and then, beginning in January, she would travel to other exciting and vibrant cities. And maybe, along the way, she would become very calm and very sophisticated about arriving in the world's most glamorous cities at midnight.

She had felt neither calm nor sophisticated when she had given the driver the address on Riverside Drive, nor when she had handed him the bridge toll right on cue; but when the cab pulled to a stop in front of the red-brick building and the fare was precisely what Alexa had written it should be, she tipped twenty percent in sophisticated appreciation of how smoothly it all had gone.

Alexa had clearly labelled each of the three keys necessary to gain access to the security building and to the double-locked apartment. There were lights on in the apartment, as she had promised there would be, set to a timer that magically sensed when the sun rose and fell. Catherine didn't need to look at the detailed floor plan of the apartment Alexa had drawn. Like the address, she knew it by heart. But, as she wandered from the foyer to the living room, along the plush-carpeted hallway lined with walls of springtime flowers, she discovered that the apartment was much larger than she had imagined it would be— and so bright and cheerful.

Catherine's sapphire eyes misted with emotion when she saw the pastel ribbons and words of welcome on the beautiful piano. She set down her suitcase and approached the magnificent instrument, her delicate fingers touching first the sign, and then the elaborate bow, and then the satiny veneer of the expensive wood.

She was exhausted, but she knew she would play tonight anyway. She had to. It had been two days, and her music was so necessary to her now. She would play, even though she was already exhausted, and even though she knew, too, that once started she might well play all night. First, she would unpack, and shower, and then . . .

As she crossed the living room to get her suitcase and find the hallway that led to her bedroom, her eyes fell on the coffee table. There, beside a vase of roses, was Alexa's purse, and, beside that, a man's wallet. Alexa was here, and she was not alone. She had unwittingly intruded on Alexa's privacy! Even though Alexa had said she would be in Maryland, she should have called to be sure.

So much for sophistication, Catherine thought miserably as she retreated swiftly to the beautiful bedroom of lilacs far away from where Alexa slept with her overnight guest.

As always, on their weekends together, James awakened long before Alexa. After he had showered and dressed, he stood over the bed, and, as she moved slightly, like a kitten stretching and then curling back into a cozy sleep, he tucked the covers over her beautiful naked body and kissed the smile that touched her lovely lips.

"It's the crack of dawn, isn't it?"

"A little past. I'll go get *The Times* and croissants and coffee, OK?"

"Hmmmmm," Alexa purred. She allowed herself this luxury once a week, a languid counterbalance to her high energy life, a dreamy lazy day in bed to recharge her batteries. As far as she could tell, James never recharged his extraordinarily high energy batteries, at least not with sleep. Sailing, not sleep, she decided, was the counterbalance to the relentless intensity of his life. James never slept late, not even on their weekends together, but he would return to her bed and . . . "Then you'll come back and wake me up properly?"

"You know I will."

His wallet was in the living room, but long before he reached the coffee table he had stopped his graceful stride. She was silhouetted by the pale golden rays of dawn that filtered through the lace curtains. Her hair was like his, midnight black and shining, and, like his, still damp from a recent shower. As she bent her head toward the keyboard, the glistening black spilled forward, obscuring his view of her profile with a veil of luxuriant curls. Her face was hidden, but her hands were fully exposed. Her delicate white fingers danced, touching the ivory keys with exquisite caresses—like whispered kisses—but not depressing them.

No sound came from the piano, but it hardly mattered. Simply watching the dance of her lovely fingers was mesmerizing . . . magical. James was quite content to watch in silence, and he did until the compelling need to see her face urged him on his legitimate mission across the living room to his wallet.

He wanted to see this black-haired Alexa, and he had invaded her privacy long enough without making his presence known. He crossed the room, expecting his movement to alert her, but she was lost in the magnificent music that surely swirled in her mind even though the room was silent. So he simply stood, staring at her boldly, content to wait until she sensed his stare, having no wish for that to happen soon because he was as happily lost in watching her as she was happily lost in her music.

He could see her face now, a wonderful view because the rich black curls that would have fallen into her eyes were held captive by a gold barrette, and he realized that the resemblance he had anticipated didn't exist at all. The Taylor sisters did not look alike; but there was a striking similarity nonetheless in the expression each wore as she so dazzlingly practiced her art—a bewitching mixture of determination and hope, concentration and dreams, perfectionism and magic. Like Alexa, Cat was at once performer and audience, focused on her performance, wanting to make it perfect, and yet lost, too, in the magnificence of the creation. Alexa gave life and spirit and soul to the beautifully scripted words she spoke. Cat quite obviously did the same for the notes she played.

So this was Alexa's little sister.

Catherine sensed his presence then and her graceful hands abruptly halted their delicate dance. *And it was as if the music had stopped.* The soundless room suddenly seemed more still. The magic vanished.

162

Until she looked up at him.

And then there was new, quite unexpected magic as he saw the bright blue eyes, dark-circled from lack of sleep, surprised, questioning, and so magnificently innocent.

Alexa had described Cat's eyes to him—the brilliant blue of a winter sky after a snowstorm—but he had discounted that description as he had discounted all the remarkable words she had used to describe her little sister. Now James gazed at the remarkable eyes and realized that Alexa's words were only the beginning of the image. The blue was indeed the brilliant blue of a winter sky; but there was more in the magnificent sapphire . . . a crystal clarity, a bright hopefulness, and, like her snow-white skin, an astonishing purity.

James remembered his worry that Alexa's sister would be self-absorbed, insensitive, dazzlingly confident. But she was none of those things. She was, as Alexa had tried to tell him, quite timid; and too, when it mattered, as it had that day at the polo field, she was quite brave. He saw both timidity and bravery now, because even though her bright-blue eyes courageously held his intense appraising gaze, her snow-white cheeks blushed a soft, timid pink.

"Hello. You must be Catherine," he said finally, deciding that she *should* be Catherine not Cat, but then wondering, "Or do you prefer Cat?"

"Catherine is fine," she replied, for the first time ever preferring her given name to Alexa's nickname, because of the way "Catherine" sounded when he spoke it.

"Good. I'm James."

"Hi." Catherine smiled a brave yet uncertain hello to the handsome man who gazed at her so intently.

She had never before met any of Alexa's "men." Whenever Alexa returned to Topeka, she always came alone, cheerfully explaining to the curious neighbors that whichever handsome leading man to whom she was currently romantically linked by the entertainment press was simply a good friend. "Nothing serious," she would announce with a laugh. "I'm still married to my career!"

Alexa never brought her lovers to Topeka, but now Catherine was in New York, in Alexa's apartment, and here was this most handsome man, gazing at her, and . . .

How she must look to him! Catherine remembered with dismay her wet hair, and the bangs unceremoniously restrained off her face, and her sweatshirt and jeans, and the extra pounds she now carried. Was the curiosity in his dark blue eyes simply amazement at the contrast between her—who he believed to be Alexa's sister—and the beautiful provocative woman with whom he had spent a night of passion? Should she confess everything? *I'm the ugly duckling, you see, but it doesn't reflect on Alexa at all, because she's not really my sister . . .*

Catherine might have blurted out that confession, or simply dashed out of the living room in mortification, but the powerful feelings that compelled her to stay overrode the impulses that urged her to hide, and all words remained very

164

far from the surface, drowned deep in her over-whelming shyness. She neither ran away nor spoke; but somehow she willed her fingers to unclasp the barrette that held her bangs, freeing the black curls to partially curtain her so very exposed eyes. Then she just sat, quite still, even though her heart raced with sudden restless energy.

James's heart raced too. The racing had begun the moment her surprised blue eyes had first met his, and it had intensified as he had become so very aware of her embarrassment. Her embar-rassment, and his own . . .

Alexa's lovely naked body was covered, of course, but she slept contentedly in the bedroom where they had made love, and where her clothes were scattered still, a flamboyant symbol of the urgency of their passion. James could not send this innocent young woman into Alexa's bedroom, and he even felt awkward about returning there himself to awaken her sleeping sister. Not that it wasn't abundantly obvious that he and Alexa were lovers, or that he saw anything but acceptance in the innocent blue eyes, but still . . .

"Alexa is sleeping," he said finally, after making a solemn vow that there would never again be a night when he made love with Alexa in one bedroom while Catherine slept in another. "I'm going out to get the paper, and fresh-ground coffee, and croissants. Come with me, Cather-ine."

It was a command, gently given. But even if James had posed it as a question, she would have gone with him; because all the warnings that reminded her of how she looked, and how impossible it would be for her to find words to say to him, would have been silenced by whatever it was that would have compelled her to answer "yes."

Chapter 10

It wasn't yet seven A.M., but the June sun was already warm. Basking in the warmth of the light blue summer sky, the sometimes harsh and menacing city felt friendly and safe. The fragrance of freshly baked bread erased all memories of exhaust fumes and diesel, and the balmy air was alive with the songs of seagulls and the soft thud of jogging shoes on pavement.

They bought the Sunday *Times* from a corner newsstand, and croissants and fresh-ground coffee from a nearby bakery. Then, wanting to allow time for Alexa to awaken and make the discovery of Catherine's arrival before they returned, James suggested that they sit for a while on a bench by the river.

"Alexa will be so thrilled that you're here," he told her when they were seated.

"Do you think so?" she asked, the flicker of hope fading swiftly to doubt as she remembered that she had intruded on Alexa's intimate privacy with *him.* Surely that intrusion alone might make her very angry.

"I know so. Now you'll have some time together before she has to be in Washington and your classes begin at Juilliard."

"She told you about Juilliard?"

"About Juilliard, and the album you're recording, and your upcoming concert tour. You're going to be very busy."

Catherine shrugged, smiled a lovely embarrassed smile, then turned her eyes from him to the early morning activity of the river. Already a small fleet of brightly colored sailboats glided across the shimmering water.

"Are you a sailor?" James asked.

"No. Well, I don't know. I've never sailed."

"So you might be."

"I guess. It looks so peaceful."

"It is. Very."

"You're a sailor?" she asked bravely, turning once again to him.

"An avid one. Which means, when you're ready to give sailing a try, I should be the one to introduce you to it."

"Oh, no . . ."

"No?"

"Does Alexa like to sail?"

"Alexa *will* sail, although she gets a little restless. However, with you there to talk to that wouldn't be a problem." James paused as he saw the sapphire surprise at his confidence that her older sister's restlessness would be calmed by her presence. He smiled, underscoring that confidence, and asked, "So, would you like to give it a try sometime?"

167

"Yes, I would. Very much," Catherine answered softly.

"Good. Synchronizing schedules may be tricky, but, if we haven't found a time before August, there's a party then, to which you are invited, at my parents' home in Maryland. It will be the third weekend, the nineteenth and—"

"Cat!"

"Alexa," Catherine whispered. She turned in the direction of the familiar voice and stood as Alexa approached. "Hi."

"Hi." Alexa gave Catherine a brief hug and forced her smile not to wobble and her eyes not to reveal her concern. Something was terribly wrong! Cat's dark-circled eyes told of her sleeplessness, and there was heaviness now, a sallow, unhealthy, *troubled* layer where before there had been only soft, sensual, beautiful plumpness. What had happened to disrupt Cat's calm serenity so dramatically? Would Cat tell her? Alexa hoped so. She smiled reassuringly to the tired blue eyes hidden beneath the dark black curls. "I'm so glad you're here!"

"Me, too. The apartment is so beautiful, and my bedroom, and the piano . . . Thank you."

"You're welcome." Alexa turned to James, thanking him with a soft smile and then teasing lightly, "I had a feeling, when I awakened and discovered that Cat had arrived and you both were gone, that you might be watching the sailboats."

"It seemed like a good place to enjoy the morning sunshine."

"James is a sailing fanatic," Alexa explained to Catherine.

"She already knows that," James replied with a smile. Then, turning to Catherine, he added, "And, I hope, she's already accepted an invitation to go sailing—at the party at Inverness in August if not before."

"Yes," Catherine answered, a soft reply that was unwittingly embellished by a lovely smile and rosy-pink cheeks.

James returned to the apartment with them for a leisurely cup of coffee, then made the gracious exit he had been planning ever since Alexa had appeared at the river. He had known for weeks how important this time was for Alexa, and now he knew it was terribly important for Catherine, too. He had seen her reaction when Alexa had called her name—the sudden tension, the delicate hands curled into tight fists—and her grateful relief when her big sister had been so obviously happy to see her.

James knew one sister well, and the other sister hardly at all, but he wanted to reassure them both, "This will be fine, you'll see, because both of you want to be close." But he knew that wanting wasn't enough. And now he knew, too, that Catherine had secrets and doubts, just as Alexa did. Somehow they had to find a way through the treacherous emotional mine field of their past. Could it be navigated safely? James didn't know. He couldn't reassure. All he could do was leave them alone so that they could begin to try.

James left, and Alexa and Catherine were alone, and . . .

"This is so nice of you," Catherine murmured over and over as together they pored over the maps Alexa had made, personalized expressly for her little sister's new life in Manhattan. The safe, *safest*, routes to Juilliard and the recording studio were charted in vivid colors; and there were also safe, colorful paths to the best places to shop, or browse, or simply see the sights of the vibrant city.

So nice, Catherine whispered to the woman she loved and admired, and who seemed genuinely happy to see her. But would Alexa's warmth turn to ice if she knew that her gracious welcome was for a stranger, not a sister? The question spun in Catherine's mind, tormenting her, distracting her. She was so unused to deception, and here she was deceiving Alexa, of all people! But she couldn't tell Alexa the truth, not now, not yet. The conflict raged within her, depleting the energy she needed to find interesting *other* topics to discuss with Alexa and driving her even deeper into silence.

"What did you think of James?" Alexa asked, when she had said all she could think of to say about the maps she had made. She wanted to ask Cat what had happened to make her beautiful eyes so terribly troubled. Maybe someday she could ask such a question, and maybe someday her little sister would believe that she could trust her enough to tell her everything. But, Alexa reminded herself sadly, Cat has no reason to

170

believe that now. So she found a safe topic to fill the lingering awkward silence: James, a recent memory shared by the Taylor sisters, warm, pleasant, and quite untarnished by the past.

"I think he's wonderful," Catherine answered swiftly, relieved to be able to speak an unequivocal truth.

"I think he's wonderful, too."

"You're in love with him," Catherine added softly. It was a statement not a question, because the affection between Alexa and James had been so obvious. They hadn't been physically affectionate in front of her at all, but their eyes and their smiles and the tenderness in their voices betrayed their true feelings. Alexa loved James, and James loved Alexa. And there was more: James's love for Alexa cast a magical net so wide that, at its very edges, there was even a gentle kindness in his dark blue eyes *for her*. "And he's in love with you."

For a moment, Alexa was taken aback, surprised by both the words and the honesty. But as she gazed at the eyes that met hers with solemn sapphire candor, she suddenly saw the twelve-year-old sister with whom there had been the fragile beginnings of friendship that distant spring. Cat had been so honest then, a little girl who had not yet learned the coy games that little girls learn and women perfect. The lovely unaffected honesty was there still, Alexa realized, because Cat had spent her life playing the music she loved, and she had never learned to play the social games at all.

"I had forgotten how direct you are, Cat,"

Alexa teased fondly. But even the obvious fondness didn't prevent sudden flickers of worry in Catherine's eyes.

"Oh, I'm sorry. I guess I shouldn't have—"

"Yes you *should* have," Alexa interjected emphatically. She added softly, "I want us to be able to talk about the important things in our lives, Cat."

"I want that, too."

"Do you? I'm so glad." Alexa smiled, somehow managing to hold the smile even though her confidence wavered as she thought about what she could say to Cat about James.

He *was* one of the very important things in her life, of course, but her little sister had announced with surprising certainty that she and James were "in love"; and Alexa knew they weren't. They were the skeptic and cynic, after all. Neither even *believed* in falling in love. Admittedly, she had already decided that one day her gentle, wonderful, skeptical friend *would* fall in love, and she had even privately wondered about the woman who would steal James's heart. One day, Alexa was very sure, James would find a consuming love. And what about her? Did her newfound belief in the possibility of love for skeptical James extend even to cynical her? No, not yet. And yet, *because of James*, she was beginning to believe in something she had never before imagined possible: herself, and her worthiness.

One day the skeptic, and perhaps even the cynic, might fall in love. But, even though they were wonderful friends and wonderful lovers, she and James were not *in love* with each other. But

172

how did she explain that truth to the innocent blue eyes that gazed at her now? Alexa had no doubt that her little sister believed in love, and would find a perfect one; and she had no doubt either that Cat would make love only with the man who was that perfect and forever love.

But I'm not so perfect, Cat, Alexa thought. I never have been. And I have made a solemn vow to be honest with you, even though I know that the honest revelation of my flaws may disappoint.

"James is very important to me," she said finally to the earnest and attentive sapphire. "He is an important part of my life and always will be. I don't think that James and I will be together forever, Cat, but I do know that whatever happens between us, I will always care about him and his happiness."

"But that's love, isn't it?"

"Is it?"

"I think so. I think that when you love someone, you care about that person's happiness even if you're not destined to be together."

"Have you ever been in love, Cat?" Alexa asked, suddenly wondering if it could possibly have been a disastrous, and not perfect, love affair that had so dramatically disrupted the serenity of her sister's life.

"Me?" Catherine's eyes widened with surprise. "Oh, no . . ."

"Is everything all right?" Alexa pressed gently.

"It will be," Catherine answered quietly. *Please, please, please.* "I'm very glad to be here."

"And I'm very glad that you are. And so is James. Now that you've met him, I'll give you his unlisted phone numbers at work and at home. You really should feel free to call him any time. I know he'll be calling to check on you, too."

"No! Please don't ask James to call me. I know he's very busy, and I'll be fine. He doesn't need to worry about me."

"I wasn't going to ask him to call, Cat. But I know he will want to, without me asking."

"Then, would you please ask him *not* to?"

"All right, if that's what you'd prefer."

"Yes. Please."

"All right," Alexa assured again. After a thoughtful silence, she asked, "What about the party at his parents' home in Maryland?"

"I'd like to go to the party . . . if you're going."

"Of course I am. I have a promise etched in stone from the producer that I'm off for the entire weekend. Cat, you need to know that Hillary Ballinger will be there. She's married to Senator Robert McAllister now, and James and Robert are friends."

"Have you seen her?"

"I have, and it wasn't wonderful, but it was OK."

"Then it's OK with me, too."

"So?" James asked when he called from San Francisco Wednesday evening.

"So, we're having a nice time."

"Good. Am I interrupting?"

"No. I'm in my bedroom reading a script and she's practicing."

"Has she mastered Manhattan?"

"She will have, at least the necessary routes,

by the time we go to Maryland. We're going to spend Saturday night at RoseCliff, then she'll return by herself and we'll both settle into our long, hot, busy summers."

"You know that I'm available if she needs anything. Will you tell her that?"

"I already have. She thinks you're wonderful, by the way . . ."

"But?"

"But she asked me to ask you not to call."

"Did she give a reason?"

"No. But I think she's a little—a lot—overwhelmed by you, and I think she's embarrassed about her appearance."

"Her appearance?"

"Her weight. She's planning to diet this summer in addition to everything else."

"I didn't notice that she was overweight," James said with quiet surprise. He believed that Catherine must truly be overweight, because Alexa's tone conveyed such loving concern; but he, the man whose lovers had been the most sleek and beautiful women in the world, hadn't noticed. What he had seen, what he remembered with vivid and enchanting clarity, were bright blue eyes, and snow white skin, and flushed pink cheeks, and black velvet hair, and delicate dancing hands, and brave-and-timid innocence. That was his memory of Catherine, and it was lovely and gentle. But, he realized, her memory of him was obviously uncomfortable and embarrassed. "Is she planning to come to the party at Inverness?"

"Yes. In fact, that weekend is the date by which

all the major goals of her summer will have been met. Her French paper will be in the mail for Oberlin on that Friday, and a third of the new pieces she needs to learn for the tour will have been perfected, and her classes at Juilliard will be under control, and a sensible number of pounds will have been lost."

"It sounds as though you won't be seeing much of her this summer," James observed gently, even though he heard no disappointment in Alexa's voice.

"No. We may not actually see each other again until the weekend at Inverness, but we plan to spend some money on phone bills."

"Without the answered-in-French switchboard?"

"Without that." Alexa added softly, "And, I think, with a new closeness to the voice at the other end of the phone."

Even though she had never dieted before, Catherine knew how to do it sensibly. The nation's obsession with thinness, and concerns about the extremes to which teenaged girls would go to be thin, resulted in the addition of nutrition and proper diet techniques to the curricula of most high school health classes. Catherine knew how to diet sensibly, by eating small portions of nutritious food, and exercising, and modifying untoward behaviors; and that was how she dieted for the first week.

Then, even though she knew it was dangerous, she stopped eating altogether. The decision to diet incautiously—to lose as much weight as quickly as she could—matched the incautiousness of the decision to diet in the first place. She had always been plump, of course, and the plumpness itself prevented comparisons to slender Alexa. Would they be studied more closely for similarities if she was thin? What if the face that emerged from beneath the soft protective layers of flesh was so strikingly different from Alexa's that even Alexa herself began to wonder?

It was a terrifying worry, but a worry that was, remarkably, overridden by an even more compelling wish to look the best she possibly could. For herself, whoever *she* was. And for Alexa, who might be more proud of her. And . . . for James.

After two days without food, the gnawing hunger stopped and Catherine felt an astonishing clarity. All her senses were heightened. The world seemed brighter, more vivid, and her music rang with such purity, and the warm summer wind caressed her skin with such tingling delicacy, and sleep felt luxurious, and water tasted sweet, and . . .

Sometimes the clarity clouded slightly—a sudden breathlessness, a little dizziness on standing, a whisper of confusion or forgetfulness. Catherine knew the meaning of those clouds—signs that she needed food—and she begrudgingly obeyed the signs, providing a little necessary fuel for the body that had, for that blurry moment, needed more energy than was readily available from its stores.

She decided that had her demands for energy not been so high, she might have been able to fast entirely. But she needed energy for her classes, and the new pieces she was learning, and the French paper she was writing, and the frequent meetings with her manager at Fordyce who was arranging the concert tour. Her demands for energy were high, which meant that occasionally she had to eat; and yet, paradoxically, in the midst of days with little or no food, there came sudden, powerful, almost euphoric bursts of new energy. It was that omnipotent, euphoric energy that prompted her to agree to more and more appearances on the tour, until finally she was left with only a three week break between the end of her solidly booked North American tour in June and the beginning of her equally committed European tour in July.

Catherine's baggy clothes told her that she was losing weight, lots of it, and in the shower her hands soaped a new and different body. There were vestiges of her plump self, soft full breasts and curved hips, but mostly there was boniness and a very slender waist and thighs that no longer touched. She knew, from her baggy clothes and soapy hands, about the new body that was emerging as the fat melted away; but until ten days before the party at Inverness, she had no idea about her new face.

When she finally forced herself to sit before the mirrored antique vanity in her bedroom, Catherine saw the face of a woman—a *woman*—and a stranger. The woman bore no resemblance to Alexa, of course, nor did she look like the plump little girl who had gazed back at her on the rare occasions in the past twenty-one years that she had glanced at herself in a mirror. This woman with the rich black velvet hair and high aristocratic cheekbones and huge sapphire blue eyes and full provocative lips was a stranger—a hauntingly beautiful stranger who could turn heads and draw smiles, like the surprising appreciative smiles that had been following her around Manhattan for the past few weeks.

Catherine's initial appraisal of the strange and beautiful woman in the mirror was analytical. Then, quite suddenly, the appraisal became personal, and startling. *This is who I am.* Since May, she had known who she *wasn't,* neither the daughter nor the sister she had believed herself to be. Now, as she gazed at this new face, she wondered, for the first time, about the mother who had abandoned her.

Did you look like this? she silently asked the image in the mirror. On impulse, she removed the sapphire necklace from its hiding place in a remote corner of the vanity's top drawer and held it to her slender ivory neck. She stared at the reflection of the precious gems, an exact match of her own sapphire eyes, and wondered if this necklace, a gift from her father to her mother, had been created because the color was an exact match, too, of her mother's eyes.

As she gazed at her image in the mirror, her starved-for-days vision blurred, blurring the image, changing it, aging it slightly until . . . Was she looking at her mother? Did she have questions for that beautiful woman?

"Oh, yes, I have questions for you, Mother," she whispered. "What was wrong with me that you could so easily give me away? What was it

179

about me that made you unable to love me enough to keep me? Do you know, Mother," she asked softly, "how much I hate you?"

"Truly an exquisite piece," the jeweller at Tiffany raved as he examined the sapphire necklace through his magnifying glass. "The stones all appear to be flawless. Are they?"

"I don't know."

"It would say on the appraisal." He saw her confusion and wondered for a moment if this beautiful woman dressed in baggy jeans was a cat burglar, a jewel thief who had come to Tiffany to sell this stolen work of art. He had assumed that she was the owner—a mistress, most likely, of one of Manhattan's wealthiest men—dressed waif-like as a disguise. He had assumed that the necklace was hers, and that she wanted to sell it, the affair over, or, perhaps, because she needed money for the cocaine that was possibly the only nourishment she provided her thin body.

"I don't have the appraisal. It was a gift."

"Yes. Of course. Did you wish to sell it?"

"No."

"To have it appraised then?"

"I just wanted to know if you recognized it. I had hoped to trace it to its original owner."

"Oh. Well, the design, the simple elegance of a heart pendant suspended on a strand of precious gems, is quite traditional. All the major jewellers would have similar pieces. The extraordinary quality and color of the sapphires might be a clue, depending on what records were kept by the designer."

"I have no idea who designed it," Catherine said quietly. Just as she had no idea why she was here. She only knew that something very powerful—surely anger, not sentiment—had compelled her to leave the mirrored vanity in her apartment moments after whispering to the blurry image and to come here to ask these questions.

"The designer I can tell you. All jewellers engrave their initials, usually on the clasp. Let me see."

Ever since she had begun to starve herself, Catherine's heart had set a new pace, fast and unhealthy. Now, as she waited to learn the name of the jeweller who had made the necklace, her already racing heart began to flutter, leaving her lightheaded and breathless. I will eat some sugar and some protein, she silently promised her swirling head and galloping heart, just as soon as I learn the name.

"This is probably not the original clasp," the jeweller said after several moments. "It looks very new."

"The necklace hasn't been worn for twenty-one years."

"Oh. Well, anyway, it must be a replacement clasp because I don't find any jeweller's initials. You know about the words that are engraved on the clasp?"

"Words? No. What do they say?"

"Something in French."

"May I look?"

Catherine held the magnifying glass in her hands, willing them to stop trembling just for

181

a moment, just long enough for the tiny words engraved in gold to come into focus.

Then there they were: *Je t'aimerai toujours.* "I will love you always" engraved in the language that she, the little girl from Kansas, so inexplicably loved and spoke more fluently, more effortlessly, than she spoke English.

Je t'aimerai toujours. Was it a promise from her father to her mother? Yes, of course. It was surely *not* a promise from her mother to her. Or if it was a promise of forever love from her mother, it was a false one, *a lie.*

As Catherine left Tiffany to find something to calm her fluttering heart, she left with the certain knowledge that the sapphire necklace could never lead her to her mother. And that was just as well. In fact, it was quite comforting to have an answer—"It's no use!"—to future renegade impulses from her heart that might urge her again to search for someone she did not truly wish to find.

Part Two

Chapter 11

Inverness Estate, Maryland . . . August 1989

"Your parents are wonderful. You come by your niceness honestly," Alexa told James as he drove her back to RoseCliff following Sunday evening dinner with Arthur and Marion Sterling at Inverness. "Not to mention your good looks."

"Thank you. They liked you, too, of course. Why wouldn't they? Maybe we can do this again before the party."

"I'd like that. Speaking of the party, when I spoke to Cat last night she asked me what clothes to bring . . . and I wasn't sure."

James heard the uncertainty in her last words and gave her a quizzical glance.

"OK, I confess, I'm a country girl from Kansas and the only house parties I'm familiar with are in the movies. So, will this be like the picnic at Twelve Oaks in *Gone With The Wind?* You know, tightly-corseted women in hoop-skirted frocks who flirt outrageously, eat nothing, and retire for naps while the menfolk smoke cigars, drink brandy, and discuss politics? Or will it be like an Agatha Christie murder mystery in which a group of people with intertwining secrets arrive at a remote clifftop mansion, sip champagne, and eye each other sinisterly as they wait for the drama to unfold?"

"Neither—although I have not yet exacted a promise from you that you won't eye Hillary sinisterly."

"You know I couldn't make such a promise, sugar," Alexa drawled, batting her long eyelashes as she mimicked Hillary's Southern accent perfectly.

"I think you'll be shamed into impeccable behavior because of Brynne, whom you will like very much, not to mention my parents and your little sister and—"

"I'm sure I will! So, how about some impeccable attire to match?"

"OK. The garden party on Sunday will be fairly dressy—like a formal summer wedding—but Saturday will be very casual. Sundresses, shorts, swimsuits, whatever."

"Swimsuits," Alexa mused provocatively, "I wonder how Hillary looks in a swimsuit these days."

"Sensational, I would imagine. Not as sensational as you, naturally, but sensational nonetheless. However, Hillary won't be appearing in a swimsuit."

"No? Why not? Improper First Lady attire?" Alexa's tease faded as she saw the seriousness in his handsome face and sensed that he was debating how much to say. After a thoughtful silence, she guessed softly, "It's something to do with Robert, isn't it? Because he has scars from Vietnam?"

"Yes."

"Oh." Alexa frowned softly, sympathetically. She hadn't planned to wear a swimsuit anyway, of course, because of Cat. Her little sister reported that her diet was going well, but even with a perfect body Alexa knew that timid Cat would not feel comfortable appearing in a swimsuit amongst strangers. She hadn't planned to wear a swimsuit because of Cat, and now, because of the dirt-poor country boy who had traded in the combat zone of his childhood for an even more horrible one, there was yet another important reason not to. "So, no swimsuits, snazzy for Sunday, casual for Saturday. That's easy. I'll tell Cat."

"How is she?"

"She sounds fine, peppy and positive. Her French paper is virtually done, her classes and new pieces are under control, and she says she's happy with her diet."

"Good. Oh, be sure to remind her—and yourself—to pack jeans, sweaters, and tennis shoes for our sail."

"Aye, aye, Captain."

Catherine would have liked to spend the Friday night before the party with Alexa at RoseCliff. She would have liked to see again the bountiful garden of roses, and she would have very much liked to have had an evening alone with Alexa.

But Catherine knew with absolute certainty that she didn't have the strength to climb the three flights of stairs to the clifftop cottage. So she flew to Washington on Saturday morning instead, arriving with only enough time to drive directly from National airport to Inverness. Alexa was already at the gate when the plane landed and the passengers began to disembark. She smiled admiringly at the stunningly beautiful woman who was approaching her . . . who was vaguely familiar . . . who was her baby sister!

"Cat! You're so *gorgeous*. But . . ."

"But what?" Catherine asked anxiously.

"But you've lost far too much weight in such a short period of time . . . haven't you?"

"No. I'm fine, really, Alexa."

"Well, you certainly look fine." Alexa tilted her golden head and carefully studied Cat's face, ignoring the flickers of sapphire worry. Finally, smiling, she said, "I hadn't realized it before, but you've got Mom's cheekbones—high, classically sculpted, incredibly patrician. I always secretly wished that I'd inherited them, but now I see that they look far better on you."

"Thank you," Catherine murmured softly, breathing finally, a breath of pure relief. But the wonderful relief was fleeting. As a sudden sternness subdued Alexa's smile, Catherine felt sharp claws of fear mercilessly clutch her ever-empty stomach. Had Alexa realized that her enthusiastic acceptance of her newly thin and dramatically changed little sister had been far too hasty? Was she about to declare that, on closer scrutiny, the lovely aristocratic cheekbones didn't really resemble Jane's after all? In fact, there was really nothing familiar looking about her, no family resemblance whatsoever.

But Alexa's sudden solemnity wasn't a prelude to a pronouncement that Catherine was an impostor. It was another worry altogether, a gentle, loving, sisterly one.

"You just stopped eating didn't you? Don't answer. I know you and your incredible discipline. But, Cat, you've lost enough weight now, haven't you?"

"I guess," Catherine replied, although she wasn't entirely certain. Losing weight had become so easy. Why not lose a few more pounds? She had lost all urge to eat, now eating only when breathlessness or weakness warned her that she must. And when she did eat the necessary nourishment, the uncomfortable fullness made food feel far more like medication than pleasure.

"*Yes*. Any more would be too much. You could not look more stunning, Cat. Wait until James sees you!"

"Hello, Alexa, dear," Marion Sterling said affectionately when they arrived at Inverness. Marion's welcoming smile and twinkling blue eyes first greeted the Taylor sister she already liked so much and then fell on her little sister. "And you must be Catherine. Welcome. We're absolutely delighted that you were able to join us this weekend."

"Thank you," Catherine whispered softly as she met James's mother. As with James, she instantly felt the warmth and kindness, a magical net of affection cast for Alexa but which captured her—a most willing captive—as well. "It's so nice of you to include me."

"It's our pleasure."

"Are we the last to arrive?" Alexa asked. "We ran into a bit more traffic than I had anticipated for a Saturday morning."

"You are the last to arrive, but you're not the least bit late. Luncheon won't be served for another hour. Why don't you get settled and then join the rest of us on the south veranda?"

Catherine and Alexa were led to their adjacent suites by one of the many staff brought in for the weekend of entertaining at Inverness. Alexa knew already that she would not be sharing her room in the mansion's east wing with James. On this weekend, at this house party in Maryland, only wedded couples were sharing beds. Alexa knew . . . and approved. Inverness was Marion and Arthur's home, after all, and, although her own parents were almost a generation younger than James's, it would have been the same in Topeka. Besides, having a room next to Cat's would be fun. Perhaps they would stay up until all hours discussing their impressions of the day.

Alexa unpacked her small suitcase quickly, brushed her long golden hair, gave herself a critical but ultimately approving glance in the full length mirror, and left her suite to find Cat. She was unpacking still, quite unaware of Alexa's sudden appearance in the open doorway. For several moments, Alexa simply watched, startled anew by the change in her little sister's appearance. The plump, luxuriant, sensuous beauty had given way to an even more beautiful one, slightly haunting, elegant and mysterious. Even the way Cat moved had changed. Her motions were slower now and ballerina graceful. Alexa had no idea that her sister's new gracefulness—so elegant and so regal—was simply a manifestation of her critically limited energy and her starving

190

body's instinctive attempt to conserve whatever energy it could.

"Hi," Alexa said finally, when it became obvious that Cat wasn't about to sense her presence. "Aren't these rooms luxurious?"

"Hi." Catherine greeted Alexa and then responded softly to her question, "Oh, yes, very luxurious."

"Are you about ready to join the others?"

"I thought I'd change first."

"Really?" Alexa asked with surprise. Cat looked so beautiful in the simple elegance of the cream-colored silk blouse and blue linen skirt that it seemed a shame to change. "What you're wearing is fine . . . stunning."

"Thanks, but I think I'd like to change into a dress. Marion said luncheon wouldn't be for an hour, so there's time, isn't there?"

"Sure. Plenty of time."

"Then I will change," Catherine said decisively as she moved to the closet where she had hung her new clothes. How long it had taken her to select her wardrobe for this weekend! The selections had been hers, even though at each Fifth Avenue boutique the saleswomen had been very eager to help. More than one had shrewdly deduced, with knowing and appreciative smiles, that she must be Eileen Ford's newest discovery, and all had tried to dress her model-thin body in the latest fashions. Catherine looked stunning in the summer collections of Armani, Karan, and Klein, but, she explained with quiet apology, the ultra-chic clothes weren't really *her*. For her entire life, she had dressed of necessity, without a thought to fashion or style, but with her new shape came new attention to clothes. She had a definite preference, she discovered, and it was a preference for traditional elegance. She withdrew from the closet a very soft, very feminine, very demure floral print dress and held it for Alexa to see. "I thought this."

"That's beautiful." Alexa tugged at her lower lip, suddenly uncertain about what to do. Sisters undoubtedly dressed and undressed in front of each other all the time, but the Taylor sisters never had. "Should I go on ahead?"

"Oh, no," Catherine replied swiftly. "Would you mind waiting?"

"Not at all."

Alexa sat on the bed, determined neither to stare nor to avert her gaze entirely while her little sister changed. But, drawn by powerful magnets of concern and curiosity, it was virtually impossible to not to spend more time looking than not. It was concern that first drew Alexa's gaze, because as Cat shed the layers of silk and linen her true thinness was so abundantly obvious; and it was curiosity that held it, because her little sister's shape was so unlike her own. Alexa's sleek, perfect, golden body was made for scant bikinis and provocative gowns. There was no golden sleekness to Cat's new shape; but, Alexa thought, the snow white skin and curves that were softly rounded despite her thinness sent a message of pure femininity.

"Are you looking forward to the weekend?" Alexa asked impulsively, aware of the lingering silence and the intensity of her own stares.

"Oh, yes, of course. Have you already met everyone?"

"Everyone except Brynne—Robert's sister—and her husband Stephen. James says they both are very nice, although we may not really get to know Stephen. He's an architect in Richmond, where he and Brynne live, and he's in the midst of some project that will prevent him from arriving until the party tomorrow. So, today it will be Brynne, and the Sterlings—you'll like Arthur as much as Marion—and the McAllisters, and Elliot Archer."

"Elliot Archer?"

"I may not have mentioned Elliot before because James wasn't certain he'd be able to come. He's something like the nation's—which I think also means the world's—leading expert on terrorism. He's in his midfifties, although he looks much younger, never married, very dashing. I think he began his career as a secret agent, an authentic James Bond, and he still has that intriguing allure. I met him last week. He's very nice, too. I'm sure you'll like him." Alexa's description of Elliot stopped abruptly and she said quietly, "That dress is sensational on you."

"Thank you. I was wondering if . . . ?"

"Yes?"

"Well, I've never worn make-up. I went to the cosmetic counters at some of the department stores but what they put on me seemed like too much. I thought maybe you could suggest something."

Catherine's voice trailed off, and for a moment Alexa was silent, moved by her little sister's uncertain request for her advice, and eager to be needed, but confronted with the truth: brilliant blue eyes framed by long midnight-black lashes, lovely pink cheeks, and full rosy lips. Finally, she said honestly, "You don't need make-up, Cat."

"I don't?"

"No. You have Mom's high aristocratic cheek-bones, and like me you've inherited Dad's natural coloring."

"Here you are," Marion greeted Alexa and Catherine warmly when they appeared on the veranda. At the arrival of the beautiful Taylor sisters, conversations halted in mid-sentence and all attention focused on the house party's final two guests. "Now, let's see, who knows whom?"

"I know Alexa," the very handsome silver-haired man standing beside Marion admitted with a welcoming smile.

"Hello, Arthur," Alexa replied. "Arthur, I'd like you to meet my sister, Cat."

"Welcome, Cat."

"Thank you," Catherine answered softly to James's father. "Arthur."

"And this is Robert," Arthur said, gesturing to the man beside him, continuing the introductions as if they were in a reception line at a wedding.

"Hello, Robert."

"Hello, Cat." As Robert smiled warmly at Alexa's stunningly beautiful little sister, he wondered, not for the first time in the three months since he had last seen her, what reception he would get from Alexa herself. Until that afternoon, after her performance, she had always greeted him with magnificent emerald ice. But, for those brief moments, the ice had melted into something even more magnificent, a warm, welcoming emerald glow. Welcoming, and memorable. How well Robert remembered those moments, and how he had hoped that today the ice would be defrosted still. And now, as he left the luminous sapphire eyes and met the sparkling emerald ones, he saw quite eloquently, quite wonderfully, that they, too, remembered. "Hello, Alexa."

"Hello, Robert," she answered softly, luxuriating for a moment in the smiling dark eyes. Finally, she forced herself to leave that welcoming warmth to turn to his wife's always cool disdain, and, with carefully rehearsed off-handedness, she asked. "You remember Cat, don't you, Hillary?"

"Of course I do. How lovely to see you again, Cat."

"It's lovely to see you, too, Hillary," Catherine echoed politely, even though the sight of the senator's beautiful wife caused a pulsing thunder in her brain that made her far more dizzy than the lightheadedness which had been her constant companion since the third week of her diet. Catherine had been worried about seeing Alexa for fear that Alexa would guess she was not truly her little sister; and she had been worried about seeing James, worried yet eager, for reasons she could not define. But her greatest fear about today had been the fear of seeing Hillary again. What if the cruel girl from Dallas had grown into a cruel woman who would turn to the other guests, as she had turned to her teenaged friends at the polo field that day, and bluntly demand, "I ask you all, do these two look one tiny little bit like sisters? Isn't it obvious? They can't be. One of them is an impostor!" Amidst the dizzying thunder, Catherine bravely met Hillary's sable-colored eyes and felt the heat of her appraising patrician stare. Appraising and approving . . .

"My mother is in absolute heaven that you've agreed to spend a second week performing with the Dallas symphony this spring," Hillary gushed graciously. "Not that two weeks is enough, mind you, but at least it's better than just the one."

"Oh, good. I'm glad," Catherine murmured softly, quite unaware that she had agreed to a second week in Dallas. During her starvation-induced euphoria, she had simply empowered the Fordyce Agency to fill every second of her concert tour, and they had. She was unaware that she was scheduled to spend two weeks in Dallas next spring, but she was glad, *so very glad*, that Hillary had chosen to embrace her accomplishments and overlook her appearance.

"And this is my sister Brynne," Robert said after a moment. "Brynne, Alexa and Cat."

There could be no doubt that Brynne and Robert McAllister were brother and sister. They shared the same rich dark brown hair, and sensitive dark brown eyes, and elegantly sculptured features. But it was remarkable, Alexa thought, that the features that were so strong and handsome in Robert could soften into such delicate prettiness in Brynne. Brynne's dark eyes sparkled with radiant warmth, and there was such a generosity about her, such a glowing aura of kindness, that, as James had confidently predicted, Alexa found herself liking her *instantly.*

"Hello, Brynne."

"Hello, Alexa. Hello, Cat."

As Catherine, Alexa, and Brynne embellished their formal greeting with a brief discussion of Cat's impressions of New York, and unaffected praise from Brynne about both *Majesty* and *Pennsylvania Avenue,* and a few words about the exciting architectural project that, albeit exciting, would unfortunately keep Stephen in Richmond until tomorrow, Elliot Archer awaited his turn to be introduced.

Of the necessary skills that he had acquired during his many years of intelligence work, Elliot's ability to hide his emotions was, perhaps, his most valuable. More than once—*many times more than once*—his expertise at concealing his true feelings had saved both his own life and the lives of others. In the beginning, the skill had to be practiced; but now, after so many years, it was reflexive, a virtual instinct. Still, had any eyes been watching him when he first saw Catherine Taylor, they would have seen an instant of shock followed by unmistakable flickers of emotion— love, grief, and rage. But no eyes had been focused on Elliot at that precise moment, because all had been drawn to the stunning Taylor sisters; and he had swiftly vanquished all overt signs of the waves of emotion that swept through him, even though the powerful waves crashed and pounded still . . .

Because Catherine Taylor looked so very much like

Princess Isabelle Castille. It had been over thirty years, but Elliot's memory of the lovely Princess who had given sanctuary to the woman he loved was still, always, exquisitely vivid. Isabelle's hair had been spun gold, and Catherine's beautiful face was framed in black velvet, but the remarkable sapphire eyes, the thoughtful tilt of the head, the soft smile and even softer voice were so astonishingly like Isabelle's. Had Isabelle and Alexandre had a daughter, she would surely have looked like Catherine Taylor. But, as Elliot knew only too well, the Prince and Princess of L'île had been childless. This beautiful young woman simply looked like Isabelle, and that remarkable resemblance simply triggered the waves of emotion that crashed still, even though by the time Alexa introduced her little sister to him, the handsome face of the dashing master spy was calm, smiling, inscrutable once again.

"It's nice to meet you, Cat."

"It's nice to meet you, too, Elliot." Catherine returned his pleasant smile until her restless heart, brave and timid, urged her on. There was one final hello, the greeting to the handsome man for whom it had somehow been so important for her to look her best. So that James would be proud, not embarrassed, by Alexa's little sister? And so that, perhaps, she would find the courage to speak to him? Because thin, beautiful women were always courageous and confident, *weren't they?*

"Hello, James," she said to the sensuous dark blue eyes that made all the dizzying breathlessness that had come before seem now to be the most stable of vital signs.

"Catherine," James answered softly, wanting to say a thousand things to her, some soft, some harsh, but finally simply asking gently, "Did you remember to bring jeans for our sail?"

"Yes."

"Good." After a long moment, he took his gaze from her and addressed the others. "I hope you all brought your jeans. Tonight should be ideal for sailing. The moon will be full and the breeze will be brisk and balmy."

It wasn't either the picnic at Twelve Oaks or a prelude to an Agatha Christie murder mystery, Alexa decided as the delightful afternoon drifted gently by. It was Christmas, a gathering of loved ones with no plot whatsoever and no purpose other than to be together. The others had been here before, many times, and now she and Cat had been included in this lovely gathering, and they had been made to feel so welcome. The afternoon was quite magical, as if Inverness had been showered with fairy dust, drenching everyone with pleasantness and joy. Of course, she mused wryly, the "magic" may simply be that I've been able to spend the entire afternoon floating from conversation to conversation without ever finding myself alone with Hillary . . .

"Did you visit L'île, Marion?" Hillary asked when they assembled in the formal dining room for dinner. "I remember your saying that you hoped to."

"Yes, we did."

"And? Is it really the romantic island paradise everyone says it is?"

"It truly is. Truly romantic." Marion cast an affectionate smile at Arthur. "And truly a paradise."

"L'île?" Brynne asked, her twinkling eyes communicating quite clearly, and without a flicker of embarrassment, that even if according to her sister-in-law "everyone" knew about the romantic island, *she* didn't.

Good for you, Brynne, Alexa thought, chiding herself slightly for her own hesitation in posing the same question. She had heard about a place called L'île, an island kingdom in the Mediterranean that was a favorite haunt of Europe's very rich, very famous, and often very royal. She wondered if this was the same L'île. If so, she was intrigued that Marion and Arthur had visited there and was quite eager to hear their impressions.

"The full name of the island is L'île des Arcs-en-ciel, the Island of the Rainbows," Marion explained. "L'île is located in the Mediterranean off the southern coast of France, and, like nearby Monaco, it's a principality. The royal family is Castille, as in Castille Jewels, although it is hard to imagine a more dazzling jewel than the island itself. The terrain varies from white sand beaches to luxuriant gardens to dense tropical forests, with each breathtaking spot linked to the next by paths of white marble lined with hedges of gardenias. Every vista would be a painter's delight, and I truly believe that in the flowers and sunsets on L'île I saw shades of plum and pink and gold that I've never seen before."

"You can tell Marion was impressed," Arthur offered lovingly as Marion paused for a breath. When she arched an eyebrow in response to his teasing, he admitted with a soft laugh, "And so was I."

"Tell them about Le Bijou, Arthur."

"All right. Well. Le Bijou is the hotel, the only one on the island. Like everything else, it's owned by the Castilles, and, like everything else, it is of impeccable quality and decorated with extraordinary taste—Persian rugs, jade statues, antique porcelains, and magnificent original art. Guests are made to feel quite special, and most welcome, as if there by personal invitation from the Prince and Princess. Marion and I agree that we've never stayed in a hotel as beautiful, or as luxurious, as Le Bijou."

"That's quite an endorsement," Robert said quietly, smiling slightly at the understatement. Marion and Arthur Sterling had stayed in the world's most celebrated hotels, and to be placed at the top of that elite list was quite an endorsement indeed.

As Elliot listened to the discussion of L'île, his face revealed only casual interest, even though his actual interest in the discussion was far from casual. He had never told Marion and Arthur about his great love, Geneviève Castille, or about the three enchanted weeks of love he had spent with her on the romantic island kingdom. He was glad now that he hadn't; because now he could ask, quite casually, about their impression of

Alain Castille. Alain . . . the son of Jean-Luc, whom Elliot hated still, six years after his death . . . and the son of Geneviève, whom he loved still, over thirty years after Jean-Luc had murdered her.

"Did you meet the Prince?"

"Yes. We met both Alain and his half-sister Natalie. When Alain discovered we were staying at Le Bijou, he insisted that we move to the palace. Arthur's already told you that the hotel was palatial, but the palace was even more splendid. And Alain and Natalie could not have been more gracious hosts. They behaved as if there was nothing they would rather do than show us their beautiful island. They strolled with us along the white marble paths and told us all the wonderful myths and legends of L'île."

"Myths and legends?"

"There are a great many, but the most famous, of course, is the legend of the rainbows." Marion smiled mysteriously and then continued, "Every afternoon, just before tea time, the bright blue sky turns almost black as thunderclouds appear from nowhere. The sudden darkness is dramatic but cozy. The ambient temperature remains warm, and of course the rain is welcome because it nourishes the magnificent tropical flowers. The cloudburst lasts less than an hour, and when it's over the rainbows come out."

"More than one rainbow," Arthur embellished, wishing, as he knew Marion wished, that their words could even begin to convey the true splendor. "Sometimes five, six, even seven, all

202

overlapping, blending together until the entire sky is filled with the brilliant colors."

"The rainbows begin in the sea and arch to the center of the island where they all converge in a huge cave." Marion elaborated. "The enormous cave was once completely filled with jewels—sapphires, rubies, emeralds, amethysts—which, according to legend, were in reality small glittering splinters of rainbow."

"What a lovely image," Catherine whispered.

"Yes, isn't it? On one of our walks, Alain and Natalie took us to the cave."

"And?"

"Not a jewel. There once *were* jewels in the cave, Alain explained. However, he admitted, the precious gems weren't crystallized bits of rainbows. Instead, because of L'île's strategic location along the ancient trade routes, it's most likely that roguish Castille ancestors intercepted jewel-bearing vessels, stole their precious cargoes, and hid the gems in the cave. At which point, in his telling of the true history of L'île, Alain Castille quoted Balzac." Marion looked questioningly at her extremely well-educated son and teased lightly, "Do you know the quote, James?"

"Hopefully I will at least recognize it," James countered amiably.

"Cat knows," Alexa murmured quietly. She had no intention of putting her little sister on the spot, of course, but asking Cat about something French was like asking her to play "Chopsticks" . . . very easy . . . second nature.

Catherine did know, although she apologized

a little in advance, "Only yesterday I mailed my French term paper to Oberlin. There was quite a bit of Balzac in it. I think the quotation you mean is 'Behind every great fortune there is a crime.' "

"Yes."

"How gracious of Alain to admit to the crime," Elliot said quietly, even though his heart ached as he thought about the history of the Castilles—a history of great fortunes and even greater crimes.

"Alain is a very gracious young man."

"Is Alain the creative genius behind Castille Jewels?" Hillary asked.

"I imagine that it's Alain who insists, as he obviously insists with everything else on L'île, that the quality is impeccable. But I think Natalie is the talented designer. When we toured the design studio on the island and the jewelry boutique in the hotel, it was she who suddenly became the expert."

"Well," Hillary sighed softly as she extended her perfectly manicured left hand, "I would like to thank whoever is responsible for my wedding band. Other than Robert, that is."

"It's a Castille design?"

"Yes. Robert discovered it at the Castille boutique in Dallas two weeks before our wedding."

"It's very beautiful," Alexa said. She had noticed Hillary's ring during dinner at La Côte and had begrudgingly admired it then. The sparkling slivers of diamonds and emeralds imbedded into the shining gold were elegant, tasteful, and not, she imagined, terribly expensive—well

204

within the means of the prosecutor Robert had been when Hillary had married him.

"Thank you, Alexa." Hillary's expression conveyed approval of, not gratitude for, Alexa's compliment. "I don't know when Robert and I will have time to visit L'île, but I would certainly like to send my thanks to Princess Natalie. Do you anticipate seeing her again, Marion?"

"Yes. Alain has invited us to spend Christmas at the palace. James plans to join us, beginning with a sail from Nice to L'île." A warm glow filled Marion's dark blue eyes as she gazed at the much loved faces around her. "I just had the most wonderful idea. Wouldn't it be marvelous if we all met on L'île sometime? I know it's probably impossible with everyone's busy schedules, but wouldn't it be lovely?"

Chapter 12

"So," James said as the summer sky faded from blue to pink. "Time to go sailing. Alexa?"

"Oh, no, thank you," she sighed contentedly. "I'm much too mellow to move."

James got variations of the same answer from the others, including Arthur who was an avid sailor. James shrugged amiably with each refusal, and, smiling, finally announced to the brilliant blue eyes that had accepted his invitation weeks before, "I guess it's just us, Catherine."

"Oh. Well. Maybe . . ." Her words faltered quickly under his intense gaze.

"I'll wait here while you go change into your jeans," James said firmly as his eyes sent the same gentle command they had sent once before, *Come with me, Catherine.*

"OK," she agreed quietly, somehow hiding her sudden panic. She had wanted to go sailing tonight, of course. She had been looking forward to it for weeks. And this afternoon and evening had made her all the more eager. She had barely spoken a word all day, but it hadn't mattered. The others had chattered, and she had been part of the conversations with her attentive eyes and lovely smiles, and that was all that had been required of her. And it had been wonderful . . . magical. There had been even more magic— because, a few times, James had smiled at her, and she thought, yes, maybe, he approved of the way she looked.

How she had looked forward to the sail! James and Alexa would talk in their easy, clever way, and she would listen and smile, and . . . and now she and James were going to be alone! Catherine had already learned that her new appearance did not bring with it a new talent for lively, effortless conversation. If anything, she was even more shy with him now, because the dark blue eyes were far more intense than she had remembered.

Just borrow the clever line from Alexa, reason urged. Just tell him, with a soft purr if you can, that you're far too mellow to move, too.

That's what she should have done, but she didn't. And as she changed into her jeans with the slow graceful movements that were eloquent clues to her limited energy, she wondered with renewed panic how she would find the energy to think of words to say to him, and then the energy to speak them, all the while fighting to calm her racing heart.

Catherine wondered, but she had no answers. She only knew that she couldn't say no.

You can't do this! Her mind sent new and urgent warnings as she and James began the three flight descent from the cliff to the cove where *Night Wind* was moored. You can get down the stairs, but there is *no way* you can climb back up! Remember the reason you didn't spend last night with Alexa at RoseCliff?

I can do it! a defiant voice answered. I *will* do it.

When they reached the sailboat, Catherine sat in the cockpit while James cast off the lines and raised the sails. She marvelled at his graceful strength as he so effortlessly rigged the boat; and when he was out of her view she simply listened to the wonderful symphony of new sounds—ropes being coiled on varnished decks, sails unfurling in the night breeze, waves lapping gently against the hull. Once the sails were set and the lines were cast off, James joined her in the cockpit and expertly guided the sleek sailboat out of the cove and into moon-drenched Chesapeake Bay.

They sailed for a long time without any words at all, sharing with their soft smiles the wonder of the silent power as the boat glided swiftly through the dark water.

"So?" James asked finally. "First impressions?"

"I love it."

"So do I."

"Alexa says that sometime you are going to spend a year sailing around the world."

"I hope to." James smiled. "I think that sounds like a one-year prison sentence to your sister."

"Really?"

"I imagine it might sound that way to you, too."

"No," she answered softly. "Why?"

"It would mean a year away from your music. Or is your music always with you?" he asked, remembering the June morning when her delicate fingers had whispered soft kisses on the keys, and the room had been filled with passion and emotion even though there had been no sounds. "Do you hear it even when you aren't playing?"

"I guess," she answered slowly, "that my music is with me even when I'm not playing, but it's a feeling more than a sound."

"A peaceful feeling?"

"Oh yes." The greatest peace, she thought. The only peace, the only place where I know that I truly belong. "Is that what sailing is for you? Peaceful?"

"Very peaceful." Very peaceful and very private, he thought. At least, that was how it was when he sailed by himself. Whenever others joined him, the mood inevitably changed; the simple presence of another person disrupted the absolute peace and invaded—even if a friendly and welcome invasion—his privacy. The most exquisite tranquillity, James had discovered, could not be shared. *Until now* . . . with Catherine. He felt the extraordinary peacefulness now, with her; but there was a restlessness, too, because of her. The completely new and quite astonishing restlessness urged him, a powerful wonderful urge, to sail out of the bay and into the ocean and beyond—right now, with Catherine.

James gazed at the moonlit sapphire eyes, to see if they too felt the extraordinary peace—and just maybe, the enchanting restlessness—but in the lingering silence a frown had crossed her lovely face. She seemed to be searching, struggling.

"What are you thinking?" he asked gently.

That I can't think of what to say to you! I'm trying, but everything I think of seems so silly and naive. If only . . . Catherine finally answered his question with a question, her soft voice hopeful, "Do you speak French?"

"Not really. I had a year in high school and know some of the usual phrases, but that's about it. Why?"

"Because . . . I think I speak French better, more fluently, than I speak English." Maybe, James, if I could speak to you in French I could be more clever. Clever at all, she amended miserably.

"You speak perfectly fluent English, but I think it's intriguing that you would speak French with even a matching fluency. Why do you?"

Because it's my heritage. The thought came swiftly, and with equal swiftness Catherine banished that agonizing truth and spoke a far less

209

painful one. "For the past three school years I lived in a house where we spoke exclusively French. And I've been thinking in French still this summer because my term paper was written in French."

"Thinking in French?"

"Yes." She paused for a moment, thinking in French, and then explained slowly, "Whenever someone says something to me in English, I—automatically, I guess—translate it into French. And I always think about what I'm going to say in French first, and then translate it into English."

"Is that what you did just now?"

"Yes." Catherine sighed softly. "I feel, sometimes, that I lose something in the translation."

"Really? I don't think so, Catherine." James smiled at her until she smiled back, a slightly wobbly smile, but a very lovely one. Then, putting her at ease with his indisputably nonfluent French, and hoping it proved to her that it didn't matter, he asked, *"Voulez-vous* a mug of hot chocolate? You have to say yes—oui—because you haven't truly experienced night sailing without one."

"Alors, oui, merci." Her eyes sparkled and the wobbliness of the smile magically vanished. "Shall I make it?"

"No. You steer."

"Me? How?"

"Come here."

James stood as he spoke and beckoned for her to take the place where he had been sitting. After she did, she curled her slender ivory fingers around the wooden spokes that were still warm from the heat of his strong hands.

"Now," he instructed softly as he looked at the ribbon of gold that rippled across the inky black water, "just follow the moonbeam."

The suggestion that they have hot chocolate had been intentionally casual, although James had been prepared to gently but firmly insist. He wanted to get some calories into her! He had watched, throughout the day, as she artfully pretended to eat, but in fact ate almost nothing. As he waited for the water to become piping hot, he considered preparing a platter from the fruit, cheeses, smoked salmon, and crackers that had been boarded for those among tomorrow's guests who chose to sail. He finally decided against the elaborate platter, worrying that it might only embarrass her. She would *have* to drink the mug of thick rich hot chocolate he made for her, and that would be a good start.

"My mother's recipe," he told her when he returned to the cockpit and handed her a mug. "It has a little cinnamon in it."

"Thank you," she said as she moved away from the helm, gratefully relinquishing it to him, and took the huge warm mug in her delicate hands. "Your mother, your parents are so nice."

"Thank you. I think so, too."

"You're very close to them, aren't you?"

"Yes. Very. How about you and your parents?" James knew the answer to his question, of course. He had learned from Alexa about the closeness of the quiet, talented parents and their quiet, talented youngest daughter. Alexa had shared with him the darkest secrets of her heart, secrets he had sworn never to reveal, especially, most especially, to Catherine. And he would never break that solemn vow. This question about her parents betrayed no trust; although, admittedly, he posed it because he already knew that its answer was one that Catherine could discuss easily, joyfully, with sparkling happy eyes. But as she considered the question, James saw no joy, only sadness, and a deep, deep pain. "Catherine?"

"My parents and I used to be very close," she admitted quietly.

"But something happened?"

"Yes. Something happened, and then I moved to New York, and . . ." And she hadn't spoken to Jane and Alexander since May. She had written, of course, because she didn't want them to worry. But the letters since May bore little resemblance to the long, exuberant ones she had always written before. The new letters were short, and free of emotion or embellishment, as if anything more might be an imposition on their time that she no longer had the right to make.

"And you miss them."

"Yes. I miss them very much."

"Do they know that?"

"I'm not sure. I've been thinking about calling to tell them, but somehow . . ."

"I think you should call them, Catherine. I think that is something they would very much like to hear."

★　★　★

212

They sailed until midnight. After James secured *Night Wind* to the wharf, explaining the knots to her because she wanted to know, they began the long climb back to the mansion.

You *can* do it, Catherine's mind, or perhaps her heart, sternly reminded her body. But quickly, very quickly, the body that had been betrayed by her, betrayed her in return. It was an overwhelming mutiny, every starved, rebellious cell screaming and gasping at once.

Her lungs gasped for air, but there wasn't enough! And her fluttering heart took flight, carrying her with it, floating, floating away!

"Catherine!" James's strong arms were around her in an instant, catching her before she fell and then holding her very close . . . so close that he could feel the terror of her heart—a frightened sparrow trying frantically to flee her chest—and the coolness of her skin and the fragile body that was so terribly light and thin. Light and thin, and soft and lovely. He held her very close, as if contact with his strong body would transfer desperately needed strength to her. But it didn't. He felt her becoming weaker not stronger. His lips brushed the silkiness of her hair as he spoke, "Come over here, to the bench, and sit."

He held her still, even when she was seated, and felt her frantic attempts to regain control of her heart and lungs. It seemed like forever, an eternity of silent prayers, but finally her gasping began to slow and she somehow found the energy to raise her spinning head and speak.

"I guess I'm a little out of shape."

"Dammit, Catherine, you're starving yourself!" Her voice had been soft and trembling, and now his voice trembled, too, with the sudden anger borne of immense fear.

"No," she countered softly, pulling away.

"Yes." James had known it the instant he saw her, and he had spent most of the day debating what to do. Should he speak to Alexa, or to Catherine? Alexa had asked him privately, "Doesn't Cat look stunning?"; but he had seen flickers of emerald worry that suggested that she, too, knew her little sister's weight loss was far too rapid. James had decided he would discuss it with Alexa, gently encouraging her to speak aloud her worries to Catherine, but he hadn't yet had a chance. And now, because it was a matter of life and death, he was discussing it with Catherine directly.

Not discussing, *accusing,* he realized too late as he heard the harshness of his own voice and saw its effect on her lovely face. He had overwhelmed her again, as he had in June, but her embarrassment now went far beyond lovely flushed cheeks and a timid smile. Now he saw anguish on her hauntingly beautiful and terrifyingly pale face, and worse . . . because now the brilliant sapphire eyes glistened with tears.

Now he, who cared so very much about her, had done what only a cruel young Hillary had been able to do before: he had made Catherine cry.

"Catherine," he whispered softly. "You've lost a great deal of weight very quickly, perhaps too quickly."

"I'd never dieted before. Once I started, after the first few days, it was very easy."

"Easier and easier every day?"

"Yes," Catherine admitted quietly, miserably, an acknowledgment that she had permitted her starving brain to make irrational choices. It had been easy to permit those irrational choices, even though, deep inside, a voice had sent urgent warnings. She hadn't heeded the warnings and now her own gasping weakness truly terrified her. But that life-and-death terror was almost surpassed by her fear of what James thought of her. James, of all people. What if he believed that her incautious dieting was something more, something disturbed, pathologic, like anorexia or bulimia? "James, I'm not . . . I didn't do anything . . ."

"I know," he reassured gently. "You, Catherine Taylor, simply happen to share, with your older sister, extraordinary discipline and determination. Do you know what Alexa told me once, when she said she was going to spend an entire evening rehearsing her lines and I made an offhand remark about practice makes perfect?"

"Yes, I know what she told you. She said, 'No, James. *Perfect* practice makes perfect.' "

"I have the feeling that may be a Taylor sister motto. And I think, maybe, you dieted a little too perfectly."

Catherine smiled a trembling and grateful smile. "I need to begin eating again, and when I'm stronger I need to exercise so that my body can become fit and healthy at this weight."

"It sounds as though you've read the books."

"Yes. I knew how to do it sensibly. I just got carried away. Thank you for catching me." Her voice became a soft whisper at the memory. It was a gasping fluttering memory of fear, but there was more to the memory: the feeling of his arms around her, the warm strength of his body, the delicate brush of his lips against her hair, the pounding of his heart. And there had been another breathlessness, exhilarating and so wonderful, that had nothing to do with starvation or terror.

"Of course," James answered softly, remembering too that oh-so-compelling, oh-so-lovely part of the memory. After a moment, he said gently but firmly, "Now I'm going to feed you. Another mug of hot chocolate and some food. We'll have a picnic right here, and then, eventually, we'll wander slowly up these stairs. OK?"

"Yes. OK. Thank you."

"You're more than welcome." James smiled. And then, before returning to *Night Wind* to prepare their midnight picnic, his handsome face became very solemn and he said quietly, "Promise me, Catherine, that you will start eating again."

"I promise."

James held her gaze, debating for five swift heartbeats. Then he simply told her.

"I'm not sure what made you decide to lose all the weight." His words stopped, suddenly distracted by the eloquent message of her moonlit blue eyes. The lovely eyes seemed to be telling him, with innocent candor, that *he* was the reason. After a moment, he continued shakily,

"You are very beautiful now, of course, but you were very beautiful before, too."

There was more to say, a far more important truth. Your most magnificent beauty, Catherine, is who you are, deep inside.

But James didn't tell her that truth.

How could he?

Chapter 13

Alexa was awakened by a soft tap on her bedroom door. The moonlight streaming through the open windows illuminated the bedside clock: twelve-thirty. Cat, probably, coming to tell her about sailing with James. Or, perhaps, James himself. No, Alexa decided as she sashed her emerald silk robe around her slender waist, James and I aren't furtive teenagers!

Besides, she remembered with a soft smile, last night, in her bed at RoseCliff, she and James had made up in advance for the next ten nights of separation. The garden party and James's responsibilities as host would last until late Sunday night, long after she had taken Cat to the airport and returned to RoseCliff. On Monday afternoon, James would leave for Denver for four days, followed by meetings in Chicago that he expected to last all weekend. They would be apart for at least ten nights; but still, Alexa knew, it would not be James at her bedroom door. No, her most welcome late night visitor would be her little sister, and they would stay up for hours chatting about the wonderful day.

But the visitor wasn't Cat. It was Brynne. But such a different Brynne from the woman with whom Alexa had spent so many pleasant hours during the day. Brynne's rosy cheeks were ashen now, her sparkling brown eyes cloudy and bewildered, her glowing radiance merely a memory. When Alexa had last seen her, three hours before, Brynne had announced with smiling apology that she was a little tired, contently so, and was going to bed early. She *had* gone to bed, her sleep-tousled brown hair proved it, but now she wore blue jeans and an incorrectly buttoned cotton shirt, not a nightgown and robe.

"Brynne? What's wrong?"

"I need Robert. I'm sorry, Alexa, I don't know which room he and Hillary are in."

"Well, I walked upstairs with them about an hour ago, so I know. Why don't you come in and wait here while I get him?"

"Oh. All right. Thank you."

Alexa walked hurriedly along the plush Oriental rugs that covered the shining hardwood floors. As she neared the door of Robert and Hillary's bedroom, she thought briefly about her bare feet, her clinging silk nightgown and robe, and her sleep-tangled golden hair.

It didn't matter how she looked! Nor did it matter that she might be intruding on a passionate interlude between the sexy politician and his patrician wife. All that mattered was that a little sister was in trouble. A little sister, Alexa realized, who turned instantly to her older brother when she needed help. Instantly and confidently, she thought, remembering Brynne's voice when she said, "I need Robert." Brynne needed Robert, and she knew without a trace of doubt that Robert would help her.

Alexa tapped firmly on the bedroom door, deciding she would tap louder in fifteen seconds and call Robert's name if need be. But she didn't need to repeat the knock. He opened the door in seconds. His dark hair was tousled, by passion or by sleep, and he wore a belted robe over his pajamas, and his feet, like hers, were bare.

"Hi." He smiled a quizzical smile.

"Brynne needs you. I don't know what's wrong but—"

"Where is she?" Robert's smile vanished and his dark eyes filled with worry.

"In my room."

Alexa led the way to her room, but stood aside at the doorway to allow Robert to enter first. He crossed the room to the chair where Brynne sat, on its very edge, and then knelt in front of her so that their dark brown eyes could meet.

"Honey?" he asked as he covered the small hands, curled in tight bloodless fists, with his larger ones.

"I'm miscarrying."

"Oh, Brynne. I didn't know."

"No one did. Not even Stephen. I had to try, Robert, just one more time. I know I said I wasn't going to, but I was so sure that this time . . . I just had to try." Her words ended in a soft sob and tears spilled down her stricken face.

"I know. It's OK, Brynne," he assured gently. "It's OK."

Alexa moved close enough for Robert to see her, and when the dark eyes that were so concerned for his little sister finally looked up and met hers, she asked softly, "Should I get Marion?"

"Brynne? Would you like Alexa to get Marion?"

"No. There's no need to bother Marion. I just have to go to the nearest hospital."

"I'm not sure where that is, Brynne. I'll need to find James and—"

"I know where the nearest hospital is," Alexa offered. "It's in Marlboro, about ten miles away. We can take my car and I'll drive."

"Thank you." Robert stood, still holding his sister's hands. "I'm going to get changed, Brynne. It will only take a few minutes."

After Robert left, Alexa quickly changed, too, into the outfit that she would have worn had she gone sailing with Catherine and James. As she was tying her tennis shoes, Brynne stood . . . and swayed.

"Brynne?" Alexa rushed to her and urged her back onto the chair.

"I was going to get my purse."

"I'll get it for you. Here. Just sit down. I'll be right back."

Alexa found Brynne's purse on the bedside table. She grabbed it, and then on impulse walked into the dressing room to search for a sweater or jacket. She drew a soft breath when she saw the nightgown and robe on the vanity in the dressing room. Both were blood-soaked, obviously ruined, and yet they had been so carefully folded, not tossed aside.

Because the bright red stains are memories of the tiny life Brynne so obviously treasures and now may be losing, or has already lost? Has already lost, Alexa decided sadly, as she remembered the expression of hopelessness on Brynne's beautiful face, as if she already knew, as if she had had experience with such a great loss before.

When they arrived at Marlboro Hospital, Brynne was taken immediately through the "Authorized Personnel Only" doors that led into the treatment area of the Emergency Room. Robert and Alexa waited in the waiting room adjacent to the ER, where, after forty-five minutes, Brynne's doctor appeared to give them the report.

"She has miscarried."

"I see," Robert replied with quiet emotion.

"The miscarriage appears to be 'complete', which means that a D and C will probably not be necessary. I want to keep her here, though, until I get the results of the blood work that has been drawn. Once those are back, assuming they're what I expect them to be, Brynne should be ready to go home. My guess is that will be in about two hours."

"All right. May I see her?"

"Sure. She wants to see you, too. I think it would be best for her if you made the visit fairly brief. She's exhausted, and I'm hoping she'll be able to sleep if she's left alone."

"OK." Robert turned to Alexa and asked, "Do you mind waiting a little longer?"

"No, Robert, of course I don't mind."

"Shall we go?" Robert asked when he returned from seeing Brynne.

"Go?"

"To Inverness, to take you back and pick up my car."

"To pick up your car . . . and Hillary."

"Hillary?" Robert echoed with soft surprise. After a moment, he said quietly, "No."

No? Alexa felt a sudden rush of anger for her ancient enemy. Robert was here for Brynne, helping her, supporting her, loving her; and even though this was obviously terribly emotional for him, too, he hid his own sadness to be strong for his little sister. He was here for Brynne, but who was here for Robert? Where was his loving wife? Was Hillary really so selfish and so vain that she would not forfeit even a few hours of her beauty sleep to help her husband? Did she have so little sympathy and compassion for Brynne's devastating loss? Or was, perhaps, the idea of sitting in a smoky, crowded waiting room simply *too* distasteful for her patrician sensibilities?

The waiting room *was* unappealing, of course. It was now filled, like most Emergency Rooms on a Saturday night, with a boisterous, predominantly intoxicated clientele that sought medical attention for bumps and bruises acquired during an evening of injudicious partying. The waiting room was not, at the moment, a place for quiet reflection about the loss of a much wanted baby.

Brynne was protected from the noise, in a room far behind the heavy steel doors, but there would be no peace here for Robert.

And, Alexa thought as she gazed at his sensitive and so troubled eyes, he needs peace. Hillary may not be here for you, Robert, but I am. The thought was neutral enough . . . until it continued quite boldly, I *want* to be.

"I have an idea, Robert. My cottage is close by, much closer than Inverness and only a little farther away from Brynne than this noisy-and-not-so-tranquil waiting room. We can give the doctor the phone number and wait there, if you like." She smiled gently at the dark eyes that looked uncertain about imposing, and yet so very tempted. "This may sound terribly presumptuous of me, Robert, but I'm quite confident that the coffee served at RoseCliff is far better than what one can get from the coffee machines here."

"I'm sure it is, but Alexa . . ." his protest faltered because he didn't want to protest at all.

"Besides, Brynne will need a new nightgown," she said quietly. "And since I happen to be a bit of a pushover for nightgowns, especially the soft, fluffy, cozy kinds, I have a small collection of never-yet-worn ones at the cottage. I would very much like to give one of them to Brynne."

RoseCliff had been a light-hearted topic of conversation after dinner. True, her tiny cottage was far less grand than Inverness, Alexa had amiably admitted. And far less grand, too, than Clairmont, the famous Arlington estate that had been a wedding gift from Sam Ballinger to his daughter and son-in-law. But, she had added with a sparkling smile, like "Inverness"—and indeed in the same elegant script—"RoseCliff" was permanently chiseled into the granite boulders at the base of the stairs that led to the cottage. The engraving had been James's idea, and once he had her surprised yet eager approval, it was he who had commissioned the work.

"So this is RoseCliff," Robert said as he paused to admire the moonlit lettering.

"This is RoseCliff," Alexa echoed softly. She heard the attempt at a gentle tease in his voice, a valiant effort to lighten the mood, and she answered with a lovely smile that told the troubled dark eyes that the effort wasn't necessary for her, not at all, because she understood well the deep love for little sisters.

Alexa led the way up the stairs to her magnificent garden of roses and her tiny romantic cottage beyond. She made coffee, as promised, and, as promised, too, offered him the wonderful tranquillity of RoseCliff at night. They sat on the porch beneath a ceiling of stars, their faces softly illuminated by the full moon, listening to the songs of crickets, breathing the rose-fragrant night air, and talking, in quiet words punctuated by long comfortable silences, about the crickets and the roses and the moon and the stars.

Finally the words, or the silences, felt so comfortable that Robert said softly, "I want to tell you about Brynne."

"Yes," Alexa answered with matching softness. I want to hear about Brynne, Robert, she thought. And, Robert, I want to hear about you.

"Brynne and Stephen have been married for twelve years, and they've been trying for that long to have children."

"And she finally got pregnant? Only to lose the baby?"

"No. It's been more complicated, even more difficult, than that. Brynne has always been able to conceive, but for some reason her pregnancies invariably end in miscarriages."

"For some reason?"

"For some unknown reason. Brynne and Stephen have seen the best specialists and have had all the tests and procedures. Marion has made certain of that, of course, but even the best medical science has had to offer has not come up with an answer. That's why they've kept trying all these years, believing that someday . . ." Robert sighed softly. "Brynne has always been able to tell, almost immediately, when she becomes pregnant. She bonds instantly to the new life inside her, a bond of hope and joy, and when she loses the baby, it's a very great loss for her."

"Oh, Robert," Alexa whispered quietly. "Brynne would be such a wonderful mother."

"Yes. The best. And Stephen would be a wonderful father. Isn't it ironic that in an era when women can be whatever they want—when they aren't bound to spend their lives being mothers and when being a mother has even become devalued—that being a mother is all my very smart little sister wants, or has ever wanted?"

"Yes it is," Alexa agreed softly. "But, Robert,

even if Brynne and Stephen can't have their own children, they can adopt, can't they?"

"They've tried. But because Brynne was always able to get pregnant, and because she believed so strongly that eventually she *would* be able to carry a baby to term, they delayed pursuing the possibility of adopting for a long time. By the time they did, Stephen was almost forty, which put them in a low priority category with all the public agencies." A smile of gentle fondness touched his moonlit face as he continued, "I guess you've realized by now that in a way, in a very loving way, Brynne and I have ourselves been adopted by the Sterlings. Just as Marion made certain that Brynne and Stephen saw the best fertility specialists available, when the issue of adoption arose, James immediately volunteered to contact reputable attorneys throughout the country who were known to handle private adoptions."

"And that hasn't worked?"

"It almost has worked—twice. But both times—once within twenty-four hours of the baby's birth and the second time after the baby had been with them for almost six weeks—the biologic mother changed her mind."

"That can happen?"

"Absolutely. The era of closed adoptions, especially in the private arena, is rapidly vanishing. James felt terrible about what happened. He had met with both of the biologic mothers and truly believed they were confident of their decisions."

"And Brynne . . . ?"

"It was terribly painful for her, of course, another loss, but she understood completely that a mother would change her mind about giving up her baby. Anyway, the two attempts at adoption have made them very wary. I thought they'd decided to give up trying altogether, either for their own baby or adopting. It's taken such a toll on Brynne. The last time we talked about it, after she'd miscarried in March, she told me it was all over—everything, both the dream and the torment."

"But she had to try one last time."

"One last time." The crickets whirred gaily in the long silence that followed. When Robert finally spoke, his voice was very soft and his words were spoken to the twinkling stars, "I feel so helpless."

"Helpless, Robert?"

"I would do anything to put an end to Brynne's anguish, but I . . ."

"But there's nothing you can do," Alexa assured gently. "And you do help her, you know. You understand her sadness, and share it with her, and you are so gentle with her. Brynne obviously trusts you very much."

"I guess it's just that I spent so many years protecting Brynne when we were young, *trying* to protect her, and I want so very much to protect her from this pain. But I can't."

"No, you can't," she agreed quietly. And then, quite suddenly, Alexa felt it: the immense power of the emotions that Robert kept so carefully hidden, buried so very deep inside. The immense power was quite invisible, and yet she felt it, and it was almost as if his frustration and helplessness and torment were inside her, too. After a moment, she said bravely, "This is taking a toll on you, too, Robert."

"Yes it is," he confessed, as he turned from the twinkling stars to her solemn and beautiful emerald eyes. Then, even more softly, he made another confession. "I don't usually admit such things."

And then, as their eyes met and held, there was another immense invisible power, buried deep and carefully hidden, too, by both of them, until now. Now, as the dark sensuous eyes gazed into the glowing emerald ones, the fluttering of their hearts fanned the powerful emotions out of hiding, and all the wondrous desire and longing came joyfully to the surface, dangerously brave, carelessly defiant.

"You don't usually admit such things, Robert?" Alexa echoed softly, breathlessly.

"No, Alexa, I don't."

The moon watched, and seemed to approve, because it enveloped them in a golden mist within which all was possible, and there were no thoughts of consequences, and it was safe, permissible, to share the deepest secrets and desires of their hearts. And in that golden mist, Alexa saw Robert's desire for her, an intense and wondrous desire that had begun long ago and reached far beyond this moment; and Robert saw, mirrored in the joyous moonlit emerald, a desire that was as intense, and wondrous, and far-reaching as his own.

Everything was safe, all secret desires permissible; and Alexa would have so joyfully welcomed the hands and lips that would have caressed her with the same exquisite tenderness as the dark eyes that were caressing her now . . .

But then the phone rang, and she left Robert and the magical golden mist for the too bright lights of the kitchen. Robert followed, and moments later, after sharing the news with him that Brynne was ready to be discharged, she left him again, to go to her bedroom, to get the nightgown for his little sister.

When Alexa returned to the kitchen, she found Robert drying the coffee mugs he had just finished washing.

"You didn't need to do that, Robert."

"I wanted to. Besides, it's habit."

"Habit?" From his impoverished and chore-laden childhood? she wondered. Or from his life as a soldier? He certainly did not, she assumed, nor did Hillary, wash dishes at Clairmont.

"I have a small, uninspired, unnamed apartment near Capitol Hill," Robert explained with a soft smile. "The drive to the house in Arlington is over ninety minutes, without trafffic, and since I often have early morning and late night meetings, I frequently spend weeknights in town, in an apartment where I am solely responsible for washing my coffee mugs."

"I see," Alexa replied softly. And surely he would see, unless she bent her head and cast a golden veil across her emerald eyes, the dangerous wishes that leapt from her heart. There are nights, frequent nights, that you choose to spend away from Hillary? Perhaps, on one of those nights, you could come back here and we could talk again and . . . *What was she thinking?* Fortunately, she had bowed her golden head, and when she spoke finally, it was to the soft cotton garment she held in her hands. "Here is the nightgown for Brynne. I thought this one, with the roses, would be cheerful . . ."

Her words stopped at his touch, *they had to,* and she trembled as, with the exquisite tenderness she had imagined, he gently parted the curtain of silky gold. Robert trembled too, as he lifted her beautiful face to his and whispered softly, "Thank you."

"Thank you," Brynne echoed her brother's words an hour later.

They were in Brynne's bedroom at Inverness, and Robert had already bid them goodnight, and Alexa had stayed to be certain that Brynne was settled and comfortable. She was in the luxurious bed now, propped up against feather pillows, looking very young and very pretty in the soft fluffy nightgown Alexa had given her.

"You're welcome, Brynne." I wish there was more I could do for you, Alexa thought as she watched Brynne's dark brown eyes lapse quickly back into sadness after her gracious smiling thank you. "I'm so sorry."

"I know you are, Alexa," Brynne answered softly. "Thank you."

Alexa hesitated a moment, then, sensing that perhaps Brynne wanted to talk about it, she offered gently, carefully, "It just seems so terribly unfair. You would be such a wonderful mother."

"Oh, well, thank you." She frowned thoughtfully, and then confessed quietly, "I guess I do think it's terribly unfair. I guess I really do believe that Stephen and I have so much love to give." She gave her head a soft, bewildered shake. "But, for some reason, we weren't destined to have children."

"Whatever the reason is, it's a pretty faulty one." Alexa's voice was gentle, but her own annoyance at whatever unknown fate had caused this sadness for lovely Brynne was apparent.

"Yes it is, isn't it?" Brynne agreed swiftly, smiling at Alexa's bluntness, grateful to be able to acknowledge the injustice she herself sometimes felt, although rarely spoke of. "It's nice to be able to talk about this with someone other than Stephen or Robert, Alexa. It's been a source of such sadness for us all that it's been a very long time since we've simply glowered at the whimsical fates."

"I'd be happy to sit here and glower with you all night if you like." Alexa tilted her head thoughtfully at the eyes that clearly wanted to talk; and the face that so obviously needed rest. "Or, at least, for a few more minutes."

"Thank you. I would like to talk a little longer."

They talked, sharing quiet, important words and emotions, until finally, reluctantly, Brynne had to yield to the exhausted body that needed sleep.

"I'll come visit you tomorrow," Alexa promised.

"I'll be at the party."

"You will? Won't you need to stay in bed?"

"No. I'll be fine. I may do more sitting under pink umbrellas than wandering around the grounds, but I'll be OK. I don't plan to tell anyone else, not even Stephen, about the miscarriage. He didn't know I was pregnant, so . . ."

"I understand," Alexa said quietly. She had learned tonight about Brynne's great love for her husband, and she understood the wish to spare Stephen further sadness. "I understand."

"Thank you for being here tonight, Alexa."

"You're very welcome, Brynne."

As Alexa crossed the hallway from Brynne's bedroom to hers, she looked at the closed door to Cat's room. She had imagined that on this evening she and her own little sister might have stayed up until all hours chatting. But, instead, tonight she had been with Robert's little sister, and she would hear another time about Cat's sail with James.

James. What would he say if, right now, she wandered stealthily to the other wing of the mansion and confessed everything to him? How would he respond to her memory of moonlit magic at RoseCliff, and the fact that her heart raced now, still, because of Robert? James, her wonderful friend, who was not in love with her, would simply explain to her, his dark blue eyes very gentle, that whatever she'd thought she had seen in Robert's sensuous dark eyes had been purely an illusion—that she had been, quite obviously, blinded by moonlight. That was what

James would say, *wouldn't he?* He would not, surely not, be hurt, *would he?* Alexa thought not. She very much hoped not.

Still, she didn't wander to the other wing of the mansion to find James. But, she admitted to herself as she crossed instead to her own bedroom, it wasn't the fear of seeing hurt in the dark blue eyes that made her stay away, because she truly doubted that she would. It was, in fact, her reluctance to hear James tell her, however gently, that it had all been an illusion.

So, instead of finding James, Alexa went to her own bedroom, where, once inside, she was drawn to the window by a golden beam of light.

Hello, Moon, she greeted silently as her emerald eyes looked hopefully to the smiling witness to whatever it was that had happened at RoseCliff. Remember me? Could you tell me, please, did you happen to see the look in his dark brown eyes? I wasn't wrong, was I? Please? Oh, and Moon, since you're an expert on such things, and I'm merely a novice, could you tell me if these wonderful feelings that are swirling inside me still, these rushes of happiness and desire and joy, are these magnificent feelings what one feels when she's fallen in love? Yes? I thought so. And, Moon, there's just one more thing. Do you think, could you tell, was he feeling these wonderful feelings, too?

Washington's very most powerful people spent that Sunday at Inverness. They wandered among the prize-winning roses and through the elegant mansion, chatting about world-changing topics and trivial ones, sipping champagne, and sampling the endless array of gourmet delicacies presented to them on shining silver trays.

Senator and Mrs. Robert McAllister spent the day together, of course, and everyone wanted to talk to the future First Couple, and there were a great many people who wanted to meet Alexandra Taylor, too. Alexa and Robert never had a chance to speak to each other, not with words, but more than once, searching at the same moment as if by silent signal, their eyes met and smiled.

Alexa didn't speak to Robert, and Catherine didn't speak to James. She had planned to, to thank him again, but by the time she appeared for breakfast, he was already off helping Arthur make certain that the pink-umbrellaed tables were arranged just so on the emerald lawn, and that the tennis court got a final wash and the pool a final clean, and that the only slightly depleted larder on *Night Wind* was re-stocked. Before Catherine even saw him, much less found a private moment to speak to him, the guests began to arrive, and James assumed the role, with his parents, of gracious host. He was very busy after that. And, when the Secretary of State, a music afficianado, identified her as the beautiful womanly version of the teenaged Catherine Taylor he had seen win the Van Cliburn, she became very busy too.

"Guests are not obliged to give command performances at my parties," Marion intervened lightly but firmly when she overheard the Secretary's serious suggestion that Catherine give an impromptu recital on the rarely used but impeccably maintained Steinway. Marion smiled at the Secretary, a good friend for many years, and added, "No matter who makes the command."

"I wouldn't mind, Marion. Unless you'd prefer that I didn't."

"My dear Catherine," Marion answered with a twinkle. "It's taken an incredible amount of discipline for me not to ask you myself."

So Catherine played, sharing her gift, completely unruffled by her famous audience. The impromptu recital became an afternoon of music. At first, the guests who were drawn to the great room by her magic simply listened, mesmerized and enchanted. But eventually, in response to her offer to play whatever they wanted to hear, they began to make requests. Her repertoire was vast, and she delighted in playing all music, any music, from Bach and Chopin to Gershwin and rock 'n' roll.

Catherine played joyously, as always, and flawlessly, as always . . . until James appeared. Moments before, with a loving wink to his wife, the President had asked if she happened to know "I Fall to Pieces." She did, of course, and had just begun playing it when James walked in. How appropriate, she thought miserably, as she felt herself fall to pieces, *as always,* when his intense dark blue eyes fell on her. Her cheeks flushed pink, and there was the rapid fluttering of her heart that had nothing to do with starvation. She wasn't starving now, she knew, because she had eaten today, small frequent nibbles, and her body had responded with grateful, exuberant energy.

Catherine had become accustomed to the warm pink cheeks and racing heart that came without warning whenever James was near. But now, as she played, she felt even her extraordinary talent begin to fall to pieces. A delicate finger caressed the wrong key—once, then a second time! No one but she detected even the smallest stumble in the magnificent dance of her beautiful and graceful hands, of course.

But she noticed, and oh how she had wanted to play beautifully, fluently, flawlessly for him. But she couldn't. Nor could she look up and meet his eyes and smile hello and thank you. Oh, yes, she could smile a lovely smile at the President of the United States and bravely hold his admiring gaze and even talk to him while her fingers danced over the keyboard. But she *could not* look at James, not without stopping the music entirely. So she just played, her fingers dancing and stumbling, her eyes never meeting his.

James remained in the great room for only a very short time. He had agreed to take some of the guests for a dinner sail; and they were sailing still, a small blue and white speck in the distance, when Catherine and Alexa left the party.

"Mom?"

"Cat," Jane breathed. Her eyes filled with tears as her soft voice filled with joy. How patiently— and *desperately*—she and Alexander had waited for their beloved daughter to return to them. How they had wanted to rush to her and hold her in their loving arms and assure her over and over of their love. But Jane and Alexander knew it was

Catherine's journey, not theirs, to make. And they knew, too, that even once begun, her journey home—to love—would be long and difficult. But now, at least, at last, the journey had started. Jane heard the delicate hope in her daughter's voice, and "Mom" itself was a huge brave step. Since May, Catherine's letters had begun with "Hello" and *"Bonjour,"* not with the so familiar, so-taken-for-granted greetings of "Dear Mom and Dad" or, even, "Dearest Mommy and Daddy."

"Hi. Is Dad there?"

"He's on his way upstairs to the other phone."

They waited in silence until Alexander picked up the extension, and when he did Jane wondered if Catherine heard the trembling emotion in her father's quiet voice.

"How are you, Cat?"

"I'm fine, Dad. I just thought I'd call to say hi."

They talked for an hour, and there were times when Catherine's breathless descriptions of New York and the new pieces she was learning and the weekend she had just spent at Inverness felt wonderfully normal, wonderfully, hauntingly like the past. Hauntingly . . . a ghost from a past that didn't really exist. In the midst of the breathless descriptions, the painful memory of the truth would suddenly sweep through her, stopping her words mid-sentence. There would be silence then, and Jane and Alexander would wait with desperate prayers, but each time, Catherine finally spoke again.

Yes, she would send tapes of her new pieces, she promised. And, as soon as she got them from

Marion, she would send the photographs of the President, First Lady, and Alexa leaning over the piano while she played. And, she promised softly, she would call again.

She would call again. That was the most wonderful promise of all. Because it meant that Catherine's brave journey back to her parents and their love had truly begun.

Chapter 14

"You have received substantial payments— *bribes*, Senator—for your recent votes on the defense contract proposals."

"That, Ms. Winslow, is a ridiculous, not to mention libelous accusation for which you most assuredly haven't a shred of proof."

"I have more than a shred, Senator—documents that you assumed had been shredded, but which are in fact now in the possession of the Senate Ethics Committee Chairman. I happen to have copies in my office, if you would care to see them."

"You won't get away this kind of yellow journalism, Ms. Winslow."

"I'm not trying to get away with anything. You, however, did try. And now, thankfully, you've been caught."

Alexa's eyes—Stephanie Winslow's eyes— flashed at the startled and indignant face of the

"Senator." She held the look, her beautiful eyes blazing, until the director called "Cut."

"Very nice," he embellished as the actors released their gazes of hostility and replaced them with satisfied smiles. "That's a print. Lunch time, everyone. Alexa, after lunch I'd like to begin blocking the scene that takes place in your office. Are you ready to do that?"

"Sure."

"Senator McAllister!" The reporters rushed to him, encircling him the moment he emerged from the Senate Intelligence Committee meeting. "We understand that one of the agenda items for today's meeting was the hostage situation. Have there been new developments?"

"You know I can't tell you anything," he admonished amiably.

The reporters did know that, of course, which was why many of their colleagues were following the other Senators who had attended the meeting. Sometimes Senators slipped up, accidentally revealing something that shouldn't have been revealed with an unguarded expression or an injudicious comment. Sometimes the "slips" weren't even accidental; they were intentional revelations, made for personal and partisan politics. Senator Robert McAllister was one of the newest members of the Intelligence Committee, yet he had never made an injudicious remark, either by accident or design. The reporters didn't expect carelessness or political gamesmanship from Robert. But they hoped that if there was anything that could legitimately be revealed about the behind closed doors Committee meeting, they could get a quote from him, because comments from the photogenic and respected Senator from Virginia always made the evening news.

A great deal had been discussed at the meeting, but, Robert felt, even making such a nonspecific observation would be an indefensible breech of security. Robert had been to war. He saw the shades of gray in issues that many of his colleagues chose to portray as black and white— miraculously right along party lines.

"Sorry," he said. His smile to the assembled reporters acknowledged that he knew they were only trying to do their jobs just as diligently as he was trying to do his.

Then he escaped to his office to spend the lunch hour returning calls, meeting with aides, reading the never ending stacks of documents that arrived on his desk every day, and trying, as he had been trying every second of the past five days, to forget about *her.*

But how could he? She had touched a part of him that had somehow survived the ravages of his past, a delicate and hopeful place in his heart that had miraculously escaped unscathed and unscarred. Robert knew very well about the thick, constricting scars in his heart, because it was he who had put them there, forcing the tough blood-less tissue over the tender wounds of his life, sealing those hurts and protecting himself from future pain.

He had believed, until now, until Alexa, that the only truly vulnerable place left in his heart was that very special place owned by his little

240

sister. He had spent his boyhood protecting Brynne from the grim reality of their impoverished life, hiding his own tears and lovingly convincing her that *her* life could be filled with happiness long after he had privately given up all hope for his own.

Beginning as a very small boy, Robert was strong for Brynne. And as only an eighteen-year-old, he was strong for the men with whom he served in Vietnam, his mature calm lending a measure of sanity and control to a world he knew to be truly insane. He was heralded as a leader and a hero, and indeed he had courageously saved the lives and hearts and spirits of a great many men. But Robert knew the truth. His screams of pain at the horror he witnessed were silent to the men around him, but they thundered inside—until he silenced them, trapping them beneath thick scars, buried deep and forever.

Robert returned from Vietnam with an intense commitment to the vision of peace he saw for the world. He planned a quiet solitary life dedicated to public service and to the fulfillment of that vision. His heart was far too damaged, he knew, to ever fall in love, and until he met Hillary he had never even given serious thought to marriage. But beautiful, vivacious Hillary made it so very easy for him. She made it wonderfully, seductively, clear how much she wanted him; and, as a governor's daughter, she knew well the very public life a politician necessarily led, and seemed most eager and willing to share it; and, so it seemed, too, she truly believed in his important visions and his dreams. Theirs was a whirlwind romance, a glittering golden thread woven into the already vibrant tapestry of his campaign for the U.S. Senate.

Robert did not ask Hillary to marry him because she was the daughter of the very powerful Governor; it was not, *for him at least,* a marriage of political ambition. He simply wanted to marry the lovely, gracious, unselfish woman who had so enchantingly convinced him that he was not destined to live a solitary life after all. Admittedly, by their wedding day, he and Hillary had not had many truly private moments together; they had not, by that day, had a chance to share the very private intimacies of their hearts. Which was why, as he quietly spoke his solemn wedding vows to his alluring bride, he made a solemn private vow as well. He would share with her all of himself that he could. He would even, he vowed, expose his so carefully scarred wounds, enduring all that pain again, if she asked that of him.

But, as he discovered shortly after she became Mrs. Robert McAllister, Hillary couldn't care less about the boy who had been forced to become a man when he was only a frightened, starving little child. And she most certainly wanted to know *nothing* of the soldier's silent screams of horror. Her only interest, he learned, was in glittering symbols—the shining gold medals of the hero, not the thick ugly scars of the man.

Hillary did not want emotional intimacy, nor did she want any longer to be the warm, unselfish, loving woman he had courted. She reprised that enchanting role, of course, for the public appearances in which the world marvelled at their perfect marriage; and sometimes, especially in the beginning, she reprised the enchanting role just for him. Robert knew he had been tricked. But he felt a commitment to the vows he had made, and an even stronger commitment to the woman Hillary had been in the months of their dazzling whirlwind romance. He tried very hard to help her become that warm, lovely woman again—for him, for their marriage, *but mostly for herself;* but in time he finally realized that that woman was a phantom. She was neither who Hillary truly was, nor who she wanted to be. His wife was quite content, he discovered, to be the cold, vain, selfish woman she had always been.

Robert's heart was not further damaged by Hillary. She had never gotten that close. He might have lived his entire life without love, never really missing it, never knowing to search for more, never imagining that there could be *for him* the joy and happiness he had always promised Brynne. But now there was Alexa. He hadn't searched for her, hadn't known to, but now she was found, and he needed her. Oh, how he needed her.

And how much was the brilliant Senator, whose destiny it was to be President, willing to risk for this woman whose need for him could not possibly match his desperate need for her?

The answer was so simple.

Everything.

"Alexa, for you." The cameraman gestured with the telephone receiver he held in his hand.

"Oh, thanks." Alexa smiled as she walked to the backstage phone. "Hello?"

"Hi, Alexa. It's Robert."

"Hi," she whispered softly.

"I was wondering if . . . ." He paused to recapture the breath that had left him when he heard the softness in her greeting. Softness, almost relief, as if she had been waiting for his call, but had not really dared to expect it.

"Yes."

"Yes?" he echoed softly, relieved, overjoyed. Alexa was saying yes to whatever it was he was about to propose. He hadn't even planned that far, but now his mind raced. It was Thursday, and he had a dinner meeting, and he had been planning to spend the night at his apartment in town. "Tonight? It would be almost eleven before I could get there."

"That's fine. Eleven."

Alexa met him on the moonlit path of roses. For a moment, they simply stared at each other, touching only with eyes that spoke so eloquently of their joy. Then his trembling hands gently touched her face, and her trembling fingers touched his, and then she was in his arms, and their lips found each other, greeting with welcoming wonder and astonishing need. He needed to touch her and hold her and kiss her and love her, and there were words, too, that he needed her to hear. The words came from the most delicate place in his heart, the brave, hopeful place that defiantly survived unscarred because it had known somehow, miraculously, that one day there would be Alexa.

"I have missed you, Alexa," he whispered between kisses. "All my life."

Their loving couldn't be leisurely. They needed each other, all of each other, far too much and far too urgently to make slow sensual discoveries. And when, swiftly, so swiftly, they were where they both needed so desperately to be, there was something even more extraordinary than their extraordinary passion; because, when they were together, when they were one, there was the most gentle peace, the most quiet joy, the most perfect happiness.

Alexa's delicate fingers tenderly touched the long wide scar that coursed down his abdomen, and moments later her soft lips followed, caressing lovingly, asking no questions, but welcoming anything he wanted to tell her.

"I have other scars, Alexa, much deeper ones."

"If you could show them to me, Robert, perhaps I could kiss them, too."

"Oh, my darling Alexa, you already have." Robert gently drew her to him and parted her love-tangled hair until he could see her emerald eyes. And when he could, he whispered softly, "I love you, Alexa."

"Oh, Robert, I love you, too." Her lips touched his, and in a moment they would need all of each other again, but now there was a question that needed to be asked and answered, for him, for them—so that he would know without doubt that her love for him was unconditional, no matter what secrets or horrors dwelled in his past. She asked gently, "Was there something about the war, Robert?"

"No, my love. Nothing specific, no shameful secret," he assured her truthfully. "I'm just like any other man who's been a soldier, that's all."

"I don't think, Robert McAllister," she answered softly, before losing herself again in the compelling desire of his sensuous eyes, "that you are just like any other man."

"Hello, James."

"Alexa."

"Is this a bad time to call?" It was six P.M. Chicago time on Saturday, and she had reached him in his suite at the Drake Hotel.

"No, not at all. My meetings are finished for the day." James frowned slightly as he reflected that it had been almost two hours since the day's meetings had adjourned. On any other Saturday in the five months he had known her, he would have long since caught a flight from O'Hare to National to spend the night with her at RoseCliff. But today, during the past two hours, he had simply stood at the window, gazing at the panoramic view of Lake Michigan and thinking—about Alexa, and about her little sister.

"So . . . can I come up?"

"Up?"

"I'm in the lobby."

"Hi."

"Hi. Come in."

"Thank you."

James watched with surprise and interest as, after a brief awkward smile and no lingering kiss, no kiss at all, she breezed past him and into the elegant living room of his spacious suite. Alexa quite clearly had an agenda.

"So?" he asked, when he had followed her into the living room and sat on the sofa across from the one she had chosen.

"James . . . something has happened."

"I can tell," he answered quietly. Then, as he gazed at her glowing yet uncertain emerald eyes, he added, "Something good, although you're not sure that I will think so."

"Yes," she whispered, marvelling at how well he could read her, and worried anew about what she had come to say and her ability to convince him of the one necessary lie.

"Do I guess? Frankly, I can't imagine what it could be."

"That's because it's the unimaginable. I've met someone, James, and we've fallen in love."

"Fallen in love?" he echoed softly. From a distant corner of his spinning mind spun the remarkable thought that he had so carefully suppressed all week, but which now twirled free and danced in jubilant defiance, *So have I.* "Love? Cynical you?"

"Cynical me. It's all your fault, of course," she said, as she had planned to say, speaking as many truths as possible. It *was* James's fault, for introducing her to Robert, but she knew that he was responsible for her love in a far more important way. And she wanted him to know that. She said softly, "You, James Sterling, made me believe in myself. You relentlessly told me that I was nice, not cruel, worthy of loving and being loved. I don't know if you really believe it. If not, you've created a deluded, love-crazed monster."

"You know damn well I believe it."

His solemn blue eyes told her that it was true. Alexa gazed at him, searching for other messages, but he was the master negotiator now, his stunningly handsome face set in neutral: controlled, inscrutable, cool. She had flown to Chicago to tell him, face to face, that their relationship was over, because she thought it was right to do so. She had not expected drama from James, nor had she wanted it, but there hadn't been even a dark blue flicker of regret. In fact, hadn't there been, at the moment he echoed "Fallen in love" something that might almost have been relief? Alexa didn't want James to be hurt, but still . . .

"What?" he asked with a soft laugh, unable to interpret the suddenly turbulent emerald stare.

"Dammit James! Does this matter to you, even a little bit? Did you care about our relationship at all? Maybe it's not fair for me to ask, but—"

"Alexa! *Of course* I cared about us. Do you really not know that?" James waited until her glare softened and her eyes confessed, Yes, I do know. Then he added gently, "I cared very much about us. And, Alexandra Taylor, I will care, *always*, about you and your happiness."

"Cat's definition of love," Alexa murmured softly.

"Oh?"

"Yes. She says that love is when you care about someone else's happiness always, forever, whether or not you are destined to be together. Which is the way I feel about you, too. So . . ."

"So?"

"So we love each other, even though we never told each other."

"Even though we never told each other before now," James amended softly. "Do I have to care about your forever happiness from a distance, or do we remain friends? We were wonderful lovers, Alexa, but we were—*are,* I hope even better friends."

"Oh, James," she whispered, "I am so glad that you want to be my friend."

"Always." James sealed the promise with a gentle smile. Then, because it had been enough emotion for both of them, he teased lightly, "So, my friend Alexa, tell me about him."

"There isn't much to tell. We met on Thursday—two days ago!—and that was it. Love at first sight." Alexa spoke the necessary lie without a flicker, and even managed a sheepish smile when she confessed to a romantic notion she once had so defiantly scorned. The lie was necessary, she had decided. James could not know that her love was Robert. She hated the lie, but she hated her reason for it even more: *because James might not approve.* What if, despite his words of love and friendship, he believed that she was unworthy of Robert? Or, at least, that Robert's affair with her was not worth the risk to his important political career? The monsters that lurked in the shadows of her heart, symbols of her past failures and unworthiness, were there still, quieted by James's love and by Robert's; quieted, but not, perhaps never, silenced.

"Does he have a name?"

"Romeo. Appropriate, don't you think, since I've completely converted to belief in a *Romeo and Juliet* love? Besides, stealing a line from the young Ms. Capulet, 'What's in a name?' "

"This unsuccessful attempt at evasiveness means he's in one of your 'totally unsuitable' categories," James observed with a smile. Alexa had informed him once, half-teasing, half-serious, about the men who were, in her judgment, totally unsuitable for a serious romantic involvement should her cynicism toward love ever vanish. Actors were, naturally, impossible, as were, she had discovered in the past few years, politicians; the two shared, she said, an unappealing blend of supreme vanity, total self-absorption, and the unnerving ability to act their way out of any corner. Attorneys *had* been in the unsuitable category, on ill-defined "general principles," as had blue-bloods, but that was before James. Had her new love been an actor or politician or attorney or blue-blood, she would have tossed her golden mane, laughed merrily at her mistake, and confessed. But she didn't. Seeing apprehension in her lovely eyes, James guessed quietly, "He's married, isn't he?"

"Yes," Alexa admitted. She knew there were only so many lies she could tell him. She had told him the most important one—that she and her love had just met—and he had seemed to believe it. She didn't dare push her luck with less important ones.

"I thought marriage was an automatic deal breaker, Alexa."

"It used to be. But it isn't any longer. It can't be, not with him. I have to live this love for as long as I can, James, no matter what."

"It's dangerous."

"I know. Dangerous and foolish—not to mention *wrong*. That's a very deep, old-fashioned, country girl belief of mine."

"Old-fashioned, maybe, but very, *very* sound."

"Yes. But, James, I believe in my love for him more than I've ever believed in anything in my life. A consuming and compelling love wasn't going to happen to me, remember? But now it has."

"I can tell." It was so obvious. Alexa was radiant, more beautiful than ever, glowing from a deep and wondrous joy. "Just be careful, Alexa."

"I can't even promise that, James," she answered softly. She and Robert would be careful to keep their love hidden, of course; but she had no control any longer over what happened to her heart. It didn't belong to her any more.

She had given her heart to Robert. It was completely in his care.

Alexa declined James's invitation for dinner, pleading exhaustion, which was true, and a need to get back to Washington because they were filming in the morning, even though tomorrow was Sunday, which was also true. But mostly, she declined dinner because she feared that, given time and more questions and his ability to tease truths from her, he might begin to guess.

251

Alexa left, and James spent the evening, the entire sleepless night, thinking about Catherine. She had been with him all week, in enchanting thoughts that surfaced without warning—even, astonishingly, distracting him in the midst of the billion-dollar negotiations. The thoughts had been there, and he had rationed them as best he could, allowing brief enticing forays into a distant fantasy and then forcing them away, where they belonged. Eventually, when he had uninterrupted time, the lovely, renegade thoughts would be marched out, spoken to firmly, and then banished forever.

Banished forever, an act of love and will, because of Alexa, whom he loved and would never hurt. If he had met another woman and fallen instantly in love, as Alexa had, yes, then, of course, he would have gone to her and gently confessed, as she had to him, that the unimaginable had happened. And she would have been happy for him, as he had been for her.

But Catherine wasn't just another woman. She was the little sister whose birth had caused such chaos in Alexa's young life and with whom the relationship now was so important, so complicated, so fragile. James knew, with absolute certainty, that he would never have said, "I know, Alexa, that cynical you and skeptical me have never really believed in falling in love. But, you see, there is something so wonderful, so magical about your little sister . . ."

But now Alexa had found her own magical love.

And maybe, just maybe, it was the tenderness

252

that he and Alexa had felt for each other that had opened their hearts to these even greater loves. Your fault, she had told him, a teasing grateful thank-you for convincing her of her own worthiness of love. But the truth was, in caring about Alexa, in loving her, James had made very important discoveries about himself. There had always been people he loved, of course—his parents, and Elliot, and Robert and Brynne. But, until Alexa, the "niceness" she had so quickly perceived hadn't in fact been there for any other lover. He simply hadn't cared before, not really, but he had really cared about Alexa. And because of caring about her, he had made wonderful discoveries about his own capacity for gentleness and tenderness and love.

"Your fault, Alexandra, that I am now able to fall in love with your little sister," he whispered softly to the glittering Chicago skyline. And then, even more softly, he added, "Thank you."

The wonderful thoughts of Catherine, now freed of restraint, danced in his mind, twirling and spinning and leaping with joy . . . until they crashed.

What about Catherine? a voice, perhaps the voice of reason, suddenly asked. Have you forgotten how young she is, how innocent? Don't you remember that every time—*every time*—you have been together you have caused her lovely cheeks to flush with embarrassment? You overwhelm her. Alexa told you that from the very beginning, and last weekend proved it's still true. In fact—how can you have overlooked this small point?—it was just a week ago tonight that you

253

made Catherine cry. And don't you remember her reaction the following afternoon when you joined the others to hear her play? She couldn't even look at you!

Yes, Catherine is innocent, but I will be so gentle and so careful, his loving heart promised. And, yes, she is young, and yet not so young. There is sometimes such solemn wisdom in her lovely sapphire eyes, as if she has known sadnesses far beyond her years. And, yes, yes, I have embarrassed her, and I am so sorry for that. She *is* overwhelmed by me, I know that's true. But I am overwhelmed by her, too. And, perhaps, we are both simply overwhelmed by the magic. She feels it, too, I know she does. I see the wonder in her sparkling eyes and in her soft beautiful smile. And I think I know why she didn't look at me when she was playing the piano last Sunday afternoon. It's the same reason that I had to force thoughts of her from my mind while I worked this week. The distraction is so great, so enchanting, so compelling that it demands all attention.

You sound very confident of your feelings for Catherine, the voice of reason observed. But are you so very certain that this is what she wants?

I am very confident of my feelings. And, yes, I believe that this is what she wants, too. But, he vowed solemnly, if our love is not what Catherine wants, I promise I will leave her alone. We will do what she wants. The choices of the heart will be hers.

James wanted to go to her soon, *now*, but as a final begrudging concession to reason, he decided that there needed to be time between the end of his relationship with Alexa and the beginning of his love with her little sister.

Time . . . weeks . . . precious time away from precious Catherine.

Chapter 15

Manhattan . . . October 1989

"Hello, Catherine? It's James."

"James."

"How are you?"

"I'm fine. Thank you." She could have embellished truthfully, "I'm truly fine, James, slender still, but strong and healthy and fit." But Catherine knew that he wasn't calling about her, not really. He was calling about Alexa. Even though Alexa had assured her, more than once, that his heart hadn't been broken, that obviously wasn't the case. And now he was calling to ask for her help.

"Good. I wondered if you'd like to go sailing with me on Saturday."

"Oh," she whispered softly, torn, as always, by conflicting answers when it came to James. Yes, because I want to see you. And no, because I have nothing to say that will help you. Alexa is very much in love.

"Or Sunday. Whichever is better for you."

"Saturday would be fine," she heard herself say, a brave and foolish answer from her heart.

"Good. I'm borrowing a boat from a friend. It's moored at the Southampton Club on Long Island. We should leave Manhattan about eleven. Is that OK?"

"Yes. That's fine."

"Hi."

"Hi." James smiled, so happy to see her, and for an enchanting moment he was lost in her bright blue eyes. Her eyes sparkled, so happy to see him, too, but surrounding the shimmering sapphire were dark circles and beneath them the always pink cheeks were ashen. "Catherine? What's wrong? Are you ill?"

"I'm fine. It's . . . nothing. What a glorious day for sailing! I just need to get a jacket from the closet, then I'll be ready to go."

"OK," he agreed uneasily, his impulse to press the issue intercepted by his reluctance to embarrass her—again. As she moved to the closet to get her jacket, he saw her slender body stiffen and her delicate fingers dig mercilessly into her snow white palms.

She's in pain, he realized. It was intermittent, he decided as her body relaxed just a little and her virtuoso fingers uncurled to reach for her jacket. Intermittent, coming in excruciating waves and then receding; but her pale drawn face and dark-circled eyes gave eloquent testimony to the fact that the pain had been with her all night.

"Catherine? Did you try to reach me to cancel? I was in my office this morning."

256

"No. I didn't try to reach you."

"Oh." Whatever it was, no matter the severity, she hadn't wanted to cancel their date. The realization filled him with both sadness and joy. "But maybe we should reschedule?"

"Yes. I guess we should." Catherine backed away from the closet, closed the door, and looked up bravely into his eyes. "Was there something you wanted to ask me about Alexa?"

"About Alexa?"

"Yes. About Alexa and . . ." She shrugged apologetically.

"About Alexa and her new love? No, not a thing. Why?"

"I thought that was why you called."

"No. I talk to your sister all the time. I have worries, as I'm sure you do, about the wisdom of what she's doing, but I'm delighted at how happy she is and hope her happiness will last forever." He gazed at her beautiful surprised eyes and added quietly, "The reason I asked you to go sailing with me, Catherine, is because I wanted to see you."

"Oh." Her reply began as a lovely breath of happiness, but it became a sharp gasp as a knife twisted deep inside her.

"Catherine, please, let me help you," James said softly. "Do you know what's wrong?"

"Yes. I know, and it will be gone in a few more hours." It should have been gone already! The severe cramping usually only lasted about eight hours, and it had already been nearly twelve. She had spent every pain-tossed moment of her sleepless night finding comfort in the certainty that it would all be over by morning, long before he arrived. She would be tired for their sail, but at least the cramps would have subsided. But they hadn't! The sharp claws dug into her still, first clutching and then, once their grip was deep and firm, twisting, causing even greater pain, stealing her breath and her strength.

"It's happened before?"

"Yes," she admitted, and, just for a heartbeat, her ashen cheeks flushed pink. "It's nothing, really, James. It's . . . I'm just having my period."

As the embarrassed blush vanished, sucked away by another wave of pain, he felt a most unusual mixture of helplessness and enchantment. Helplessness, because he wanted to stop her discomfort *now;* and enchantment, because it was the age of tampon ads on billboards and cocktail party conversations about PMS, but somehow that had passed her by. To lovely innocent Catherine, this was very private, very intimate.

"Hey, Catherine," he said gently when he sensed with grateful relief that the most recent wave of pain seemed to have retreated. "Remember my mother, the gynecologist? Admittedly, menstrual periods weren't frequent topics of conversation at the dinner table, but . . ." He paused, because his words had brought from her a trembling smile. Menstrual periods had *never* been dinner table conversation at Inverness, of course, and what he knew on the subject he had learned in vivid, uninhibited detail from women he had dated. But still . . . "I'm not embarrassed,

Catherine. Please don't you be. Are your periods always this painful?"

"Yes, although it's lasting longer than usual this time. I think that might be because this is my first period since June. They stopped altogether while I was dieting."

"Have you seen anyone?"

"I saw a doctor at the student health center at Oberlin. She didn't think it was endometriosis, but she thought I should see a specialist when I got here and that I should probably start taking birth control pills."

"Did she give you the name of a specialist?"

"Yes, and I'll make an appointment for this week."

"Good. Now, what pain medications do you have?"

"Aspirin. It's not doing much, but I'm sure the cramps will stop soon."

"Have you had anything to drink?"

"To drink?"

"Vodka? Bourbon?"

"No. Why?"

James suppressed his surprise. He had known about the salutary effects of alcohol on menstrual cramps for years, probably since high school. But, apparently, Catherine hadn't learned this from her friends either in high school or college; nor had she learned it from her big sister, who, he knew, "treated" the mild to moderate cramps she had on the first day of her period with two glasses of Dom Pérignon.

"Alcohol seems to help," he explained, in answer to her question. Then, smiling gently, he offered quietly, "So, Catherine, shall I ply you with liquor?"

"OK. I don't know if there's even any . . ." She tilted her head, a thoughtful acknowledgment of what they both knew, that he was more familiar with Alexa's apartment than she. After a moment, she said softly, "I guess you do."

"Why don't you go into the living room, and I'll find some and bring it to you? Do you have a preference?"

"No. I've never really had more than a taste of anything."

"Oh. Well. Bourbon, then."

James knew there was bourbon here, his favorite brand, mild and rich and smooth. As soon as Catherine left to wait for him in the living room, he found the bourbon and a Saint Louis crystal highball glass and poured the drink undiluted and without ice.

"Here you go," he said when he joined her in the living room, where she was seated on the sofa, and handed her the glass. "Sip."

"Thank you. OK."

As Catherine sipped the expensive liquor under James's watchful gaze, she cast shy, apologetic smiles as if to say, Maybe I won't feel any effect. Maybe . . .

The bourbon hit her sleep-deprived and pain-exhausted body with a smooth rush of heat, filling her, bathing her, gently transporting her to a place where her mind floated, and there was no pain. The ferocious claws that had dug mercilessly into her for the past twelve hours magically withdrew, and into the tender wounds where the sharp claws

260

had been, flowed a soothing, liquid warmth. She felt warm, and floating, and amazingly, wonderfully bold.

"Better?" James asked as he watched her eyes widen.

"Yes. I can't believe it. Thank you." She set the glass of bourbon down on the coffee table and announced, "I'm ready to go sailing."

He would love to have taken her sailing as planned. But James knew that the exhilarating rush from the alcohol, coupled with the euphoric relief that the pain was blocked, would soon give way to the legacy of fatigue from her sleepless night.

"I think bed would be better, don't you?"

For a magnificent moment her sapphire eyes filled with wonder, as if she thought he was suggesting that they go to bed together and welcomed the suggestion with desire and joy. It was only a moment, and when it was over, in a flutter of long black lashes and pink flushed cheeks, James wondered if it had only been a mirage. A mirage that made his heart race.

"Yes," she answered softly, finally. "I guess it would."

"Will you call me when you wake up, no matter what time?"

"OK. I don't have your number."

"Is that why you didn't call to cancel?"

"No. I didn't want to cancel."

"Because you thought I needed to talk to you about Alexa?"

"Yes." She lifted her eyes bravely to his and

added softly, truthfully, "But mostly because I wanted to see you."

"Hi, James. It's Catherine. You told me to call no matter how late." It was after midnight, and she had just awakened, rested, refreshed, and free of pain.

"Yes. How are you?"

"Fine. I just woke up and I'm fine. Thank you."

"Good. I'm glad. Fine enough to have brunch with me tomorrow—no, today? I was going to suggest a sail, but the weather forecasters are talking fairly confidently about storms heading this way. So, how about trying Long Island's most famous champagne brunch? It happens to be in the Azalea Room at the Southampton Club, which means we could bring our sailing clothes, just in case, and sail after brunch if the weather looks clear when we get there . . ."

"I'd better not drink any of this," Catherine said with a soft smile as her delicate finger traced a line along the crystal champagne flute that had just been placed in front of her on the pink linen tablecloth.

"No champagne?"

"I discovered yesterday that alcohol makes me far too honest."

"Too honest?" James asked softly as he wondered which boldness from yesterday she decided had been too honest. Was it the soft confession that she had accepted his invitation to go sailing with him because she wanted to see him? Or the provocative sapphire wonder when he had suggested bed? And what as yet unspoken truth prevented her from drinking champagne today? Was it, perhaps, her version of the complicated history of the Taylor sisters? "Is it really possible to be too honest?" "I think," she answered slowly, "there are some truths that need time before they can be told."

"Yes. I think so, too," he agreed gently. It was too soon, he knew, to tell her all the truths about his feelings for her. Some day, when she was ready, he would tell her those wonderful, joyous truths. And some day, he hoped, she would tell him the hidden truths which, unlike his joyous ones, were so obviously deeply troubling. Take all the time you need, lovely Catherine, but please know that you can trust me with all the secrets of your heart. "You really had very little alcohol yesterday, you know."

"I know."

Catherine knew it had taken only a few sips for the bourbon to work its magic on her pain. And what about the other magic, the warm, exhilarating rushes of pure joy, and the wonderful soft laughter that splashed merrily from a sparkling fountain of happiness deep within her? That magic, she knew, had nothing to do with alcohol. That magic was James. So gently, his dark blue eyes and warm smile lured her from her shyness, welcoming all her words, all her thoughts, all her truths.

But there were words she did not yet have the courage to speak to him. I'm adopted. My real mother didn't love me enough to keep me, you see. I'm not sure who I am, James, not yet, but each day I'm learning a little more. Catherine didn't have the courage to tell him that truth, not yet, or perhaps it was simply that she didn't have the courage to tell him the rest. There is something I have learned, James, about myself, a wonderful recent discovery. I have learned that when I am with you, I am everything I want to be.

Catherine didn't tell James her secrets on that stormy day. They talked instead of music and sailing, and raindrops and roses, and storm clouds and waves. And woven into the afternoon of soft smiles and softer laughter were invitations for future times to be together. Yes, she told him, she would love to see the Ring cycle at the Met, yes, all four operas. And she would love to dine with him at Manhattan's most famous restaurants, and view the Impressionist exhibit at the art museum, and. . .

Catherine answered yes to all his invitations, a joyous happy yes, and her beautiful honest eyes embellished, telling him the most important truth, the only truth he needed to know, Yes, James, I want to be with you.

Chapter 16

Washington, D.C. . . . December 1989

"All weekend?" Alexa echoed softly.

It was the first Tuesday in December. In the three months of their love, she and Robert had never had a weekend together. Their loving had been on weeknights only, in rare, precious hours stolen from darkness. And in those cherished late-night hours, they shared an emotional intimacy that was exquisitely gentle and tender; and they shared, too, a breathless passion that was still as desperate, as urgent and as furtive, as it had been the first night.

Their desperate, furtive passion was a symbol, Alexa had decided, of what they both knew but neither said: their secret love could not endure. Their love was safe now, a secret easily kept because no one knew to search for it. The Washington press pursued Robert relentlessly in hopes of getting quotable quotes from the nation's brightest political star. But it would never have occurred to a single reporter, not even the most aggressive gossip columnist, to investigate the Senator's personal life. Why bother? Anyone in Washington who had ever seen them together, and virtually all the reporters had, knew that Robert and Hillary McAllister had a perfect marriage.

The secret love of Robert and Alexa would be quite safe—until Robert made his bid for the Presidency. Then, every detail of his life, no matter how personal, would be in the public domain. He would be pursued constantly, both by the political press and the legion of spies hired by the other party who had been given the virtually impossible task of finding even the tiniest chink in his impeccable armor. If Robert became the party's nominee for the 1996 election, which most political analysts predicted, their secret love was safe for at least four more years, perhaps almost five. And if he didn't run until the year 2000 . . .

Would she be willing to live this love of dark, desperate, stolen moments for four more years, or even eight? *Oh yes.* She would love him, whenever she could, for as long as she could.

And now he was telling her that beginning three days from now they would have a weekend together.

"All weekend," Robert whispered as his tender kisses wandered from her tear-dampened eyes to her kiss-dampened mouth. "All weekend, my love."

"Oh, no!"

"Darling?"

"I have to work on Saturday! We're filming on location at the Supreme Court. I have all of Friday off, but I have to work on Saturday."

"Then, on Friday, you make dinner for me. I'll be here in time for dinner, I promise," Robert replied, kissing away her frown. "And I'll make dinner for you on Saturday. And on Sunday, my love . . ."

All weekend, my love, he had promised, and her emerald eyes had filled with such lovely joy at the promise. How eagerly he awaited the moment when he could promise her, All of our lives, my love.

Maybe this weekend I will be able to make that promise, Robert thought, as, hours later, he held her in his arms as she slept. She was a portrait of peace and happiness, her golden hair haloing her beautiful face, a soft hopeful smile on her lips. As he gently touched the golden silk, her lovely smile grew, reaching to him from sleep, as if she had been dreaming about what he had been thinking—the time when, at last, they could be together always.

Robert had never discussed his joyous plans to spend his life with her—but, of course, she knew—and he wanted to make no specific promises until Hillary had agreed to a divorce. He had decided to wait until the Christmas holidays to approach Hillary. The Senate would be in recess then, and Alexa would be in Topeka; and, *if all went well,* Hillary could go to Dallas as always, to the lavish parties she loved, while he remained in Washington and moved out of the house. The decision to wait until the holidays had been a practical one, and not the least bit cruel. Christmas held no special sentiment for Senator and Mrs. McAllister, *no time did.*

But now, as Robert held the woman he loved and thought about the many Washington parties that he and Hillary would be expected to attend in the upcoming weeks, he made a new decision. He would talk to Hillary about the divorce very soon, this Thursday, the evening before she left for her weekend at the spa. He couldn't, wouldn't, live the public charade any longer.

It had always amazed Robert that no one could tell that the perfect script followed by the perfect First Couple-to-be was just a sham, a performance without heart or soul. He had survived it in the past, before Alexa, because his heart had been empty then, and the charade hadn't really mattered. But now his heart was filled, overflowing, with love for Alexa; and even if the sham hadn't been apparent in the past, it certainly should have been now, because he scarcely looked at Hillary any more; and yet, they were Washington's darlings, the picture perfect couple *still.*

It was time, now, for the charade to end; and, *if all went well,* it would. It was a very big "if." Robert knew that Hillary wouldn't "give" him a divorce. He would have to pay for it. The cost, he knew, might be quite high, because he wanted more than just a divorce: he wanted a quiet, private one. What he wanted had nothing to do with his political career, of course; it had only to do with Alexa. He knew that a highly publicized divorce, starring the talented actress in the real life role as "the other woman," would be devastating for her.

Robert knew that Hillary would have a price for what he wanted. He had to steel himself to weather her insults and her fury until she told him what it was; and then, for Alexa, for her protection and her happiness, he had to be prepared to pay.

"I love you," he whispered softly to his sleeping love. I love you, and, my darling, maybe this weekend I will have wonderful news for us.

Hillary always spent the first weekend in December at the Willows, the ultra-exclusive spa forty miles north of Savannah that catered to the South's richest women. She was a guest at the lavishly restored antebellum mansion at least four times a year, a tradition that had begun as a gift from her mother the day she turned sixteen. Hillary never really felt improved after her visits to the Willows. Indeed, the spa's many beauty, health, and fitness experts were hard pressed to find ways to enhance the perfect face, skin, nails, and body with which she always arrived. But she faithfully returned to the Willows nonetheless, because rich, beautiful, and influential women, like her, did such things.

Now, for the first time ever, Hillary had wondered if she should cancel her reservation for this booked-years-in-advance weekend before the all-important holiday social season began. She knew full well that if she spent the weekend at the Willows, Robert would spend it with Alexa at RoseCliff. And if she cancelled? Robert would spend the weekend at Clairmont working in his study, and when they shared their silent meals, she would see in his solemn eyes how much he longed to be with *her.* And she might even see something worse: the dark turbulence that made her fear that Robert was going to tell her about his affair.

As if she didn't already know! Months ago, she had followed him to the tiny cottage perched high on the cliffs. And, for months, she had churned with a hatred for Alexa that made all previous emotions about her long-time rival seem trivial; and she hated Robert, too, for doing this to *her*. She knew that their paltry affair would end, of course, *it had to;* but that would not put an end to Hillary's fury that Robert had risked scandal—risked the Presidency—for Alexa! How could he? How *dare* he?

Hillary had finally decided not to cancel her weekend at the Willows. The more Robert was with Alexa, she had reasoned, the sooner he would tire of her. And, she had wondered grimly as she gazed at her beautiful face in the mirror, were those really tiny little lines she saw now in her always flawless skin? Worry lines, *hatred* lines? Even more reasons to hate Alexa and Robert, she had decided; and more reasons, too, to spend a lavish rejuvenating weekend at the spa.

On Thursday evening, the night before her morning departure for Savannah, Hillary sat in the Florentine drawing room at Clairmont glancing through a stack of engraved, mostly gilt-edged, invitations. She expertly sorted the various soirées, receptions, galas, and black-tie charity balls in her mind, instantly recognizing the socially and politically important ones and dismissing the ones that weren't pure "A-list." And, as she sorted, she planned which ravishing designer gown she would wear to each, never needing to repeat, scowling as she imagined the conversation with Robert in which he would question her conspicuous extravagances and suggest yet again that, at the very least, she wear more American creations and fewer original designs of Givenchy, Chanel, and LaCroix.

Hillary's scowl at that imagined conversation—how dare he make any suggestions whatsoever?—deepened as she reached the engraved invitation to *Pennsylvania Avenue*'s "When You Wish Upon a Star" charity gala to be held on Saturday the sixteenth. She started to rip the invitation in half, on the way to a hundred tiny pieces, but she was stopped mid-ravage by a wonderful image.

Senator and Mrs. Robert McAllister would go to the gala this year. Alexa would be there, of course, wearing something trashy, tasteless crimson satin, perhaps, plunged to the navel. And she would be wearing her new gown of ivory silk, intricately sewn with the most delicate pearl and silver beads, like dewdrops on roses, endlessly pure, timelessly elegant. She would wear her sable-brown hair in a demure chignon, away from her beautiful face, to fully reveal her emerald earrings, the only jewelry she would wear, *except,* of course, the most important piece of all: the gold and emerald wedding band that would be a reminder to both her wandering husband and his brazen slut of precisely who and what she was.

Hillary's reverie was interrupted by the sound of approaching footsteps. Robert? At home on a Thursday night? Home, instead of RoseCliff? *Good,* she thought triumphantly. At last.

"Hello, Robert," she said, with cool surprise when he appeared in the doorway, not leaving the silk sofa to greet him, and, in fact, after a moment glancing back to the stack of invitations in her hands.

"Hello, Hillary. I'm here because I need to talk to you."

"Oh?"

"Do I have your attention?"

"Yes." She smiled prettily, disingenously, as she looked up. "Of course."

"OK, then, the reason I've come here tonight is to tell you that I want a divorce."

"You're joking."

"No. You know that I'm not. And you know, too, that the joke is the marriage. We have both known that for a very long time."

"Do you honestly think I will give you a divorce, Robert?"

No, he thought. I know that you will not. But that's why I'm here, to learn your price for my freedom and Alexa's privacy. He said quietly, "You don't really have a choice, Hillary. I can file the papers just as easily as you can. I had hoped, I do hope, however, that we can reach an amicable agreement."

"There's someone else, isn't there?" she demanded suddenly, as if the horrifying thought had just occurred to her. "That's what this is *really* about, isn't it?"

"What this is really about, Hillary, is a marriage that exists in name only and needs to end. Yes,

I have met someone, and I plan to marry her, but she is not the reason our marriage failed. It failed long ago, long before I ever met her."

"Who is she?"

"It doesn't matter who she is."

"Really? I sincerely doubt that the many reporters assigned to cover our very ugly and very public divorce would agree with you. My guess is that they would be most interested in every sordid detail about your mistress. Our divorce *would* be very ugly and very public, Robert, I promise you that. Your constituency has a right to know what kind of man you really are. As you know, womanizers aren't doing terribly well at the voting booths these days." Hillary stood up then and walked toward him slowly, allowing the effect of her threat to settle, reveling in her triumph. Finally she continued almost condescendingly to the man who had apparently, astonishingly, forgotten that he *could not* leave her, "Divorcing me, Senator McAllister, would cost you the Presidency."

Robert held her angry yet triumphant glare for several moments before replying very quietly, "Then so be it."

His quiet words instantly shattered both her confidence and her anger, leaving her only with trembling fear. He was really going to leave her, and she was powerless to stop him, *because* he was willing to give up everything—*everything*—to spend his life with her most bitter enemy.

She spun away from him, suddenly needing support for her trembling body, and finding it a few staggering feet away against the marble mantlepiece. Her eyes focused vaguely on the expensive adornments on the Italian marble the Orrefors vase, the antique clock, the Boehm rose. How she wanted to hurl them at him! But, if she did, he would leave now, immediately and forever. He would waste no time in filing for the divorce, and all would be lost. She needed time to think, to plan, to somehow find a way to stop the divorce entirely.

Anger had never worked with Robert, nor had tears or threats, nor, not for a very long time, had seduction. But he was, she knew, a fair and reasonable man; and in the long, silent moments before she was steady enough to face him again, her spinning mind searched frantically for, and finally found, fair and reasonable appeals to make to her fair and reasonable husband.

"I don't want to fight with you," she said softly when, eventually, she turned back to him.

"I don't want to fight, either, Hillary."

"I will give you the divorce, uncontested and without a whisper of publicity, but I need time. Don't worry, I'm not talking about a reconciliation. I have a little pride, you know. I just need time to adjust, to decide what I'm going to do and if I'll even feel comfortable being in Washington any longer."

Robert's heart raced at "uncontested and without a whisper of publicity." Hillary had agreed, in principle, to the quiet divorce he wanted, and now she was beginning to tell him her price. He asked with amazing calm, "How much time did you have in mind?"

"Until the end of May."

"That's almost six months."

"I need that much time, Robert. And there is the celebration for my father's birthday in Dallas over Memorial Day weekend. You know what an important event that will be for him, and you've already agreed to give one of the major speeches. If we could just keep up appearances until Memorial Day, it would give me time to make plans and it would make that weekend untarnished for my father."

Robert reeled inwardly at "keeping up appearances." But, surely, the public charade would be more endurable once the private charade was over.

"Nothing is going to change between now and then, Hillary."

"I know that."

"Is there anything else you want?"

"Yes. Does anyone know about . . . her?"

"I don't think so. No."

"Then I have a final request. I would like to know that people aren't gossiping about me."

"You want me to stop seeing her until after we've separated."

"Yes."

Now he knew the full price for a quiet divorce: six months away from Alexa. *Six months.* It was a long time, but he knew it was not an unreasonable request. It would take Hillary a while to adjust. His vain, spoiled wife was quite unused to being denied anything, and even though this was not the loss of a love, for pretentious and ambitious Hillary it was a loss of great magnitude nonetheless. *Away from Alexa.* Was that too high a price to pay? No, he decided, and he knew that Alexa would agree. "We've been waiting all our lives for each other, Robert," she would say softly as her emerald eyes filled with joy. "Can I wait six more months until our forever? Of course I can."

"I would need to see her one more time, Hillary, to explain."

"Of course."

"And if I agree to keep up appearances and stop seeing her, at the end of May you will give me a quiet, uncontested divorce," he said quietly, holding Hillary's eyes, searching for deceit, and seeing none.

"Yes, Robert," she answered with matching quiet and without a flicker. "I promise that I will."

Six months, Hillary thought as she paced restlessly in her bedroom. Six months with which to do what? *Nothing,* she realized miserably, except to hope that Robert would come to his senses, or that Alexa would become impatient with the wait and find a new love.

Hillary paced, and, as the winter night grew colder and darker, completely black, so too did her thoughts. Cold, and dark, and black, and suddenly quite hopeful. Maybe something terrible—terribly wonderful—would happen to Alexa.

Maybe Alexa would die.

Robert might have left the following morning without seeing Hillary, but, shortly before seven, as he was finishing a cup of coffee before beginning the long drive from Arlington to the capital, the phone rang, and, moments later, she appeared in the kitchen.

"Good morning, Robert."

"Good morning, Hillary."

"Did I hear the phone?"

"Yes. I have to go to Camp David for the weekend."

"Leaving now?"

"Leaving at two this afternoon. What time is your flight for Savannah?"

"At ten." But I won't be leaving this morning for a weekend at the Willows after all, she thought. She wasn't certain yet what she was going to do, but she felt quite confident that she had suddenly been presented with a chance to control her own destiny.

As soon as Robert left, Hillary made two phone calls. Then, after dressing elegantly, she drove from Arlington to the Washington studio where *Pennsylvania Avenue* was filmed, gave her name to the studio security guard and announced that Alexa was expecting her. She was, she explained truthfully, a co-hostess for a benefit for the homeless. Then, lying effortlessly, she further told him that Alexa had said she would be willing to appear at the event.

"There must be some mistake, ma'am. Ms. Taylor isn't scheduled to work today."

"You're kidding." Hillary's beautiful smile became a beautiful frown as she followed the guard's eyes to the schedule he held. She saw that Alexa had worked late last night, was off today, and if her quick glance at the much marked up schedule was correct, would be working most of tomorrow. Good . . . *perfect*. "I spoke to Alexa last week. Perhaps her schedule changed since then and she forgot to call me."

"Probably. Shall I tell her you were here?"

"No. Thank you. I'll reach her myself."

As Hillary sped along the interstate from Washington, D. C. toward Maryland, she caught sight of a police car hidden beside the road. Her eyes swept to the speedometer—sixty-eight!—and then to the rearview mirror as she pressed her suede pump to the brake. For ten breath-held seconds she waited for the police car to follow her, lights flashing, siren blaring, and steeled herself for a condescending "Now, Mrs. McAllister" lecture. But when the car didn't follow, she vowed to look frequently at the speedometer to be certain that her gold-tone Mercedes didn't fly toward RoseCliff as swiftly as her thoughts were flying.

Slow down, she told herself. And, as she slowed the car, gaining control, her thoughts came under control, too. She had raced to the studio because it seemed necessary to speak to Alexa before Robert did. But, she realized, it didn't matter.

By the time she began the three flight climb up the stairs to Alexa's secluded cottage, she felt amazingly calm. Why not? Even if her plan backfired she could lose no more than she had already lost—*everything*—and if it succeeded, her most bitter enemy might unwittingly become her greatest ally. As she climbed the stairs, Hillary noticed the roses. They were barren now, carefully draped in burlap for winter, their thorns hidden. You have to keep your thorns hidden, she reminded herself. You have to.

"Hillary."

"May I come in?" Hillary's calm stumbled briefly at the sight of Alexa, her golden hair tousled from sleep, her robe cinched tightly around her narrow waist; and there was a little more faltering when she left the colorless winter day behind and entered the romantic, pastel love nest.

"Of course. I'm surprised to see you."

"Wives and mistresses don't usually meet for coffee?" she asked, discovering to her relief that "mistress," spoken with glacial contempt, had a tranquilizing effect, helping her restore the necessary calm control. "No, I suppose not. Well, we can forgo the coffee."

"Hillary, I don't know what—"

"For heaven's sake, let's don't spend any time pretending it hasn't happened! I know all about you and Robert. He hasn't called you yet this morning, has he?" She paused, deliberately considering her own question, and then mused with a coy smile, "Or perhaps he *has* called and you still don't know what's happened. I guess that's the reason I'm here, Alexa. Robert may not tell you, and I want to make very certain that you know the truth."

"The truth," Alexa echoed numbly.

"Yes." Hillary smiled. She felt wonderful now, and oh-so-confident having the ever-confident Alexa at such a distinct disadvantage. Be careful, she warned herself. Don't overplay your hand.

Be haughty and disdainful. "Did Robert ever happen to tell you why he chose you to have an affair with?"

"No." *Chose?* Neither of us chose! Our love happened because it was meant to happen.

"It wasn't by accident. Robert wanted to punish me, and I'd told him enough about our days at Ballinger for him to know that of all the women on earth it would hurt me the most to know that he had been unfaithful with you."

"Why would Robert want to hurt you?"

"Because I hurt him. He really told you none of this, did he? Of course not, because you might have been suspicious of his motives from the outset. Robert had an affair with you to get even with me—for the affair I've been having. I'm not the least bit proud of what I did. I was a little bored, I guess, and a little petulant about how hard he was working and how little time he had for me. And remember, Alexa, unlike you I didn't spend my past sleeping with everything in pants. So I allowed myself a foolish affair. I didn't even know Robert knew about it until last night." She sighed, softly, sadly, her dark sable eyes conveying deep regret for her own foolishness. "You can tell from the dark circles beneath my eyes that I didn't sleep, neither of us did, because we spent all night talking about what we had done, and what we want to do now. And what we want, after we've had a little time just to ourselves, is to begin our family. We've delayed because of Brynne, because she has desperately wanted children and has been unable to have them. Well, that's really none of your business.

All that you need to know is that it's over, Alexa, not me and Robert, but *you* and Robert."

"But for some reason you don't think he'll tell me."

"He'll tell you something that will cause your affair to end, but it may not be the truth. He's very politic and probably more than a little embarrassed. He'll find a graceful way out. I'm very certain he won't admit that he used you, or that our marriage is stronger now than ever."

"But you're telling me."

"Yes. Because we have been at war for a long time, Alexa, and I want you to know that in this final and most important battle you have lost. It's a luxury for me to tell you, an indulgence, but not a great risk."

"You don't think I'll go public with this."

"No. I don't think so. I doubt you could destroy Robert's career even if you did. The other woman—the immoral seductress—is never a sympathetic role. You're a star, of course, but so is he, and he's also the great political hope for very many people. Destroying him, even attempting to, would ruin your career in the process. Maybe you don't care about that, or have so little pride that you might confess to a sordid affair in which you were the loser, but there's your sister to think about."

"What about Cat?"

"She'd defend you, I'm sure, as she did years ago, but I wonder if you want to drag her and her career through the shame? Your little sister is a lady. And you, Alexa, are a whore. You'll never be anything else."

"Get out."

"Well," Hillary continued smoothly, ignoring Alexa's trembling command but glancing at her diamond Chopard watch as if it might be nearing time for her to leave anyway. "I'd better be going. Robert's leaving work early today, at two, so that we can get to Dallas in time for a champagne and candlelight dinner. You look surprised, Alexa. Oh, that's right, this was going to be your weekend with Robert while I was at the spa. Well, plans have changed. We're spending the weekend in the bridal suite at the Mansion, the same hotel where we spent our wedding night. That was Robert's idea. Very romantic, don't you think?"

"Get out."

"Yes, we have the reservation," the desk clerk at Dallas' famous Mansion on Turtle Creek confirmed when Alexa called pretending she was Senator McAllister's secretary. "The bridal suite, as per the Senator's request."

"Thank you."

Her hands trembled as she returned the receiver to the cradle. She had believed Hillary's eyes and tone and confidence, but until that moment she hadn't believed her devastating words. *I still don't believe them.* And I won't, until I hear them from Robert. He will tell me the truth, whatever it is, I know he will.

In their months of love, Robert had never once mentioned Hillary or his marriage. Alexa had simply assumed, because of *their* desperate and passionate love, that his marriage was loveless; but, she had assumed, too, that in spite of its unhappiness, it would endure, would have to, because of his political career. And she had been willing, so very willing, to be Robert's hidden love, forever, because she believed so much in their love.

But what if he truly loved Hillary? What if he had come to her, as Hillary claimed, simply to hurt the wife who had hurt him so much? What if his desperate passion for her was really a disguised desperation for Hillary?

"No! I don't believe it!" Alexa cried defiantly to the gray sky, darkening now even though it was still before noon, an ominous black harbinger of a long cold winter. "Call me, Robert, please. And please, whatever the truth is, even if it's exactly as Hillary has said, please tell me."

Robert called at one-fifty. In the crush of compressing the obligations of his day so that he could leave for Camp David at two, he had been unable to find a private moment earlier in which to call her. His office phone had rung incessantly, including several aggravating crank calls from a caller who remained on the line but said nothing, and there had been a steady stream of people who needed his attention. It had been a frustratingly rushed day, but every time he had felt his sleep-deprived temper begin to fray, Robert had reminded himself of what Hillary had promised last night. He wanted to tell Alexa now, but there wasn't time; and, he thought, they were words that needed to be whispered softly, between kisses, as he held her for the last time before their six months apart.

As Robert dialed the number to RoseCliff, the warm joy of their love, the antidote to every frustration and every problem in his life, drifted over him.

His voice smiled, a gentle tender smile, when she answered.

"Hello, darling."

"Robert." Alexa curled her aching body in the tenderness of his voice and her mind banished the memory of Hillary. It hadn't happened. It was just a mirage, just a lie. "How is your day going? Do you still think you'll be able to get here for dinner?"

"Oh, Alexa, this weekend isn't going to happen."

"Why not?" No! Please, *no*.

"The President wants me at Camp David."

"Is it something top secret? No media coverage?" No way to prove or disprove?

"What? Oh, yes, I imagine so. Alexa? I'm very sorry," he said gently, surprised by the sudden edge in her voice. He had expected disappointment, but not the sudden disappearance of gentleness.

"So am I."

"Darling, I need to go now. The limousine is waiting. I should be back late Sunday night. I'll call you, if it's not too late. OK?"

"OK."

"I love you, Alexa."

I love you too.

Chapter 17

The annoying crank calls to Robert's office had been made by Hillary. She recorded his voice, the polite "Hello" that, on repeated calls, degenerated into impatient demands "Hello? *Hello?* Who is this?" She made the recordings on a high quality hand-held recorder, one of many Robert kept around the house for dictation, and using another one made a careful single recording of two pleasant "Hellos" back to back, then a pause, then increasing annoyance, and in the background, she added her own voice, purring seductively, "Robert, who is it? Tell them to send us more champagne!"

Hillary made the recordings, packed a large suitcase, took a limousine to National, and by late afternoon was settled in the first class cabin of the flight to Dallas sipping champagne and silently toasting both the expensive empty seat beside her and whatever international crisis had taken Robert to Camp David. A few hours later, she was in the lavish lobby of the luxurious Mansion on Turtle Creek, preparing to casually murmur to the hotel receptionist that her husband was on a later flight. But no explanation was necessary. Apparently it was simply assumed that the important and busy Senator had been unavoidably delayed.

And then she was in the romantic bridal suite,

her mission accomplished, and all that was left to do was reminisce about the exhilarating and triumphant day. She had moved with swift confidence from task to task, propelled by powerful bursts of adrenaline, and further energized by each successfully completed phase of her desperate plan. *I, not Alexa, should have been an actress,* she had decided after her performance at RoseCliff. *Or a secret agent,* she had mused as she listened to the tape she had made of Robert. *Or a criminal, a rare and extraordinary criminal who is bright enough and clever enough to commit the perfect crime.*

The wonderful exhilaration was with her as long as the adrenaline was, and the potent substance continued to spurt, in thrilling rushes, as long as there was yet another obstacle to conquer. But when she was safe in the bridal suite, all obstacles conquered, the adrenaline evaporated and took with it the sensation of euphoria.

Reality crashed quickly and mercilessly. Here she was, alone in a bridal suite because her husband did not want her, sipping Dom Pérignon, foolishly musing about how she had missed her calling as an actress, a secret agent, a criminal. *Your calling,* reality reminded her harshly, *what you were bred to be from the moment you were born, is the wife of a powerful man like Robert McAllister. And you have failed.* This desperate plan will not work. Perhaps you planted a seed of doubt in Alexa's mind, but beyond that all you have done is shown that you can make a few simple recordings on a tape recorder—idiot's work—on the vanishingly remote chance that Alexa will call. After performing that ridiculously simple and probably useless task, you bought and used two expensive airline tickets; and then, for your dazzling encore, you flew to Dallas and checked into a bridal suite with a phantom companion.

And here you are! Alone in a luxurious room, surrounded by flowers and champagne and caviar, with the silly tape recording strategically positioned by the phone. And you're even wearing a provocative silk negligee! For whom? For your phantom companion, of course . . .

Because Robert doesn't want you.

Robert only wants Alexa

Hillary drank the champagne, trying to revive the wonderful feelings that had propelled her on her mission, but the alcohol made her far more sober than drunk, far more depressed than cheerful.

When she awakened the following morning, all the illusions were gone. She was no longer a talented actress. She was, instead, simply an understudy, destined never to get a chance to perform, reading her lines without heart. She ordered breakfast for two, Eggs Benedict and more Dom Pérignon, and as she picked at the elegant food, she glowered at the silk sheeted bed where she and Robert were supposed to be spending a weekend of passion.

Alexa, Alexa, how I hate you!

The telephone rang at four, startling her. The concierge? Calling to see if everything was satisfactory? Or Housekeeping wondering politely, discreetly, if the lovers wouldn't like new silk sheets, more plush towels, fresh terry cloth robes? No, Hillary told her racing heart. No one within the hotel would dare intrude on their privacy. The call had to be from outside the hotel.

And there was only one person it could be.

Her slender, perfectly manicured fingers became clumsy as she fumbled to activate the tape recorder's play button just as she lifted the receiver. She had set the volume soft, as if the phone were intruding on intimacy, and held it a slight distance from the receiver. As she listened to the wonderfully convincing recording of Robert answering the phone, and her own voice whispering seductively for more champagne, and heard nothing but the magnificent sound of silence on the other end, her heart began to race. And then, moments later, her heart became almost airborne, fluttering away, as she heard the even more magnificent sound of the silent caller hanging up, a quiet somber disconnect, long before the tape even ended.

Alexa. Oh, Alexa, did my perfect, desperate crime really work?

The adrenaline was back, celebrating her triumph with her, as she paced back and forth on the deep pile carpet. Hillary tempered her own euphoria, long before the adrelanine vanished, with a stern reminder that there was a scene to be played out that was completely beyond her control—the scene between Robert and Alexa. How she wished she could script that scene!

But she couldn't. She had done all she could do. Now, she just had to hope.

"Hi," Robert said when Alexa answered the phone *finally* at midnight Sunday night. She usually answered on the first ring, and as the phone rang and rang unanswered, fear began to creep into his mind, the heart-stopping fear that an obsessed fan had discovered the remote clifftop cottage where she felt so safe. "Were you asleep?"

"No." She had barely slept Friday night; and last night, after her call to the bridal suite at the Mansion, she had spent the entire night chiding herself, and the tears that would not stop, for her foolishness. Now some new masochistic urge made her ask, "How was your trip?"

"Successful, I think. Darling, I have something wonderful to tell you." Robert paused, expecting her to urge him to come over, even though it was quite late, but she was silent. "Alexa? Shall I come over?"

"No. I have a very early call tomorrow morning. Could you just tell me over the phone?"

"Alexa?"

"Please." Please, let's get this over with quickly! I can't possibly see you. I can't endure a gentle loving good-bye.

"OK. Well, my lovely Alexa, will you marry me?"

Yes, her heart answered instantly, but her fatigued mind intervened warily. "Marry?"

"Yes. Of course," he answered lovingly, surprised at her surprise and worried about whatever else it was—that edge again—that he heard in her voice.

"You're already married, Robert."

"Hillary has agreed to give me a divorce."

"When did she agree to that?"

"Thursday night."

"Did you tell her about me?"

"I told her I was in love with another woman."

"Did you tell her it was me?"

"No."

Lies! her mind screamed.

"And she agreed to a divorce, just like that?"

"No. She asked that she and I stay together until after Memorial Day. She wants time to plan what she's going to do, and there is a celebration for her father in Dallas that weekend. As soon as that's over, she has promised to give me a quiet divorce."

"I see. During which time we don't see each other?"

"She asked that."

So this was how he was going to do it. Did he actually believe her love for him was so fragile that in less than six months she would have found someone new? Or, perhaps, that simply because of this request she would cast him aside in an angry show of pique? Apparently, because this was how he planned to let *her* end their love: and it meant that he didn't know, must never have known, how much she loved him. She would wait six months, six years if need be, but somehow he had determined six months would be enough to drive her away. And what if she said, "Yes, of course I'll wait"? Would he call in May with a request for an extension? Or might there be a final call in which he confessed sadly that Hillary was pregnant—he had slept with her just one time, an idiotic mistake, because he missed *her* so much?

Alexa had believed the pain she had felt all weekend could get no worse, but now it did; because now the loss was far greater than simply the end of their love; now, whatever love there had been was brutally betrayed. It was cruel, so terribly cruel, for him to have asked her to marry him! From her anguish came a remarkable strength, defiant and proud. She would not let Senator Robert McAllister know of her foolishness. She was an actress, after all, and she was an expert at hiding her pain beneath dazzling layers of golden confidence.

"Oh, Robert," she purred softly, the bewitching yet menacing purr of a tigress luring her prey. "I'm so flattered by your offer of marriage."

"Flattered?"

"And embarrassed. It was a game, Robert, a game between me and Hillary. She and I have been rivals for a very long time. Didn't she tell you the story before we had dinner last spring? We were in high school together in Dallas, at Ballinger. She made me feel quite unwelcome there, and I retaliated by taking her friends, including her boyfriend, away from her. It may sound like a silly childish game, but I assure you, the emotions behind it weren't silly at all."

"What are you saying, Alexa? That you had

291

an affair with me because of some rivalry with Hillary? That I was a pawn in some petty game?"

"I'm not proud of it, Robert, but I honestly didn't know it would go this far. If I'd had any idea at all that you were thinking about marriage . . ."

How could you *not* have known? he wondered, stunned. Wasn't it so passionately, and so desperately, obvious in every moment we had together that I wanted to spend my life with you? But those precious moments of love had been spent with Alexa, not with the stranger who was speaking to him now in the purring voice he had never heard before.

"Robert, please don't misunderstand," the strange voice continued. "Our affair was not a hardship for me. I enjoyed every minute I was with you. You're a wonderful man, but you're Hillary's kind of man, not mine. Please be assured that I care very much about your political career and would never do anything to harm you."

But you have harmed me very much. I love you, Alexa, *oh, how I love you,* and for you my love was all a game?

"Alexa," he whispered softly, the soft whisper of love that he had whispered to her in bed, a whisper of love to a woman who existed somewhere, didn't she? He needed desperately to reach that lovely, loving woman now. *"Alexa."*

Oh, Robert, her loving heart answered in silent anguish. How she had loved the man who spoke to her so softly, his desperate need matching her own. How much she would need to believe, for the rest of her life, that that man had existed somewhere deep inside Senator Robert McAllister, a wonderful part of him that *had* loved her as she had loved him. Why couldn't *that* man have said a sad, loving, truthful farewell? She would never have betrayed him. Didn't he know that?

"I'm very sorry, Robert. Good-bye."

"It's over, Cat," Alexa told her little sister when she called the Riverside Drive apartment ten days later.

"Over?"

"Affairs with married men aren't destined to survive. I knew that going into it."

"Are you all right, Alexa?"

"Sure!" she answered brightly, even though with each passing day the bright cheeriness was more difficult to force, dimming despite her immense effort, and draining her energy so that now she actually felt ill. She was worse now than she had been ten days ago. The shock and numbness had faded, leaving her with pure, unrelenting pain. After a moment, she confessed softly, her voice flooded with tears, "No, Cat, I'm not all right. I'm very sad."

"Oh, Alexa. How can I help you?"

"You can simply remind me, whenever I begin to feel even the least bit sorry for myself, that I got precisely what I deserved."

"But I don't believe that!"

"I know," Alexa answered gratefully. From the very beginning of her affair, her little sister, like James, had cared only about her happiness.

"You loved him, Alexa, and love is right, not wrong. And . . . you never deserve to be sad."

"Thank you. It's just all so fresh. I guess what I need now is for a little—a lot of—time to pass." She sighed, and added, "And I need to get out of this town. I am very much looking forward to Christmas in Topeka."

"So am I."

"And then, beginning late next month, after we're done with *Pennsylvania Avenue* for another season, I may do something like wander around the world. I've thought about doing it before, but I've always had projects scheduled during the hiatus. Now I have no projects scheduled, and I even have an extra month off because we're not resuming production again until August. That gives me six months with nothing to do." *Nothing to do except what you've been promising yourself for years you were going to do: spend time getting to know Alexa.* She clamped down on a flicker of panic, the lazy yawn of a slumbering monster, and continued, "So, in six weeks I'll suddenly have plenty of time and space, both of which I need. But, right now, what I need most is James."

"James?" Catherine echoed softly. *But,* her heart began to protest until her brain intervened, *But what? But James is yours?* Hardly! He has never even kissed you, remember? He has just made you feel wonderful and special and so very happy. But that's because *he* is so wonderful and special—a wonderful, special man who has been looking out for the naive little sister of the beautiful sophisticated woman he has always loved. And now Alexa is free, and she wants him again,

294

and when confident dazzling Alexa beckons . . . "You need James?"

"Yes. I need him to escort me to the 'When You Wish Upon a Star' gala," Alexa answered casually, even though her need was not casual at all. Senator and Mrs. Robert McAllister would be at the gala this year, she was sure of it. Hillary would *want* to be there this year, to gloat and parade her triumph, and Robert really could not afford to miss the important event for the fourth year in a row. "It's this Saturday evening. I can't remember when James is planning to fly to Paris."

Catherine knew James's plans. She knew that beginning later tonight, he would be in New Orleans for four days; and that he was returning on Saturday, in time for dinner with her; and that on Sunday he was flying to Paris to spend the holidays with Arthur and Marion on L'île, and that, after Saturday night, she would probably never see him again—because following Christmas with her family in Topeka, she would travel to San Francisco, where, on New Year's Eve at the Opera House, she would make her professional debut.

James had asked her, more than once, if she was going to give him a copy of the itinerary for her eleven month booked-solid concert tour of North America and Europe. And he had talked to her, more than once, *so often,* about meeting her for dinner wherever she was. But Catherine hadn't dared believe that that would ever happen. She had only bravely prepared her heart to say good-bye to him at dinner this Saturday. And now even the farewell dinner would never happen, because Saturday night was when Alexa needed him.

"You haven't spoken to him?"

"Not yet. We played telephone tag this morning, and I've been on location all afternoon. I assume he'll call me tonight."

"Yes, I'm sure he will."

She just wanted to say good-bye to him. Good-bye, and thank you. She realized, as she wove hurriedly through the rush hour crowd, that she had forgotten the scarf she had knitted for him, and forgotten, too, the copy of the itinerary she had made for him, finally, just today. But if she was to catch him before he left for the airport, and perhaps she was already too late, she couldn't take the time to go back for either. No matter! He wouldn't need the itinerary now, and the scarf was unimportant, too, a sentimental memory of their midnight sail last summer. Maybe, some faraway day, she would send the scarf to him accompanied by a letter that would thank him more eloquently than she would ever be able to do in person.

"I'm Catherine Taylor," she told the receptionist who was obviously just preparing to leave for the day. "I wondered if I could see Mr. Sterling, if he's still here?"

"One moment, please." The receptionist pressed the single button that connected her phone to the one in his private office. "Ms. Taylor is here. Oh. OK. I'll send her right back."

James assumed his visitor would be Alexa. Perhaps her attempts to reach him this morning had been to announce that she had a free evening and was flying to New York to toast the festive season with him as they drank hot buttered rum and watched the iceskaters glide to the sound of Christmas carols in Rockefeller Center. As he waited for her, he prepared himself for her exasperation when she learned that he was just about to leave for LaGuardia. But the beautiful woman who appeared in his doorway wasn't the one who had greeted him last spring with the confident, provocative proposal for a swift and satisfying merger.

It was her little sister, not so confident, but in that lovely uncertainty oh-so-provocative.

"Catherine," he said with soft surprise. Smiling welcomingly at the uncertain sapphire, he walked over to her, and as he helped her remove her coat, he gently added, "Hi."

"Hi. Thank you." She felt a wonderful rush of warmth at his smile, and at the surprised dark blue eyes that seemed so happy to see her. It wasn't until he left her to hang her coat that she brought herself to quietly ask, "Have you spoken to Alexa?"

"No. She called earlier, but we missed." James finished hanging the coat and returned to her. "Why?"

"Her relationship is over."

"Oh," he said with quiet sympathy. He knew how devastating this would be for Alexa. He saw a reflection of that immense loss in her little sister's lovely worried eyes. "How is she?"

"Very sad. James, she needs you."

"I think she probably needs both of us."

"She needs you to escort her to a gala in Washington this Saturday night."

James knew that Catherine had never told her older sister about any of their dates. Alexa would have mentioned it to him if she had. That was fine with him, more than fine, wonderful. He loved the privacy of their relationship and was very happy to share it with no one but Catherine. But now . . .

"Did you tell Alexa that I already have plans for Saturday?"

"No. I thought, James, if you want to cancel our dinner, it's fine. I understand."

"What do you understand, Catherine?"

"I understand about you and Alexa. Now that she's free again . . ."

"You think that Alexa and I will pick up where we left off, as if nothing has changed?" he asked softly, his heart racing as he saw the lovely hope in her beautiful eyes at his question. I think there are some truths that need time before they can be told, she had said on a stormy afternoon, and he had agreed. But now, lovely Catherine, it is time, isn't it? "Is that what you want?"

"No," she whispered the brave and confident truth to the man who had been so careful not to rush her, so careful to allow all the choices of the heart to be hers. But the dark blue eyes weren't careful now. They told her, quite eloquently, and quite urgently, of his desire and his love. "No, James, that's not what I want."

"That's not what I want either, Catherine," he said very quietly. "You see, I am completely enchanted by Alexa's little sister."

"You are?"

"You know I am."

Her full, soft lips had never kissed before, but they knew by a deep, wonderful instinct how to greet the lips of the man she loved. The greeting was soft at first, the most tender of hellos, and then, soft still, and tender, and so welcoming, the kiss became warmer and deeper. Her delicate snow white fingers caressed their own wondrous hello, greeting his face and weaving gently into his coal black hair, and, in touching James, her talented fingers discovered a joy, a gift, that was far more magnificent than her magnificent music.

Their lips kissed hello, and then their bodies did, in a kiss that began gently, too, but became closer and closer, until her heart pounded against his chest, triggering the terrifying memory of the only other time he had held her. On that August night, her fluttering heart had sent a frantic message of starvation, and even though what he felt now were surely just the strong, confident heartbeats of joy and desire, James pulled away, just a little, to look at her. And what he saw was glistening sapphire desire, and then a brief flicker of surprise and disappointment that he had stopped the kiss, and then pure desire and happiness again. Catherine was healthy and fit, as was he.

Although we are both starving, he thought, a most wonderful hunger—for each other.

"I have wanted to kiss you for a very long time, Catherine."

"I've wanted you to."

"Have you?"

"Yes. For a very long time." She looked up at him and smiled. Her smile was lovely, innocent, and yet so seductive in its unashamed messages of desire. She whispered softly, "I need to be kissed again, James. It's already been too long between kisses."

"Far too long," he agreed with a soft laugh as his lips touched hers.

Then he was lost again in her lovely eager warmth, and he had no wish ever to be found, but . . .

"Oh, darling," he sighed softly, holding her close, his lips kissing her silky black hair as he spoke. "I have a plane to catch. I can't even take a later flight because we're having a strategy meeting the moment I arrive. I'll call you from New Orleans, a thousand times, and I will see you Saturday night." He found her eyes then and asked, "OK?"

"OK to you leaving me now for New Orleans, and to calling me a thousand times," she answered with soft joy. Her lovely blue eyes became thoughtful as she added quietly, "But Alexa needs you Saturday night. Could you come for brunch at the apartment on Sunday before your flight to Paris?"

"Of course I can," he replied gently, not questioning her decision about Saturday night, seeing from her beautiful eyes that it was a generous decision of love—for the sister whose life was not so happy now. He had to leave for the airport, soon, but he had to kiss her again, and he did, a good-bye kiss, reluctant and lingering, but a kiss that held the tender promise that soon, very soon, they would be kissing hello again. And then he really had to leave, but there was one last thing. "Catherine?"

"Yes?"

"I love you."

"Oh, James, I love you, too."

Chapter 18

Alexa had mentally rehearsed an angry tirade to deliver to James about the man for whom he had such great respect. But when he arrived at RoseCliff, and she saw his gentle concern, she just fell gratefully into his willingly offered arms. Because, more than anything, she needed to be held by someone who loved her.

"I'm so sorry, Alexa," he whispered as she curled against him.

"Me, too." She looked up at him, smiled a wobbly smile, and offered softly, "I won't say you didn't warn me."

"You know I hoped it would work out for you."

"I know." She lingered a moment longer in the luxurious shelter of his arms, and then with a sigh, dreading the evening that lay ahead, but knowing it was almost time to go, she pulled away. "Thank you for doing this tonight, James. I just don't have the energy to go by myself."

It was a quiet confession, but an enormous one, a symbol of how truly fragile she was. James knew she would dazzle at the gala, but now she was confessing to him what an effort it would be. Just to dazzle from a distance would require all of her precarious energy. She would have none left over to ward off all the men who would want to flirt with her. And men would want her tonight, perhaps more than ever, because on this night whose theme was "When You Wish Upon a Star," in her gown of soft emerald silk with her flowing golden hair, she was a romantic vision of dreams come true.

"I'll stick very close, Alexa."

"I was thinking . . ."

"Yes?"

"If you could hold my hand and not let go?"

"I can do that." James sealed the promise with a smile. Then, he asked gently, "Would you like to tell me about the bastard?"

"No. Thank you."

James kept his word. He held Alexa's hand and didn't let go. She drew strength from the strong hand that held hers as they wandered through the glittering sea of the famous and powerful, and she drew even more strength as they danced, their bodies moving together gracefully with chaste but intimate familiarity.

I can do this, Alexa thought. I can make it through tonight even if Robert is here. I'm sure of it.

"James? Alexa?"

The sound of Hillary's voice, and then the sight of Robert and Hillary slow dancing just a few feet away, instantly shattered her foolish confidence. But still, *somehow*, with her hand in James's, Alexa crossed the dance floor to greet Senator and Mrs. McAllister. And somehow, miraculously, when she spoke her voice sounded cheerful and gay.

"How lovely to see you, Hillary." She smiled pleasantly at Hillary and then, holding the smile, she turned to Robert. "Hello, Senator."

"Hello, Alexa," he replied quietly, even though his heart screamed with pain. There were no protective scars yet on the wound created by Alexa, and Robert wondered if there ever would be. After a moment, he shifted his gaze from the woman he loved to his friend. "Hello, James."

"Hello, Robert. Hillary."

"You finally made it to the gala," Alexa observed lightly. Then, like a gracious hostess, because after all this was *Pennsylvania Avenue's* charity ball, she added, "I'm so glad."

"So are we," Hillary answered with matching graciousness. "And it's so nice to see you, James. Are you still planning to join Marion and Arthur on L'île for the holidays?"

"That's the plan. I fly to Paris tomorrow and on Tuesday we'll set sail from Nice."

"Wonderful," Hillary murmured, although what was wonderful, she thought, was the way James held Alexa's hand, and the way they had been slow dancing together. The stunning couple had drawn stares, all admiring—except for Robert's, which had been a gaze of pure pain. After a moment, casually hiding her private hope of revealing even more evidence of Alexa's faithlessness, she asked, "Will you be going to L'île, too, Alexa?"

303

"No. I only have five days off. I'm going to spend Christmas in Topeka with my family."

"How nice. Well, James, please give Marion and Arthur our love. And," she added softly, "please remember to tell Princess Natalie how delighted I am with my romantic Castille wedding ring."

Hillary believed she had won. She believed it before the gala, and as she and Robert drove back to Arlington afterward, she believed it even more. His foolish affair with Alexa was over. Her plan had worked perfectly. She had won . . . and Robert looked as if he had lost everything. That would change, she assured herself. In time, this unfortunate episode in their marriage would be long forgotten, *assuming* that the pain in his dark eyes wasn't simply anguish that he and Alexa would be separated for five months.

"Robert?"

"Hmmmm?" he answered distractedly, even though he was a little relieved to be pulled away from the tormenting images of James and Alexa that had been blazing in his mind. Some of the images were simply scenes he had witnessed— Alexa teasing James, flirting with James, dancing with James. But there were other images, far worse—Alexa making love with James, last night, tonight, all the nights he hadn't been with her this fall. He had seen tonight, in his friend's steady untroubled gaze, that James had not known about their affair. Did that mean that, all this time,

304

Alexa been playing with them both? "Did you say something, Hillary?"

"You're obviously suffering, Robert, and I can't stand watching it. If it's going to be this painful for you to be apart from whoever she is for the next five months, well . . . my father and I *will* survive."

"It's not a problem."

"No?"

"No. The affair is over."

"The married man was Robert?" James demanded angrily as he drove her back to RoseCliff shortly before midnight.

"What makes you say that?"

"Don't play with me, Alexa."

"Was it so terribly obvious?"

"No," he admitted, his tone softening as he heard the hopelessness in her question, as if now she had lost her ability as an actress in addition to losing everything else. "I don't think it would have been obvious to anyone who wasn't holding a hand that suddenly became ice. And then," he teased gently, "there was the small matter of fingernails that were digging for some mysterious treasure buried very deep in my palm."

"I'm sorry."

"I wish you'd told me."

"I was afraid you wouldn't approve."

"I might have questioned your motives, given your feelings about Hillary."

"I didn't have any motives," she said quietly. "I just loved him, that's all."

"And you still do."

"Yes, James, and I still do."

James warmed milk for her while she showered and changed into a new nightgown, fluffy, modest, never worn for a lover. He watched her drink the milk and then tucked her into her bed, gently refusing her halfhearted plea, a cry of loneliness far more than passion, that he join her.

After she fell asleep, he drove to Inverness.

I was afraid you wouldn't approve, Alexa had said in defense of not telling him about her affair with Robert. Would she approve of his love for her little sister? he wondered. Probably not, at least not right away. Alexa would worry about his restlessness, his need for challenges and privacy, his own admission that he doubted he could ever fall in love. In short, she would worry about Catherine's happiness.

You don't need to worry, he would assure her when the time came. No one cares more about Catherine's happiness than I. James wondered when he would speak those words to Alexa. It didn't matter. For now, for as long as Catherine wanted it to be that way, their love was secret, a private treasure to be shared with no one but each other.

"Did I awaken you, darling?" he asked softly, when he called her from Inverness, as he had told her he would, and as she had wanted him to, no matter how late.

"No. I was practicing. How was the evening?"

"It was OK. I'm glad you'll be together at

Christmas. Right now, Alexa very much needs to be with people who love her. Especially her little sister." James expected a soft reply, but he only heard surprising silence, and finally asked gently, "Catherine?"

"Yes?"

"Do you know what I need?"

"No, what?"

"What I need, my love, is to see you as much as possible between our brunch tomorrow morning and the time I put you on your flight to Topeka Tuesday afternoon."

"James," she whispered with quiet disbelief and joy. "But . . ."

"It's just about breakfast time in Paris. I think I'll call my parents right now and arrange to meet them Wednesday on L'île instead of sailing with them from Nice."

"Do you think they'll mind?"

"Not at all." If they knew the reason, he thought lovingly, they would be overjoyed.

James and Catherine had presents for each other, gifts of love that had been in the making long before they had spoken their love aloud, because they had both known about their love for a very long time.

"Merry Christmas, darling," he said as he handed her a small gift-wrapped box. The beautiful wrapping, gold foil adorned with delicate satin ribbons in all the colors of a rainbow, signified a gift of jewels from Castille.

"Oh," she whispered when she saw the earrings, two perfectly matched sapphires the rare and precious color of her eyes. "James, they're beautiful."

James looked from the brilliant sapphires to the brilliant sapphire eyes and saw that the search he had commissioned Castille's Fifth Avenue jeweller to undertake had been worth it: the flawless gems perfectly matched her flawless eyes. As he smiled at her beautiful eyes, he saw a small but unmistakable ripple of uncertainty in the shimmering blue.

"Catherine?"

"They're magnificent. Thank you." Her eyes left his and fell for a thoughtful moment on the stunning earrings. She touched the precious stones with her delicate fingers; but instead of putting them on, she placed the small velvet box on the table and reached for the gift-wrapped package for him. Meeting his eyes again, and smiling softly, she said, "This is for you. It's not so magnificent . . ."

But the scarf Catherine had made was far more magnificent, James thought, and far more valuable than the sapphires. She had sketched the scene herself—*Night Wind* gliding across the sea on a shimmering moonbeam of gold; and then, the needles dancing in her delicate virtuoso fingers, she had knitted it.

"Catherine . . ." he faltered, truly at a loss for words.

"Do you like it?"

"I love it, darling. I love it."

"I'm so glad."

"But you, my love, are uncertain about the

earrings," he said gently. "They are very returnable, Catherine. I'll take them back tomorrow."

"Oh, no, James. I'm not uncertain about the earrings at all. It's just . . ." She frowned, sighed softly, and admitted quietly, "It's just that there's something I need to tell you about me . . . and Alexa."

Good, James thought. At last, my lovely Catherine, you are going to trust me with the troubling secrets of your heart. "Tell me, darling."

"I will. In a moment. I have to get something from my bedroom first."

As he waited, James thought about what he would hear: Catherine's version of the history of the Taylor sisters. He didn't expect to be terribly surprised, he knew Alexa's version after all, but when Catherine returned from her bedroom, James was truly stunned. He watched in silent amazement as her trembling fingers positioned a dazzling sapphire necklace around the velvet box that still held the earrings he had given her. The necklace and earrings looked like a set, perfectly matched, made for each other, *made for Catherine.*

"This necklace belonged to my mother," she began, speaking first to the necklace she wished she had never seen. Then she looked bravely at him and said softly, "I never knew my mother, James. She gave me away when I was a week old. Alexa isn't really my sister."

Catherine told him the simple truths very quickly. And then, for the next hours, she told him about her complicated and confusing emotions: her bewildering pain, her frantic desperation as she felt herself being torn away from Jane and Alexander, her love for Alexa and her great fear of telling her the truth, and her deep bitterness toward the mother who had abandoned her.

"Oh, Catherine, I'm so sorry that this has caused you such sadness."

"I'm better now, James, much better. I felt so lost at first, and so alone and afraid. Do you remember when we were sailing that night and you told me I should call my parents to tell them I missed them?"

"I remember that you had been thinking about calling them anyway."

"Yes, well, but it helped me to hear that you thought they would want to know."

"And they did."

"Yes. I guess. I never actually told them I missed them, but I'm sure they know. We've talked quite a few times since then, and each time I feel closer. I haven't seen them since May."

"But you will in two days. And?"

"And I'm a little afraid." She paused, and then smiled a lovely smile of hope. "But mostly, I'm very excited."

"They love you," James said softly, confidently. "And so does Alexa."

"Oh, I hope so. But, James, it's still too soon for me to tell her the truth. I want to tell her, someday, but I need to wait until it feels more safe."

James nodded in silent agreement that she wait, but his concern was for Alexa, not Catherine. Alexa's love for Catherine wouldn't change, he knew, but Alexa was so very fragile now. She had just lost Robert, and even though the truth about Catherine shouldn't feel like a loss, he knew that right now to Alexa it would.

"I'm so glad you felt it was safe to tell me."

"Even though you thought you knew who I was and now . . . ?"

"I know who you are, Catherine. I have always known. You're the woman I love with all my heart."

"Oh, James . . ."

His lips found hers, as they had many times already on this snowy afternoon, but now the kiss was different, more tender, more passionate, and more deep . . . a kiss without secrets or shadows . . . a kiss of boundless forever love.

"Tomorrow, darling, I'll return the earrings," he whispered, finally pulling away from the kiss because suddenly kissing Catherine had become too much, *and not enough.*

"Oh, no, James."

She reached then for the velvet box and removed the magnificent earrings. They were designed for pierced ears, as hers were, but because of their great value, the tiny solid gold backings screwed, not slid, onto the posts.

"There," she said when her delicate fingers had finished fastening the brilliant gems. "I know I won't ever wear the necklace, James, but I'll wear my earrings always."

"They aren't actually for every day, do you think?" he teased gently.

"No," she admitted. "I guess not."

"I thought you could wear them for concerts."

"Yes. For concerts . . . and for kissing . . . and

for making love," she said softly. "Make love to me, James."

"Oh, Catherine, there's no hurry. We've just discovered kissing. I think I could kiss you forever."

"Forever? Just kissing?"

"No," James confessed softly. "But . . ."

"We have these two precious, private days, James, and we love each other. Why wouldn't we spend this time sharing everything we can share, all our love, all our joy?"

"Why wouldn't we," he echoed gently as he smiled at her beautiful innocent eyes. So innocent . . .

"I've been on the pill for over two months," Catherine said, interpreting, incorrectly, the sudden worry on his handsome face.

"I wasn't thinking about that. It's just that I don't want to hurt you, not for an instant, and . . ."

"How could our loving possibly hurt me?"

It was all new for Catherine, and for James making love with the woman he loved was all new, too. They discovered each other with wondrous joy, treasuring each discovery, marveling at their desire and their love. Catherine trembled at the patient and gentle exploration of his loving hands and tender lips; and she gave everything to him, every gift she had to give, hiding no secrets of her lush and lovely snow white body, unashamed of her passion for him.

When it was time for both of them, when they needed to share all that could be shared, a loving frown of worry touched his handsome face. She

312

greeted his frown with a soft smile, and then she greeted him, arching to him, welcoming him with confident joy.

"I love you, Catherine," he whispered. *Oh, I don't want to hurt you.*

"I love you, James." *How could our loving possibly hurt me?*

It didn't hurt. There wasn't pain, just a surprising tearing heat that was quickly, so quickly, forgotten, because then they were one, as close as they could be, and that was the greatest wonder of all.

For a timeless moment, neither moved, nor spoke, nor even breathed. They simply gazed at each other with silent, reverent wonder as their loving eyes eloquently acknowledged their joy.

They moved again finally, because they had to, urged on by their magnificent crescendoing desires . . . and they spoke, the most tender whispers of love . . . and they breathed, too . . . but soon, and over and over, James and Catherine were breathless again.

During those two days and nights of exquisite intimacy and passion, they loved, and made love, and made wonderful plans for their love. They poured over Catherine's itinerary, city by fabulous city, and city by city, they planned where they would dine, and the sights they would see, and the walks they would take. It seemed to Catherine that he planned to be with her in every city, every week, and when she mentioned that to him, a loving tease filled with hope, he promised that

313

he would arrange his work so that he could be with her as often as possible.

"Maybe I should stop working altogether," he suggested softly, "and simply become a Catherine Taylor 'groupie.'"

"That would be wonderful."

"Yes, but as a 'groupie' I would expect to hear your performances. And," he added quietly, "the one time I heard you play, I thought my presence distracted you."

"Oh, yes, it did."

"Would it now?"

"I don't know. Shall we see?"

She played Mozart's "Sonata in C Major," one of the pieces she would perform on New Year's Eve in San Francisco. As he listened, James began to appreciate the true measure of her extraordinary gift. It *is* a gift, he realized, a gift that she so generously shares with her audience, graciously inviting whoever is listening to journey with her on her magnificent emotional voyage. He was traveling with her now, as first they paid a soft, delicate visit to hope, and then, in a cascading journey that felt like a waterfall, they spilled down to sadness, and then they flew, dancing, leaping, soaring to joy, and . . .

And suddenly the stunning journey stopped.

"Oh, Catherine," James whispered sadly, "it does distract you to have me listen."

"I think it's something I can conquer in a concert hall filled with hundreds of patrons. But today, James," she said softly, "if I'm over here playing, and you're over there listening, then I'm not where I should be."

"Then come to me, my love."

As Catherine left the piano to be in his loving arms, she realized the truly immense signficance of what she had done. Today she was choosing James over her music. And she knew, without a doubt, without a fear, that given the choice between her music and James, she would choose James . . . always.

"I'm going out to get us some croissants," he announced at nine-thirty on Tuesday morning. He added lovingly, "I admit it's a fairly transparent excuse to get to wear my scarf."

"I see," Catherine laughed softly as she kissed him good-bye.

She wondered, as she closed the apartment door behind him, if the real reason he was leaving her, if only for fifteen minutes, was to begin to prepare them both for the almost two-week separation that would start at four this afternoon. They had already promised each other, over and over, that they would never spend another Christmas apart; but neither had suggested altering plans for this Christmas. This was a special and important Christmas for both of them—a private time alone with the parents they loved.

When the phone rang five minutes after James left, Catherine was certain it would be him, calling on the pretext of asking if she wanted cream cheese or raspberry croissants, but really calling to tell her something she felt too—that it had only been five minutes and already he missed her desperately.

"Hello?" she answered with a soft loving laugh.

"Is this Catherine Taylor?"

"Yes."

"Catherine, this is Elliot Archer. We met last summer at Inverness."

"Yes, of course. Hello, Elliot."

"I'm afraid I have some very bad news. About two hours ago, there was an explosion on the boat that the Sterlings were sailing from Nice to L'île."

"Oh, no."

"The explosion was probably caused by a leak in the gas line to the stove." Elliot paused briefly to fight the sudden rush of emotion that swept through him. "It would have been impossible for anyone to survive the blast. Robert McAllister suggested that we call you before notifying Alexa, in case you'd like to be with her when she is told about James."

"About James?"

"Arthur and Marion have been found. The divers are still searching for James, but as I said, it would have been impossible for anyone to survive the blast."

"James wasn't on the sailboat, Elliot."

"Robert saw him in Washington Saturday night and James told him then that he was leaving the next day for Paris."

"Yes, but he didn't leave then after all. He's still in New York. He was going to fly to Nice this afternoon."

"Are you sure?"

"Yes."

"Thank God." After a moment, Elliot continued quietly, "Well. I'd better let him know."

"I'll tell him, Elliot. I'll tell him and have him call you."

"Oh. All right, Catherine. I'll be in my office. He knows the number."

After the conversation ended, Elliot realized it had happened once again. Once again, Catherine Taylor had triggered his long-ago memories of Isabelle Castille. In August, the memories had been triggered by the astonishing physical resemblance, but now it was Catherine's great inner beauty that reminded him of Isabelle. It had been Princess Isabelle, after all, who had flown to London to tell him of Geneviève's death. She hadn't needed to, of course, but she had, because she knew how devastating the news would be for him, and she had wanted to help him with his grief, if she possibly could.

And now Elliot heard in Catherine's soft voice the same gentle wish, a wish to help James, if she could.

"Oh, James."

"What's the matter, darling?"

"It's your parents. Oh, James, there was an explosion on the sailboat."

"Catherine?"

"They were killed," she said very softly, very gently. She saw his shock, and even though he didn't ask the questions, she knew he needed to hear more words, as she had needed to, more proof. She explained quietly, "Elliot says it was probably the gas stove. He called here, thinking you were with them, wanting me to fly to Washington to be there when Alexa was told. Oh, my love, I'm so sorry."

Catherine's lovely eyes glistened with tears, and as the numbing waves of shock began to ebb, James felt moist heat in his own eyes. Tears were so unfamiliar to him that he couldn't remember how long it had been since he had felt them; and so unfamiliar, too, that his first impulse was to hide them.

Hide his tears from the woman he loved?

No, he thought as the tears spilled freely. I do not need to hide my tears from Catherine.

"Mother was probably making her famous hot chocolate," he said quietly an hour later.

Catherine answered as she had answered all his words and tears—with love. She had held him, and she had tenderly kissed his tear-dampened cheeks, and now she smiled softly, as he did, as they remembered lovely Marion.

It was another hour before James called Elliot. Both men focused on details, not emotion; a brief review of the facts that Elliot knew, and a brief discussion, too, of the plans for the memorial service that would be held two days before Christmas. The arrangements for the service, and for the reception to follow, were already being made by the ever-efficient Office of Protocol.

"I'll fly to Washington sometime after four this afternoon, Elliot. I'll call you when I arrive."

"After four?" Catherine asked as soon as he replaced the receiver.

"After I put you on the flight to Topeka."

"I'm going with you to Washington."

"No."

"Yes!"

"No. Catherine, listen to me. You need to be with your parents." His words were stopped by a rush of emotion. How he wished he had told his own parents his reason for not sailing with them to L'île! If he had told them, then perhaps, as his mother had been making the hot chocolate, they might have been joyfully speculating about their black-haired, blue-eyed grandchildren laughing and frolicking at Inverness. James had planned to tell Marion and Arthur about his love for Catherine when he saw them. But now it was too late, and his voice was hoarse with impassioned emotion as he continued, "Darling, being with your parents is more important now than ever, don't you think?"

"I will be with them, James, in a few days. Maybe we both will be," she added softly. "But right now I need to be with you."

"You are with me, Catherine. You are always with me. All I need is to be able to talk to you, darling, and I will call you every night. That's all I need, or want." James smiled at her worried sapphire eyes. "Besides, even though I need no more than to be able to talk to you, Elliot will be there, and Robert and Brynne."

"And Alexa."

"She needs to be in Topeka, too."

"She will be, but not until the twenty-fourth."

Three hours after James kissed her good-bye, Catherine saw the beloved parents she hadn't seen since May. She had such vivid memories of them, a lifetime of seeing their loving faces. But now, even from a distance, they looked different, less vivid than she had remembered, and a little faded and worn.

Was it that they were older? Had the past seven months aged them so? she wondered sadly. No, she realized as she drew closer. The difference she saw wasn't age at all. It was the expression of uncertainty in their gentle eyes.

Uncertainty? About her? About her love?

Catherine rushed to Jane and Alexander then, and as she did she soared over the deep abyss that had separated her from her parents for so long. By the time she reached them, she was far far beyond the treacherous abyss, and she whispered over and over as she hugged them, "Oh, Mom, oh Daddy, I love you both so very much."

Chapter 19

The memorial service and reception were over, and only those closest to James remained at Inverness. They—Alexa and Elliot, and Robert and Hillary, and Brynne and Stephen—sat in the elegant great room with him; and on this sad day, all petty wars and all bitter betrayals were put aside, and all eyes filled only with honest emotional messages of grief for the loss of Marion and Arthur.

"There's something you all need to know," Elliot said.

"What is it?" James asked tiredly. He was exhausted. He had uttered a thousand gracious thank-yous to those who had come to offer their condolences, and all he wanted now was to call Catherine. He had missed her terribly in the past few days, but he had not for one moment wished that she had been in Washington during this time of such sadness.

"The explosion on the sailboat wasn't caused by a leak in the gas line, James. It was caused by a bomb."

For a stunned moment, no one spoke, but the thoughts that suddenly swirled in their minds were remarkably the same. Marion and Arthur's death hadn't been simply an accident, an inexplicable tragedy caused by some unknown and whimsical fate.

Someone had known that Marion and Arthur would die.

Someone had wanted it.

Someone had caused it.

"A bomb?" Brynne echoed finally.

"How long have you known, Elliot?" Robert asked.

"A few hours. We're going to have to let the press know tomorrow, so I wanted you all to know tonight."

"Has anyone claimed responsibility?"

"No. Not yet."

"What *do* you know, Elliot?"

"Very little, James."

"Because the trail is cold now."

"No. The explosion was investigated as possible sabotage from the very beginning. The best agents in Europe have been working on it. So far, we have nothing. The sailboat had been moored in one of the busiest marinas on the Côte d'Azur, lots of traffic, lots of tourists, many people with potential access."

The room fell silent again, and again the thoughts of the assembled group were remarkably the same, drifting to the summer evening only four months before when Marion had raved about L'île. How eagerly she had anticipated her return visit to the romantic island of rainbows, and how her dark blue eyes had sparkled as she had wished aloud that some day, despite the busy schedules of their successful lives, they could all find time to meet for a holiday on L'île.

But now Marion's wish would never come true.

Because someone had decided it was time for Marion Sterling to die.

"I think you all should go now," James said quietly. In the silence, he had stood up and walked to the windows, and now his quiet words were spoken to the dark gray winter sky. After a moment, he added, "It's getting dark and the wind seems very strong. There may be a storm on the way."

"Maybe we should all stay here tonight, James," Brynne offered.

"No. Thank you," he whispered tightly. "No."

James's need for privacy was so obvious that eventually they all complied. Alexa was the last to leave, kissing him softly on the cheek before she returned to RoseCliff to finish packing for her early morning flight to Topeka.

The winds were too strong and too dangerous, and the vast blackness of the winter night was broken only by a thin sliver of moon, but still he sailed. And as he guided *Night Wind* through the treacherous darkness, he struggled, too, with the dark and treacherous emotions that swirled within him. The emotions were new and very powerful. Without even a whisper of mercy, they violently trampled all the gentler emotions of his heart, crushing them, proclaiming them gone forever—they had to be!—because everything had changed.

James wore the beautiful scarf Catherine had made for him, and as *Night Wind* raced across the inky sea, he reached to touch the soft wool, as if reaching to touch her, needing her soft warmth. But he couldn't feel the softness or the warmth. His fingers were numb, chilled to ghostly whiteness by the icy wind, the delicate nerve-endings unable to feel anything but frigid pain.

His most gentle emotions were crushed by powerful new ones . . . and warmth and softness seemed far beyond his reach . . . and a deep ominous voice shouted above the howling winter wind that his greatest loss was yet to come.

"I know about the bomb, James," Catherine said gently when he called, finally, five hours after she had learned the devastating news from Alexa. She had tried during those five hours to reach him, but there had been no answer at Inverness. "Were you sailing?"

"Yes."

"James?" she asked softly, urging him to talk to her as he had every other night, sharing his emotions, his sadness, his loss.

"I won't be able to be in San Francisco for your debut after all, Catherine."

"It's too soon to know that for sure, isn't it?" she asked quietly, fighting ominous ripples of panic as she felt him pulling away from her. She fought the ripples, and very bravely she began to fight *for him*. She continued softly, "In the meantime, I'm coming to Washington. My visit with my parents has been wonderful but—"

"No," he interjected harshly. Then, hearing his own harshness, he added gently, "No, darling. Elliot and I will be going to France."

He was going, that was decided, although he knew he needed Elliot's help if his trip was going to have any value.

"Oh! When?"

"Hopefully tomorrow."

"Oh." He was already so very far away. She reached for him with a whisper of love, "James . . ."

"Oh, Catherine," he answered softly. "I need to go to France. I'm not sure when I'll be back, but my love, no matter what, I will call you in your suite at the Fairmont after your dazzling debut. At midnight on New Year's Eve, OK?"

"OK. James?"

"Yes?"

"Somehow, this will be all right, won't it?"

James heard the uncertainty in her voice, and

he knew that what she was really asking was if *they* would be all right, if their gentle love would survive the ravages of his rage.

He knew his lovely Catherine was asking for a promise.

And James didn't make promises he couldn't keep.

"I'll call you, darling, on New Year's Eve."

"I'm going to France with you," James said as he entered Elliot's office, unannounced, at eight the following morning.

"I'm not going to France, James."

"*What?*"

"I told you last night. The best agents in Europe are investigating."

"You're an expert—*the* expert—on terrorism."

"And I promise you that once we have any data, even the slightest clue, I will become intimately involved. But there's nothing yet. You know—at least you *should* know because I loved your parents very much—that if my participation in the field would help I would have been on a plane long ago."

"Yes, I do know that, Elliot," James replied quietly. "So, all we can do is wait?"

"Wait for what, James?" Elliot knew the answer to his question. He knew the wishes that swirled in James's heart; and he knew, too, that James might not speak them. So he spoke them for him. "Wait until the terrorists are found and then murder them in cold blood?"

"Right now that sounds very good," James

325

admitted quietly, deeply troubled by his own bloodthirstiness and very relieved that Elliot seemed to understand.

"Right now it sounds very good to me, too. But I know about the intoxication of revenge. You become convinced somehow that there will be pleasure in it. And, perhaps even worse, you begin to believe that everything will be better after. But nothing is better, and that makes the emptiness even greater." Elliot sighed softly. "Revenge changes nothing, James. Your loss is still the same, still as great, still as irrevocable. Revenge doesn't help the pain, and it can cause great harm by tainting the memory of those you loved with hatred and rage."

As James listened to Elliot's quiet and impassioned words, he realized how little he really knew him. James had always known *how* Elliot had chosen to spend his life—never marrying, in constant danger, risking life and defying death with casual calm—but now, for the first time, he realized there must have been an intensely personal and emotional reason *why* he had made such a choice.

"Elliot?"

"I know whereof I speak, James." Elliot quietly acknowledged the existence of a reason, but the finality of his tone closed the subject.

"I have to do something, Elliot. I have to be involved."

"I don't need more agents, and even if I did I sure as hell wouldn't let you anywhere near this investigation." Elliot held up his hand, stopping James's protest. "I'm not going to license you to kill, James, but I—this country—could use your help."

"My help?"

"Your knowledge of international law coupled with your skill and finesse in negotiating would make your services very valuable to the State Department."

"Was there something specific you had in mind?"

"If it were entirely up to me, I'd send you to Central America with the team that's going back down in the middle of January. The cease-fire dialogue has reached an impasse—again—and I think we need a new face at the negotiating table. However, there are any number of equally critical cease-fire and treaty negotiations, not to mention the hostage situation, on-going throughout the world, and it might be decided that you'd be of greater value elsewhere."

"You seem quite confident that this is something I could do."

"I am *absolutely* confident that it is. Except for the modestness of the surroundings, and the relatively small amount you would be paid as a government consultant, I don't think you'd notice a great difference between this and the work you've always done. The principles that govern negotiations between nations, James, are virtually identical to those governing negotiations among billion-dollar corporations."

"Money, territory, and power?"

"Yes. Money, territory, and power. We use those three as currency—we have to—but in so doing we hope to secure far more elusive and far more valuable treasures."

"Like peace and freedom," James offered quietly.

"Like peace and freedom," Elliot echoed with matching quiet.

The idea of working as a negotiator for the government appealed to James very much. If there was really something that he could do that might curb terrorism and insure a world in which loving couples could always sail in complete safety to paradise islands, he would gladly do it. And there was something else, far less valiant, that appealed, too. He and Elliot would be working together, and Elliot would keep him informed about the investigation into his parents' murder, and someday he would look into the evil eyes of whoever had willed their death, and if this bloodthirstiness still churned within him . . .

"I'm very interested, Elliot."

"Good. This really hadn't occurred to you before, had it?"

"No. Why?"

"I had always assumed that your work, especially since it so frequently has involved international conglomerates, was part of a very smart plan to prepare you to be Secretary of State when Robert becomes President. Your parents didn't think it was, and I guess they were right."

"You discussed this with them?"

"With them, and with the people who have asked me repeatedly when I was planning to recruit you."

"But you said nothing to me."

"No, because there's another rather critical difference between this work and what you've done in boardrooms, James. This can be extremely dangerous. You can, and will be, face to face with some of world's most volatile people; and you will be on their turf, in some of the world's most unstable places."

"So you were protecting me. And my parents," James added softly. *And now it is they who have been murdered.* The thought swept him swiftly back to the unspeakable crime itself, and he asked, almost urgently, "Do you really have no idea who is responsible for the bomb, Elliot?"

"None. Calls claiming responsibility will start pouring in as soon as word gets out that it was a bomb, but those late calls are usually simply opportunistic. Any legitimate claim should have come in by now." He frowned, then added quietly, "I don't know, James, somehow this feels personal."

"Personal?"

"Yes. An attack intended to make a political statement against the United States would have been staged in Paris, in or near the embassy, not while your father was on vacation, and especially not with your mother on board. This feels more like a vendetta to me, very personal, something like a disgruntled—and psychopathic—embassy employee."

"I was supposed to be on board, too, Elliot," James reminded him, his words causing a new anguish. *What if. . .* "What if I was the intended target?"

"That's something you and I need to discuss,

although I think it's extremely unlikely. You're so accessible here. Why assume the unnecessary risk of planting a bomb in a busy marina halfway around the world? I honestly don't think that you were the target. However, I still need to know what negotiations you've handled over the last couple of years, and, more importantly, your current projects."

"There's nothing current. I wrapped up a deal last Saturday in New Orleans and have a stack of proposals on my desk that I was going to look at in January." James frowned as he remembered how he had planned to screen the proposals. He would have looked for those that were challenging, of course, but he would have had Catherine's concert tour itinerary on his desk and would have made decisions that would have permitted him to be with her as often as possible.

The memory came with great pain, because James knew now, already, that all the wonderful plans he and Catherine had made for their love would never happen. He knew now, already, that he had to say good-bye to her and their magical love. Her world was, and always should be, a gentle world of love and joy; and for now, and perhaps forever, the world in which he was compelled to live was an angry world of murder and terror and revenge; and his ugly world belonged nowhere near her lovely one. And for now, and perhaps forever, he had to devote his time and energy to that harsh and tormented world, not to creating a quiet and gentle life of love with Catherine.

"James?"

"Sorry," he answered, apologizing for his distracted silence. Remembering what they had been discussing, he observed quietly, "You didn't mention last night that you would be needing information about my work."

"I knew you would be here this morning."

James nodded solemnly. "Yes. I am here, Elliot. And I have no outstanding projects. So, I'm available to go to Central America, or wherever, in January."

"I think this might be a very good time to take that sailing trip around the world you've always talked about."

"You know I can't do that. You know I have to do something."

"Yes," Elliot answered softly. "I know. OK. I need to talk to a few people. As soon as I've done that, I'll give you a call."

"Good. In the meantime, I'll get the information you need from my office."

"OK. Oh, and James, we need to see the letters of condolence you receive. The ones from Europe are obviously of greatest interest, but I'd like to have all of them screened."

"All right."

"Has anything arrived yet from Prince Alain?"

"I honestly don't know. I haven't looked."

Catherine sat by the telephone in her suite at the Fairmont, waiting for his midnight call, watching the hands of her clock move so slowly toward twelve. The knock on the door didn't register at first, and when it did, she moved to

331

open it reluctantly. It would be a bouquet of winter roses and a brief message of apology . . .

But it was the man she loved, his blue eyes dark-circled, his beloved face pale and drawn. James was here, now, but Catherine was very certain that he hadn't been in the audience at her concert this evening. She would have known, and she would have left the stage, in the middle of her dazzling performance, to go to him. He must have known that. That must have been why he had stayed away.

"Oh," she breathed as she gently touched the taut skin beneath his eyes with her delicate and loving fingers. "Oh, you're here."

Catherine led him into her suite and into her bed, and James followed, so willingly, as she led him to the magical place of peace and joy that was their love. He had believed that that gentle, fragile place was gone, trampled by the monstrous emotions that raged within him now. But for one night of exquisite intimacy and passion, the monsters were still, the nightmares were banished, and the churning restlessness was calmed . . . and there was only the gentle tenderness of their love.

"Good morning," she said softly when she walked into the living room of her suite and found him standing by the window.

"Good morning," he answered gently, turning away from the bright blue splendor of the first day of the New Year to the far more magnificent bright blue splendor of her eyes.

"Are you leaving so soon?" He was fully

dressed, and she was in her robe, her silky black hair softly tangled from their night of love.

"Yes. Darling, I only came to say good-bye."

"Good-bye?" Catherine echoed softly, even though part of her had sensed, in the intense emotion of his loving, that that was what he had been telling her.

"Yes. Good-bye," James answered quietly. Then he began to explain, slowly, gently, wanting her to understand, as he did, why he *had* to say good-bye to her and their love. "Their death—their murder—has changed me, Catherine. I'm angry, and restless, and consumed by ugly yet very powerful thoughts and emotions. I don't know if I could conquer my rage even if I tried, but the truth is, my love, that as painful—and even terrifying—as the emotions are, I don't want to force them away. I don't want to ever feel calm or complacent about what was done to my parents."

"I don't want to ever feel complacent about what was done to them either, James. Their death has changed me, too. I'm angry, too."

"Do you want to find whoever killed them and point a gun at his heart and pull the trigger and watch him die?"

"No," she answered softly. "And I can't believe that's what you want, not really."

"It is what I want, Catherine. Really. Believe it," James said quietly. It was the truth, such an ugly truth. Surely now he would see sad comprehension on her beautiful face. Surely now she would understand that his monstrous thoughts and emotions—and, perhaps, someday his deeds—had no place in her gentle lovely world. But James didn't see comprehension. He only saw love.

"Is that where you're going, James? To find whoever planted the bomb?"

"No. That's Elliot's job, although he has promised to keep me informed. In the meantime, I'm going to work as a negotiator for the State Department. Maybe there's something I can do that will help prevent a similar tragedy from occurring to someone else. My intentions aren't terribly noble, Catherine, I just have to do something. It's my need as much as anything."

"I understand why you have to do that, James," she said softly, and then, more softly, "But I don't understand why you're saying goodbye."

"Because, Catherine, I'm no longer the man I want to be for you, or for our love. All my gentleness is gone."

"Your gentleness wasn't gone last night."

"No, but I wonder if I was only borrowing from you. Maybe, my darling, if I clung to you the restless rage would be quieted for a while. But it would come back eventually, and eventually my bitterness and anger would consume us both. I love you far too much, Catherine, to let that happen."

"You can't love someone too much."

"Oh, yes, darling, you can. I want your life to be filled with joy, not with nightmares and hatred and rage. I don't want this unhappiness for you, Catherine. Don't you understand?"

As she gazed at the man she would always love

with all her heart, she tried to understand. But she couldn't. How could this be a reason to end their love?

"And would you leave me, James, if you were dying? To spare me that unhappiness?"

"I'm not dying, Catherine."

Yes you are! her heart cried. You are dying— your gentle loving heart is dying—and you have decided not to share that pain and sadness with me. Because you want only joy and happiness for me, but . . .

"But what about what I want, James?" she asked suddenly, urgently. "Doesn't that matter?"

Once he had vowed, a most solemn promise of love, to do only and always what Catherine wanted. All the choices of the heart would be hers, he had promised. She wanted their love still, despite everything. But it was not what he wanted for her. And now, very softly, very quietly, James broke his solemn vow.

"No, Catherine, it doesn't matter."

There had been confusion and uncertainty on Catherine's beautiful face when she had asked her urgent question. But now, as she heard his quiet and resolute answer, the confusion and uncertainty vanished, and he saw comprehension . . . *at last.*

"I trusted you with all my secrets, James, all my anger and all my pain, but you don't trust my love enough to share your sadness with me."

"It's not a matter of trust."

"No," she agreed softly, sadly. "It's a matter of love. You never really loved me."

"Oh, Catherine, I loved you. I will always love you."

I will always love you. The words echoed in her mind long after James was gone. How well she knew those false promises of love! I will always love you. *Je t'aimerai toujours.*

Long ago, she had been abandoned by someone who claimed to have loved her, but didn't. Now, once again, she had been left in the name of love. And now, once again, she had not really been abandoned because there had been *too much* love, but because there had not been enough.

Chapter 20

Inverness Estate, Maryland . . . February 1990

"Elliot? This is Alexa Taylor."

"Hello, Alexa."

"I was calling about James." It had been almost six weeks since the bitter cold January night when he had said good-bye. At first his good-bye had frightened her. It had sounded so ominous, so permanent, as if he wasn't certain he would ever return. James had reassured her quickly, scolding her for being melodramatic. And yet, still, on that night, he had reminded her very gently that he loved her, and he had told her even more gently that Robert McAllister was a fool to have ever let her go. "Is he all right, Elliot?"

"Yes. He's fine, Alexa."

"Oh, good. Would it be possible for me to get in touch with him?"

"Can you tell me why?"

"No. Well. Would it matter?"

"Maybe. How urgently do you need him? I expect him back in less than two weeks. Can whatever it is wait until then?"

"Yes," she answered, although *it* wasn't waiting. The tiny new life inside her was growing every day. "If you speak to him in the meantime, though, will you tell him that I'm at Inverness?"

James had given her a set of keys to the mansion, and the code for the alarm, and he had told her that she should feel free to go to Inverness whenever she needed time away from the love nest that held such bittersweet memories of Robert. Alexa was there when James called three days after her conversation with Elliot.

"You're answering my phone with a British accent?"

"Well, yes, I am. Hi."

"Hi. Elliot said you called?"

"Yes. I need some legal help."

"*Alexa.* You called Elliot because you want me to negotiate a contract for you?"

"No. It's something else. Something very important. I'm not trying to be coy, James. It's just something I need to discuss with you in person. I called Elliot because I needed to know if you would be back in the foreseeable future."

"I will be."

"Victorious as always?" Alexa teased, a gentle tease that suddenly transported them both back to the happy, uncomplicated time when they had been lovers.

"Victories don't come so easily in this arena," James admitted quietly. "The name of the game is patience and compromise."

"Not two of your favorites."

"No. But I'm learning."

In fact, he had already been proclaimed a master by the State Department veterans. His cool was, as it always had been, absolutely unshakable. He was an elegant sculpture of ice that never melted, not even in the sweltering jungle heat, and not even when agreements that seemed *so close* suddenly dissolved like mirages in the desert. The consensus was that they were making progress, astonishing progress, and in a month they would return and try again. James was learning patience and compromise. And he was learning, too, the stark truth about the hope for world peace. It could happen only as long as one understood that for each small painstaking step forward, there might be a giant step back, and that then one had to be willing to begin the patient, steady, tireless march all over again.

"Robert's baby?" James asked abruptly when he saw Alexa and her very obvious pregnancy ten days later.

"Yes. Of course."

"How did it happen?"

"The usual way."

"*Not* the usual way, Alexandra. You were always so fanatically careful. Or was this planned?"

"*No.* You know that nothing except abstinence is one hundred percent effective. I wasn't careless, James," she said quietly, truthfully. "It just happened."

"OK," he said, his voice softening finally as he looked at Alexa, who he loved and was so vulnerable now, so fragile, so very much in need of his help. But how could he help her, when his own emotions were so raw and frayed? Somehow a little gentleness surfaced as he asked, "So . . . now what?"

"Now I need you to handle the adoption for me."

"The adoption?"

"I want Brynne and Stephen to have the baby, James. I know how desperately they have wanted children, and been unable to, and I know what wonderful, loving parents they would be."

"That's all very true, Alexa, but don't you think you should discuss this with Robert?"

"With Robert? He didn't want me, remember? There's no reason for him to ever know about the baby." Besides, she thought, as she had thought so often in the past weeks, I think Robert would want this, too, for his little sister, and for the tiny, precious treasure of love that is growing inside me. "This is my decision to make, James."

"Then I think you should think about it."

"I *have* thought about it. I have thought about nothing else since the moment I learned I was pregnant. I've made the decision that I believe is the best one for the baby. Being with Brynne is being with family, after all, and with Brynne and Stephen the baby's life will be so happy, so filled with love and so untouched by questions or uncertainties about its absentee father."

"But what about the uncertainties of being adopted?"

"The uncertainties of being adopted?" Alexa echoed with a thoughtful frown. "I guess there could be uncertainties for Brynne and Stephen, but can't you eliminate them by making it a closed adoption? Isn't there a legal way to have the documents sealed forever? I want you to be able to assure Brynne and Stephen that there is no way that their baby can ever be taken away from them."

"I can do the legal paperwork, yes, but Alexa, I can't assure them that the baby won't ever be taken away."

"You can't?"

"No, darling," James said gently to the obviously confused emerald. He reminded even more gently, "Because the baby's mother, *you*, will know where her baby is."

"Oh, yes, but I would never . . . In August, while you and Cat were sailing, Brynne had a miscarriage. I was with her. I watched as she realized that her dream was over, it had to be, because the pain was simply too great. I will never try to take this baby away from Brynne, James," Alexa promised quietly, a solemn promise from the heart. "You just have to believe it."

As he gazed at her lovely thoughtful eyes, James knew that Alexa would keep her sacred vow, no

340

matter what, not even at the cost of great anguish to herself. He could truthfully assure Brynne and Stephen that the baby's mother would never appear to claim her child, but did that confident knowledge mean that the secret was completely safe?

"Who else knows about the baby, Alexa?"

"No one else knows, James, and no one, except for the doctor, ever will. I haven't even looked for a doctor yet. I thought you might know someone?"

"Yes, I do," he answered, thinking immediately of Dr. Lawton, one of his mother's closest and most respected colleagues, and a longtime friend of the Sterling family. Family . . . "You're not planning to tell your parents or Catherine?"

"No. I've decided it would be best not to. I hate the lie, but . . ." Alexa gave a soft shrug. "My parents and Cat think that as of four weeks ago I'm on a six-month jaunt around the world. And, thanks to Barbara Walters, as of Academy Award night in late March, most of America will think so, too."

"Barbara Walters?"

"For her Oscar Special this year, she's doing interviews with Meryl Streep and Jessica Lange and me. My interview was taped on the set in late January, just before we finished filming for the season. The pregnancy was quite hidden then, even though I had all sorts of precarious emotions floating very near the surface. But still, I suppose because it was so important, I managed not to cry at all during the interview and spent a great deal of time raving about my upcoming around-the-world adventure. I supposedly left on Valentine's Day, which is when I moved here. My mail has been held since then, and all my bills have been paid in advance, and the Marlboro Nursery will take care of my roses. I bought a first class around-the-world airplane ticket, with unlimited stopovers, and I withdrew seventy-five thousand dollars in cash from my bank."

"Why did you do that?"

"So that if anyone ever tried to prove where I'd been, I could just say I'd paid for everything in cash and that's why there was no trail of credit card receipts."

"Why *would* anyone try to prove where you'd been, Alexa? Did someone else know about your affair with Robert?"

"I'm just being careful for the baby's sake, that's all," she answered without answering. Then she lifted her face to him and asked softly, hopefully, "Will you help me with this, James?"

James hesitated, torn by conflicting emotions. He believed her decision was confident and firm, a solemn and generous decision of love. And he knew, as she did, that with Brynne and Stephen the baby's life would be filled, overflowing, with happiness and love. And what great joy this would bring to Brynne and Stephen, and even to Robert. *But . . .*

"James?"

"Yes, Alexa," he answered finally. "I will help you."

I will help you because Catherine, for whom this would cause such immense sadness, will never know.

★ ★ ★

342

"What exotic place are you in now?" Catherine asked when Alexa reached her in her suite at the Four Seasons Hotel in Seattle in April.

"No exotic place," Alexa confessed softly. She had been debating telling her sister the truth for weeks. The debate had been silent, never involving James, an emotional struggle between her vow to be honest with Cat and her almost lifelong habit of hiding her flaws from those she loved because of her great fear of disappointing them. But for her baby sister, this would not be the revelation of new flaws. Surely Cat already believed that it would be best for a baby to have a mother other than Alexa. "I'm in Maryland. I've been here all the time. Cat, I'm pregnant."

"Pregnant?"

"The baby's due in June." Alexa paused briefly and added quietly, "And will be adopted."

"Adopted? Oh, Alexa, no." *No!* "Why?"

"Because it's best for the baby."

"Best for the baby?"

"Yes." She reminded softly, "I wouldn't be a very good mother."

"You would be a wonderful mother, Alexa!"

"Oh, no, Cat," Alexa countered swiftly, her emerald eyes filling with tears at her little sister's surprising confidence in her. "I wouldn't be. And it would be best for the baby to have a mother and father, and—"

"Best for the baby, or best for you? Because it would be a bother for you to raise a baby?"

"A bother? *No.*"

"Then keep her, Alexa, or let Mom and Dad

raise her. I know they would welcome her and love her."

"Her?"

"The baby."

"No, Cat. I can't ask that of them. And, please, I don't want them to know. I just wanted you to know . . ." *I just wanted you to know, and to understand, and to love me still.*

"And now that I know, Alexa, I will help you. I'll cancel the rest of my tour, right away, and move into RoseCliff with you, and after the baby's born I can help you take care of it."

"Oh, Cat, thank you, but no. The way you can help me is by understanding that this is what I truly believe is best for the baby."

"But I don't understand, Alexa."

"Will you try?" she asked softly as fresh tears flooded her eyes. This had been such a foolish mistake. The love and confidence had vanished from Cat's voice, and all Alexa heard now was disappointment. "Will you think about it and call me back? I'm at Inverness."

"Inverness?"

"Yes. I'm quite hidden. The doctor, a friend of Marion's, even comes here to see me." Alexa paused and then, because she knew her little sister had always thought he was wonderful, she added quietly, "James is going to handle the adoption for me."

"James?" It was a whisper of pain. James is going to handle the adoption? James is with you? "I thought James was out of the country."

"He got back about three weeks ago. He's leaving again at the end of next week, but he should be back by the middle of May, several weeks before the baby is due."

Every day, every second of every day and every night, Catherine had missed him, and wondered about him, and worried about him. Her desperate longing came alive in her music, stunning her audiences more than ever before, as they journeyed with her from the joyous ecstasy of her remembered love to the anguished sadness of that love's loss. Recently, in the breathtaking voyages, there had been something new, a delicate, trembling hopefulness as Catherine courageously dared to believe that her precious love would return to her.

I will always love you, James had promised. At the time, his promise of love had only been a haunting reminder of the mother who had abandoned her. But, in soft, defiant whispers, Catherine's loving heart had convinced her to believe that he would return. She herself had once been swept away from those she loved by powerful emotions she could not control. She had needed time apart from Jane and Alexander then, but finally, because her love for them was strong and deep and real, she had made the journey back to their love.

It will be the same for James, she had so bravely decided. *He will find his way back to our love. He will trust me and allow me to help him with his anguish.*

But now James had returned *to Alexa,* to help her, as he always did when she needed him. James was helping Alexa. And, the most painful realization of all, by being with her in the private hours they spent together at Inverness, James was allowing Alexa to help him as well.

"Cat?" Alexa asked into the long silence that had fallen.

"It's wrong, Alexa. It's wrong for you to give your baby away." *And it's so very wrong for James to help you!*

"Cat, please!"

"I'm sorry, but that's what I believe."

"Cat . . ."

"I have to go."

"*Why* did you tell her?" James demanded angrily.

"Because she's my sister and I wanted to be honest with her and I foolishly believed . . ." Alexa sighed softly. "It was a mistake."

"Maybe the mistake is what you're planning to do, Alexa."

"No." She met his intense gaze with clear emerald eyes that didn't flicker. "*No.*"

Alexa's eyes had been clear and unflickering from the beginning, her decision firm and resolute. James had suggested that they wait, perhaps until after the baby was born, before mentioning anything to Brynne and Stephen, but she had been adamant that he tell them right away. And so he had, and now, sometimes, Alexa even referred to the baby as Brynne's. But did she really not hear the new gentle softness in her own voice? James wondered. Was she truly unaware of the bond of love between herself and the tiny life inside her? Whenever he tried to tell her, her magnificent green eyes turned to ice, as they did now, warning him away.

"We're going for a long walk, James. You're not invited because you're glowering and that bothers the baby."

He was glowering; but, after Alexa left, his expression softened to loving concern for Catherine. How terribly upset she must be. How painfully torn between her love for Alexa and the secrets of her own gentle heart. How sad she must be, how confused, how alone.

James wanted to go to her. He wanted to hold her and kiss her and love away her sadness. But he didn't trust himself to go to Catherine. He didn't trust himself not to succumb to his desperate need for her—a need that would, he knew, ultimately only drown her, as he was drowning, still, more and more every day, in the tormented depths of his rage.

James knew he couldn't, shouldn't, go to Catherine. But he could talk to her, couldn't he? He could try to help her understand. Alexa hadn't told him where she was, but James had her itinerary in his dresser drawer beneath the carefully folded scarf she had made for him. He took neither the scarf nor the itinerary with him on his treacherous travels, of course. He carried no symbols of Catherine or their love with him at all, because, should he be taken hostage, he wanted no links of danger to her.

Catherine was in Seattle, James discovered. Before dialing the number of the Four Seasons Hotel, his mind drifted to the wonderful plans they had made for their love in the Emerald City.

They would go to the top of the Space Needle, of course, and wander through Pike Place Market, and take a wind-blown ferry boat ride, and visit the Locks, followed by lunch at Hiram's, and . . .

The strident sound of the telephone didn't startle her. Indeed, for several moments it simply blended into the strident thoughts that had screamed in her mind ever since her conversation with Alexa. When she finally realized that it was the phone, she quickly realized even more: it would be James, and he would keep calling until she answered.

"Hello."

"Hello, Catherine. I want to help you understand."

"I'm fine, James," she answered swiftly, wanting, *needing*, to stop the gentleness in his voice, because it caused such pain. "I do understand."

"It's her decision, darling, and hers alone. It has to be. She can't make it based on what you—"

"Did you tell her about me?"

"No, of course not. Of course I didn't tell her. You know that." *Don't* you know that, Catherine? Don't you know, my love, that I would never betray your precious secret? He was about to ask her, to be certain, but Catherine spoke first, a soft, devastating question.

"Is it your baby, James?" Oh, how she hadn't wanted to ask that! But it had been there from the beginning, one of the very first screams, and it had only grown louder, more taunting and demanding, as the minutes passed.

"No, Catherine, how could it be?" James asked with an astonished ache. When Alexa's baby was conceived, you and I were in love, remember?

"But it could be—once could have been—yours." Catherine no longer recognized the voice that was speaking. But it was a voice she would come to know very well. It was her new voice, the one that would be with her for the rest of her life, the voice that no longer held any hope for the love of Catherine and James. The strange voice continued calmly, "If you pretended this baby was yours, James, no one would ever guess that it wasn't. Maybe Alexa is afraid of raising the baby by herself and if . . ." Even the new voice, empty of all hope, couldn't finish the sentence.

Catherine couldn't finish the sentence, but James knew what the words would have been. After many silent moments, he asked very quietly, "Is that what you want, Catherine? Do you want me to marry Alexa?"

Oh, no, James, her defiant heart cried. That's not what I want. But what I want, I cannot have. I want you, and you are gone. I can't have that wish, but I have another wish, a desperate wish for Alexa's baby to be with her mother, where she should be, and if this is a way that that can happen . . .

"Yes, James. That's what I want."

Chapter 21

Dallas . . . May 1990

"Robert?" Hillary asked when she walked into their bedroom suite in her parents' mansion in Highland Park and found her husband packing his suitcase. It was the Sunday of Memorial Day weekend. The festivities celebrating Sam Ballinger's sixty-fifth birthday had been flawless, capped with an eloquent speech given last evening by his son-in-law. The public celebration was over, but Hillary had assumed they would stay in Dallas another day. The Senate wasn't scheduled to reconvene until Tuesday, after all, and the Gorbachevs weren't due to arrive in Washington until Wednesday evening. "What are you doing?"

Robert looked up at her with surprise.

"The celebration is over, so I'm leaving, as we agreed. I should be completely moved out of the house in Arlington by tomorrow night."

"Moved out?"

"Don't do this, Hillary," Robert said, his voice quiet but edged with icy warning. He had survived the past six months, *barely*, living for this day when he would be free at last of his loveless marriage, and free at last to mourn the loss of his beloved Alexa in private. "Don't

350

pretend, not even for a moment, that you thought we weren't getting divorced after all."

"You told me your affair was over!"

"Yes, and I also told you from the very beginning that our marriage was a travesty and that it had failed long before I met her. The fact that you may believe, or can even pretend to believe, that there is any marriage left after the past six months simply proves how very little we ever had."

"It was all a lie, wasn't it, Robert?" Hillary demanded, her sable eyes flashing with indignant rage. "She *has* been waiting for you, hasn't she? Maybe not even waiting. Maybe you've been seeing her still all this time even though you promised you wouldn't. If you've broken your promise to me Robert—"

"I haven't broken any promises, Hillary. No one is waiting for me."

"Then, Robert . . ."

"Stop," he commanded, startling her into sudden silence. "Let it go, Hillary, just let it go gracefully. I'm sure that you would prefer to file the divorce papers, and that's acceptable to me, but please do it soon. I don't want anything, of course." Except my freedom, he thought. *Beginning right now.* "Good-bye, Hillary."

"Robert!" she cried, but he was gone, racing away from her, with no destination other than *not* to be with her. *Because of Alexa.* Alexa was gone from his life, but still Robert preferred to be alone, with only the memories of his lost love, than to spend another minute with her.

"How I hate you, Alexa!" Hillary hissed as

she hurled a crystal decanter across the room, shattering an antique mirror into hundreds of sharp glittering pieces. "How I hate you!"

Robert didn't breathe comfortably until the plane left the tarmac at the Dallas–Fort Worth airport. He took a deep breath then, and wondered as he did if it was the first unconstricted breath he had taken since December.

The bright May sunshine streamed through the airplane window, glinting off his scuffed gold wedding ring. Robert stared at the ring, as if noticing it for the first time. He hadn't, he realized now, thought about it at all when he and Alexa had been together, because for him, for so very long, it had been a symbol of nothing.

But had Alexa noticed? Had it bothered her? Should he have taken the ring off before their nights together? Robert stopped the questions abruptly. They were, after all, questions about the Alexa who had never really existed—the lovely vulnerable woman whom he had loved so desperately. The real Alexa, the clever confident woman who had simply been playing with him, would not have been bothered by his wedding ring. Indeed, she would probably have enjoyed seeing the ring on the hand that caressed her so urgently, a golden symbol of her triumph over Hillary.

Robert removed the ring and forced his thoughts away from the past and into the future . . . to his most welcome privacy and solitude . . . to the work in which he believed so strongly . . . and to the wonderful joy that would soon be coming into his life. Soon, very soon, Brynne's baby would arrive.

A soft smile touched his handsome face as he anticipated that great happiness, wavering slightly as worry crept in. James had assured them all that the mother's decision was firm, and that once the baby was given to Brynne and Stephen there would be no way for her to ever to find her adopted child, but still . . .

It will be fine, Robert decided firmly. It *has* to be. Brynne has suffered enough losses. We all have.

"Alexa?" James tapped on the door of her bathroom as he called her name. It was two A.M. and her lights were on and he had heard water running. Neither the lights nor the water had awakened him in his own room two spacious bedrooms away. He was awake already, driven gasping from sleep by the tormenting nightmares that had been his constant companions since December—except for the one magnificent night when they had been banished by Catherine's love. As he had gazed out his bedroom window, he'd seen the golden beam of light from Alexa's room. She was awake, too, and probably restless. Perhaps, she'd like to play a little backgammon.

"James? I'll be out in a minute. I've already called Dr. Lawton. He's going to meet us at the hospital."

"You're in labor?"

"The real thing," she replied as she opened the bathroom door. "So, how do I look? Doctor Lawton said that this kind of hair dye—it will wash out in six washes—is safe, and it makes a good disguise, don't you think? I have some horn-rimmed glasses for you to wear, a very scholarly look. James?"

James didn't answer, he couldn't, because he was too stunned by her midnight black hair, still damp from the dying, her blackened eyebrows and lashes, and her eyes, tinted sapphire blue by contact lenses.

"I'd never really seen the resemblance before either," Alexa said quietly, correctly interpreting his astonished impression that it was Catherine not Alexa who stood before him. She had never seen the resemblance before, but as she had gazed at herself in the mirror, checking her disguise, Alexa had seen very clearly the little sister with whom her impulsive decision to reveal the truth had caused such irreparable harm.

"Nor had I," James whispered finally. He knew full well that any resemblance—beyond the Taylor sister look of determination—should not have been there. And it never had been, until tonight. But tonight Alexa looked like Catherine, and James was left with the horrifying feeling that it was Catherine not Alexa he was taking to the hospital to have the baby she would give up for adoption.

"So, shall we go?" Alexa asked, her voice now quite matter-of-fact and quite empty of emotion. "Doctor Lawton has notified the hospital that we'll be arriving. We're the Smiths, by the way, James and Juliet."

★　★　★

They hadn't discussed James's role, other than to accompany her to the hospital and then take the baby to Brynne and Stephen in Richmond. But, as he had done in December when Alexa needed him, he had taken her hand and not let go. And, as in December, at some point in the night her fingers began to dig deep into his palm. But James didn't even notice. Tonight he was witnessing a miracle—the miracle his mother had described so often and always with such great awe.

"A healthy girl," Dr. Lawton announced quietly moments after the baby was born. He and Alexa had agreed in advance that he would tell her the sex and health of her infant, and nothing more.

"A beautiful little girl," the delivery room nurse embellished enthusiastically.

Dr. Lawton grimaced slightly at the nurse's words. He hadn't told her that the baby was to be adopted, because he hadn't wanted to draw any special attention to Alexa. *Not* that Alexa was recognizable, not at all; and even James was quite transformed by the glasses.

The baby cried then, an announcement that her voyage from the warm cave where she had lived for nine months had been made safely. An announcement, and a question. Where was the other comforting heartbeat she knew so well?

"May I see her?" Alexa asked softly, all the softnesses that had touched her voice all spring now combining in the gentlest of sounds.

"Of course," the nurse answered warmly. "Let me just get her ready."

In a few moments, the little girl, clean and dry and wrapped in a pre-warmed blanket, was cradled gently in her mother's arms. As James watched Alexa's trembling fingers touch her daughter's soft cheeks, and saw all the love Alexa had so defiantly denied, he began to plan the very difficult words he would speak to Brynne and Stephen and Robert. Brynne's heart would be broken, again, and Stephen's and Robert's. But there would be joy for Alexa, and for Catherine. Hearts would break . . . and, perhaps, hearts would mend.

But even as James thought about the words he would say, he saw the subtle change in Alexa's expression. A moment later, she touched her lips to her daughter's forehead, an exquisitely tender kiss of love, and then looked at the nurse and whispered, as she handed the baby to her, "Thank you."

"She'll be waiting for you in the newborn nursery."

Alexa nodded absently, but her eyes followed the nurse and her baby until they left the delivery room. Then they were alone, the three people who knew the truth, Dr. Lawton, Alexa, and James.

"Will I be able to leave tonight, Doctor?" Alexa asked. The plan, assuming all went well, had been that she would return to Inverness as soon as the delivery was over.

"Yes."

"Why don't you stay here with the baby, Alexa?" James suggested quietly.

"Don't call me Alexa!" she warned urgently.

"It's just the three of us—"

"—just the two of you," Dr. Lawton interjected. "I'm going to give you a little privacy."

"Alexa," James continued after the doctor left, firmly repeating her name as a reminder of who she was. Alexa, not Juliet, a mother who had just given birth to her baby—*her* baby—not a romantic heroine performing a carefully scripted role to perfection. "Alexa . . ."

"I haven't changed my mind, James, and I'm not going to." Even though my heart wants me to! Her heart wanted her to, but it was a battle Alexa allowed her logical mind, once again, to win—for her baby. It's wrong, Cat had said, and Alexa knew now that her little sister had been right, at least partially. It *was* wrong for her, for her heart; but it was right, *best*, for her daughter. Wasn't it? Yes. *Yes* "Please call Brynne and Stephen right now."

"No."

"Damn you." Her tinted sapphire eyes filled with tears and she whispered, "Please don't do this to me, James."

"I want you to spend the night here and see her again."

"No. It's too risky for me to be here. Someone might recognize me."

"OK. I'll bring her to Inverness tomorrow as soon as she's been discharged. You need to see her again. Alexa, you need to think about this!"

"I don't need to see her again." The memory of the moments she had touched and kissed and smiled hello to the lovely little girl who had been

conceived in such love would live in her heart
. . . always. "And I *have* thought about it."

"You've thought about all the reasons to give
her to Brynne. But, Alexa, I don't think you've
thought about all the reasons not to."

"Very selfish reasons, James, and very
emotional ones."

"Maybe if we got married . . ." He hadn't
asked her before. He was convinced it would not
have changed her decision, and he had his own
reasons—selfish and emotional—for not wanting
to spend his life as Catherine's brother-in-law.
"Will you marry me, Alexa?"

"Oh, you're such a nice man," she whispered
as she gazed through tears at her beloved friend.
James was so tormented, battling his own
demons, but he had still found the energy and
emotion to help her. For a moment—a lovely
dream—Alexa considered his proposal. *I could
spend my life loving my daughter.* But then she
forced the dream away. It was such a selfish
dream, and so unfair, to everyone but her. Could
she really ask James to spend his life pretending
to be the father of his best friend's baby? Could
she really ask him to live his life with her, and
deprive him of a chance at the kind of love she
had felt with Robert? It was unfair to ask that of
him, even though he was offering, but it was most
unfair to her baby. The best life for her daughter,
the most happiness, would be to live with parents
who loved each other as deeply as she had loved
Robert. And that was far more than anything she
could offer, either with James or without him.

"Please call Brynne and Stephen, James. I'm not going to change my mind."

"Please tell me," Alexa said thirty-six hours later when James returned from Richmond.

"Why are you doing this?"

"I want to know that Brynne and Stephen were happy."

"They were happy beyond words," James answered truthfully. The look in Brynne's eyes had been astonishingly close to the look he had seen in Alexa's eyes when she held her baby daughter—as if Brynne had spent the past months bonding with the baby girl, too. And of course she had. Brynne knew very well what it felt like to have a new life growing inside her. "Beyond words."

"Have they picked a name?"

"Dammit, Alexa!" James growled, and then felt instantly guilty. Alexa looked like death. After two washings, the midnight black hair had faded only to dirty gray, and her eyes, thankfully no longer sapphire, were gray-green, the emerald now filled with dark clouds of grief. He wondered, as he had been wondering, if he should have been more forceful about her seeing the baby another time, or if he should have insisted that she marry him. He repeated, very softly, "Dammit, Alexa."

"Just tell me, James, and then I'll never ask another question about her. I know that because of your friendship with Brynne and Robert you will watch her grow. I promise that I won't spend our lifetime asking you to be my spy." It was a solemn promise to them all, to James, to Brynne, to her baby, and to herself. "Just tell me her name. Please."

James gave a soft sigh and said gently, "They named her Kathryn, after Stephen's mother. It's spelled with a K and a Y."

"Are they going to call her Kat?"

"No. They're going to call her Katie."

For a long time Alexa said nothing. She just gazed out the window to the rose garden and far far beyond, her lovely eyes envisioning a distant dream. As he watched, James witnessed an act of will that consumed every ounce of energy left in her soul. When she finally looked back at him, her emerald eyes were sad but very clear.

"Will you take me for a sail, James?"

"Of course I will."

"This Tuesday, Elliot?"

"Yes. We need to be in Damascus by Thursday, so we should leave Tuesday." Elliot heard James's hesitation and added quietly, "You don't have to do this, James. In fact, maybe it's time for you to return to private life."

Private life? James mused. No. Those memories were far too painful. He felt much less pain when he was in places steeped in hatred, not in places that reminded him of love. He needed to work, needed to look into the eyes of the kind of people who might have ordered the death of his parents, and with those evil people he needed to make slow determined negotiations toward peace. He was restless, eager to flee the memories, but it had only been a week since Alexa's delivery,

360

and even though she was valiantly fighting her sadness, she was still so very fragile.

"Let me call you back, Elliot."

"Sure."

James replaced the receiver and looked up to see Alexa. She had been outside, lying in the warm June sun, hoping to turn her pale white skin into glowing gold. In the six weeks remaining before *Pennsylvania Avenue* resumed production, she needed to lose weight—an easy task because she had no hunger; and—an impossible task—she needed to become the relaxed, confident, carefree woman who had spent the past six months traipsing around the world. Alexa had been dutifully lying in the sun when Elliot called, but she had been drawn from the rose-fragrant veranda by the sound of the telephone and the hope that it was Cat, calling at last.

But Cat wasn't going to call.

"Elliot?" Alexa said, chastising herself for her foolish hope that she and her sister would ever reconcile. "Word about your parents?"

"No. Still absolutely nothing."

"He needs you?"

"Yes. But . . ."

"But you're worried about me." She smiled bravely. "I think it's time for me to return to RoseCliff."

"If anyone saw you . . ."

"No one will. If you could just buy food to last me about three weeks, I should be very presentable after that."

★ ★ ★

James knew Catherine was in Denver. Tomorrow she would give the final concert of her North American tour, and in three weeks she would begin her tour in Europe. What wonderful plans they had made for these next three weeks. A few days in romantic, charming Aspen, they had decided, and then . . .

James stopped the distant memory of love, but he did not stop the decision to call her.

"It's James, Catherine."

"James."

"Alexa had her baby—a baby girl—a week ago, and she has been adopted by very loving parents." He paused, sighed softly, and said quietly, "Alexa needs you, Catherine. Alexa needs her sister."

"Is she at Inverness?" *With you?* If I go to see Alexa—and, oh, how I have thought about calling her!—will I see you, too?

"No. She's at RoseCliff."

The knock at her cottage door startled and then terrified her. What if it was Hillary? *What if it was Robert?*

Alexa cowered in the kitchen, out of sight. She was unable to see the intruder at the door, but she would be able to catch a glimpse when whoever it was began to leave.

Go away, whoever you are!

"Alexa? Are you here? Alexa?"

"Cat?" she whispered as she rushed to the door. "Cat."

"Hi." Catherine's heart wept when she saw the haunted emerald eyes. Oh, Alexa, I should have been here a long time ago! "May I come in?"

"Of course." As she opened the door to her small cottage, Alexa said softly, "Cat, there's no one else here. I had a baby girl . . . and I gave her away."

"I know. Alexa, I've come to apologize. I should have accepted your decision and supported you."

"How *could* you have supported me, Cat?"

Alexa's tone was sad and bewildered, but the words cut through Catherine like the sharpest of knives, plunging with surgical precision into an already bleeding wound in her loving heart. Was it true? Had James revealed to Alexa the secret of her own adoption? Had he broken that solemn promise of love?

"What do you mean?"

"I mean that somehow you knew what I was doing was wrong. Somehow you knew how difficult it would be for me. How did you know that, Cat? You have always been so wise."

"I'm not wise, Alexa."

"But you knew, without ever having been a mother yourself, that giving away a baby is . . ." Alexa softly shook her head. There were no words, only emotions. "Somehow you knew."

"No," Catherine whispered. I never knew about the mother's pain, only the baby's. But now, as she heard Alexa's anguish and saw her haunted eyes, she wondered, Did my own mother suffer like this? Is it possible that she really did love me?

"Cat?" Alexa asked softly, as the sapphire eyes

363

she had seen cry only once before suddenly filled with tears.

"I never knew until now about the mother's loss. I only knew about the baby's." She turned away from Alexa then and moved to the nearby picture window that gave a breathtaking view of roses and sky and sea. Catherine didn't see the view, her eyes were blurred with fresh tears, and she barely heard her own words above the thundering of her heart. "I knew how the baby felt because I'm adopted. I'm not really your sister, Alexa."

"Yes you are! I was there, Cat. I was in Kansas City when you were born. I saw you the moment you were released from the hospital." How vividly she remembered that day. How vividly, too, she remembered her own desperate words, She's not my sister! I don't want her! And now, on this day, even more desperately, Alexa's heart cried, I want her to be my sister, please, *please!* She whispered softly, pleadingly, lovingly, "You're my baby sister, Cat."

At the softness in her voice, Catherine turned back to Alexa and confessed bravely, "No, Alexa, I'm not. I've only wanted to be. Your real baby sister died."

"No," Alexa protested quietly.

"Yes," Catherine countered gently, her heart swelling with hope as Alexa greeted the revelation with sadness and defiance, not even a flicker of the relief she had always feared. "On the day she was discharged, Mom visited the newborn nursery. She was looking for the courage to tell you what had happened, and instead . . ."

Catherine told Alexa everything she knew about that day. It was the same story she had told James, the identical story told by Jane to her. But now, as she spoke of the mother who had claimed to love her but had given her away because of some mysterious danger, Catherine's voice was soft, not bitter. And now, there were bewildering questions in her heart where before there had only been the confident answer: she didn't really love me.

"Do you know how often I've wondered if *I* was adopted?" Alexa asked softly when Catherine's story had finished.

"You?"

"Yes. I was the misfit in the family. You and Mom and Dad were so alike, so gifted and talented, and I—"

"Oh, but Alexa, you were everything! You were very talented too, of course, and you were also beautiful and confident and vivacious. I was always so proud of you!"

"Were you? Oh, Cat, and I was so jealous of you."

"Jealous? Of me?"

"Of course. And," Alexa confessed softly, fearfully, "I guess because I was so jealous, I was also very cruel to you. I didn't want you to be my sister. Don't you remember?"

Catherine heard both Alexa's fear that she would remember, and her great hope that she wouldn't. She wanted to assure, No, Alexa, I don't remember. But today, beginning today and forever, there could be no more lies, not even the most gentle lies of love.

"I remember, Alexa," she admitted, continuing swiftly, lovingly, "But I understood. I was so quiet and so shy. I thought it was embarrassing for you to be my sister."

"Embarrassing? Oh, Cat, no, never. I always thought you were perfect, a serene, perfect, beautiful princess." Alexa gave a wry trembling smile of pain. "You must have been relieved to learn that you weren't truly related to me."

"No!"

"No?" *Even now?* Alexa wondered, but was afraid to ask. Instead, very quietly, she tried to explain what she had done and why. "I love my baby, Cat. I will always love her. I gave her away because I believed it was best for her, even though it wasn't best for me. I gave her away, and it feels as though I have given away my heart."

Hot tears spilled from Catherine's eyes as she listened to Alexa's words. They were familiar words, engraved in gold on the clasp of a sapphire necklace given by another mother to her baby girl: *Je t'aimerai toujours.* And there were other words, forgotten—dismissed as false!—until now, the words her mother had spoken to Jane when she had given her the necklace: "We had one heart, her father and I, and now we give that heart to her."

"I'm comforted," Alexa continued quietly, "by the knowledge that her life will be safe and happy and filled with love. She'll probably never even know I existed. The adoption was closed, all records sealed, and her parents may choose never to tell her she was adopted."

"Does that matter to you?"

"When I held her, I had a sudden impulse to request that she be told. I wanted her to know that I loved her and that I believed with all my heart that what I was doing was best for her. I didn't make the request, and I think it's better that I didn't . . . because now she can never hate me."

Or love you. The thought came to Catherine without warning, an astonishing thought trembling with emotion.

"You hate your mother, don't you, Cat?"

"I guess I did, but . . ." But now, she thought, I wish, somehow, I could let her know that I understand. I wish I could reassure her that my life has been happy, as she hoped it would be, and that I have been safe and loved.

"Cat, if you can, forgive her," Alexa said softly, and, even more softly, she implored, "And, then, if it is possible, please forgive me."

"Forgive *you*, Alexa? I'm the one who needs to be forgiven. I'm the one who always wanted to be your sister, and yet I wasn't a very good sister when you needed me."

"But you are my sister," Alexa whispered, a soft statement, not a question, just a most gentle whisper of love. "*You are* my sister."

Part Three

Part Three

Chapter 22

Damascus, Syria . . . July 1990

"Where next?" James asked Elliot as they dined together in Elliot's hotel room.

It was a celebration of sorts. They had finally accomplished all they could have reasonably hoped to accomplish, a small hopeful step. It had taken a month and every ounce of James's energy to maintain his famous cool, and now, already, he was asking about the next project.

"How about a sailing voyage around the world?" Elliot offered quietly.

"No. This is good for me, Elliot."

"I'm not sure of that, James," Elliot replied truthfully. Every day he saw more of himself in James—the fearlessness of a man who, having already lost everything, has nothing more to lose.

"*I'm* sure."

"Well. It sure as hell is good for the future of the free world."

"Good. So, where next?"

"Colombia, but not until late August. There's nothing until then, and the Colombia effort will probably consume all fall, so how about a one-month sailing voyage in the meantime?"

"I probably won't sail, but maybe I will stay over here—Europe—for a while."

"That sounds good."

"I thought I'd visit L'île."

"You won't find anything there, James." Elliot's smile faded. "I thought we had an agreement that I would keep you informed, and that you would stay away from the investigation. I know it's been seven months, and we still don't have a damned thing, but—"

"Elliot," James interjected. "My reason for going to L'île is purely sentimental, because they loved the island so much. I guess it should have occurred to me, but hadn't, that the bomb might have been connected to their intended visit. It obviously has occurred to you, though. Why, Elliot? Something more than the simple reason that L'île was their destination?"

"Yes, although nothing more specific than the bloody history of the damned place."

"The bloody history of L'île? Mother and Father described it as a paradise."

"L'île is a paradise, but from time to time the island's tranquil beauty has been shattered by its rulers. There have been benevolent Castilles, of course, but there have also been treacherous ones."

"Alain?" James asked with surprise. He remembered how gracious his parents had found the Prince to be. And he remembered, too, the thoughtful letter of condolence he had received from Alain after their death.

"As far as the intelligence community of the free world is concerned, no, Alain Castille is not treacherous. "

"But the intelligence community has made a point of finding out. Why?"

"Because of Jean-Luc, Alain's father. Jean-Luc was banished from L'île by his older brother, Alexandre, and during his years of exile on the French Riviera, he created an empire of power and terror. When he returned to L'île—as monarch, because Alexandre died without an heir—Jean-Luc's enormous power became even stronger and more dangerous. As L'île's head of state, the terrorist Jean-Luc enjoyed diplomatic immunity and protection. We couldn't assassinate him. We could only watch and hope like hell that he didn't arm one of the most strategically important islands in the Mediterranean with nuclear warheads. *We* couldn't assassinate him, but, fortunately, someone did. We still don't know the identity of the assassin, but Jean-Luc had plenty of enemies, including former 'friends' whom he had betrayed. Anyway, he was killed, seven years ago, when his sabotaged plane dove into the sea."

"And?"

"And Alain Castille assumed the throne and the criminal activities appeared to vanish."

"Appeared to."

"That was the question seven years ago. Jean-Luc never concealed what he was doing. That was part of his megalomania. He flaunted his power and corruption and delighted in the fact that the civilized world was powerless to stop him. When Alain assumed the throne, the question was had the criminal activities truly ceased, or was Alain simply far more subtle, and therefore far more dangerous, than Jean-Luc? Alain has been watched very carefully, and there is no evidence whatsoever that he is continuing Jean-Luc's menace."

"But you're telling me this."

"Because I don't want you to hear about it and think you've made an important discovery. The treachery of selected members of L'île's royal family is old news."

"Have you ever met Alain, Elliot?"

"No."

"But you've been to L'île?"

"Yes. Many, many years ago. Before Jean-Luc."

"Why don't you come with me?" James suggested. As he watched Elliot's reaction to his suggestion, he saw the well-trained eyes of the master spy cloud ever so slightly and felt a sense of déjà vu. He had seen the same look when Elliot had spoken with quiet emotion about the emptiness of revenge. There had been something personal then, a distant yet still so painful loss, and there was something very personal and very painful now—something to do with L'île. "Elliot?"

"The difference between consultant negotiators and paid civil servants is that we have to show up on a regular basis," Elliot countered lightly. "You go, James. I think you will find it very peaceful."

Peaceful? James wondered. His memories of peace were far, far away. He churned with angry energy still, although in recent months his monstrous emotions raged a little less, as if battered by frustration, and they had given way, in small begrudging growls, to an emptiness which felt almost worse than the restless rage—less vital somehow, less alive. The thundering emotions had subsided slightly, and in the relative quiet he had begun to hear the soft voices of his gentler emotions, trampled but miraculously still alive, a resilient chorus of remembered joy that urged him to go to her.

Go to Catherine, the soft voices sang. Go to your love.

But James knew that he had nothing to offer her. He had even less now, more emptiness, less life, than he had had on the morning he said good-bye. He wondered if, as Elliot suggested, he could perhaps find a little peace on L'île—peace *at least* for the soft voices of love.

And if the voices weren't quiet? If the romantic island paradise simply made the gentle memories of love sing with greater confidence? James had no answer for those questions. But he knew—and the resilient chorus *knew* that he knew—where Catherine was. She had been in Paris last week, and next week she would perform for the Princess of Wales at the Royal Albert Hall, and this week she was in Vienna . . .

The vision in Alain Castille's long-lashed dark brown eyes was perfect, and from the box seats reserved for royalty at the Staatsoper in Vienna he had a perfect view of the stage; but still, after willing his hand not to tremble, the Prince of L'île des Arcs-en-ciel gestured for the opera glasses that rested in his Natalie's lap.

Natalie always brought opera glasses. Playfully, yet discreetly, she would eye the jewels of the other patrons, casting scowls of mock petulance at her half brother when she spotted a design that wasn't Castille. Natalie didn't share Alain's great passion for music, but she very much enjoyed accompanying him on his frequent excursions to attend concerts throughout Europe.

She handed the opera glasses to Alain and watched with surprise and curiosity as he focused on the beautiful pianist who was dazzling the audience with her stunningly emotional performance of the "Mephisto Waltz." As Natalie watched, Alain's darkly handsome features settled into a somber grimness. His aristocratic profile resembled that of an ancient Greek statue, she thought, the solemn marble face of a general preparing to lead his men into a battle from which they might never return, committed to that path because there was no noble choice other than to defend the homeland.

It cannot be! Alain's mind protested defiantly. It cannot be!

But it was. An almost identical face, framed in spun gold not black velvet, had been indelibly etched in his mind for over twenty years. How vividly Alain remembered the moment when he had overheard Isabelle accuse Jean-Luc of murdering his mother. Jean-Luc's massive hands would have crushed Isabelle's slender throat had he run—and he had wanted to, far away and forever!—but he could not let Isabelle die at Jean-Luc's hands as, apparently, his own mother had. He had feigned innocence, interrupting them as if he had only just arrived and overheard nothing, even though his own small heart was filled with a loathing for Jean-Luc that far exceeded all the hatred that had come before.

After Isabelle left, Jean-Luc had told him the story of the missing princess. On that day, and on so many other days, he had been forced to stand in front of the portrait of Isabelle and listen to Jean-Luc's obsessive madness about her and her missing yet so menacing daughter. Each time Jean-Luc told the entire story anew—as if Alain had never heard it before—a ritual repetition that felt almost religious, a terrifying pagan religion in which Isabelle was both goddess and sorceress.

"Isabelle deserves to die," Jean-Luc had whispered, his voice always trembling with pleasure and then fading to a wistful sadness, because it was a pleasure to be postponed, like that of lovers unable yet to share their passion. "But, until the missing princess is found, Isabelle must live. She will lead us to her daughter and then they both must die."

As they had stood before the portrait of Isabelle, Jean-Luc had commanded solemn promises from the boy who would one day be Prince of L'île. "You must make it your mission, Alain, to find the princess and see that she is destroyed. L'île belongs to you, my son, and to your little sister. Natalie need never know the threat exists. You must protect L'île, and you must protect her. It is your duty. Swear to me that you will."

Alain had made the promises, knowing full well the only vow he would ever keep was to protect his half sister, and he spent the next six years tormented by the eventual consequences of his lies. Surely the blatant lies to his father would doom him to hell, and he would spend eternity with the man he hated.

When he was sixteen, Alain—Alain's soul—escaped the torment; because, when he was sixteen, he discovered that he was not Jean-Luc's son. It was an assignment to be completed over the Christmas holidays, while he was home from the exclusive boarding school in Switzerland where he spent the school year with other sons of princes and kings. He was to make a diagram of his royal pedigree, with eye and hair color, and handedness, and blood types, if available. His mother's blood type existed somewhere, kept because she was the mother of the future monarch, although he did not dare ask Jean-Luc's permission to search for it. But he did learn Jean-Luc's blood type: O. There was no doubt. Only a month before, Jean-Luc had been shot, a nonlethal wound from a now dead enemy, and he had required blood transfusions. Jean-Luc's blood type was O; and, as Alain already knew from class, repeating the test twice because it was so rare, his own blood type was AB. Which meant that Jean-Luc could *not* be his father.

Alain returned to Switzerland with a falsified pedigree, assigning type A to Jean-Luc and type B to his mother. Ten years later, when one of Jean-Luc's enemies finally succeeded in killing him and Alain returned to L'île as Prince, he found his mother's medical records and discovered that at least part of the pedigree had been true: Geneviève Castille's blood type had been B. Alain unsealed a second set of medical records, desperately hoping to learn that he wasn't an impostor prince after all, but instead the son of Alexandre, the older brother of the missing princess, and hence L'île's most legitimate heir. How joyfully he would search for his missing little sister then! But Alexandre's blood type, typed repeatedly because of all the transfusions he had received as he was dying of leukemia, was O, like Jean-Luc's.

There was not a drop of Castille blood in Alain's veins. He was neither half brother to Natalie nor cousin to the missing princess. He was an impostor. He should have told Natalie; but she was only seventeen when Jean-Luc died, too young and innocent to deal with the empire of terror that was her father's legacy. And he should have told Isabelle and offered to help her in her search for L'île's legitimate monarch; but he only told the men Jean-Luc had assigned to shadow her to cease their ominous vigil.

Alain told no one. He only waited, and with each passing day he grew more confident that his secret would be safe forever. It was his destiny, he decided to believe, to rule the island he loved so much. He was the rightful owner, even though an impostor prince, because it was *he* who had lovingly restored L'île after Jean-Luc's reign of destruction, *he* who had enabled the island's beauty to bloom anew, like a hopeful spring flower awakening from the harshest of winters.

In the seven years of his reign, Alain had come to believe that L'île was truly his kingdom.

And now he was looking at the woman who could take it all away from him. Alain was certain it was she. She had Isabelle's lovely face and her brilliant blue eyes, *and*, most telling of all, she wore the same sapphire necklace that Isabelle had worn in the portrait. Jean-Luc had obviously not known that Isabelle had given the necklace to her daughter, but nonetheless, he had spent hours raving about the fortune Alexandre had spent finding the perfect gems. What foolishness! he had scoffed. What silly romanticism for a woman who should have been—as all women should be—simply a possession, to have, to use, but never to treasure. This was the same necklace, Alain had no doubt. His trained eyes appreciated the rare color and quality of the precious stones even through the opera glasses. And there were earrings, too, never mentioned by Jean-Luc, but quite obviously designed as companions to the necklace.

Alain knew other details about Isabelle's daughter: her age, her date of birth in a Chicago hospital, her disappearance sometime in the next four weeks along a path that meandered between Chicago and New York. He glanced at the program, a final desperate hope, but the brief biography of the gifted twenty-two-year-old from Kansas only confirmed what he already knew. It was she, the woman who could take from him all that he loved, and who could, as her father had done to Jean-Luc, banish him from L'île forever.

Catherine Taylor obviously did not know of her birthright. Perhaps she did not even know of her adoption. Would she stumble on the truth as she traveled throughout Europe, dazzling the most dazzling royalty with her great gift? Would Rainier, perhaps, be struck by her similarity to Isabelle and even give a frowning glance to the necklace? Yes, but her lovely face and the extraordinary necklace would evoke only fleeting ripples of emotion, vague bittersweet feelings that would vanish long before they became thoughts. And even if a thought formed—How much she looks like Isabelle Castille!—it would go no farther than an intriguing impression. Because no one, Alain was quite certain, knew that Alexandre and Isabelle had had a child. And what about Isabelle herself? What if *she* happened to see this daughter who was so obviously her own? But Isabelle lived a quiet life in the country, with her husband, almost never venturing from her secluded Loire Valley château.

You are safe, Alain assured himself. Catherine Taylor does not know who she is, and there is no one but you who can tell her.

Twenty-two years before, when ten-year-old Alain had sensed danger for Isabelle, he had vanquished his own fear and bravely intervened. Now all the danger was for him, and it was wise, and not uncourageous, to quietly flee.

But Alain was drawn to Catherine. He needed to meet his beautiful enemy.

"Do you remember where the reception is?" Alain asked Natalie as the applause following Catherine's second encore finally began to fade.

"At the Imperial Hotel. Why, Alain, are you thinking we should go?"

"You sound so surprised."

"Just because my older brother's aversion to such things, unless protocol mandates, is legendary?" she teased.

Alain conceded her point with a fond smile. It was quite true that, although just as legendary were his regal graciousness and elegant charm, he almost always greatly preferred privacy to lavish galas; he almost always chose a quiet dinner by himself, or with his little sister, over mingling with strangers. But tonight was an exception, because of the black-haired, blue-eyed stranger who wasn't really a stranger at all.

"I'd like to meet Catherine Taylor," he explained calmly to Natalie's smiling, interested eyes.

"She's really gifted, isn't she?"

"Yes."

"And very beautiful."

"I suppose she is. I thought I might ask her to join us for a late supper after the reception."

"But surely she will already have plans for this evening."

"Yes. Well, tomorrow then," Alain said quietly with a small smile, a gentle apology, although most of his handsome face was set in stony resolve. He had not forgotten that he and Natalie were scheduled to fly to Paris in the morning to meet with the jewellers at the Castille boutique in the Place Vendôme, but his dark eyes sent a clear message that this was more important. "I would like to hear her play again anyway."

"You and your music, Alain!" Natalie replied with a soft tease. She teased because she knew quite well that a pout would not change Alain's

382

mind, nothing would, and she had no wish to annoy him. *"Bien!* But I'm going on to Paris as scheduled. The designers are expecting us—"

"—you—"

"They like to see you."

"I'll come the day after tomorrow."

"Saturday?"

"We'll make a special trip next month. *D'accord?"*

"D'accord."

The reception celebrating Catherine Taylor's debut performance in Vienna was held in the Grande Salon of the Imperial Hotel. The guest list boasted the rich, the famous, the noble, and the royal; an elite assembly of people whose love of music was as authentic as the original designer gowns and glittering flawless gems they wore. They had come to honor Catherine, because these elegant patrons of the arts were authentically grateful that she had honored them with her great gift.

By the time Natalie and Alain arrived, Catherine was already surrounded by admirers. She smiled softly, graciously, at the lavish words of praise, receiving each new compliment with almost surprised gratitude. *Like the true princess she is,* Alain thought uneasily, observing her demure graciousness from a short distance away as he and Natalie politely waited for an opportunity to approach her. Catherine stood with quiet, regal dignity, straight and proud in a long gown of pale blue silk, her midnight black hair swirled atop her head in rich, luxuriant curls. The legitimate princess of L'île des Arcs-en-ciel didn't wear a crown of jewels, of course, only the stunning sapphires at her neck and ears; but as the chandelier's golden light filtered through its crystal prisms, the luminous gold was transformed into brilliant colors that fell on her shining black hair like a glittering crown of rainbows.

Alain and Natalie would have politely awaited their turn to meet the virtuoso. But when the reception's hostess, a baroness, spotted them, her aristocratic face registered such pure delight that they had come that the other guests surrounding Catherine followed her delighted gaze, and, also recognizing the Prince and Princess allowed them to approach at once.

Catherine watched with appreciative interest as Alain and Natalie drew near. Such a stunning couple, she thought. He, tall, dark, and handsome, and so elegant in the black silk tuxedo; and she, an auburn-haired vision of grace and beauty in her flowing gown of spun-gold chiffon.

"May I introduce Princess Natalie," the baroness beamed happily.

"Hello." Catherine smiled warmly at the remarkable gold-flecked brown eyes that smiled warmly in return.

"And Prince Alain," the baroness added.

"Oh." Catherine's voice filled with soft surprise when she heard his name. "Natalie" by itself hadn't triggered any memories, but combined with "Alain" it certainly did. "From L'île des Arcs-en-ciel?"

"Yes," Alain replied quietly, even though his heart pounded uneasily at the sudden sadness in her sapphire eyes. It was sadness, not possessiveness, he thought, but quite clearly L'île meant something to Catherine Taylor, something he needed to find out, something, perhaps, that Natalie should not hear. Alain immediately abandoned plans to even ask about a late supper tonight. He and Catherine would dine together, sometime. He would stay in Vienna until they did.

Alain and Natalie and Catherine talked for a while, about her performance, about Vienna, about the priceless tapestries that lined the salon walls. Finally, because he knew that there were others waiting patiently to meet her, Alain asked Catherine if she would like to have dinner with him the following night.

Yes, she told him without hesitation. Catherine knew Alain had sensed something in her reaction to L'île, and that it had worried him, and that she needed to explain about Marion and Arthur. And she knew, too, that it needed to be done quietly and in private, not in the midst of this festive gala. Her performance for the following day would be in the afternoon, so they agreed that Alain would call for her at her hotel at eight.

They chatted a little longer, and then Alain and Natalie were gone, and Catherine met a hundred more dazzling people; and it was only much later, in the privacy of her suite, that she had a chance to reflect on the fact that she had made plans to dine with a handsome prince. In the past six months, as she touched all corners of North America with her breathtaking talent, Catherine had been wined and dined by the very rich and very famous, and she had become quite expert at communicating with beautiful gracious smiles and very few words.

But did that mean she was now the sophisticated woman she had imagined herself becoming as she had gazed for the first time at the midnight glitter of Manhattan? Yes, perhaps she was that woman, at least on the surface. She was quite fearless now, unafraid of glamorous new cities and glamorous new people—even the most handsome of princes. Her cheeks didn't flush pink with sudden embarrassment any more, and the wide-eyed innocence had long since vanished from her sapphire eyes, and the rich black curls that had once been a necessary veil for those timid blue eyes were pulled bravely off her face and twirled into lustrous knots of black silk on top of her head. That elegant calm gave her the look, the *illusion*, of sophistication, she supposed. But, of course, she knew the truth. The look of unblushing serenity came simply, painfully, from the loss of her love.

A truly sophisticated woman wouldn't love, *still*, a man who didn't love her, would she? No, absolutely not. Nor would she unknot the elegant chignons, allowing the long black hair to cascade over her shoulders and be caressed by the wind, *as if she were sailing*, as she walked for hours on end trying to soothe the emotional wounds that were reopened every time she played her music.

Catherine knew she wasn't sophisticated, not really, but still it was now possible for her to conceal her shyness and her fear beneath the elegant calm and to dine with a handsome prince.

She needed to see Alain again, to explain that she had known Marion and Arthur; but, astonishingly, she was looking forward to their dinner. Why was dining with Alain suddenly more appealing than the long solitary walk that had become almost necessary after each emotionally exhausting performance? *Why?* Because, astonishingly, almost immediately, she had felt comfortable with him.

But why? . . . Mais pourquoi?

And then she knew: because the so very comfortable conversation with Alain Castille had been in French. The baroness's introduction had been in English, she was certain of that. But, at some point, they had shifted to French. Which one of them, Alain or she, had spoken the first word in the beautiful language of love? Catherine couldn't remember. But why hadn't Alain remarked on her flawless French? Surely it must have been a surprise to hear such fluency from a country girl from Kansas.

Perhaps, Catherine mused, Alain hadn't realized, as she hadn't, until after. She wondered if he, like she, had been struck by how wonderfully comfortable their conversation had been.

Catherine frowned slightly, a frown of surprise not worry, when she entered her elegant suite at seven the following evening. The heavy brocade drapes were drawn, blocking out the summer twilight and the view of the gardens below. On previous evenings, the maids had left the drapes open, and she had stood by the windows and watched the drama of the sky fade from blue to pink to gray. Now the room was dark and shadowy. Well, she couldn't have lingered tonight anyway, and the drapes needed to be drawn while she got ready for her dinner with Alain.

As Catherine crossed the suite toward the dressing room, one of the shadows came alive, leaping at her as she passed. She sensed the soundless motion, but before she could turn toward it she was trapped by strong arms, restraining her and holding a rag tightly—too tightly, she couldn't breathe!—over her nose and mouth.

Just before she was enveloped by darkness, Catherine saw the faces of the people she loved, and in her mind she called to them, I love you, Mom. I love you, Dad. I love you, Alexa.

I love you, James.

"Catherine!" She was in a dream from which she could not awaken. Above her, beyond the dream, voices were calling to her, anxious voices, and one that was more calm, and vaguely familiar, a comforting voice that spoke to her in French.

"Alain," she whispered as her heavy lids opened, finally, to his beckoning voice.

"Are you all right, Catherine?"

"Yes. I guess. What happened . . . ?" As she asked the question, she felt a strange hot dampness on her neck and reached to touch it—*blood!* And there was even more blood, she realized as she stared at her delicate fingers, because there were cuts on them as well.

"A burglar," the hotel's security chief answered, his voice filled with relief that she had awakened and deep chagrin at what had happened. Catherine Taylor was not the only victim of theft this evening. The burglar had stolen a passkey from a maid; and while the maid had frantically searched for it, thinking she had simply carelessly misplaced it, he had entered several suites, all uninhabited except Catherine's, and stolen money, gems, and watches. The chief continued in French, because that was the language the beautiful woman spoke to the Prince, *"Mademoiselle Taylor, je suis désolé."*

As the ether that had caused her swift unconsciousness began to wear off, Catherine's understanding of what had happened to her became crystal clear. She had surprised the burglar, who, after subduing her with ether and a knife had stolen the sapphire necklace that she had only just started wearing, a symbol of a love that might have existed after all. Now the necklace was gone, and gone, too, were the sapphire earrings, another symbol from another love. Her earlobes were unhurt, without blood or pain. The burglar had obviously been familiar with expensive gems and their settings and had taken the time to carefully unscrew the gold backings from their delicate posts.

"I would like to take her to the hospital now," the hotel's doctor said. "Thankfully, the knife wounds are superficial, but they need to be cleaned and sutured. And even though it appears that her unconsciousness was due to the ether, not a blow to the head, I would like to observe her overnight in the hospital."

"May I come in?"

"Alain. Yes, of course." It had been hours since she had been taken by ambulance from the hotel to the hospital, hours that she had spent, until now, attended by a careful and thorough team of doctors and nurses. Had Alain been waiting all this time?

"How are you, Catherine?"

"I'm fine. I think this night in the hospital is quite unnecessary, but . . ."

"Better to be safe."

"Yes. I guess." Her smile faded slightly as she followed his concerned dark brown eyes to her bandaged hands. "The cuts weren't deep, no damage to nerves or tendons, but the doctors say it will be several weeks before I can play again."

"Will you return to the States?"

"I'm not sure. I haven't thought that far ahead yet."

"Well, then, may I suggest that you spend at least part—and hopefully all—of your convalescence on L'île?"

"On L'île?"

"The tranquil beauty of the island can cure the deepest of wounds. Do you know about L'île, Catherine? Not everyone does, but I got the impression when we met that you had some special knowledge." *What do you know, Princess Catherine, about your magical kingdom of rainbows?*

"Not a special knowledge, Alain. It's just that I knew Marion and Arthur Sterling."

390

"Oh," Alain whispered softly. "How?"

"My sister Alexa and their son James are very close. Last summer, I spent a weekend at Arthur and Marion's home in Maryland. They were such wonderful people."

"Yes, they were. Their death was a great tragedy." Alain's expression grew solemn and reflective, adding strength and detracting nothing from his handsomeness. After a moment he asked gently, "Does the remembered sadness of their death make you reluctant to visit L'île, Catherine?"

"No, just the opposite, Alain. I would very much like to see the paradise Arthur and Marion loved so much."

Chapter 23

L'île des Arcs-en-ciel . . . July 1990

"The Prince is in Vienna until tomorrow," James was told when his call was connected to Alain's private secretary. The secretary recognized James's name, of course, and immediately extended the gracious welcome that Alain had promised in his letter of condolence. "But the Princess is in residence, *monsieur,* and she will be so pleased to receive you today."

When James arrived at the palace an hour later, he was escorted from the main entrance through a marble courtyard ablaze with bougainvillea and into a private sitting room overlooking the sea. The vista was a tableau of brilliant shades of shimmering blue—as the bright azure sky kissed the sunlit sapphire sea. Breathtakingly beautiful, James thought, a thought he had had a hundred times during the three days he had already spent wandering around L'île. Truly a paradise . . .

"Monsieur Sterling?"

James turned from the breathtaking natural beauty to yet another of L'île's extraordinary treasures—Princess Natalie Castille. There was indeed a great richness about her, the beautiful light brown eyes flecked with gold, the aristocratic features that were at once delicate and sensuous, the luxuriant mane of auburn hair that glittered with all the colors of fire.

"Your Highness."

"Please call me Natalie."

"I'm James."

"How terrible we—my brother Alain and I—feel about your parents, James. They were such very lovely people." Natalie spoke softly and emotionally. Her voice was elegant, accented only with the accent of impeccable education, and her English was flawless, although, because she spoke it so infrequently, slightly formal. "We anticipated their visit, and yours, last Christmas with much joy. How fortunate that you weren't with them on the sailboat."

As Natalie spoke the last words, her expression was both sympathetic and wise—as if she well knew that there had been times in the tormented months of rage since his parents' murder that James had wondered if he had truly been fortunate to have escaped death himself. After a solemn moment, she freed her beautiful face of all sadness and asked, "Have you just arrived? Alain and I hope that you will stay here, at the palace, during your visit."

"I actually arrived a few days ago. I have a magnificent room at the hotel."

"A few days ago. Have you spent those days exploring the island?"

"Yes. I think I've walked along every beautiful path."

"Searching for clues?" Natalie asked softly, without censure.

"Clues?"

"Our father was a very evil man, James," she said quietly. "Alain and I know that. We lived with his madness, after all. We understand the scrutiny that must be given us as his children. It is part of his legacy to us. Although Alain and I never speak of it, I know we have both searched our own souls fearing that we will find some trace of Jean-Luc's evil within us." Smiling softly, she added, "I believe that we have both escaped his madness. Our true inheritance is this tranquil island, not our father's treachery. My half brother is not a terrorist, James. You will see that at once when you meet him. So, you have searched for clues and found nothing sinister. But, has anyone given you a guided tour?"

"No."

"Then it shall be my pleasure to tell you the stories that accompany the mystical beauty of our island. Alain will not be back until noon tomorrow. If you like, since you have already walked all the paths, in the morning we can sail and you can view the island from the sea."

For the rest of the afternoon and during an elegant dinner that evening at the palace, Natalie told James the enchanting myths and legends of L'île. The following morning, as he expertly guided Alain's sleek sailboat across the shimmering sea, she told him about the not-so-enchanting childhood of the children of Jean-Luc Castille.

"The palace was like a fortress under siege. There were heavily armed guards everywhere, in every room, at every corner, behind every door."

"And now there are no armed guards at all."

"No. No guards for the palace and no bodyguards for Alain or me. It's an obvious reaction to a childhood in which there was so very little freedom. Alain and I enjoy great freedom now, but we are careful, of course, because our wealth makes us targets for kidnapping. We avoid excessive publicity, and whenever we leave L'île, we always travel in our own jets."

"More than one jet?"

"Yes," Natalie admitted with a sparkling smile. "We each have one. Alain and I like to travel together, but there are times—such as now—when he wanted to remain in Vienna and I needed to go to Paris on business. We began the trip in his jet but had to call for mine."

"It sounds as though you and Alain are very good friends."

"Yes, we are. I suppose we're like soldiers bonded by war. And yet," she added thoughtfully, "although Alain and I had similar childhoods, we didn't actually *share* the experience. Alain is six years older than I. From an early age, he was sent off to schools for princes and kings. We had almost nothing to do with each other until I was a teenager. I was in boarding school by then, too, and I was considered quite wild. My wildness was really little more than normal teenage behavior, but was nonetheless regarded as unbecoming a princess."

"More infringement on normal freedoms."

"Yes. I was rebelling, I suppose, and trying, too, to get attention. No one here even noticed, except, to my great surprise, my older quite proper and quite princely brother. Alain and I became friends then, even though my wildness didn't instantly vanish. More than once Alain had to ride in on his white charger and prevent me from a foolish and defiant marriage. He still protects me, although I'm long since grown and not the least bit wild any more."

"Not about to plunge into an unwise marriage?"

"Oh no." Natalie smiled an untroubled smile. "Not about to plunge into any marriage. I'm only twenty-six, so there's no rush, but I'm not sure I ever will marry. My vision of marriage is far from appealing. Alain's mother died shortly after his birth—and Jean-Luc forbade anyone to mention her name—and the relationship between my mother and Jean-Luc was turbulent at best. There is, of course, historical precedent for daughters of such tyrannical monarchs as Henry the Eighth never choosing to marry."

"Indeed. And what about Alain? Will he ever marry?"

"Eventually he will, he *must,* to father L'île's next ruler. But I don't think it will be for a very long time. Alain was engaged to be married once."

"Oh?"

"Yes. Her name was Monique. She was with French intelligence, a beautiful secret agent sent to investigate Alain shortly after Jean-Luc died."

"Alain knew that?"

"Not before he fell in love with her."

"And he was furious when he discovered her true identity?"

"Furious? No. Alain never gets furious."

"Did you ride in on your white charger and put an end to his foolishness?"

"Oh, no. I was thrilled about Monique. She was very lovely and very much in love with Alain. It would have been a perfect marriage. Monique told Alain the truth, and they planned to marry, but . . ." Natalie's beautiful face clouded with sadness. "She and Alain were driving from Saint Paul de Vence to Monte Carlo. There was a terrible car accident and Monique died."

"Was Alain injured?"

"No. He and Monique were driving in separate cars. They had planned to return one of the cars to the airport in Nice en route to Monaco. Alain was following her when the accident occurred. He was merely a helpless witness to the horrible tragedy." She shook her head softly at the devastating image. "Alain will marry someday, to give

L'île its next monarch, but I am quite certain that he will never again plan to marry for love."

"Natalie is sailing," Alain said, gesturing toward the boat in the distance as they drove from the landing strip to the palace. "Do you sail, Catherine?"

"Yes." At least I used to, she amended silently. I used to sail with the man I love . . . *loved.* She banished the memory, or maybe it was simply banished for her, because as she turned her eyes to the beauty of the island, Catherine felt the most amazing sense of peace. She whispered softly, "Alain."

"I knew that you would like it."

Throughout the breathtaking drive and as he showed her the elegant marble palace, Catherine simply whispered, over and over, Alain, *Oh, Alain,* as she marvelled at the splendor.

"And this, Catherine, is the music room. You can practice here once your fingers begin to heal."

"C'est magnifique."

"Oui. D'accord. It is my favorite room in the palace. From here, while you're sitting at the piano, you can see the rainbows. They are right there, close enough to touch, and they fill this entire window."

"And where is the cave? Marion said there was a cave that was once filled with precious jewels— glittering splinters from the rainbows."

"It's just beyond that hill. If you like, I'll take you there."

"Oh, yes, I would like that."

"Marion told you the legend of the rainbows,

Catherine, but did she tell you the truth about the treasure trove of jewels?"

"Yes, she did. But now that I'm here on this magical island, Alain, I think I believe that the wonderful legend is really true," she answered softly. After a moment, she returned her gaze to the azure sky which, in just a few hours, would suddenly scowl with dark storm clouds, and then would cry warm, nourishing tears, and then, the tempest over, would smile again, the brilliant azure now gift-wrapped with rainbows.

As Alain saw Catherine's obvious enchantment with the island—*her* island—he remembered the confession he had made to Marion Sterling, borrowing from Balzac, "Behind every great fortune there is a crime." There had been many thieves in L'île des Arcs-en-ciel's royal family. There were the ancient Castilles, who plundered the tiny vessels laden with treasure chests of gold and gems as they made their dangerous voyages along the trade routes from the Orient. And there was the modern Castille, Jean-Luc, who had plundered hope and dreams and beauty and peace.

But now, even though no Castille blood flowed in his veins, it was he, Alain, who proved to be the greatest thief of them all. Because it was he, the impostor prince, who had stolen by far the most precious treasure—the magnificent island itself.

"Alain!"

Alain smiled with relief as Natalie's voice interrupted his troubling thoughts. Catherine smiled too in anticipation of seeing Alain's sister again. But as she turned her smile faltered.

"James."

"Hello, Catherine," James replied softly, as startled as she. Natalie had mentioned that Alain might be returning from Vienna with a guest, but . . .

Now here was Catherine. She was so beautiful still, so very beautiful, but in the almost seven months since he had said good-bye to their love, she had changed. Her blushing innocence was gone, and her sapphire eyes seemed so wary and watchful, as if on alert for someone who might hurt her. *Oh, Catherine, I never meant to hurt you!* James wanted her to see that message in his eyes, but she wouldn't hold his gaze. Finally, reluctantly, his own troubled blue eyes fell, and when they did there was a new worry. The white gauze bandage on her neck had been hidden by the black velvet hair which, much longer now, tumbled in a luxuriant cascade of soft curls almost to her breasts. But as she had tilted her head, *shying away from him,* he saw a corner of the bandage.

"What happened?"

"I . . . Oh, James, you haven't met Alain."

The two men greeted each other with polite formality, and Alain offered sympathetic words about Marion and Arthur, and then the conversation returned to Catherine's wounds.

"A burglar entered Catherine's suite at her hotel in Vienna and stole her jewels from her," Alain explained quietly.

"Oh, no," Natalie whispered.

"I'm not badly hurt," Catherine assured. "The burglar used ether, but he had a knife, too, and I must have struggled before the drug took effect. The cuts on my neck and fingers aren't deep, everything will heal, but it will be a few weeks before I can resume the concert tour."

"And will you spend those weeks here, with us, I hope."

"Thank you, Natalie. Alain, too, has made that very generous offer." Catherine had accepted Alain's offer for "a few days only," although until James had appeared she had already been wondering if she would ever want to leave this beautiful, peaceful place. But now the peace was shattered, and she wanted, needed, to get away from the dark blue eyes that were staring at her with such gentle concern.

"What was stolen, Catherine?" Natalie asked. Then, frowning, she added, "Not that magnificent necklace you wore at the concert, I hope. I noticed it, of course. The color and quality of the sapphires were exquisite."

"Yes. The sapphire necklace was stolen, as were a pair of sapphire earrings." Catherine looked at James then, a brave look of proud defiance. Yes, James, I wore the earrings still. I didn't wear them because of some foolish hope that you would return to me, but as a memory of a love that meant so very much to me . . . even though it did not have the same meaning for you.

"You must let us replace the stolen jewels," Natalie said. "I have a memory of the necklace and with your memory, too, I should be able to sketch it. And the earrings—"

400

"Thank you, Natalie, but no," Catherine replied, her refusal polite yet firm, just as it had been when Alain had made the same gracious offer. "I don't plan to replace either of them. Both the necklace and the earrings were symbols of distant memories . . . and I think the time has come to let those memories go."

"Then you must let me design something else for you," Natalie offered. "A symbol of a new memory—your first visit to L'île—created from all the colors of the rainbow."

Following the lavish luncheon in the palace's summer dining room, Natalie and Alain retreated to his study for a brief but necessary discussion of her trip to the Castille boutique in Paris, leaving Catherine and James alone. After a few moments of silence, in which sapphire met dark blue briefly and then fell, Catherine turned away from him and walked to the window overlooking the sea. She tried to find peace in the tranquil beauty, but it was impossible, because she was so aware of him, across the room . . . and then standing behind her.

"I'm going to leave as soon as Natalie and Alain return," James said quietly. "I just wanted to say good-bye."

"Good-bye," she whispered, without turning to face him, as her heart cried, How many times must we say good-bye, James?

"Catherine?"

She had to turn then, because she had always been compelled to follow the soft commands of his voice, and when she did she met dark blue eyes that were filled with concern.

"May I look?" he asked gently as he gestured to the bandages on her neck.

How she ached at his gentleness, *for* his gentleness. Oh, James, please go away! But Catherine knew that he wouldn't leave until she had complied with his request, so she began to reach for the tape that secured the white gauze to her snow white skin. But her delicate fingers were clumsy now, wrapped in bulky bandages themselves, and trembling, because of him; and finally it was his strong and tender fingers, trembling, too, that gently peeled back the gauze.

James saw that the wound was superficial, just as she had said it was. The burglar's razor sharp knife had made a thin straight incision, almost surgical, across the right side of her lovely neck. In time, the scar would be almost invisible, a slender white thread the color of her skin; but now the wound was dark red, a vivid reminder of the recent violence. As James looked at the wounds, he felt powerful rushes of anger at whoever had harmed her, and an even more powerful—but impossible—wish to be with her and to protect her always.

"I had the impression earlier, as you were describing what happened, that you didn't remember struggling with the knife," he said finally.

"No, I don't remember struggling—I don't even have a clear memory of the knife—but I must have struggled." As she answered, Catherine pulled away from the oh-so-painful

402

tenderness of his touch and firmly pressed the tape back onto her neck.

"You have to be so careful," he said softly.

"I *am* careful, James," she countered swiftly, amazed at the swiftness and effortlessness of her lie. She wasn't careful at all, of course. She wandered the dark streets of unknown cities at all hours of the night, oblivious to her surroundings and the lurking dangers, wholly absorbed in the impossible task of trying to free her heart from the memories of love, of him.

"Good. I'm glad," he said gently, wanting impossible wishes, but knowing the truth, that he had to leave soon, *now*, for himself, for his heart, and, as was so painfully clear from the wary sapphire eyes, *for her.* "Well. I'd better go. I'll find Alain's study and say good-bye to them on my way out."

"James?"

"Yes?"

"Thank you for calling me about Alexa. I went to see her—I suppose you've talked to her and already know that." Catherine fought yet another wave of pain as his blue eyes told her, gently, apologetically, that yes, he did already know. "Anyway, we're close now, very close, and I just wanted to thank you."

"You're welcome."

"And James?"

"Yes?"

"Thank you for helping her. I should have been there for her and I wasn't . . . but you were. I'm very sorry that I was angry with you about that."

As he gazed at the woman he would always

love, James wondered if she had other regrets. Did she regret her suggestion that he marry Alexa? Did she regret that their love was just a memory whose time had come to be forgotten? The questions were self-indulgent *and* self-destructive, because he already knew the answers. From the first moment she had seen him again, Catherine's beautiful sapphire eyes had quite eloquently conveyed their wariness of him, and it had been very obvious that she was far, far away from their love.

Which is where she should be, James reminded himself sternly. I have nothing to offer her. And even though I will never forget it, will never want to, it is best for lovely Catherine that she is able to forget our magical love.

After a moment he whispered softly, "Good-bye, Catherine."

"I think, Catherine, that Alexa was not the only sister who was very close to James Sterling," Alain suggested quietly a week later.

They were sitting on the cliff above the sea watching the splendor of the rainbows. They had come here every afternoon, while the sun was still golden in the azure sky, and when the storm clouds gathered and the rain began to fall, they sought shelter in the nearby gazebo. They weathered the storm there, warm and dry in the midst of nature's torrential drama. As soon as the rain relented, they returned to the cliff's very edge, as close as they could be to the rainbows that were born in the sapphire sea and arched above them, a canopy of the most brilliant colors, as they reached to the legendary cave of glittering gems at the center of L'île's tropical emerald forest.

Every afternoon Alain and Catherine had come here to share the splendor of the rainbows; and to share, too, quiet words and gentle smiles. Catherine felt so comfortable with Alain, and so wonderfully safe—a safety and comfort which, she knew, went far beyond the simple, effortless joy of speaking to him in French. Alain was like L'île itself, she had decided. Warm, and welcoming, and possessed with wondrous powers of healing. Here, on this enchanted island of rainbows, her knife wounds were healing far more quickly than the doctors had predicted; and here, too, even her broken heart was finally beginning to mend. All her wounds were healing here, because of the wondrous healing powers of the island, and the wondrous healing powers of its gentle Prince.

They had shared the splendor of the rainbows, and quiet words and gentle smiles. And now, quietly and gently, Alain was asking her about the secret love that had been known only to herself, and to James. Would she share that painful secret of her heart with Alain? Yes, she thought as she drew her sapphire eyes from the shimmering rainbows to him. I will share that secret, and perhaps others, with you, Alain. But what of *your* troubling secrets, gentle Prince? I know you have them, and that they torment you, even though you artfully conceal them in the shadows of your dark eyes. Will you, in time, trust me enough to tell me? I hope so. And, in the meantime, I will trust you.

"You are right, Alain," she began softly. "Alexa was not the only sister who was close to James. I was once very much in love with him myself . . ."

Chapter 24

Washington, D.C. . . . September 1990

The days were unusually warm for mid-September in Washington, but on either side of daylight the crisp air sent whispers of autumn, promises of rust-colored leaves, golden harvest moons, cozy woolen scarves, and bright rosy cheeks. For Robert, as he jogged along the Potomac and inhaled the cool dawn air, the unmistakable taste of autumn triggered memories of love. He had spent last autumn loving Alexa, and he had been with her on glorious mornings like this, tenderly and reluctantly kissing her good-bye as the sun began to lighten the autumn sky.

Robert didn't need the autumn air to remind him of Alexa, of course. She was with him always. But now, as he inhaled, he felt himself succumbing to the restless urgings he had battled all summer. He needed to talk to her, if she would agree. He needed her to show him the woman she had claimed to be, the woman for whom their love had been simply a game.

Robert needed to be shown that woman, because still, no matter how hard he tried, whenever he conjured up images of Alexa, he only saw visions of love.

A long night of filming lay ahead for the cast and crew of *Pennsylvania Avenue,* which was why, the director announced, they would take a full hour for the dinner break. The break was only ten minutes old when the stage manager knocked on the door of Alexa's dressing room.

"Senator Robert McAllister is here to see you," he announced with obvious enthusiasm when she opened the door.

"Senator McAllister?" Alexa echoed weakly.

"That's right! I think this is the first time he's ever stopped by."

Yes, Alexa thought, this is the first time the distinguished Senator from Virginia has ever visited the set of *Pennsylvania Avenue.* But why is he here now? Was he coming to tell her the truth at last? Or did he want to resume where they had left off, his marriage to Hillary rocky again, or perhaps so unshakably stable that he needed a little diversion?

If either of those was the reason, Alexa had no wish to see him. It was far too late to hear the truth she already knew, and even though she had once been so willing to spend her entire life loving him only in precious stolen moments, if that was all they could ever have, and even though she loved him still, resuming her affair with him was

407

impossible. She had given her heart once to Robert, and it had been completely in his care. But now that fragile and broken thing, whose only signs of life were piercing quivers of pain, was hers again; and Alexa knew she had to protect it from further harm.

But what if Robert had somehow found out about Katie? What if his visit had something to do with her daughter's happiness? That terrifying worry made her own immense pain at seeing him again quite inconsequential.

"So, shall I tell him you'll see him?"

"Yes. I will see him."

In the few minutes before Robert knocked on her dressing room door, Alexa summoned all her talent and let her memory travel to the time before love when her emerald eyes had been able to flash with confident icy contempt at his arrogance.

But he didn't look arrogant now! His tired brown eyes looked only uncertain and sad. And the emerald ice, such a thin fragile layer, was melted instantly by the warmth inside her, the defiant embers of love that would not die.

"Hello, Alexa."

"Hello, Robert."

"I wondered," he began softly. "I wondered if, sometime, we could talk."

"Talk about what, Robert?"

"About us."

His voice was so gentle, but the words felt like the heaviest of weights, pressing down on her delicate shoulders and slender legs until she knew she could no longer bear the oppressive weight while standing. Somehow she willed her wobbly legs to move, away from him and to the nearby couch. But even when she was seated the weight was still there, bending her head, casting a most welcome curtain of golden silk across her face. Oh, Robert, I don't have the strength to talk about us. Once I prayed that no matter what the truth, you would tell me, as proof of our love and our trust, but now it's far too late. Just seeing you causes so much pain, too much.

After a moment, Robert moved beside her, and, after another moment, he very tenderly parted the silky gold. The gesture was painfully familiar to both of them, because this most gentle caress of love had been made so often after their passionate loving, when he needed once again to see her glowing emerald eyes. "Alexa?"

"Don't! Please." As she lifted her head in proud defiance, her gaze fell on the hand that had touched her. "You're not wearing your wedding ring."

Oh, Alexa, his heart cried. He had come to see the woman who had been playing with him, a woman who, had she even noticed the ring, would certainly never have cared. But that woman wasn't here. Only Alexa, the lovely, vulnerable woman whom he loved so desperately, was here.

"Oh, Alexa," he whispered softly. "Did it bother you that I wore the ring last fall? I didn't even think about it, darling. I should have. I'm very sorry."

"No, it didn't bother me," she truthfully told the so very worried, *so very beloved,* sensitive dark eyes. "But please, Robert, tell me why you're not wearing it now."

"You know why," he said gently, as delicate whispers of hope began to tremble deep within him. He gazed at her beautiful, confused face and said quietly, "Hillary and I are getting divorced. I told you that in December, darling, the night I returned from Camp David . . . the night I asked you to marry me."

"But it wasn't true!" *It can't be true!* the protest came from the heart that had suffered enough pain already; a heart that could not possibly endure learning that her precious daughter had been lost because of . . . *No!* She reminded him urgently, "You weren't at Camp David that weekend. You were in Dallas, with Hillary, in the bridal suite at the Mansion on Turtle Creek. Robert, I heard your voice!"

"No, my love. I was at Camp David, somehow keeping my mind on my work, but filled with such joy because Hillary had agreed to give me a quiet divorce." Robert's dark eyes were soft as he spoke of that remembered joy. But they hardened, as did his voice, when he spoke again. "Tell me what she did." *Tell me how Hillary destroyed that magnificent joy.*

"She came to RoseCliff on that Friday morning. She said that you had told her about our affair, and that you'd told her, too, that you'd only slept with me because of an affair she'd had that had hurt you deeply. She said you'd reconciled and were going to spend the weekend in Dallas, a second honeymoon, and I called . . ." Alexa couldn't continue, because his dark, angry eyes told her so painfully, so eloquently, that all Hillary's words had been lies.

"She must have recorded my voice," Robert said with quiet rage as he remembered. "Before I left for Camp David, there were repeated calls to my office in which the caller never spoke, but remained on the line." He paused, fighting the rage, amazed by its strength and its power, but needing now to say soft, gentle words to his love. "My marriage to Hillary was never really a marriage. I should have told you that, and that I was going to divorce her, but it never occurred to me that you didn't already know. I've never loved anyone but you, Alexa. I've never, not for one second, my darling, stopped loving you, and, I guess, I've never stopped dreaming that somehow, someday, you would agree to spend your life with me."

Robert drew a soft, shaky breath as he watched the golden curtain of silk fall once again across her beautiful face, intentionally cast as she bowed her head in response to his impassioned words of love. Was it too late? his heart cried. Had she stopped loving him? Had Hillary won after all? He believed he had seen love in the beautiful emerald eyes, but now . . . Now she was in hiding, where she wanted to be, and this time he couldn't part the silky curtain. This time, all he could do was wait until she was ready to tell him her decision.

I still love you, Robert. Oh, how I love you! The fragile, broken heart that had for so long been filled with pain cried now to be filled once again with love, only with love. But there were other emotions, powerful and dangerous and damaging, that vied for space in her delicate

411

heart: rage, hatred, and bitterness toward Hillary, whose cruel trickery and deceit had cost her the loss of her daughter. Now as Alexa felt the rage and hatred and bitterness fight aggressively to establish firm footing in her fragile heart, some deep instinct, perhaps that wounded heart's deepest instinct for survival, warned her not to let those ravaging emotions in; because all the hatred and rage in the world would not change the truth: she had made a solemn promise of love never to reclaim Katie, and she would not ever break that solemn vow.

Alexa's damaged heart cried desperately to be filled only with the most gentle and joyous of love, and that was what she wanted, too. But how, *how*, could she possibly conquer the rage and hatred and bitterness that so boldly and so powerfully demanded their rightful place? Vanquishing the powerful and so damaging emotions seemed an impossible task, and she felt her gentle life of love with Robert becoming just a lovely dream very far beyond her reach . . .

But then, quite suddenly, Alexa was touched by a distant memory of love. The image of her twelve-year-old sister and her earnest sapphire eyes and her soft voice was clear and bright and so powerful that Alexa felt the angry emotions begin to miraculously melt away. She waited for many disbelieving moments, fearing that they would return with a vengeance, but they didn't; and finally she looked up to the man she loved.

"I think we should forgive Hillary," she said quietly, using the same words Cat had spoken to her so many years ago. Smiling lovingly at

Robert's surprised and skeptical brown eyes, she continued, "That's advice my very wise little sister once gave me. She said that we should forgive Hillary, and that we should feel sorry for her, because she must be very unhappy to be so cruel. I want to forgive her, Robert. I need to. And, I guess, I do feel sorry for her, because she will never know the kind of happiness that we have. I've never been in love with anyone but you. James was, and is, my wonderful friend, but there has been nothing more than friendship since I fell in love with you. He was with me at the gala that night because I didn't have the strength to be there alone, knowing that I would see you with Hillary." She smiled at the dark eyes that now filled with such desire and such joy and said softly, "I've never stopped loving you either, Robert, not for a second."

"Oh, Alexa, I love you," he whispered emotionally as his tender hands cupped her beautiful face. His dark eyes met her emerald ones, joyfully mirroring her happiness and her love, and vanquishing all flickers of rage. Their eyes should have been exact mirror images, but, Robert realized, there was something else in Alexa's beautiful eyes, something that shouldn't have been there. He had seen it—the deep, deep pain—the moment he had first seen her again; but it should have been conquered now, by their wondrous love and joy, and yet it lingered, a ripple of pain and sadness very deep, but very real, in the glistening emerald. Lovely, generous Alexa could forgive, but there was obviously something she could not forget. He would love her, with every ounce of his soul, and someday she would share the sadness with him, and they would conquer it together or perhaps it would simply be loved away. But, until the pain vanished from the beloved emerald, he would never forgive Hillary for this unknown harm she had done to his lovely Alexa. He smiled at his beautiful love, wanting to love away all sadness, and whispered again, "I love you."

"Oh, Robert, I love you, too."

Their lips met and kissed the gentlest of hellos, a tender welcome home, my love, and a promise of forever. After a few loving moments, the kiss ended and she simply curled against him, where she needed to be, nestling as close as she could, safe in his strong and gentle arms. And, as her golden head rested softly against his chest, she heard the joyous songs of his heart, *Welcome home.*

Robert didn't speak for a while, swept by the immeasurable joy of the moment, holding her again, knowing it would be forever. Finally, when he was able to speak, he shared with her the new joy that would be a part of that wondrous forever happiness.

"In June, Brynne and Stephen adopted a baby girl. Did James tell you?"

"No," Alexa answered softly, because somehow her swirling mind remembered that James would never have revealed such a confidence. And then, she heard herself say, "How wonderful for them."

"So wonderful," Robert echoed, his lips gently caressing the golden head curled under his chin.

"Oh, Alexa, wait until you meet little Katie. This summer, when I missed you so much, and I wondered how I would survive, I would drive to Richmond for the weekend, or even just for the day, and seeing that lovely little girl was an island of such peace and happiness."

There is so much love in Robert's gentle voice for his baby daughter! her heart cried. Alexa feared he might feel her trembling, but she couldn't pull away, not even a little, because then he might search for the eyes he must not see.

"Did I ever tell you, my darling Alexa, that I never believed my commitment to the vision of peace I have for the world could have become stronger or deeper than it was—but that it did the moment I fell in love with you?"

"No," she whispered, almost finding the courage to look up at him then, because those gentle words of love were more than enough to explain the tears that spilled so freely. But she didn't look up, and it was very lucky that she didn't, because of what he would have seen in the glistening emerald had he been gazing at her as he said the next . . .

"Well, it did. And after that, I was certain it would get no stronger. But it did, Alexa, the moment I first held Katie. She is so innocent, a joyous treasure of hope and promise. The first time I held her, I made a solemn promise that I would do whatever I could to make this world a peaceful, lovely place for her to spend her precious life."

Oh, Robert, I made solemn promises, too, to

Katie, and to Brynne, and to my heart, and to you.

The dinner break ended far too quickly. But, he teased lovingly before leaving her dressing room, if she hadn't had to return to work, he would never have let her go, and then he wouldn't have been able to go to his apartment and get all his things so that they could begin tonight, at RoseCliff, to spend the rest of their lives together.

Robert needed to get his things, and he needed to talk to Hillary. He had hidden his rage, for Alexa; but as he remembered the anguished sadness in her eyes, the painful symbol of some unknown wound that was still unhealed despite the wondrous joy of their rediscovered love, the rage came back in dizzying waves, so strongly that he abandoned his plan to drive to Arlington. He would call her instead. He had no wish to see Hillary ever again, and, as the powerful waves swept through him, he became even a little afraid of what might happen if he did.

"I have to hand it to you, Hillary."

"Robert?" Hillary recognized his voice . . . barely. The usually rich voice was just a skeleton now, ice-cold and stripped of all warmth or compassion.

"I knew very well, from firsthand experience, how deceitful you could be, and how vain and selfish and spoiled you were. But I truly underestimated the extent to which you would go in order to get what you wanted."

416

"I *know* I haven't filed for the divorce yet, Robert! I should have, and I will. I promise."

"No, Hillary, *I* will file, as soon as possible," he said with the omniously quiet control of the most icy rage. "But let me make a promise to you, and believe me, it is a promise I will keep. The moment we are divorced, the moment I am finally free of you, I will marry Alexa, who I love with all my heart."

"Thompson!" Robert called to the man walking twenty feet ahead of him.

At the sound of his name, Thompson Hall turned around, and when he saw that the greeting had come from the party's favorite son, a warm, welcoming smile crossed his face. Robert was the shining star, the great hope, and as one of the party's top political strategists, Thompson was going to help make it happen. *Not*, he well knew, that Robert McAllister would need much help. Thompson would just be going along for the dazzling ride of power and prestige.

"Good morning, Robert."

"Good morning. Do you have a minute?"

"For you? Always."

They walked together to the privacy of Robert's office, chatting about nothing of consequence until the heavy oak door was closed securely behind them. Then Robert got right to the point.

"Hillary and I are getting divorced, Tom. My attorney will file the divorce papers at the Arlington courthouse either late this afternoon or first thing tomorrow morning. I imagine that the court reporters will notice the filing, so I wanted you and the PR people to know in advance. I doubt there will be more than a few ripples of curiosity, but it seems prudent to have an answer prepared."

"An answer? What possible answer can there be?"

"How about the truth? Hillary and I made the decision to divorce almost ten months ago. We stayed together until late May, in large part because of the celebration for Sam, and have been living apart since then."

"Robert, you really must rethink this."

"That's the truth, and frankly it's already far more than anyone really needs to know."

"No, I meant you need to rethink the divorce."

"I beg your pardon?"

"Divorcing Hillary is politically very unwise. Are you sure you can't come up with some arrangement short of divorce?"

"The reason I am telling you this, Tom, is to advise you. I am not asking for your advice. Hillary and I are getting divorced. Period. Marriages fail. The country is grown-up enough to accept that, and if not—"

"If not?"

"If not, there are many ways that I can help realize the visions we all share for the nation, and for the world, that do not require election to public office."

"You can't be serious."

"I am . . . absolutely." Robert gave a dismissive gesture, the subject closed, and then continued with an easy smile, "I probably should tell you now, to give you time to adjust since these revelations are clearly difficult for you, that I am planning to marry Alexa Taylor as soon as the divorce is final."

"Alexa Taylor? As in the star of *Pennsylvania Avenue?*"

"Yes." Robert paused, steadying his eyes and voice before speaking the next. He disliked the lie, any lie, but this had seemed so very important to Alexa that he had quickly and gently agreed to it. "Our relationship began this summer, after Hillary and I had already separated, and shortly after Alexa's return from her trip around the world. We've managed to keep our love quite private, and that's how we would like it to remain for as long as possible."

Thompson Hall staggered out of Robert's office as if he had been struck a close-to-lethal blow. The entire political party *had* been struck, of course, and for Thompson the blow was personal as well. As an advisor to the President he would wield enormous power, but if Robert McAllister's career was sabotaged by an unwise marriage . . .

Something had to be done. Thompson considered having the party's most influential leaders discuss the matter with Robert. Divorcing Hillary was bad enough, they would tell him, as Thompson had, but marrying Alexa Taylor was political suicide. Yes, of course, Alexa was a celebrity in her own right and immensely popular. And yes, there was the very recent precedent of a First Lady who had been an actress—not to mention her actor husband—but the Reagans had come from a different era in Hollywood altogether. An actress Alexa's age, Thompson knew, did not conform to the nation's image of a First Lady. But Thompson hadn't dared voice his own concerns about Alexa's suitability as a wife, and he guessed other party members might be equally reluctant.

The only hope, he realized, was Robert's fiancée herself. Alexa had to be approached carefully, diplomatically, he knew, and it was he who had to do it . . .

Alexa was just about to leave the studio when Thompson called. She had never met him, but she was well aware of his important role in the party, and well aware, too, that Robert had planned to tell him about both his divorce and their marriage. When Thompson said he needed to meet with her privately, Alexa told him that Robert wouldn't be home until very late and gave him directions to RoseCliff.

"This country needs Robert McAllister, Ms. Taylor."

"I know that, Mr. Hall."

"I hoped you did. That makes my mission a little easier."

"Your mission?" Alexa echoed uneasily.

"I need to ask you to reconsider your plans to marry Robert."

"I see. You believe that I'm a political liability?"

"I'm afraid that you are. You're an actress, Ms. Taylor. Although your lifestyle may be fascinating and glamorous to middle America . . ."

"It is not a lifestyle becoming a First Lady? A little too much sex and cocaine?"

"Alexa," Thompson soothed patiently, his voice gratingly condescending. "When Robert runs for President, the other party—the bad guys—will spare no expense to find out every detail of your life. They know that uncovering some distant scandal about you—nude photos taken when you were a starving young actress, an episode of experimentation with drugs—is their only hope of defeating Robert. They know they won't find skeletons in Robert's closet, so they'll make an exhaustively detailed search of yours."

"And they will find no skeletons, Thompson," Alexa soothed patiently in return, addressing him by his first name, as he had addressed her, and perfectly matching his tone of condescension. "I don't use drugs, and I never have. I was very lucky with my career. I never starved. I never had to make compromises."

"So every moment of your entire life could be replayed before the America public? Because it will be."

"Every moment. Yes."

"Well, great, that's an immense relief." He smiled broadly, but it was a political smile, not a genuine one, and it didn't diminish in the least as he added, "Then you won't mind at all that I'm having you investigated."

"You're *what?*"

"Having you investigated." Thompson's smile vanished as he observed with quiet menace, "And, apparently, you do mind. That suggests to me that there is something to be found."

"No. I very much resent, however, the invasion of my privacy, and I'm sure Robert won't stand for it."

"Robert would be annoyed as hell, but he *would* stand for it. Admittedly, I had hoped to keep this between the two of us, but if you want him to know, I can very easily defend my reason for having it done. As I told you, it's going to happen someday, and it's just smart politics for us find out in advance if there's something—perhaps an incident you've completely forgotten—that might be twisted in a way that could cause great harm. If we know in advance, we can control the damage and make sure the proper spin is put on the story. Robert would think it's premature for me to be doing this now, and he would be furious that I believe if we discover something truly damaging you should reconsider your marriage plans, but he knows full well it will be done eventually. So, Ms. Taylor, I can defend my reason for investigating you, but what is your defense for not wanting it done?"

"It annoys me, just as it would annoy Robert. Nothing more." Alexa gave a soft shrug, as if it couldn't matter less. "So, go ahead, have me investigated."

"Are you planning to tell Robert?"

"I guess not, as long as you agree to come to me first if you find anything at all that troubles you."

"I will come to you, providing you promise that if there is something which, in my judgment, would harm Robert's career, you will give your marriage plans serious reconsideration."

"That's an easy promise for me to make, Mr. Hall, because I know you will find nothing."

"Then I will be the first to wish you all the best in your marriage."

"Thank you." Alexa smiled, and after a moment asked very casually, "How long will the investigation take?"

"A few months. It should certainly be completed by Christmas."

You really want to find something, don't you, Thompson Hall? Alexa thought as she heard him leave, his car roaring away, and then screeching and skidding as he took the first treacherous curve far too fast.

As masterful as he was politically, his eyes had betrayed him when he vowed that he would be the first to wish her all the best should the investigation uncover nothing of concern. Alexa knew that he disapproved of her, and always would, but in a strange way she found his enmity very comforting. Thompson would have her investigated as an enemy would, meticulously searching for flaws, overlooking nothing, pursuing all clues. If her so carefully hidden secret could be discovered, his compulsive investigation would find it. But, if her precious secret remained hidden, she could put that tormenting worry to rest forever. She would know that Katie was safe, and always would be; and safe, too, would be her own life and love with Robert.

Thompson had told her that the investigation would be completed by Christmas. But, would she have already learned, long before Christmas, that she had to leave Robert and their love? In three weeks they were spending the weekend in Richmond with Brynne and Stephen and Katie. Would she learn, on that weekend, that she would have to say good-bye to Robert to protect herself from the anguish of being forever merely just a visitor in her beloved daughter's life?

Chapter 25

"Welcome!" Brynne's dark brown eyes sparkled as she greeted Robert and Alexa. "Stephen and I are so thrilled about you two!"

"Thank you, Brynne. I feel very lucky," Alexa answered softly, trying to focus on Brynne but so very distracted by the knowledge that a precious little girl was somewhere quite near. She kept her hands buried deep in her coat pockets, far away from Robert's. Her fingers had betrayed her before, by turning to ice and digging deeply into a man's palms, and she knew that they would have betrayed her now, a trembling clutch of joy and fear, had Robert held them.

"I'm the lucky one," Robert said quietly.

"Yes you are, Robert," Brynne concurred with a loving sisterly tease. "And don't you forget it!"

"I won't. Not ever, not for a second." He spoke the last, very softly, to Alexa. "We seem to be missing a husband and a daughter. My guess is that they're together somewhere."

"Naturally. They're in Katie's room."

"As you'll soon see, Alexa, from all the toys and blankets and pillows, the description 'Katie's room' applies to every single room in this house," Robert explained with a gentle smile.

"True enough," Brynne admitted with a soft laugh. "But right now, she's in her very own bedroom. She and her Daddy, who doesn't have the wonderful luxury of being able to be with her all day every day, have been playing since dawn, without a nap. Now he's trying to convince her that just a little nap might be a good idea. He's been up there quite a while, which means it may not be working, even though Katie's very sleepy."

"So sleepy that her big brown eyes have finally fluttered closed, despite her very strong will," Stephen said as he appeared in the foyer and smiled warm welcomes to Robert and Alexa. "I promised her that when she awakened she'd see her Uncle Robert and meet her Aunt Alexa. She fell asleep quite happy."

"There is a one hundred percent likelihood that Stephen and I will spend every minute between now and the time Katie joins us talking about her," Brynne confessed lovingly.

"There's nothing wrong with that," Robert said.

"No, I know there isn't. But we really do want to hear about the two of you and your plans."

"Our plans are very simple, and very wonderful. Alexa and I are going to spend the rest of our lives together. We're planning to be married on Valentine's Day."

"Very romantic." Brynne smiled, then added quietly, "And probably more sensible than your original plan of getting married the second the divorce is final."

"Yes," Robert agreed, as he had agreed when Alexa had said the same thing, between tender kisses, two weeks before. Getting married the moment the divorce was final would draw the kind of attention they had so far managed to completely avoid, she had said; and by February, *Pennsylvania Avenue* would be through filming for the season and she could spend every moment being his *wife;* and, besides, she had added softly, the divorce of Robert and Hillary McAllister was final on December nineteenth, the anniversary of Marion and Arthur Sterling's death.

"How is your sister?" Brynne asked Alexa an hour later. The men were out, buying wine for dinner, and they were in the kitchen, Brynne rolling pie crust, Alexa watching.

"She's fine," Alexa answered softly as the words "your sister" created waves of emotion. The waves were gentle, the emotion loving, because of Cat's visit to RoseCliff in June and the many transatlantic conversations they had had since then. Alexa had told her little sister the truth about Robert, that he had been her secret love and was the father of her baby; and Cat had accepted that difficult revelation with love, and empathy, and a wish, as always, for Alexa's happiness. "I think Cat's in love, too. I think she's fallen in love with Alain Castille."

"The Prince of L'île? Really?"

"Yes, really. She's on tour in Europe now, and it seems that Alain manages to attend virtually every concert, and on the rare days that she's not performing, she's at the palace." Alexa smiled. "She sounds very happy, and I think the relationship is quite serious."

"I remember how much Marion and Arthur liked Alain, how gracious and charming they thought he was. They would probably think this was wonderful."

"Yes, I think they would," Alexa agreed quietly. Frowning, she added, "But I've been a little uncertain about telling James about Cat and Alain, because I'm sure that any mention of L'île would trigger memories of the tragedy."

"So you haven't told him?"

"No, but I haven't actually had a chance to. He's been away for months, working on some very important negotiations in Colombia. He doesn't even know about Robert and me yet."

"Will that be a problem? You and James—"

"No, it won't be a problem. James and I are very good friends. We haven't been more than that for a long time."

"How is he, Alexa?" Brynne asked suddenly. "I used to feel close to him, but since Arthur and Marion's death, he's been so far away, both literally and emotionally. I'm sure Robert told you that it was James who handled Katie's adoption for us, and it was even he who brought her here to us." She sighed softly. "James has done *so much* for Stephen and me. I wish there was something we could do for him. What do you think? Is there something?"

"I don't know, Brynne. He's always been very private, and since Marion and Arthur's death, he's been even more—" Alexa was stopped mid-sentence by the almost imperceptible sound, a sound only a mother could hear, a sound heard by both Alexa and Brynne.

"Did you hear her, too?" Brynne asked, surprised. Even Stephen didn't always hear the very first noises Katie made when she awakened and wondered where her parents were.

"I guess so."

"She's just awakening, still finding her baby bearings. I like to get to her before she's fully awake, so she won't be upset. Not," Brynne added with a soft smile, "that I've ever delayed getting to her long enough to know if she even gets upset."

Brynne was midway through the lattice on the top of the cherry pie, but she simply left that unimportant project and began to cross the kitchen to quickly wash the flour off her hands before going to Katie.

"I'd be happy to go get her," Alexa offered softly. "Unless you think it might upset her."

"Oh, thank you. No, it won't upset her. She seems to know right away when she meets someone who loves her. And," Brynne added, her soft voice filled with pride and love, "I'm pretty sure you're going to love our little girl."

"I'm pretty sure I will, too."

"OK, so I'll finish with the pie crust while you get Katie. Her room is upstairs, the second door on the left."

Katie was cooing soft hellos to her room as she floated from her happy dreams to the reality of

428

her safe and happy life. Alexa stood in the doorway for a moment, listening to her daughter's happy sounds, then walked with legs as unsteady as her trembling emotions to the pink and white crib.

Oh, you're so very pretty, aren't you? Alexa asked silently as she gazed through a blur of tears at the smiling little girl. She saw Robert in Katie's pretty face, Robert and Brynne, and although others would have seen her own delicate features had they known to look, Alexa saw no resemblance to herself at all.

So very pretty, and so very happy, she thought as Katie's dark brown eyes sparkled a curious untroubled welcome to the new face that smiled at her with such love. Alexa's face was quite unfamiliar to Katie, of course. Even if the tiny infant had been able to make a memory of the face that had gazed so lovingly at her in those few moments after her birth, she would have remembered a face with black hair and blue eyes, not the one she saw now. This face, with golden hair and glistening green eyes, was a face that Katie could greet with a curious untroubled smile.

No troubles for you, my darling, Alexa thought, a wish and a promise. Only happiness for you, my little love. Then, whispering softly, she spoke for the first time, "Hello, little Katie."

Alexa's whisper was filled with the same softness with which she had spoken to her daughter in the months before Katie's birth and for those few precious moments they had together after Katie was born. At the sound of Alexa's soft loving voice, a flicker of confusion crossed Katie's face and her big brown eyes strained to focus more clearly on the unfamiliar face hovering over her.

Oh, is it possible? Does she recognize my voice? Alexa wondered as a fresh flood of hot tears spilled down her cheeks. And then gently, so very gently, she lifted her daughter out of the crib and curled her into her arms. Katie's eyes remained intently focused on Alexa's face and now her tiny hands reached eagerly for the tear-dampened cheeks, touching, patting softly, searching.

"Oh, Katie, Katie," Alexa whispered. But her loving voice only caused more confusion. *Confusion,* not happiness, not joy. I must say no more words, she told herself. I want no worries for Katie, no confusion, no sadness, not even for a moment, even if . . .

Did this mean she would have to say good-bye to Robert and their love after all? Before today Alexa had wondered if she might have to leave him to protect herself. But she knew now, already, that that wouldn't be necessary. The great joy of seeing Katie *far* outweighed the immense loss.

But, from the moment she had first learned of her pregnancy, every decision Alexa had made had been made for her baby's happiness. Would it be best for Katie never to hear her voice again? Would there always be, for Katie, something troubling and confusing about her Aunt Alexa?

Alexa said no more words. She just cuddled Katie close to her, softly kissing her dark curls as she rocked her gently and memorized the precious moment—Katie's soft warmth, her delicate sweetness—as she battled the fear that it would be their last.

That was how Brynne found them many minutes later, the pie crust long since finished. Neither Alexa nor Katie sensed her appearance in the open doorway; so, for a while, Brynne simply watched, smiling softly at the exquisite tenderness and love that she saw.

How lovely and loving Alexa is, Brynne thought as she watched the gentle scene and remembered Alexa's kindness to her on a most sad August night. How lucky Robert is to have found her. What happiness there will be now, at last, for my beloved brother.

As Brynne gazed from Alexa to the precious bundle she cradled so gently, her thoughts flowed from Robert and Alexa's happiness to her own. How blessed she was. The miracle of Katie was a bountiful joy beyond words. And yet, as if that immense joy weren't enough, more than enough, there was now another little miracle, a tiny new life, living, flourishing, within her.

Brynne had told no one about the tiny new life—except Katie. "Oh, Katie, Katie," she would say. "You're going to have a little sister or brother. A little sister, you think? Yes, I think so too. And I think, also, my precious little miracle," she would add with soft wonder, "that, somehow, this new baby is here because of you. Maybe she hears how much fun we're having, and feels all the love inside me because of you, and maybe, my Katie, that's why she's decided to grow big and strong."

Brynne's baby was eighteen weeks old, exactly

Katie's age, a treasure of love created the night Katie was born, after James called, because she and Stephen had forgotten, on that night of immense joy, to take the precautions they had so carefully taken to prevent the sadness of future losses. This baby had already survived six weeks longer than the babies they had lost, and the doctor was very optimistic, but Brynne hadn't yet told Stephen. She wouldn't, not until she was sure, and that would probably be long before he even began to guess, because the little life inside her was curled, safe and protected, very low in her welcoming pelvis.

For now she would only share the secret with the beloved bundle cradled so gently in Alexa's arms; the beloved little girl who, now, Brynne needed very much to cuddle herself.

"I don't hear a fussy baby," she said softly.

As Brynne's voice broke the magical spell, there was, for Alexa, who had lost all sense of time, a moment of confusion. But there was no confusion for Katie. At the sound of Brynne's voice, her brown eyes sparkled with joy—her whole pretty face sparkled!—and she turned excitedly toward the soft, loving voice she knew so well: the voice of her mother.

"Not a fussy baby at all," Alexa agreed quietly, focusing quickly and watching Katie carefully as she spoke. One delicate dark brown eyebrow furrowed, just a little, the smallest ripple, but Katie's eager attention remained on Brynne. Whatever had been vaguely troubling about her own voice seemed quite forgotten in the memories of pure joy that were evoked by Brynne's.

"She's never a fussy baby," Brynne said as she reached for her excited daughter. When she held Katie in her arms, the two pairs of happy brown eyes met, and noses rubbed softly, as she asked, "How's my baby girl? Did you have a nice nap? Oh, Katie-Kate, look at your pink sleepy cheeks! You needed a good rest, because you and your Daddy had such fun, didn't you?"

Brynne exchanged gleeful greetings with Katie for several moments before looking back at Alexa. But when she finally did look, a thoughtful frown touched her pretty face.

"Have you been crying, Alexa?"

"Happy tears, Brynne. I'm so happy for you and Stephen . . . and Katie."

"Thank you," Brynne whispered as her own eyes misted. "I still don't really believe it's happened. My heart stops every time the telephone rings."

"But I thought the adoption was closed. I thought James had made certain the biologic mother could never find her."

"Yes, that's right, he did. But still . . ."

"She's your daughter, Brynne," Alexa said with quiet confidence. I made a promise of love, and I will never break that solemn vow. She was speaking in a normal voice now, not the special voice that was just for her baby girl, and she saw with exhilarating relief that this voice triggered for Katie no confusing memories at all. Her heart raced with joy as she repeated, in the voice that meant she didn't have to say good-bye to Katie, "She's your daughter."

James returned from Colombia on November first. The only mail of interest waiting for him at Inverness was a hand-delivered note dated two weeks before: *James, I have wonderful news. Call me. Love, Alexa.* She would not reveal her news over the phone to him, but thirty minutes after his call to RoseCliff, she was at the door of his mansion.

"Oh, James, how can I help you?" she asked when she saw him. He looked so exhausted, his handsome face so drawn, his dark blue eyes drained of color until they were almost gray.

"Help me?"

"You've helped me so much and I . . ."

"I'm OK, Alexa. I'm just very tired." He tried smiling, and failed, because it had been so long since he had smiled, but he said truthfully, "Actually, the negotiations are really going quite well. We're going to regroup for a couple of weeks and then return to give a final push. Hopefully, we'll have a signed agreement before Christmas."

"Oh, good. It would be nice if you were here at Christmas."

"So . . . tell me your wonderful news."

"My wonderful news is that Robert and I are going to be married on Valentine's Day. We want you to be the best man, of course, and Cat and Brynne will be—"

"Does he know?"

"No, James, he doesn't know. And I'm never going to tell him."

434

"He needs to know, Alexa."

"I can't tell him. I thought I might be able to, but two weeks ago we drove to Richmond to see Katie. Robert loves her *so much,* and she loves him. It's almost as if they both somehow know. But they don't know, and they never will, and this way it can always be a wonderful, joyous, untroubled love. If Robert knew the truth, it would cause him such terrible sadness." Alexa shrugged softly, as if her next words might make no sense to James, and then continued quietly, "I love Robert far too much to tell him, James. I would say good-bye to him forever before I would cause him such pain."

Alexa had shrugged, as if he might not understand, but of course James understood perfectly. Oh, yes, Alexa, I know all about loving someone too much to want to cause them sadness or pain. That's the reason I said good-bye to Catherine, who I loved, *love,* so very much.

"Oh, Alexa," he sighed softly.

"What, James?"

"I have this vague memory of a time when everything seemed uncomplicated and happy. The memory is so distant, I wonder if the time ever truly existed."

"It did exist, and it will exist again. Everything is going to be better, James, for both of us. It *has* to be," she said firmly. Then, smiling a beautiful dreamy smile, she predicted with quiet confidence, "Everything will be much better by Christmas."

"That's the second time you've mentioned Christmas, Alexa. Is there a reason?"

"Yes, in fact there are several reasons. First of all, you'll be here, having returned triumphant from Colombia. And Cat will be here, because she's going to perform at the traditional White House Christmas Concert. And my parents will be here. I'd very much like you to meet them."

"And I'd very much like to."

"Good. I'm glad. Let's see, there are more reasons. Oh, yes, Robert's divorce will be final." Alexa smiled happily and forced herself to hold the radiant smile as she casually said the next, "And, by Christmas, as much as he hates to admit it, and probably *won't* admit it to me, Thompson Hall will have discovered that I'm an entirely suitable spouse for Robert."

"What does that mean?"

"You know who Thompson Hall is, don't you?"

"Yes, of course."

"Well. He's having me investigated, to see if I'm really future First Lady material. It made me angry at first, but it's something that would be done eventually by someone, and it will be the most wonderful Christmas present of all to know without a flicker of doubt that no one can find out about Katie—*ever.*"

"But we already know that. Aside from Dr. Lawton, whose ethics are without question, the only people who knew about your pregnancy are people who love you very much. And the same is true for the people who knew about your affair with Robert." James's dark blue eyes searched her emerald ones, and when the emerald faltered under the intense blue gaze, he asked sharply, "Alexa?"

"Hillary knew about our affair."

"*What?*"

"In fact, it was cruel and clever Hillary who orchestrated our break-up."

"She knew before the evening at the gala?"

"Yes. She's a terrific actress, isn't she? Maybe if you'd been holding *her* hand that night, you would have felt it turn to ice." Alexa added lightly, trying to soften his angry blue glare, "Of course, Hillary's hands are probably always icy."

"This changes everything, Alexa."

"No, it doesn't. Hillary knows nothing about the baby. She believed she had successfully ended our affair. And you know as well as I that she wasn't prowling around here last spring. Besides, James, if Hillary knew anything she would have long since used the information."

"Really? Have you forgotten so quickly about your longtime enemy? I think, and this is based on what *you* told me about Hillary as a teenager, that it's quite possible she would hold onto the information, savoring it until just the perfect moment. Like the eve of your marriage, maybe? Or, perhaps, the day of Robert's nomination for the Presidency? Or the moment just before his inauguration? Do you have any reason to believe that Hillary would balk at destroying Brynne, Stephen, and Katie along with you and Robert?"

"Hillary doesn't know!"

"You don't know that. Dammit, Alexa, have you forgotten why you gave Katie to Brynne and Stephen? So she would be safe, and happy, and untouched by scandal or uncertainty, remember? Do you want her to become known as the little girl who cost her father the Presidency?"

"*No!* That will never happen, James. I won't let it happen," she said softly, solemnly. "If Hillary knows—and I truly believe that she doesn't—she will tell Thompson Hall or me. I *do* know Hillary, and I'm very sure that I'm the only one she would really want to hurt. I also have no doubt that what would give her the greatest pleasure would be to prevent my marriage to Robert. If Hillary knows, she'll tell Thompson or me, and she'll do it fairly soon, *before* the divorce is final."

"And?"

"And if she goes to Thompson instead of coming to me, he'll tell me. He agreed that if he uncovered anything worrisome, he would come to me first, to try to convince me not to marry Robert."

"*And?*"

"If Thompson Hall discovers anything that could even remotely lead to Katie, I will tell Robert good-bye."

James knew it was true. He saw in the beautiful emerald a look he had seen once before, on the day she had asked him to handle Katie's adoption; a look that said, quite eloquently, that she would keep the solemn promise from her heart, no matter what, even at the cost of great anguish to herself.

Chapter 26

L'île des Arcs-en-ciel . . . December 1990

Alain and Catherine sat at their special place on the cliff above the sea watching the brilliant rainbows fade gently into the pink winter twilight. They sat in silence, as they often did, as they shared the magnificence before them. But, on this warm winter evening, the silence wasn't comfortable as always; it was troubled, a trouble to match the dark worry Catherine saw on Alain's handsome face. In less than an hour his private jet would carry her swiftly to Paris, and from there she would fly to Washington. They would be apart for ten days, the longest separation since their gentle love began. It could be their impending separation that was troubling him, she supposed, but she sensed it was something more. Something he would tell her, Catherine knew, because in their love there were no secrets that weren't shared.

"Alain?" she asked softly.

"There's something I'd like you to think about while you're away, Catherine."

"All right," she agreed as she saw uncertainty in his dark eyes. The uncertainty didn't need to be there. Alain could tell her anything. Smiling, she urged gently, "What is it?"

"I was wondering," Alain said very quietly to

her welcoming sapphire eyes, "if, while you're away, you'd think about marrying me."

"Oh, Alain," she whispered, her surprised blue eyes sparkling with happiness, giving him his answer before she spoke it aloud. "I don't need ten days to think about it. Yes, I will marry you."

"Yes?"

"Of course I will," she repeated softly as he drew her gently into his arms. "I love you, Alain."

"And I love you, Catherine," he whispered as his lips tenderly caressed her silky black hair. After a moment, he found her shimmering blue eyes. "I love you, and for the next ten days I shall miss you very much."

"And I'll miss you," she admitted softly. Then, smiling, she reminded lovingly, "But you'll be very busy spending time with the friends you've ignored all fall because you've been with me."

"True, and you'll have a wonderful time visiting with Alexa and your parents." Alain smiled, and added softly, "But this will be the last Christmas we spend apart."

Alain's promise was tender and loving, but Catherine suddenly felt a tremor of ice, the chilly stirring of almost forgotten ghosts. Just a year ago, *on this same Sunday in December,* James had made the same loving promise to her.

"Yes, our last Christmas spent apart," she echoed quietly, still chilled by the icy ghosts of the love of Catherine and James. Their wonderful, private love had been so secret that when it died only they knew it had ever even existed. Such secrecy scared her now, as if hidden loves could not survive, and Catherine wanted this warm,

440

gentle love with Alain to last forever. "May I tell Alexa and my parents that we plan to marry?"

"Of course. And may I tell Natalie? She'll be so thrilled. Already she thinks of you as a sister."

"Oh, yes, please tell her."

"She'll want to be involved in the design of your engagement ring."

"Yes, she will, won't she?" Catherine asked with a soft laugh of fondness for her future sister-in-law. Natalie was a gifted designer, bold and innovative. She could design a breathtaking engagement ring, a true work of art, but . . .

"But, Catherine, the ring should be what you want," Alain quietly addressed her unspoken worry that what Natalie might design would be magnificent, but not her, not *them.*

"And what you want."

"I was thinking, perhaps, a bouquet of emeralds and rubies."

"I love you," she said softly in response to the gentle tease. A bouquet of emeralds and rubies would be a disaster, of course, but Alain was simply suggesting something as far removed as possible from the obvious: exquisite blue sapphires to match her exquisite blue eyes. She had told him about the sapphires she had received before in the name of love, from her mother and from James, and she knew his tease was his gentle way of telling her that he would never give her gems that would recall those other sadnesses.

"I love you, too, Catherine." Alain took her slender left hand in his and after a moment admitted quietly, "I actually have been thinking about your engagement ring."

"Yes?"

"I thought a diamond, simple and elegant, a flawless brilliant cut solitaire in a delicate setting of white and yellow gold."

"Oh, Alain, that would be lovely."

"Is there no respect whatsoever for days on which divorces are final?" Alexa demanded with an exasperated laugh as she replaced the receiver of the phone and turned to Catherine, with whom, until the telephone rang, she had been enjoying a leisurely breakfast in RoseCliff's cheery kitchen.

"What horrible thing is happening?" Catherine asked.

"They want me to work today! Cat, did I or did I not return after eleven o'clock last night with a solemn promise from the director that in exchange for the late shoot I would have today off?"

"Yes, you did. But now they need you?"

"Just until mid-afternoon, they claim. And—I guess I should get this in writing!—they are now saying that if we can finish the scene they want to shoot today, they won't need me again this week, which means I'll be off until after Christmas."

"That sounds good."

"It sounds very good, doesn't it? Much too good to pass up. So, I guess I'll need to have you drop me off on your way to the White House, and when I'm finished I'll get a ride or take a taxi home."

"I should be done with the rehearsal by noon,

Alexa. Why don't I just plan to go back to the studio and wait for you?"

"Oh, no, Cat, if you don't mind, you'll need to meet James."

"James?" she echoed softly.

"Yes. He called me yesterday afternoon at the studio. Whatever it was he was negotiating in Colombia is finished, triumphantly, and he's arriving home today. His flight is scheduled to land at Dulles at one-fifteen, and I told him I'd be there to meet him."

"Do you usually meet him?"

"No. But it was just a year ago today that his parents were killed, and I thought . . ." Alexa shrugged. "I didn't say that to him, of course, and I don't know if he'll be even more sad about them today than any other day, but . . ."

"But what?" Catherine asked quietly.

"But he didn't tell me not to meet him. No matter what, it's Christmas and James is alone. I'm hoping he'll join us for Christmas dinner. I thought I'd invite him when I saw him today, but maybe you could? Cat, can you meet him? Do you mind?"

"No, of course I don't mind."

"Great. Thanks. Invite him for dinner tonight, too, if you like. Robert thought he'd be able to get here by six."

They had talked, when they had made the wonderful plans for their love, about how terribly romantic it was going to be greeting each other at airports. They would never be apart for more than a week, they had promised, and at the time each had wondered privately if even a week would be far too long to endure.

And now Catherine hadn't seen James since they had said good-bye on L'île in July . . . and it had been precisely a year to the day since the wonderful plans for their secret love had begun to die.

But when James walked off the plane and saw her waiting for him, it was as if the past year had never happened and their joyous, magical love was alive, *flourishing,* still. He hadn't expected her to be there, of course, and in the unguarded moment of surprise, his defiant heart responded before his mind, sending its bold and illogical wishes with swift joy to his dark blue eyes, filling them with unconcealed desire and love. And, in that same moment, even though she had given it fair warning that she would be seeing him, Catherine's heart answered with its own bold and defiant joy, sending messages to her sparkling sapphire eyes that precisely mirrored the wonderful wishes and desires in his.

The magnificent moment couldn't last. Quickly, *too* quickly, their minds intervened, subduing their fluttering joyous hearts with stern reminders of the truth, and by the time James reached her, they each acknowledged the wonderful and wondrous moment, *that should never have happened,* with smiles that were apologetic, and very, very gentle.

"Hello, Catherine," he said softly.

"Hi. Alexa had to work after all."

★   ★   ★

They talked a little, and filled the silences with more gentle smiles, and soon Catherine was slowing the car to a stop in front of the mansion at Inverness. She hadn't invited James for Christmas dinner with her family yet, much less for dinner with Robert and Alexa at RoseCliff tonight. Nor had she told him the news that would surely be mentioned at both gatherings . . .

"James?"

"Yes?"

"Alain has asked me to marry him, and I've told him yes."

"Alain? Alain Castille?"

"Yes." Catherine frowned. "I guess Alexa hadn't mentioned to you that Alain and I have been seeing each other?"

"No."

"Oh." She looked bravely into his surprised blue eyes. "I think you're supposed to wish me all the best."

"Catherine . . ."

"Yes?"

"How well do you know him?"

"I know him very well, James," she assured softly, with a grateful smile for his gentle concern.

"Good." James hesitated a moment and then asked quietly, "Do you know about his father?"

"Yes, I know about Jean-Luc. I know all about his treachery and his madness. But how do you know about Jean-Luc, James? Oh, no," she whispered as she found an answer to her own question. "Is that why you were on L'île in July? To investigate Alain?"

"No. Elliot told me a little of L'île's history

before I visited, that's all." James hesitated again, knowing he had very little right to pry and yet remembering so clearly what Natalie had told him that morning as they had sailed: *Alain will marry someday, to give L'île its next monarch, but I am quite certain that he will never again plan to marry for love.* After a moment he said gently, "Actually, it was Natalie who told me about Alain. Catherine, she told me that he had been engaged once before."

As the meaning of James's words settled, Catherine was swept by waves of emotion; powerful, unfamiliar rushes of anger, and the more familiar, more delicate whispers of sadness. The emotions swirled together, battling to be heard. The more powerful, anger, spoke first.

"And that he loved Monique very much? And that when she died so tragically, while he watched in helpless horror, that he was quite confident he would never fall in love again? Oh, yes, I know that." As Catherine paused, the anger washed away as swiftly as it had appeared, and when she spoke again it was with a soft, bewildered voice of sadness. "Is it so impossible for you to imagine, James, that someone could truly love me? Just because you couldn't—"

"I loved you, Catherine. You know that."

"I suppose I believed you did," she answered, her voice still soft and sad. But then it was anger's turn to speak again, and it rushed back with a vengeance, crushing all delicacy and bringing with it the aching memories of how hurt she had been when he left her. James had hurt her, *so much,* and now she heard herself speaking hurtful words to him, words that flowed with astonishing effortlessness from her heart to her lips on a gushing river of pain, "But I was so naive then, James. I didn't really know about love when we were together. But now I do. I've learned the truth about love from Alain. He knows everything about me, *everything,* and I know all his secrets, too. His life has been filled with terrible tragedies, but, unlike you, he is not afraid to share even his darkest emotions. Alain trusts me and our love enough to share both his joy and his pain. You only wanted to share the joy, James, and now I know that that's not really love."

"Oh, Catherine."

"Be happy for me, James!" she defiantly commanded the stricken blue eyes. "You wouldn't let me love you when you needed my love and I was so willing to give it, remember? Alain loves me as you never did. He wouldn't send me away if he were dying. He would allow me to love him."

"I loved you, Catherine," James whispered softly. "How can you believe that I didn't?"

"It doesn't really matter now, does it?"

Yes, his heart screamed. Yes it matters! I loved you . . . I love you . . . I will always love you.

"No," he answered quietly before turning to get out of the car. "I guess not."

Alexa was at RoseCliff, puttering in the kitchen, when Catherine returned from Inverness.

"How is he?"

"Fine."

447

"Is he coming for dinner?"

"No. Not tonight, and I forgot to ask him about Christmas."

"Are you OK, Cat?"

"Sure. I think I need a long hot shower."

"Be my guest. Is it getting cold outside?"

"Oh, yes, I guess." Catherine felt chilled, but the icy shivers which swept through her had nothing to do with the rapidly darkening sky or the frigid winter wind. The shivers were simply the restless and tormented swirlings of the ghosts of a dead love. The icy ghosts had been sleeping, but they were awake now, wide awake, and they were very upset.

"They're predicting snow tonight. It's not supposed to start until after midnight, but if it comes earlier it might be best for Robert to spend the night here."

"He can spend the night here anyway, Alexa. Really, it wouldn't bother me at all." It only bothered me when it was James in your bed, she thought. James, *James* . . .

Catherine took a long shower and dressed for dinner. The outside world might be preparing for a winter snowstorm, but RoseCliff was warm and cozy, as always, and Catherine knew she would be quite comfortable in silk.

"Gorgeous dress," Alexa said when Catherine reappeared. She smiled questioningly, because her little sister had been in her bedroom for almost an hour, but Catherine simply returned the smile.

"Thank you."

448

"I'm having tea. Would you like some?"

"Sure. I'll get it. Shall I get some more for you?"

"Yes. Thanks."

Catherine poured the tea, and they sat in the romantic living room and gazed at the swirling gray drama unfolding over Chesapeake Bay. The snow was still a long way off, but the storm clouds already stretched ominous dark fingers across the sky.

The telephone rang as Catherine and Alexa were discussing the plans for their parents' visit which was to begin early the next morning. Jane and Alexander would tour the set of *Pennsylvania Avenue,* of course, and Robert would show them the sights on Capitol Hill, and after Catherine's concert at the White House they were all dining with the President and First Lady . . .

"Your Prince or mine?" Alexa teased gaily when their conversation was interrupted by the ringing telephone.

"I'll answer it," Catherine said, hoping, indeed, that it would be her Prince. She needed Alain's warmth to melt the icy ghosts. She needed to be reminded of a safe gentle love . . . not a dangerous and magical one. "Hello?"

"Once upon a time there was a beautiful little girl whose mother didn't want her."

"Who is this?"

"If you want to know what became of the abandoned baby come to the Marlboro Marina now."

"Who . . ." Catherine began again, but stopped because the voice was gone, the message delivered, the connection severed.

449

"Cat? Who was it?" Alexa asked as waves of fear washed through her. Thompson Hall? Hillary? For months, every time the phone had rung, her heart had raced, and she had said a silent prayer before answering it—just as, she supposed, Brynne always did, too. As if the silent prayer could change the message of the ringing phone! But Alexa had forgotten this time, because Robert's divorce was final today, and surely she would have heard by now if Thompson had found anything, and it was almost Christmas, and everything was going to be fine . . . "Cat?"

"Oh, Alexa."

Catherine took a soft breath and told her exactly what the caller had said. As she watched Alexa's emerald eyes, she saw first the loss of hope, the *end* of hope; and then, after only a moment, she saw familiar Alexa determination.

"I'm going to the Marina."

"I'm going with you." Catherine underscored her words by handing Alexa one of the two winter coats that hung on the antique coat hook and putting the other one on herself.

"No, Cat," Alexa said quietly. "Please stay here. Please stay here and call James and tell him what has happened."

"James, but not Robert?"

"No, not Robert. I've never told him about the baby, Cat. I can't tell him."

"Because she's Katie?" Catherine asked gently. It was a guess, of course, but . . . "Robert talked about her so much at dinner Monday night, and you'd never even mentioned Brynne's

450

adopted daughter to me, so I wondered if maybe she was your baby."

"Yes, Cat, she is," Alexa admitted softly. "Katie is our little girl. I haven't told Robert. I can't. It would hurt him too much."

"But Alexa . . ."

"I have to go. Please, Cat, will you stay here and call James?"

"What can James do?"

"I don't know. But, please, just call him. I have to go now. Where are the car keys?"

"In my purse. Here." As Catherine gave Alexa the keys, she said, "Alexa, this will be all right, you'll see."

"No, Cat," Alexa answered quietly. "I don't think it will be."

Chapter 27

As soon as Alexa disappeared down the stairs and out of sight, Catherine dialed the once-familiar number to Inverness.

"James?"

"Catherine, I—"

"Alexa needs your help. She just got a call from someone who knows about the baby."

"Let me speak to her, please."

"She's gone. The message was for her to go to the Marlboro Marina."

"And she did?"

"I couldn't stop her, James. She . . ." Whatever

451

Catherine had been about to say was swept away by a sudden overwhelming fear. She didn't remember hearing a sound, but there must have been one, because as she was trying to decipher her immense and inexplicable fear, she heard the crash. "No!"

"Catherine? What is it?"

"It was . . . a crash. Oh, James, *no.*"

"I'm on my way. I'll call the paramedics and the police from my car phone." James wanted her to wait at RoseCliff, but he knew she wouldn't, so he whispered softly, "Catherine, darling, be careful."

Catherine wasn't careful. When she reached the foot of the stairs, she dashed across the parking area and directly onto the winding road, running down the middle because it was the shortest route to Alexa.

But there was no Alexa, just an ominous plume of gray-black smoke, darker even than the stormy winter sky, a sinister flare that rose from the car burning on the beach below. Catherine reached the edge of the cliff and would have found a way down the treacherous granite wall—even though there was none—but Alexa wasn't in the inferno on the beach. Her motionless body lay just six feet away, on a ledge beneath where Catherine stood. After quickly removing her coat and tossing it onto the pavement as a marker for James and the paramedics, she scrambled down the cliff to Alexa.

"Alexa," she whispered to the face that was already ashen from internal blood loss. She was unconscious, but alive. Her chest lifted and fell in rapid shallow gasps, and her pulse beat frantically in her neck. Catherine was careful not to move her, but gently, so gently, she touched her warm cheek to Alexa's cold one and whispered, "I love you, Alexa. Help is on the way, so please fight as hard as you can. Oh, Alexa, I love you. Please fight. *Please.*"

The paramedics from Marlboro arrived within five minutes. By the time James arrived, having made the twenty-minute drive from Inverness in thirteen, Alexa's dangerously low blood pressure was being supported by intravenous fluids and pressors, her neck and back had been stabilized, and the Trauma Team at Memorial Hospital, having been notified that she obviously had internal bleeding, had communicated in return that there would be surgeons and an OR waiting for her.

Alexa was still on the ledge when James arrived, and Catherine was still there, too, kneeling on the cold hard granite as close to Alexa as she could be without interfering in the lifesaving efforts of the paramedics. Catherine didn't interfere, but her delicate hand found a way through the wall of backs to gently touch Alexa's golden hair.

The small ledge had become even smaller with the addition of paramedics and their equipment. James wanted to climb down, to be with Alexa and Catherine, but there was no room; and he would have been stopped, anyway, because there was a police lieutenant who had been awaiting his arrival with interest.

"Are you the one who called?"

"Yes. I'm James Sterling."

"Lieutenant Ed Baker. How did you know to call, Mr. Sterling?"

"I was talking to Alexa's sister Catherine on the phone when she heard the crash."

"That's Catherine on the ledge?"

"Yes."

"Good. I'll need to talk to her. I've only been here about five minutes, but already there are some things that bother me a whole lot about this accident."

"Like what?"

"Like the fact that there are no skid marks on the pavement, and the tracks of the wheels indicate that the car went straight off the cliff."

"*Meaning?*"

"Meaning, did Alexa Taylor drive off the cliff on purpose?"

"No."

"You sound confident."

"I am confident. I know Alexa very well. She would not take her own life." Or would she? James wondered. Had the call signaled an end— *the* end—to her? I will tell Robert good-bye, she had vowed, if her precious secret was ever discovered. Was this her good-bye? Good-bye to Robert and Katie, and good-bye to her own anguish? *A love to die for, James?* Alexa had teased a million years ago, long before either she or James had believed in love. Now, to protect the man she loved and his precious daughter had she given her own life? No, James thought. Please, *no.* "She would not."

"Well, good. I'm glad to hear that. I'm a real fan of hers, and I'd hate to think she was so

454

unhappy. Still, something happened. Something made her drive like a bat out of hell and lose control of her car. Maybe her sister knows what it was."

"Maybe," James agreed quietly. But maybe, he thought, if I can talk to Catherine first, she won't tell you what it was. "May I speak with Catherine first, Lieutenant? She may be in shock, and I would like to explain to her why you need to talk to her."

"Sure."

At that moment, the paramedics stood, ready to move Alexa off the ledge and into the waiting ambulance. Catherine stood, too, and as she did, Lieutenant Baker and James both moved forward, as if to stop her, even though she was far away from them. The movement was instinctive, protective, because they saw how precariously near the edge she was. She had been safe, kneeling on the granite, but now her trembling body wavered, and if she stepped back at all, even an inch to give the paramedics more room to maneuver, the fall would be instantly lethal.

But even though her eyes remained focused on Alexa, Catherine seemed to know her own proximity to disaster, and she didn't step back. She stood her ground and, very softly, asked the paramedics if she would be able to ride in the ambulance with Alexa. No, they told her, a police offficer would drive her if she needed a ride. Catherine touched Alexa for as long as she could, and then the physical bond was broken, and moments later Alexa was gone, her departure signalled by the harsh sound of blaring sirens.

Alexa was gone, but Catherine hadn't moved from her precarious perch on the ledge. James climbed down to her, and, as he approached, he saw the immense despair in her bewildered blue eyes. She looked so lost, and so fragile. Her delicate slender body, clothed only in sheer silk, shivered from the winter wind, and from the even greater chills of shock and grief. James wanted to rush to her, but she was still one terrifying step from eternity, and he was afraid of startling her, afraid even that she might back away at the sight of him. *Why wouldn't she?*

"Catherine?" he asked softly.

She didn't back away. She hesitated only a moment and then fell into his arms, allowing him to cradle her trembling body against his strong warmth.

"Oh, Catherine," he whispered into her wind-tossed, silky black hair. "She's going to be fine, darling."

"She has to be, James."

"She will be." It was a wish, not a promise, because he had seen Alexa's deathly paleness before the ambulance left.

James didn't want to let Catherine go, not ever, not ever again. But her shivering body needed even more than his loving warmth could provide. And he knew, soon and together, they would have to make a very important decision. He released her from his arms reluctantly and helped her into the coat she had tossed as a marker for the paramedics. After gently buttoning the buttons for her, he cupped her cold lovely face in his warm hands. His voice was soft, because he was speaking to Catherine, not because he worried that his important words would be overheard. The police were far away, talking among themselves, and even their loud voices were muffled by the winter wind.

"Darling, the police lieutenant needs to speak with you about what happened just before Alexa left RoseCliff."

"Oh." After a thoughtful moment, she added, "I see."

She *did* see, he realized. He had been worried that her shock and grief might make her unable to truly understand. But she understood, without further words from him, and as he watched, James witnessed an act of love—for Alexa. Her brilliant blue eyes told him, even before she spoke, that she had willed the shock from her mind.

"I know about Katie, James. Alexa told me just before . . ." She fought the rush of emotion and continued quietly, "I'm going to protect her secret. I have to."

"OK. I agree. After you talk to Lieutenant Baker, I'll drive you to the hospital. We'll make a brief stop at Marlboro Marina on the way."

"Yes." She smiled softly, grateful that perhaps in this small way, by simply protecting her precious secret, she was helping Alexa. "OK."

Lieutenant Baker was waiting by his car. He smiled sympathetically as Catherine and James approached.

"I just have a few questions, Ms. Taylor. I'm sorry, but they're necessary."

"I understand."

"OK. Now, it's obvious from the physical evidence—the distance the car traveled in the air before landing on the beach—that your sister was driving very fast. I'm trying to figure out why. You were with her right before she left the cottage?"

"Yes."

"Had she been drinking?"

"Drinking? No. Well, she and I were having tea."

"Did she, had she, taken any drugs? Cocaine or something?"

"No. Alexa doesn't ever use drugs, and she rarely drinks."

"You were having tea and then she suddenly left, driving very fast. Why?"

"Alexa received a phone call just before she left the cottage," Catherine answered, realizing she needed to provide some explanation.

"Do you have any idea who the caller was or what was said?"

"No."

"But the call upset her?"

"Yes."

"Was she on her way to meet the caller?"

"I think so."

"Do you know where?"

"No."

"Had she been getting calls, do you know? Perhaps there was an obsessed fan?"

"I don't know. I've only been visiting with her for the past three days. She didn't mention anything that was worrying her."

"But she got a call, out of the blue, that upset her enough to make her dash out of the cottage and drive so recklessly that she . . . I'm sorry, Ms. Taylor."

"Does it really matter what the caller said?"

"Probably not," Lieutenant Baker agreed easily. Then his expression changed, very slightly, even though his calm tone still sent the message that his questions were simply routine. "I just need to ask you about the car, Ms. Taylor."

"The car?"

"Do you know when Alexa last drove it?"

"Alexa? Last night. She returned from the studio about eleven."

"And as far as you know the car was working fine then?"

"Yes, And it was working fine all day today."

"Today?"

"Yes. I had it today."

"Oh. I see. What time did you return to the cottage?"

"Just before three."

"And the call came?"

"At four."

"OK. That's all for now. I know you want to get to the hospital. If you think of anything else, here's my card. Please give me a call."

James had no fear of who would be waiting in the parking lot at the Marlboro Marina. It would be Hillary, he imagined, or perhaps Thompson Hall. He planned a very brief conversation with whoever it was, just long enough to say he knew all about the blackmail call.

But the parking lot at the Marlboro Marina was quite deserted.

Had Hillary or Thompson heard the scream of sirens on the nearby road to RoseCliff and fled upon realizing that the call intended merely to blackmail Alexa out of her marriage to Robert had in fact precipitated a horrible tragedy? he wondered. Yes, perhaps, *probably*. But, as James surveyed the empty parking lot, Lieutenant Baker's words came back to him, taking on new meaning, a meaning that matched the police officer's somber expression as he had asked so seemingly casually about the car. There were no skid marks, he had said, *as if Alexa hadn't even attempted to stop,* and the tire tracks were straight, *as if she hadn't even tried to swerve away from the lethal cliff.*

James had assumed that Alexa had neither braked nor swerved because by the time her distracted mind realized the car was out of control she somehow knew her only hope was to jump. But what if she had tried to brake or swerve, and *couldn't?* What if the reason that no one was waiting here for Alexa was that the caller *knew* she would not survive the drive down the winding road from RoseCliff to the Marina? It seemed unimaginable—it *was*—and yet clearly the astute Lieutenant Baker had been considering the possibility from the very beginning.

"What, James?" Catherine asked softly, pulled from her own desperate thoughts as she sensed his sudden tension.

"Catherine, we need to tell Lieutenant Baker the caller wanted Alexa to come here."

"Why?"

"Because the police need to get fingerprints

460

from the pay phone." Even as he said it, James knew what a futile exercise it was likely to be: a call from a murderer, made simply to lure Alexa into a drive of death, would surely *not* have been made from here. Dusting for prints seemed futile, but James was unwilling to take the chance that he might be wrong.

"I thought we decided that we didn't want the police to know the details of the call. If they find the person who called, James, they will find out about Katie."

"Yes, but Catherine . . ." James sighed softly. "Darling, what I believe is that Alexa was upset, and driving carelessly, and that what happened was a terrible accident."

"That's what I believe, too."

"But, Catherine, we have to consider the possibility that whoever made the call may have also tampered with her car."

"No, James," she whispered, a soft plea from her heart. One year ago today, their world had been torn apart by an act of unspeakable brutality. It couldn't be happening again. *Please.*

"I don't think the police need to know what the caller said, but I think you should tell Lieutenant Baker that you now remember Alexa mentioning that she was coming here," James continued quietly, resolutely, even though all he really wanted to do was to hold her and reassure her. But he couldn't, so he urged gently, "Help me with this, Catherine. Doesn't that seem like what we should do? Doesn't that seem best, safest, for Alexa while we're waiting to know for certain that it was an accident?"

"Yes, I guess, it does," she said finally. "Yes. All right. I agree."

"OK. Good. Was the caller a man or a woman?"

"It was a whisper." Catherine frowned, searching for a clue, an impression, something. But there was nothing. "I don't know. I can't even guess."

"Did you notice if anyone was following you when you left me at Inverness?"

"No," she answered softly. "I didn't notice anything. I was just thinking about what we—I—had said. James, I'm sorry."

"I'm sorry, too, Catherine."

Chapter 28

Memorial Hospital's eighth-floor Intensive Care Unit waiting room was indistinguishable from the one on the first floor adjacent to the Operating Room. Both rooms were windowless and sparsely furnished with well-worn vinyl couches, institutional clocks, and coffee tables littered with frequently clutched but rarely read magazines. The two waiting rooms were essentially identical. But, nonetheless, when Catherine, Robert, and James received word, just after midnight, that they would be continuing their vigil in the bland room eight floors up, they greeted the news with unconcealed tears of joy.

Alexa had survived her first hurdle.

462

"We're closing now," the trauma chief told them. Even if they hadn't understood the surgical jargon, they would have known from the surgeon's fatigued but triumphant face that the report was good. "Alexa was terribly lucky. The internal bleeding was very significant, but we were able to oversew the hepatic and splenic lacerations, so no removal of organs was necessary."

The trauma chief was the first in a series of physicians to appear throughout the long night and give reports on Alexa's progress.

"She has multiple rib fractures," the pulmonary specialist informed them at one A.M. "The lung tissue beneath the fractures is injured, which means we will keep her on the ventilator for a while. This will insure adequate ventilation to the damaged areas, and in addition, because the ventilator will do the breathing for her, it will allow her to conserve energy."

"The period of hypotension—low blood pressure—due to blood loss, coupled with the traumatic injury to muscles, has caused her kidneys to shut down," the renal specialist explained at three-thirty. "We see this quite commonly following severe injuries. Very often, and we hope this will be true for Alexa, the kidneys overcome the shock and recover completely. We will support her until that happens with careful fluid and electrolyte management, and with emergency hemodialysis if necessary."

"She's in a coma," the neurologist said at dawn, shortly before Catherine and Robert left for the airport to meet Alexander and Jane. "I've examined her very thoroughly, and an MRI scan has already been done. There's no evidence of intracranial bleeding and no indication of any permanent neurologic damage."

"So she'll wake up?" Catherine asked softly.

"Yes. She'll wake up. I can't tell you how soon. I can tell you, though, that I've taken care of many patients who have awakened from a coma and remembered the words that had been spoken to them while they were unconscious. So, talk to her. Tell Alexa what you need her to hear."

They all—her parents, her sister, the man she loved, and the man who was her friend—had emotional words of love they needed their beloved Alexa to hear; and each spent precious moments at her bedside telling her those most important words.

Catherine told Alexa of her love, and then—because what if in Alexa's silent darkness there was the tormenting worry?—she spoke words to reassure. Catherine hoped that Alexa heard her soft, private reassurance, and that the words gave her sister peace.

"James and I decided that the police didn't need to know what the caller said. I told them that it was you, not me, who answered the phone. So don't worry, Alexa, your precious secret is safe." Catherine smiled softly and continued, "James is going to find out where both Hillary and Thompson Hall were at four o'clock yesterday afternoon. Neither of them was at the Marina after your accident, but whichever one it was probably left at the sound of the sirens. The call and the clandestine meeting seem like cloak and dagger theatrics, but remember how we were sitting in the living room discussing plans for Mom and Dad's visit just before the call? Hillary or Thompson must have come to the cottage, heard our voices, and then arranged the meeting at the Marina to speak to you in private. Anyway, somehow James is going to find out where each of them was at the time of the call." She paused, and after a thoughtful moment, she added a quiet truth, "He'll be able to find out, you know he will. He's always been there when you needed him."

Robert gazed through tears at his beloved Alexa. She looked like a porcelain marionette, motionless now, because the strings attached to her pale delicate body—the intravenous lines and monitor leads—had yet to bring her to life. How he wanted to curl her broken body in his arms and carry her away . . . to RoseCliff . . . to their wonderful love.

But Robert couldn't take her away, not yet. He could only hold her lifeless hand in his and touch his warm cheek to her cool one as he spoke.

"My darling love," he whispered. "It's been almost twenty-four hours since your accident, twenty- four miraculous hours. Your kidneys are already recovering from the shock, and your hematocrit is stable, and your lungs beneath the rib fractures are expanding far better than was hoped. Everything is healing miraculously. You just need to wake up, Alexa, that's all."

Robert paused to fight a wave of trembling emotion. He didn't want her to hear his fear, only his confident love. Finally he began again, "I just spoke to Brynne. She sends her love, of course, and even though I told her that given your miraculous recovery we'll very likely spend New Year's with them as planned, she insists on coming here to visit you anyway. They'll drive up tomorrow, assuming the roads are clear and Stephen can get away early enough. She thinks they'll arrive too late to visit tomorrow night, but says she'll be here bright and early the following morning."

And you'll be wide awake by then, won't you, my darling? he pleaded silently, pausing again as his voice threatened to falter. He fought the emotion with the memory of his conversation with Brynne, her obvious love for Alexa, her confident insistence that Alexa would be fine, and the happy images Brynne had wanted him to share with her. "Brynne wanted me to tell you that Katie is absolutely enraptured by the bright lights of Christmas, especially the twinkling lights on the tree. She says she's taking thousands of pictures, so we'll be able to see her joy for ourselves."

The happy images of Katie's sparkling eyes laughing with glee at twinkling Christmas lights swept Robert swiftly, emotionally, to other happy images, future ones, magnificent dreams. "Did I tell you how much I like your parents? I know I did, a thousand times already, but in case you weren't listening before, they're wonderful, my darling. What wonderful grandparents they will be for our babies. Oh Alexa, Alexa, think of our love, our life, our babies . . .''

We have a baby, Robert! We have a beautiful little girl who is enraptured by the twinkling lights of Christmas. Alexa's emerald eyes fluttered open then, and with complete consciousness came an acute awareness of all the sensations that had previously been only a vague part of the dream world in which she had been living. She was instantly aware of the fire in her chest, and every muscle in her body felt as if she had exerted it far beyond endurance. But Alexa ignored the fire and firmly instructed her muscles to endure just a little more—for Robert.

And then, for the tear-filled dark eyes she loved so very much, Alexa found a beautiful smile.

"She's awake," Robert said emotionally when he returned to the ICU waiting room ten minutes later and gave the wonderful news to her family.

"Awake?" Jane echoed.

"Oh, Robert . . ."

"She's awake, although I think she's about to drift off to sleep. She awakened a little while ago, and I guess I should have come out the second she opened her eyes, but I couldn't bear to leave her."

"That's all right," Alexander whispered hoarsely. "Do you think she recognized you?"

"Oh, yes, I know she did," Robert answered quietly. "And I'm sure that very soon, she'll be insisting that they remove the endotracheal tube so she can talk to us."

Robert's loving face revealed neither the

urgency he felt about hearing what Alexa would say, nor the guilt. He had known, ever since he had first seen her again, that there was a deep, painful, hidden sadness. He had hoped to love it away, and in the past few months, there had been wonderful, breathtaking moments when her emerald eyes had glowed with pure joy; but, so quickly and always, the sad, painful flickers would return. And when gently, so very gently, he had urged her to tell him what troubled her so, she resolutely denied anything was wrong at all. But Robert had proof, in the beautiful eyes he knew so well; and in their loving, *her* loving, a loving that was as desperate and furtive as it had been before—as if she still did not believe their wonderful love would last. He had urged her to tell him, many times, but sometimes even his gentle questions caused whispers of emerald fear, and, instead of pushing further, he just held her.

But I should have pushed her! The tormenting thought had echoed and reechoed in his mind ever since the accident. If I *had,* might she never have taken the nearly lethal drive? Oh, did my beloved Alexa almost die to protect a secret she kept from me?

"I'm sorry to interrupt." The words came from the ICU clerk who now stood in the open doorway of the waiting room. "There's an overseas call for Catherine at the nurses' station."

"Oh. Thank you."

It would be Alain, Catherine knew. As she walked from the waiting room to the purses' station' she realized that it had been twenty-four hours, almost precisely to the minute, since she had reached for the ringing phone at RoseCliff hoping the caller would be Alain. She had needed his gentle warmth then to melt the icy ghosts that had frolicked within her after the angry, hurtful words she had spoken to James. But yesterday afternoon, the caller had been the whispering messenger of tragedy, not Alain, and since that sinister call, she and James had been gently bonded by their love for Alexa and by the precious secret they kept for her. Catherine's angry and hurtful words had long since been forgotten, perhaps even forgiven; but still, now, twenty-four hours later, the icy ghosts lingered—because, she had discovered, it was so terribly difficult to be this close to James . . . and yet so far away.

Now, twenty-four hours later, Catherine needed the warmth of Alain's gentle love still, perhaps even more now than she had needed it yesterday afternoon.

"Alain?"

"*Oui*, Catherine. How is she, *chérie*, how is Alexa?"

"Oh, Alain, she's better. She had been in a coma, but just a few minutes ago, she woke up."

"I'm so glad, darling. And I'm so sorry I wasn't with you. I only just heard the news. Have you been trying to reach me?"

"No. Your itinerary and all the phone numbers you gave me are at RoseCliff, and I've been here since the accident. I knew you'd call as soon as you heard."

"It was Natalie who heard. She just phoned me."

"You're not together?"

"No. She went to Gstaad the evening before last, as scheduled, and I decided to spend one more day in Paris. I was at Versailles all day yesterday, and although I'm sure that the radio and television carried reports of Alexa's accident last night, I spent the evening reading—and calling you. Now I know why there was no answer at RoseCliff. I'm so sorry I haven't been with you all this time, darling, but I will be there very soon, and Natalie is coming too."

"Oh, no, Alain, you don't need to come."

"I want to be with you, Catherine."

Alain's warm words didn't melt the icy ghosts. *Indeed* they only triggered more chilling memories of the other love; memories of the time of great tragedy when Catherine had wanted desperately to be with James—to love him, to help him— and James had not allowed her to be. Was she doing that now with Alain? No, not at all. Just the opposite.

"I would want you to be with me if Alexa weren't better, Alain," she said softly, truthfully. "But she *is* better. She's going to be fine."

"Cat and I were having tea, discussing plans for our parents' visit, when the phone rang." Alexa narrowed her beautiful green eyes, searching for the precise memory, and after a moment continued, "I said something like 'Your Prince or mine?' and . . ."

"And?" Lieutenant Baker urged.

"And then darkness. It was a silent darkness— and so very black—but finally it became gray and was filled with familiar voices that were calling to me. I wanted to answer them, to reassure them, but there was such heaviness." Alexa frowned at the almost desperate memory of hearing the voices of those she loved and wanting to cry out to them—Yes, I hear you, I love you, *I love you!*—but unable even to open her eyes. She shook away the memory and smiled. "And then I woke up."

"You don't remember what the caller said."

"No. My memory stops just before I answered the phone."

"You don't remember the accident at all?"

"No. Lieutenant, I'm very sorry. I remember nothing except blackness from the moment I asked 'Your Prince or mine?' until I was here in the ICU. Nothing. I'm sorry. I want to remember, but I can't."

Alexa couldn't remember, and according to the neurologist who had been caring for her, she never would.

"It's called retrograde amnesia," the doctor explained. "It means loss of memory for the event and for a period of time prior to it. It's very common in serious head injuries."

"Will she ever remember those lost minutes?"

"No. She never will."

Alexa's retrograde amnesia meant that the police investigation would close, officially ruled an accident. The car had been destroyed beyond any hope of finding evidence of tampering, had there been any, and with neither that evidence nor Alexa's clear memory of a mechanical failure, the "case" could not be pursued. *Case?* Lieutenant Baker asked himself as he signed the final page of the report. What case? Who the hell would want to murder Alexa Taylor?

Alexa's retrograde amnesia meant that the police investigation was closed, and it meant, too, that Catherine and James would need to tell her about the telephone call she could not remember. They decided to tell her together, while Robert was spending a few necessary hours in his office and while Jane and Alexander were resting in their nearby hotel.

"James and I know what the caller said, Alexa."

"So do I, Cat."

"You remember?"

"Yes. I remember the call. And I remember your telling me what you had told the police and why." She added softly, gratefully, "Thank you. Thank you both."

"You're welcome."

"Do you remember the accident, Alexa?" James asked.

She softly shook her golden head, still bewildered that, despite how hard she tried to remember, those monumental moments remained hidden, and always would. "What I told Lieutenant Baker about the blackness is true, but it began a few minutes later, just as I left the cottage. Did you find out who made the call, James?"

"No. I only found out that it couldn't have been made by either Thompson or Hillary."

"It couldn't have?"

"No. I spoke with Thompson myself. He was quite surprised by my visit, and seemed uncomfortable that I knew about his investigation of you, but he said that the investigation was completed weeks ago, before Thanksgiving, and that it turned up nothing of consequence." As James recalled the meeting with Thompson, his memory affirmed what he had concluded then: that Thompson Hall was telling the truth. James had obviously caught him off guard, and in those unguarded moments there had been barely concealed disappointment that he had found nothing to prevent the marriage, but not a flicker of guilt or deceit. "I believe him, Alexa. And, he has a fairly airtight alibi for the time of the call. He was with Robert."

"Oh. So it *has* to be Hillary."

"But it wasn't. She's in Dallas now, apparently enjoying her role as the spurned wife, or at least capitalizing on it. Anyway, because I didn't want to leave Washington, I had someone who Elliot recommended check up on her. It turns out that on the day of the accident, she was actually in Savannah at the Willows. As part of the tranquil environment of the spa, guests at the Willows don't have phones in their rooms. There's just one phone, in the main office, and Hillary didn't use it at all during her three day stay." James paused, and then added slowly, "She didn't personally make the call at four Wednesday afternoon. But, Alexa, that doesn't mean she didn't have someone make it for her, and it doesn't mean she didn't hire someone to tamper with your car."

"No one tampered with my car, James! I was upset. I was driving too fast and lost control. Fortunately, I had the sense to jump clear."

"But you don't remember that."

"No, but that's what happened. I'm sure of it. No one I know is capable of murder, James," Alexa whispered softly, wanting to believe it, no, *believing* it, because it was too horrible to believe anything else. She added with a trembling smile, "Not even Hillary. Besides, Hillary could have very easily achieved what she wanted—the end of my plans to marry Robert—by simply letting me know that she knew about the baby. She didn't need any treachery beyond words. I think, had she known, she would have told me in person, reveling in that final victory." Alexa paused, sighed softly, and continued quietly, "But someone knows, someone from the hospital, I suppose. It hardly matters who knows, or even if they know anything more than that I had a baby girl I gave away. What matters is that someone knows something, and whatever it is, it's enough . . . too much."

As Catherine heard the resignation in Alexa's voice and saw the hopelessness as the emerald eyes envisioned a life without Robert, she realized that Alexa was still planning to say good-bye to her love.

"You have to tell Robert, Alexa." Catherine's voice was soft, as always, but it was laced with urgency. "He needs to know."

"Oh, Cat, how can I tell him? The truth would cause him such sadness, such pain. I love him far too much to tell him."

"But that's wrong, Alexa, don't you see? Yes, of course, this truth will cause Robert great sadness, but not too much, not more than you yourself live with every minute of every day. And maybe if you and Robert shared the sadness, the pain would be less for both of you." Catherine sighed softly, so very aware of the intense dark blue eyes that gazed at her. *You may not believe this, James, but I do!* "Robert loves you *so much*, Alexa. I know you want to protect him, because you love him, but isn't that terribly unfair to him, and to your love?" She took a breath, and her sapphire eyes didn't look at his dark blue ones, they couldn't, as she added quietly, "Maybe all loves aren't strong enough to survive both joy and sadness, but surely the love you have with Robert is."

As Alexa listened to Catherine's soft, impassioned words, she began to feel something that felt miraculously, wonderfully, like hope.

"My wise little sister," she whispered gently.

"I'm not wise, Alexa."

"Well, I think you are. You always have been. You're right, Cat. I do need to tell Robert." *I need to,* she thought, *but can I? Yes, I can, I will.* Alexa made the silent promise to her hopeful heart, and then she sealed it bravely by saying aloud, "I'll tell him tonight, while you're at the White House. Are you going to Cat's concert, James?"

The question startled him, because he had been so lost in memories, but he recovered quickly and answered with an easy smile, "No. I actually have quite a bit of work I need to do. Elliot likes to have an unofficial record of my overall impressions of the negotiations—and the

475

negotiators—and I need to get going on that while my memories are still fresh."

And besides, he thought, Catherine hasn't invited me to attend her concert. But it would be safe now, wouldn't it, Catherine? There would be no risk, now, that you would stop playing and leave the stage to be with me, where you belong, would there? James knew the painful answers to his questions without even looking at the beloved sapphire eyes. Yes, it would be quite safe. She had a new love now, a love that she so obviously believed was far deeper and far stronger than their magical love had ever been.

Chapter 29

After James and Catherine left, Alexa refused all the afternoon's scheduled pain medications. The frequent demerol shots made her groggy, permitting her trying-to-heal body to fall easily into necessary—and almost constant—sleep; and she needed to be wide awake when she told Robert the truth. The demerol was for pain, too, the doctors said, but Alexa had already decided, even though she had never used drugs, that she must have an innate tolerance. She was receiving lots of demerol, and although it made her sleepy, it did very little to numb the pain.

Or so she thought. As the afternoon wore on, and the demerol wore off, Alexa realized that the fire in her chest had simply been a smoldering

476

ember, prevented from flaming by the narcotic, and the immense aching in her muscles had been nothing—the ache of a weekend athlete who has overexerted—compared to the bone-deep pain she felt when the drug was withdrawn. And she had been completely unaware, under the constant influence of demerol, of the recent surgical incision in her abdomen.

Now the screams of her damaged bones and nerves and muscles and skin were unmuzzled, loud and piercing, keeping her very wide awake, even though her unnumbed battle against pain expended her precious and limited energy.

She was very wide awake when Robert arrived. Her beautiful pale face was haloed by shining gold, washed and brushed by a generous nurse, and she was propped up, positioned among pillows that, without the demerol, had lost their softness against her bruised and ravaged body.

"Hello, darling." Robert greeted her lips with a gentle kiss.

"Hello," she whispered. She wanted the gentle kiss to last forever, but she knew her energy was limited, and she had made promises to her heart. "Robert?"

"Yes, my love?"

"I know what the call was about."

"Tell me, darling," he urged softly. And then, because he saw such fear in her beautiful eyes, he assured gently, "Whatever it is, Alexa, our love is stronger."

Oh, Robert, how I hope that is true! She took a soft breath, and waited for the fiery flames in her chest to fade, and then she looked into his loving eyes and said very quietly, "The call was about a beautiful baby girl who was abandoned by her mother."

"Alexa?"

"She's our daughter, Robert. Katie is our baby."

"Oh, no." It was a long, slow whisper of pain. "Oh, Alexa."

As she gazed at him through the blur of her own tears, the screams of pain from her heart drowned out even the deafening screams of pain from all the unnumbed nerves in her badly battered body. Oh, Robert, how this has hurt you! her heart cried as she saw his stricken eyes, tear-filled, too, and so very wounded. I should have said good-bye to you, my love, instead of telling you, she thought. And then, as she watched his immense pain, Alexa was suddenly swept by a new fear. Have I caused you this anguish in vain? Will we say good-bye, after all, because this is far too great a truth for you to understand or forgive?

"Oh, Robert, I'm so sorry," she whispered softly, helplessly, as she tried desperately to reach the dark eyes that were so very dark now, so very turbulent, so very far away. "When I made the decision, I believed it was the best for Katie, for her happiness. And she is happy, Robert, and so very loved."

As Robert heard the hopelessness in Alexa's voice, he pulled himself from his swirling emotions and looked at the woman he would always love with all his heart. And when he saw her despair, and her fear, he echoed gently, "Yes, so very loved, Alexa. Katie is the most loved little girl in the world."

"Brynne's little girl, Robert?"

Robert knew what his beloved Alexa was asking with her trembling question. She was asking him to live this devastating secret with her and to conquer the immense sadness and loss with their love.

No! his heart cried in swift protest. Katie is *our* baby, *our* precious little girl. She loves us, and we love her. From the very first moment I held her, and every time since, there has been something so extraordinary, a joy beyond all words; and, my darling, whenever you and Katie are together, you're in your own special world, shared by just the two of you, a secret place of love. I've seen your special love for Katie, and hers for you, and now I understand it. Oh, Alexa, Katie is our little girl!

The protests came swiftly and powerfully. *But there were other places in Robert's loving heart.* And now it was their turn to speak, reminding him of his great love for Brynne, and of all her losses, and of his vow to protect her always. The gentle voices came with images—Brynne and Stephen and Katie together—and those were such joyous, such happy images, too, of love. The voices that spoke to Robert from the place in his heart where his love for Brynne lived were gentle and very compelling, but even they might not have persuaded him to abandon his wish to claim Katie as his own.

But then another voice spoke, a gentle, quiet voice that called to him from the greatest love of all, his love for Alexa. She had made this most generous decision of love, for Katie, for Brynne, and, even, Robert realized, for him; and she had lived with the excruciating pain of that decision every second of every day, hiding it, protecting them all. Now his beloved Alexa was asking him to live that painful secret with her. And Robert knew that he would, for her, because of her; and he knew, too, that he would never, not for an instant, allow her to doubt the decision of love that she had made.

"Brynne's little girl," he echoed finally, smiling a trembling, but so confident smile of love to her lovely, tearful emerald eyes. "I love you, Alexa. I love you."

He held her then, cradling her very gently, but she pressed closer and closer, and he held her ever more tightly, until they were so close, so tight, that there was no room between them for secrets, not ever again. And even though he held her bruised and ravaged body so tightly against his own, somehow, magically, there was no physical pain . . . and even the screams of pain from her heart were silenced now by his love.

"Robert? Alexa?"

At first Brynne's soft voice was simply part of the images that swirled in their minds, because, as they held each other, vowing to keep Alexa's promise of love, the images they both saw were images of Brynne: her hopelessness and anguish at the loss of yet another small beloved life, and her radiant joy as she loved her little Katie.

But after a moment, they both realized that the

soft familiar voice wasn't part of the images at all. It was real. She was here.

"Brynne," Robert whispered as he opened his eyes and gazed beyond Alexa's golden head to the smiling, slightly apologetic face of his little sister.

"I'm intruding."

"No," Alexa assured quickly, recovering far more quickly than Robert, because she had lived this secret for so long, and because she knew that now, especially now, everything had to seem quite normal—and normally, she and Robert wouldn't have considered it an intrusion at all for the sister they both loved to have found them embracing, especially not after Brynne had just made the trip from Richmond because of her love for them. Alexa found a beautiful, welcoming smile and said, "Hi, Brynne. Come in."

"Are you sure? I know I said I thought we'd arrive too late tonight to be able to visit, but Stephen was able to get away early after all . . .''

"Come in," Robert echoed, trying to sound as calm as Alexa, but having no idea whether he succeeded because his racing heart pumped sounds of thunder to his brain.

"Well . . . OK." Brynne smiled. "Thank you. How are you doing, Alexa?"

"I'm fine, Brynne." I will be fine, Alexa thought. Until now, she had been using her determined mind to try to convince her wounded body to heal. But, she realized now, it wasn't mind over matter that would work, it was heart over matter. She would heal quickly now, her heart

481

would see to it, so that she could be home with Robert. "I'm just fine."

"Good. I'm glad." Brynne knew she had intruded on something important. Maybe it had something to do with why she was here, and maybe not. At any other time, she would have gracefully withdrawn, but tonight she had her own important words to say, in private, to Alexa; and for her own heart, and for Alexa, she needed to say them now. And so, with an uncharacteristic and almost sassy smile, she looked at her older brother and asked, "Could I talk to Alexa alone, please, just for a little while?"

Normally, Robert would have teased her about "girl talk." But he couldn't be normal, not now, not yet. Now he very much welcomed the chance for a little privacy—assuming Alexa was comfortable. I'm fine, Robert, her emerald eyes lovingly told him, I love you.

"OK," he agreed. He gestured to the briefcase he always brought with him, work to do during the long hours while Alexa slept, but when he stayed anyway to be near her, and added, "I have plenty to do. I'll be in the waiting room."

After Robert left, Brynne removed the bulky winter coat she had been wearing, and, as she did, Alexa saw that not all of the bulk was the down-filled coat.

"Brynne," she whispered as she saw her future sister-in-law's very pregnant shape.

"She's a little girl, Alexa, a very healthy, very lively little girl," Brynne said softly, her brown eyes misting at what was still an almost unbelievable joy. "I'm already seven months along and the doctors say everything is going perfectly."

"Seven months?" Alexa echoed, frowning slightly as she recalled the last time she had seen Brynne. It had been less than a month ago, at Thanksgiving. Alexa had many joyous memories of that holiday weekend in Richmond, and she had a very clear memory of Brynne, how radiant she had been, how rosy her cheeks, how glowing—joyful signs of pregnancy, even though her body had been slender as always.

"It seems I have the kind of pelvis that allows the baby to grow, healthy but almost invisible, until quite late in the pregnancy."

Alexa nodded softly, fighting a deep ache as she thought, So do I.

Brynne crossed the small room and sat in the chair by the bed, pulling it as close to Alexa as she could be. Then she began, very softly, "She was conceived the night that Katie was born, sometime very shortly after James called to tell us." The pink in Brynne's rosy cheeks deepened slightly at the intimate admission, but it was necessary, part of the words she had come to say. "Stephen and I had decided to never try again, and that night it was quite unplanned, a symbol of our joy, I guess, at the miracle of Katie. And then Katie arrived, and somehow all the happiness and love that came with her made it possible for this tiny new life to grow and flourish inside me. I truly believe that, Alexa. I truly believe that this healthy little girl, this miracle inside me, is because of the miracle of Katie." Brynne drew a soft breath, preparing her own heart, and then said very gently, "Because of Katie, and, Alexa, because of you. She's your baby girl, isn't she?"

The sudden tears in the emerald eyes gave Brynne her answer, even though it was a while before Alexa could speak, or even nod her golden head. She nodded finally, slowly, to the dark brown eyes that were tear-filled, too, and, after a few more moments, she whispered, "How did you know?"

"I didn't know, not for sure, until this moment. And it didn't even occur to me, not consciously at least, until your accident. Robert told me about the mysterious phone call that was clearly so upsetting to you, and about his own fear that there had always been a secret you'd kept from him. It all came together then, at a conscious level, even though my memory had been recording images of you and Katie together for a long time, especially that first day, when I watched you holding her and you didn't know I was there. I know you tried to hide it, and if it weren't for the accident I don't know when or if I would have realized, but now I do." Brynne paused, because even though she and Stephen had discussed it over and over, and had agreed, and even though it was what her own loving heart wanted and believed, it was still so terribly difficult. "Now I do know, Alexa, and what I want, and what Stephen wants, is for Katie to be with you."

"Oh, Brynne," she whispered, a whisper of tears and joy and disbelief. "Oh, Brynne."

"Robert loves Katie," Brynne continued, speaking more of the words she had planned to say, to convince Alexa, even though the emerald eyes needed no convincing. "It won't matter to him, not at all, who her father was. He will love her as his own."

"Robert is Katie's father," Alexa said quietly.

"Oh," Brynne breathed with a rush of emotion. With Stephen's gentle help, she had carefully prepared her heart, as much as was possible, for this conversation with Alexa. But this revelation was completely unanticipated. She had believed, because they had both told her so convincingly, that their love had begun just last summer, after Robert's separation from Hillary and two months after Katie had been born. Now, as Brynne learned this new truth, her heart and her eyes flooded with fresh tears. "Does he know?"

"I told him just before you arrived."

"And you'd decided never to tell me, hadn't you?" Brynne asked softly.

Alexa's soft shrug gave her the answer, and in the next moments of silence, as they gazed at each other through the blur of even more tears, both realized the gifts of love that each had been so willing to give, and the secrets of love that each would have been so willing to keep. In those silent moments, Brynne realized that Alexa and Robert had decided never to tell the truth about Katie, and that they would have kept that solemn vow; and, in those silent moments, Alexa realized that once Brynne had guessed the truth, even if she hadn't been blessed with the miracle that lived within her now, she would have come to her and spoken the words she had spoken tonight.

"I love you," Alexa whispered finally.

"I love you, too," Brynne answered quietly. Then, with a soft smile, she stood and announced decisively, "Well. Why don't I go get Robert? We have plans to make."

Brynne found her brother alone in the small, windowless waiting room. Robert hadn't opened his briefcase, of course. He had spent the private moments sitting with his elbows on his knees and his head in his hands, absolutely motionless, even though his heart pounded and his thoughts whirled.

"Robert?"

"Brynne," he said, looking up, his eyes unfocused at first, but focusing quickly as he saw her pregnancy. "Brynne?"

Brynne gazed at the brother who had spent his lifetime protecting her, and would have protected her still, keeping this painful secret, and said softly, lovingly, "I'm having a baby girl, a cousin for Katie."

She saw the joyous comprehension in his dark eyes, and for the first time in her life she saw tears. Always before, even as a little boy, Robert had hidden his tears from her, bravely protecting her from all the sadnesses he knew so well. But now he didn't hide his tears, these tears of joy, not sadness, and as they moved to hug each other she whispered, "Oh, Robert, what loving cousins our daughters will be."

After the White House concert, and after dining with the President and First Lady, Jane,

Alexander, and Catherine returned to their hotel, located directly across the street from Memorial Hospital. Catherine stopped briefly in her parents' room, long enough for Alexander to call the hospital to make certain that Alexa was all right, and, upon learning that she was, she kissed them good night.

But Catherine didn't go to her room down the hall. Instead, still wearing the long green velvet skirt and ivory silk blouse beneath her winter coat, she walked into the chilly midnight air and across the street to the hospital. Alexa was out of the ICU now, and on the ward, where visiting hours were more strictly enforced. The evening visiting hours had long since ended, of course; but it was Christmastime, when any patient who could be home was home, and Catherine knew that the rules had softened for those who had to remain. After waving at the nurses, and receiving friendly conspiratorial waves in return, she walked quietly to Alexa's room.

The door was ajar. Catherine drew a soft breath before looking in, a hopeful wish that she would find Alexa sleeping peacefully. That was what she hoped to find, but she had come tonight in case Alexa was still awake, unable to fall into a peaceful sleep because of tormenting memories of telling Robert the truth. Her heart skipped a sad, sympathetic beat when she saw that Alexa was awake, propped up against pillows, gazing outside at the midnight darkness. But, as she neared, Catherine saw a soft smile, dreamy and most peaceful, on Alexa's beautiful face.

"Alexa?"

"Hi" Alexa answered, turning to her with a smile of surprise and welcome. "I'm so glad you're here. I was going to ask them to bring in a phone so I could call you." Her emerald eyes misted as she said softly, "Katie is coming home to us, Cat."

"Oh, Alexa. How . . . ?"

Alexa told her in a breathless rush of joy and tears, completely ignoring, as she had ignored for hours, the flames in her chest as she drew the deep necessary breaths at the end of each rush.

"Brynne and Stephen and Katie are across the street, in the same hotel as you, and they've said you're welcome to meet your niece whenever you want."

"Really? You're sure that it's all right?"

"Yes. This is difficult for Brynne and Stephen, of course," Alexa said quietly. "But they are being so wonderful, so generous. They're going to stay here until I'm ready to be discharged, and then Katie and Robert and I will begin our life together at RoseCliff." Their life together would begin at RoseCliff, and, someday they would move into a larger home; but they would never live in the White House. It didn't matter, Robert had reminded her gently. She mattered and Katie mattered. And, he had told her between tender kisses, even though he would leave public office, he would never leave public service, nor would his commitment to helping insure a joyous and peaceful world for his wife and daughter ever waver. Alexa smiled at those loving memories, and her emerald eyes sparkled as she told Catherine the rest of the plans they had made. "Robert and I will be married as soon as it can be arranged, definitely before I leave the hospital and before you and Mom and Dad leave."

"I don't have to leave on the twenty-sixth, Alexa, and even though Dad has performances scheduled with the symphony, I'm sure they could get an alternate and—"

"Oh, no, Cat. I'm going to be ready for discharge by the twenty-sixth, or the twenty-seventh at the very latest. In fact, I was just informing my body of that when you arrived." She smiled, remembering the silent instructions she had been issuing, the joyous commands of heart over matter. She would heal, in record time, for her daughter and her husband. "And once I'm discharged, and Katie and Robert and I are at RoseCliff . . ."

"You'll be the family of three that you want to be," Catherine gently finished the thought. "And that's all you'll want or need."

"Yes," Alexa answered softly, grateful that Cat understood. "I think we need time alone together."

"I think so, too. OK. We'll all leave as scheduled on the twenty-sixth, but I'll be back, whenever you're ready for visitors, and I know that Mom and Dad will be counting the days . . ." Catherine stopped abruptly as she saw the sudden look of doubt in Alexa's face. "Alexa?"

"Oh, Cat, I'm so afraid to tell them about Katie."

"What?" Catherine asked, not questioning the reality of Alexa's fear, because she saw the sudden

489

emerald uncertainty, but amazed, astonished, that it would exist. "Afraid, Alexa? Why?"

"Because I know they'll be so disappointed—not about Katie, of course—but in me, because I gave her away."

"No, Alexa, they won't be disappointed. They'll understand perfectly why you did what you did. I know they will."

Alexa softly shook her golden head. She knew very well that she was going to once again disappoint the parents she loved so much—even though she saw such confidence in her little sister's eyes. Oh, those wise sapphire eyes. How Alexa wished she could believe them this time! But this time, Cat, she thought sadly, I know that you are wrong.

"Alexa . . ."

"Could you tell them for me, Cat?" she asked suddenly, on impulse, her voice soft, uncertain, almost desperate. Alexa knew the great love, the extraordinary closeness, between her parents and Cat. Maybe . . . "Maybe, if you explained to them they *would* understand. You know everything about why I made the decision that I made, and we were planning to tell them this visit that I knew you were adopted, remember? So, maybe, you could tell them about that, and how close we are now, and how it was because of what I did that you told me?"

Catherine knew Alexa was wrong. Their loving parents would not be disappointed. But, she wondered as she listened to Alexa's soft impassioned plea, what if *she* was wrong? She wanted to spare Alexa that sadness, all sadnesses.

"All right, Alexa," she agreed gently. "I'll tell them."

"We just met our beautiful granddaughter," Jane said, her voice filled with love and wonder as she greeted her golden-haired daughter the next morning.

"She's very lovely," Alexander added with quiet emotion.

Alexa looked at them, and even though she saw love, and not a flicker of disappointment, she whispered softly, "I'm sorry."

"Sorry, my darling. *Why?*" Jane asked, genuinely incredulous, even though she was a little prepared. After Catherine had told them everything—and they hadn't been disappointed, not for a second, only sad and concerned about the silent anguish Alexa had endured—she had told them, too, about Alexa's worry. She repeated softly, "Why, Alexa?"

"I thought you'd be disappointed that I gave her away."

"No, darling. We understand. It was a courageous choice made from the deepest of love." Jane gently touched her daughter's silky golden hair, just as she had on that distant day in the park when she had tried to gently reassure Alexa about her new little sister. "We've never been disappointed in you, Alexa."

"Oh, but you were, don't you remember? You were so terribly disappointed in me when I first saw Cat and didn't want her to be my sister. Don't you remember?"

"We'll never forget those moments, Alexa,"

Alexander answered softly. "We weren't disappointed in you, darling, not at all. We were stunned that you so confidently announced that she wasn't your little sister, and that it upset you so, and I think we were both suddenly very worried that what we thought was truly a miracle was going to be a terrible mistake."

"We lost a little of you that day, Alexa," Jane added quietly. "You were always our happy, confident, golden girl, and after that . . ." She sighed softly. They had lost a little of their precious daughter that day, and, as desperately as they had tried, they had never, not in all these years of loving her, been able to rediscover that missing piece. Looking lovingly at the emerald eyes, so very much like her own, Jane whispered gently, "We love you so much, Alexa. You've never disappointed us, you never could."

Alexa listened to their wonderful words and wanted so much to believe them. But she had such a clear memory of that distant day. There *had* been disappointment then, she knew it. But, she wondered now, had the disappointment been her own, deep inside her, terrible disappointment at the discovery of the dark, ugly monsters that dwelled in her own heart? Yes, perhaps, *yes*. There had been ugly monsters within her, lurking in the shadows of her heart; but all those monsters were gone now, never to return, conquered and vanquished by love.

"It was truly a miracle. I love my little sister so very much," she said softly, her eyes lighted from within by a deep golden glow. Then she added, even more softly, as tears fell from the luminous emerald, "And Mom? Daddy? I love you so much, too."

Tears filled all eyes, and for a moment neither Jane nor Alexander could speak, because they saw in their beloved daughter's sparkling eyes the immeasurable joy of knowing, truly knowing, that she was loved completely, unconditionally, always. At last, oh at last, the Alexa they had lost was finally found! They hadn't seen this magnificent look of pure and confident happiness on her beautiful face for such a very long time, not since . . .

"You look exactly the way you looked on that morning in May when we were driving to Kansas City," Jane began emotionally; and when she faltered, Alexander gently and emotionally, too, finished his wife's thought, "Exactly the way you looked when you announced, with your unshakable confidence, that you were going to have a baby sister."

Chapter 30

Robert and Alexa were married on Christmas Day, a wedding joyfully witnessed by little sisters and parents, but not by James. He was invited, of course, but it was easier for him, for his heart, to stay away. He spent Christmas alone at Inverness, sailing until the winter twilight. He sailed all day the following day, too, and then worked late into the night completing the meticulous notes that he presented to Elliot in his office at eight on the morning of the twenty-seventh.

"I didn't expect these so soon," Elliot said. "This must mean all is well with Alexa?"

"All is very well. In fact, she's going home today."

"Is her family still here?"

"No. They left yesterday, her parents to Topeka, and Catherine to L'île."

"To L'île," Elliot murmured thoughtfully.

James watched Elliot's expression drift to the one he had seen before, when Elliot had spoken of the beautiful island paradise, and after a moment he offered quietly, "There's something about you and L'île."

"Yes, James, there is," Elliot admitted. He had been thinking about telling James sometime—as a gentle warning perhaps—because with each passing day he saw James becoming more and more like himself. Perhaps now was the time. "It's very old history, thirty-two years old to be exact, but it's the reason I am who I am today. Back then, I was a graduate student. I had won a two year scholarship to study philosophy at Oxford and had planned, eventually, to spend an idyllic and scholarly life as a professor at an Ivy League school. Anyway, during a summer holiday, I travelled to L'île, where I met, and fell in love with, Jean-Luc's first wife, Geneviève. Jean-Luc was in exile then in the south of France, and Geneviève had fled from him, seeking sanctuary on L'île because she knew he could not follow her there."

"And she was given asylum?"

"Oh, yes. Alexandre and his wife Isabelle welcomed Geneviève." Elliot smiled with fond remembrance as he added, "They welcomed both of us actually, and gave us privacy for our love. Geneviève and I had only three weeks then, but we knew we would spend our lives together. I had to return to England, and with Alexandre's help, Geneviève was going to end her marriage to Jean-Luc and join me. But shortly after I left L'île, Geneviève discovered she was already pregnant with Jean-Luc's child, the heir he wanted so desperately. She decided to return to him, to give him his heir in exchange for her freedom." Elliot sighed heavily, a sigh weighted with bitterness and regret. "I was so naive then. I had spent my life in the cloistered world of academia. And even Alexandre had underestimated Jean-Luc's evil. But how was he to know his brother's true treachery? Geneviève was the first of the many people Jean-Luc was destined to murder."

"Jean-Luc murdered Geneviève?" James asked softly, emotionally, realizing that it must have been that brutal death that had transformed Elliot from would-be college professor to master spy; just as his own parents' brutal murder had dramatically and irrevocably changed the course of his life, and of his love.

"It was never proven, but there's no doubt. A month after Geneviève gave birth to Alain, she was shot to death in Nice, twenty miles from the villa in which she lived with Jean-Luc. Alain was with her, and I've always wondered if, on that day, she was trying to escape, taking her infant son with her after all, because she couldn't bear the thought of leaving him with Jean-Luc."

"Oh, Elliot, I'm so sorry."

"So am I, James, still, after all these years." Elliot looked thoughtfully at James, knowing he didn't need to point out the obvious: that James was travelling down the same dangerous, solitary path. It was a useful path, of course, and undeniably challenging, but the path started in the name of love inevitably led to a life without any love at all. James knew. Elliot didn't need to tell him. After a moment, Elliot smiled, and, believing he was returning to a happier topic, he asked casually, "Is Catherine giving a concert on L'île?"

"No, Elliot, Catherine is in love with Alain," James answered with quiet apology. Alain . . . the man because of whom, perhaps, your beloved Geneviève lost her life. "They plan to marry."

James expected a wince of pain, a bittersweet acknowledgment of the irony, *something* other than what he saw on Elliott's handsome face— a gentle and approving smile.

"That seems appropriate."

"Appropriate?" James echoed with amazement. For some reason, Elliot seemed quite willing to accept the marriage of Catherine and Alain; just as he himself *should* have accepted it. She had obviously found great happiness with Alain, and James wanted happiness, only happiness, for her always; but still, to him, it felt so terribly wrong. "Appropriate, Elliot? Why?"

"Because Catherine looks so astonishingly like Isabelle Castille."

"Isabelle? Alexandre's wife?" James asked, and

as he did he suddenly felt a sense of ominous urgency; a feeling that was not yet tethered to conscious thought, but was nonetheless both terrifying and foreboding.

"Yes."

"I remember your telling me in Damascus that Jean-Luc became monarch because Alexandre had no children," James said quietly, as his bright mind began to decipher the ever more urgent, ever more terrifying feelings. "When was that? When did Jean-Luc assume the throne? Do you know?"

"I know everything there is to know about Jean-Luc Castille," Elliot answered softly. "He assumed the throne on January seventh nineteen sixty-eight. Why, James?"

James didn't answer right away. He couldn't. It was impossible, and yet, if it was true . . .

"James?"

"Catherine was born that same year, five months later, in May. Her mother had blond hair and bright blue eyes, just like Catherine's, and she told Jane Taylor, to whom she gave her infant daughter, that it was too dangerous for her baby to stay with her. Catherine's mother offered Jane a velvet satchel filled with jewels, which Jane didn't take, but she did accept, to give to Catherine on her twenty-first birthday, a sapphire necklace. Jane got the feeling that Catherine's father was dead; but because her mother asked that Alexandra be Catherine's middle name, she believed that his name had been Alexander."

As Elliot listened to James's words, his expression changed from polite yet skeptical to alert, concerned, and very interested. As soon as James stopped speaking, Elliot took a small key from the top drawer of his desk and, after inserting it into a side drawer, removed the large battered envelope that contained the only tangible memories of the love that had been so brutally taken from him—a few treasured letters and a few precious photographs.

Elliot kept the envelope in his desk, an unnecessary reminder of why he did what he did, but in truth it had been years since he had opened it. Seven years, to be exact. The envelope of memories had been last opened, and then closed, perhaps forever, when he learned of Jean-Luc's death. Elliott knew there was at least one small black and white photograph of Isabelle, but, until he looked, he had forgotten entirely about the photograph from *Life* magazine. As he unfolded the magnificent picture of the Princess, he realized that his memory hadn't been playing tricks at all about Catherine's remarkable resemblance to her.

"This is Isabelle," Elliot said as he handed the *Life* photograph to James. "It was taken in the palace garden at Monaco the day that Prince Rainier married Princess Grace."

"Elliot, you know this is Catherine," James whispered. "And . . . this is the necklace she was given on her twenty-first birthday. Oh my God."

"What?"

"Last summer, when Catherine was performing in Vienna, her necklace—*this* necklace, Elliot—was stolen. It wasn't the only theft in

498

the hotel that night, but the others were probably done to cast suspicion far away."

"Far away from whom?"

"From Alain. Elliot, we need to get to Catherine—*now*. She's in very great danger. As Alexandre's daughter she, not Alain, is the legitimate heir to L'île, isn't she?"

"Yes, James, but as far as we know, Alexandre and Isabelle Castille never had a child."

"Haven't you been listening? They did, *Isabelle* did, after Alexandre died. Isabelle had to give Catherine away because she knew Jean-Luc would never allow her to take the throne from him."

"Even if that's true—and in a moment I will make a call to learn if it is true—there is no reason to assume that Alain knows."

"But Alain *does* know. Catherine told me herself that he knows everything about her." How well his aching heart remembered her words: Alain knows everything about me, James, *everything,* and I know all his secrets, too. "And she believes Alain has been honest with her, too, but in reality he has simply charmed her with lies. She's his *cousin,* after all, and he's told her none of this."

"You're painting Alain Castille to be a very evil man, James."

"Just like his father, Elliot. Alain is Jean-Luc's son, remember? He is the son of the man who murdered the woman you loved. Oh, that's it, isn't it? You're blinded to Alain's evil because he's Geneviève's son as well."

"Perhaps," Elliot admitted softly. "But, James,

I've never been the one to make decisions about Alain Castille. I've purposefully stayed very far away from the investigations and allowed others to interpret the findings without my influence. I guess I have always hoped that Geneviève's son would have more of her goodness than Jean-Luc's evil, but, James, that has always seemed to be the truth."

"Until now."

Elliot didn't answer. His answer would have been simply a wish, and what he needed to do now was begin the search for the truth. He dialed an overseas number that he knew by heart—InterPol. After a brief conversation, and a short silent wait while computers at the other end whirred, Elliot had the telephone number to the château in the Loire Valley.

Louis-Philippe's two children and five grand-children spent every other Christmas with Isabelle and Louis in their château. The grand-children were there this holiday, scampering around the vast estate, filling the silent halls with gleeful laughter. When Elliot's call came, all five grandchildren were in the kitchen helping their mothers and Isabelle prepare dinner.

Louis-Philippe answered the transatlantic call in his study. Isabelle had told him about Elliot and Geneviève, so he recognized Elliot's name at once. The solemnness in Elliot's tone made Louis-Philippe lure Isabelle from the kitchen with just a gentle smile, waiting to tell her it was Elliot until they neared the quiet study.

"Elliot Archer?" she echoed softly when Louis

told her. How long had it been? Isabelle knew the answer without thinking. Elliot had called her in late December, shortly before Alexandre's death, a gentle call of sympathy and love. She had almost told him then about her pregnancy. She might have told him, and asked for his help in hiding her, had she imagined that Jean-Luc would begin following her the instant Alexandre died. And now Elliot was calling, *almost precisely* twenty-two years later to the day, and her voice trembled just a little as she spoke into the phone, "Elliot?"

"Hello, Isabelle. I need to ask you something. I'll just ask it bluntly and if the answer is no, we'll talk of other things."

"What, Elliot?"

"I need to know, Isabelle, if you and Alexandre had a daughter."

"Oh, Elliot," she breathed, eloquently answering his question with emotion. "Have you found her? Is she well? Is she safe? Elliot!"

"Did you give her to a woman in a hospital in Kansas City, Isabelle? Did you give her the sapphire necklace?"

"Yes! *Yes!* Elliot, where is she? Please tell me!"

"She is well, Isabelle," he answered quietly. And was Catherine safe? Elliot didn't know, but he would do everything in his power to see that she was. "She is very lovely. She is very much like you."

"Elliot, I have to see her."

"You will. I'll call you back within the hour."

After he hung up, Elliot stared at the silent phone for several moments before looking at

501

James. Finally he said quietly, a soft astonished sigh, "OK. Catherine is the Princess of L'île. I'm not sure how to proceed."

"Get her the hell away from Alain."

"As far as we know, Alain has done nothing wrong. A necklace stolen on a night when other jewels were taken from other hotel guests does *not* suggest that Alain is responsible. And, James, it is *not* a crime to marry a cousin, assuming Alain even has any idea that that's what he's planning to do."

"He knows."

"We have no evidence that any crimes have been committed, James, no reason to think that Catherine is in any danger whatsoever." Even as Elliot spoke, he frowned slightly, taunted by another ghost from L'île's past.

"What, Elliot? Something is worrying you."

"I was thinking about Alexa's accident."

"Why?"

"I got the impression from the interviews I saw with Lieutenant Baker that he was worried about foul play."

"He considered the possibility because there was nothing to indicate that Alexa had tried to avert the accident. The investigation went nowhere because the car was completely destroyed and Alexa has no memory of the moments immediately preceding the crash. *Why,* Elliot?"

"I was thinking about a woman named Monique."

"The French intelligence agent who was sent

to investigate Alain and ended up falling in love with him."

"Yes. I don't remember telling you about her."

"You didn't. Natalie did."

"Did she tell you how Monique died?"

"A car accident," James whispered as a tremor of pure fear swept through him.

"Monique was an expert driver, very comfortable with the hairpin turns of the roads along the cliffs of the French Riviera. It was never really clear what made her lose control of her car that day. Alain was following in his car and was an eyewitness to what happened. He said she made no attempt to stop or swerve before the car left the cliffs, as if, perhaps, she had passed out at the wheel. The car was completely destroyed, and the police had no choice but to conclude it was an accident."

"It was Catherine, not Alexa, who answered the phone at RoseCliff," James said with quiet horror. "The message, about a beautiful little girl whose mother had abandoned her, could have been for Alexa, but it also could have been for Catherine. And it was Catherine who was driving Alexa's car that day. Alain Castille is a murderer, Elliot. He murdered Monique, and he tried to murder Catherine."

And she's with him now, halfway around the world, his mind spun with restless horror. *I should never have let her go. I should have told her that I love her. I should have asked her if we could try again.*

"OK," Elliot said calmly, even though his heart raced, too. "You use the phone in the outer office.

Get us on the afternoon Concorde. That will put us in Nice by midnight. Then call Isabelle, have her meet us in Nice, but don't let her know that our eventual destination is L'île. I don't want her going on ahead of us. As of this moment, Alain is a suspect in an attempted murder. That means I can, and immediately will, put in place a team of agents who will watch him and Catherine. He's a suspect, James, that's all. We haven't a shred of proof that any crime has been committed, and we can't move until we do. I mean it. He's like any other free man—presumed innocent until proven otherwise."

"I understand. But you're going to get the proof. You're going to find out that Alain Castille was in Washington on the day of Alexa's accident."

"I'm going to get people working on that right away. But James, if Alain was in Europe on that day, then what we're left with is the delicate issue of an innocent man who believes himself to be the legitimate monarch of L'île, and who has already lost one love, and who has, by extraordinary coincidence, fallen in love with his cousin."

"I don't think we're going to have to worry about delicacy with Alain Castille. I'm very sure he knows everything. Elliot, do you promise me that Catherine will be safe?"

"We have people on L'île, and I'll try to get someone into the palace," Elliot answered. It wasn't a promise. It was simply the best he could do. In the hours it would take to determine Alain's whereabouts on the day of Alexa's accident, he had to hope that Catherine herself would be vigilant.

At Isabelle's gentle but firm insistence, Louis-Philippe remained at the château with his children and grandchildren. I'll bring my daughter back, she told her husband. Isabelle made that brave promise, but in fact, her wishes were far less grand.

If she could just see her daughter, even from a distance, that would be so wonderful. And if somehow she could get close enough to see that there was joy in the blue eyes, proof that her baby's life had been happy, that would be a dream come true.

Isabelle's logical mind didn't dare wish for more, but her loving heart bravely did. What if they could meet and talk and touch? What if, for one precious moment, she could see love in the eyes she feared had hated her ever since they learned the truth?

When Isabelle met James Sterling at midnight in Nice, her heart began to believe in *its* wishes. This handsome man, who so obviously loved her daughter, was going to make all the wishes come true.

It wasn't until they were in their adjacent suites at Le Bijou on L'île that Elliot and James told Isabelle about the potential danger. She understood the danger perfectly, of course. She had known Jean-Luc, after all, and even though she, like Elliot, had hoped that Alain had escaped the madness, she knew it was quite likely that the little boy who had saved her life had not been able to save himself from his father's evil. She understood, and with regal dignity, she hid her heart-stopping fear.

The call for which they had been waiting, *waiting*, finally came. It was a definitive call, and it left them quite stunned.

"Alain was at Versailles all day and in his suite at the Ritz all evening. He didn't make a point of being seen, but he is recognized in Europe, especially in France, and he was definitely seen by many independent observers. There is absolutely no doubt about it, James," Elliot told the skeptical dark blue eyes. "Alain was not in Washington on the day of Alexa's accident."

"Well. That's wonderful," James said evenly. He knew, they both did, that Alain could have hired an assassin, as Jean-Luc often did. But that might take forever to uncover and he wanted to go to Catherine now. "So, it's just that delicate issue, isn't it? I'm sure I'll think of a way to handle that."

"You're going to the palace now?"

"You know I am." James stared evenly at Elliot and then, with a soft smile, turned to Isabelle. "I'm going to tell her that you're here, Isabelle. I'm going to bring her back with me."

"Oh, James. Thank you."

"Why don't you wait a little longer, James," Elliot suggested quietly.

"I thought you said Alain was in the clear."

"Yes, but there are some other things I'm having checked. I should know in about an hour."

"I'll look forward to hearing whatever it is when I get back."

Elliot gave a half-smile. The final details were the most farfetched of all. "OK. Just be careful."

"There's no danger, remember?"

Catherine finished playing Chopin's "Fantasy Impromptu" and smiled softly at Alain.

"*Magnifique,* Catherine."

"*Merci.*" She left the piano bench and joined him at the window overlooking the cove. She saw worry in his dark eyes and asked gently, "Alain?"

"There is something you need to know about me, Catherine."

"All right," she answered, a little surprised that with all they had shared, all their honesty, there was a secret, obviously very important, that Alain kept from her still. It didn't matter what it was, of course, but . . . "Tell me."

"I thought we could walk to the cave." *Where centuries ago the rogue Castilles hid their stolen treasures, and where now you will learn about the greatest thief of them all.* "We can go now, if you like."

"All right. I'll go change my shoes and get a sweater." Catherine smiled at his worried handsome face, and before leaving him, she kissed him very gently on the lips. "Wait for me here. I'll be right back."

Chapter 31

Catherine frowned as she entered her suite of rooms in the east wing of the palace. Someone

507

had drawn the heavy curtains, obscuring the lovely view and creating dark shadows. She felt the fear before her mind told her why; but eventually the memory came: the shadowy suite in Vienna.

Catherine shook off the memory as she crossed the darkened living room to the pink and cream bedroom with its satin and lace canopied bed. She saw the painting immediately, its elegantly carved gold frame propped up against the pink satin; but the magnificent painting's many meanings, and their significance, came more slowly, in layers. At first, she just saw the beauty, not even realizing for a few moments that the beauty was *hers*, a mirror image of her lovely face, framed in spun gold not black velvet. That realization was just beginning to dawn when she suddenly saw the horror.

The beauty and the horror were so out of place together . . . like carnage in paradise . . . like violence at a garden wedding . . . like a bomb on a sailboat at Christmas.

The throat of the beautiful woman in the portrait had been slashed. Fresh, glistening, bright red drops—of paint? of blood?—rolled down the painting, flowing from the slash over the sapphire necklace painted in oil and onto the real sapphire necklace—*hers*—that lay, with her sapphire earrings, on the cream-colored carpet.

"No!" the protest escaped her lips, a soft anguished scream, even though she had not yet begun to comprehend the meaning of what she saw. Catherine didn't comprehend, not yet, but she knew instinctively that it was a truth she would not want to know. It was yet another truth, she feared, that would tear her away from those she loved.

"Catherine? I thought I heard you scream," Natalie said as she rushed into the bedroom. As her eyes followed Catherine's to the portrait, she whispered softly, "Oh, no."

"Natalie? What does it mean? Do you know?"

"Oh, yes, Catherine. I know. It means our beloved Alain has gone mad," she whispered sadly. Very gently, Natalie guided Catherine away from the mutilated portrait and urged her to sit in one of the plush silk chairs. "Sit here for a moment, I think we have a moment, and I will tell you. You don't know about your real mother, do you, or about your connection to L'île?"

"No," Catherine answered shakily.

"The woman in the portrait is your mother."

"My mother?" Catherine echoed softly, starting to rise, to move, to rush back to the portrait. *My mother.*

Catherine started to rise, but she was gently yet firmly stopped by Natalie. "No, Catherine, please don't go back to look at it. I promise, when this is over, I will find you far happier portraits of her."

"Who is she, Natalie?" Catherine asked. Who is she? *Who am I?*

"Her name is Isabelle. She was married to my uncle, Alexandre. You are their daughter, Catherine, which makes you our cousin." Natalie paused a moment before quietly finishing the astonishing revelation to the stunned sapphire

509

eyes. "And that makes you, not Alain, the legitimate monarch of L'île."

No, Catherine's heart answered defiantly, understanding before her swirling mind the painful implications of Natalie's remarkable words. If Natalie knows this, then surely Alain . . . *No,* it can't be. He would have told me. Finally, fearfully, she asked softly, "Alain knows this?"

"Yes. Of course he knows," Natalie answered with gentle sympathy. "Catherine, I know how difficult this is for you, how shocking, and I'm sorry that I have to tell you everything at once, and so quickly. But I must. We have so little time. All right?"

"Yes," Catherine herself agreed, even though, with each passing second, she became more and more confident that these were truths she did not want to hear. *But she had to.* She drew a deep breath and added bravely, "All right. Tell me."

"L'île is Alain's obsession. He loves his island more than anything in the world. Everything he has done has been done to protect this paradise. He hated what our father did to the island, making it a haven for criminals and terrorists not the rendezvous for poets and lovers that it was meant to be. That is why," she explained as softly, as gently, as was possible for the words she had to speak, "when he could stand the desecration no longer, Alain murdered Jean-Luc."

"No!" Catherine countered swiftly in instant defense of the man she loved. But who was the man she loved? Where was he? Did that gentle, loving man even really exist? She had just learned that Alain had betrayed their love, in which their

510

trust had meant so very much, by concealing from her the most important secret of all; and now Natalie was telling her, her beautiful dark eyes solemn and sorrowful, that he was a murderer. Catherine knew that her Alain, the man she had loved, was not. But, she realized, she was learning now about an Alain she didn't know. "Murdered, Natalie?"

"Yes," she replied sadly. "Alain murdered Jean-Luc, and, although I'm certain it was unintentional, because she rarely accompanied Jean-Luc on his trips, he murdered my mother, too. Unlike Jean-Luc, Alain derives no pleasure from murder. Every murder he has committed has been of necessity, necessary deaths so that L'île would flourish under his loving rule."

"Every murder?" Catherine echoed with crescendoing horror, horror at the brutal facts themselves, and horror that she was beginning to believe them.

"Alain also had to kill Monique. He loved her deeply, as I know he truly loves you, Catherine." Natalie sighed softly. "But, I suppose, he feared she would discover that it was he who had assassinated Jean-Luc. Alain fears losing L'île, and it is a fear far greater than the fear of losing his own life. He fears losing L'île, and that, dearest cousin, is why he tried to murder you last Wednesday in Washington. Oh, Catherine, I'm so sorry. I should have known when Alain insisted so firmly that I go ahead to Gstaad while he remained in Paris for another day."

Natalie softly shook her fire-lit auburn hair and then made a confession laced with apology and love, "I am a little blinded by my love for my brother. You yourself know that there is such gentleness in Alain, such goodness—it is not his fault that he is condemned to suffer our father's madness! I have known of his madness, and denied it, praying it would vanish. But now the madness is out in the open, the portrait proves it. Alain's intent to murder you is clear. I fear he may have already murdered Isabelle."

"Oh, no," Catherine whispered, a soft whisper of despair.

"I don't know that he has killed her, Catherine," Natalie added swiftly. "The portrait only makes me think so. But I promise you, when all this is behind us, if Isabelle is alive, you and I will find her. Right now, my cousin, you must leave L'île."

"We both must leave, Natalie," Catherine said, her voice suddenly quite decisive and calm. She was accepting the truths now. She had to. The proof was here, in this lovely bedroom. And there was more proof echoing in her mind—the whispered message about the beautiful baby girl who had been abandoned by her mother. The message had been for her, not Alexa, and it had been delivered to her because Alain recognized her voice.

"No, Catherine. I must stay with Alain. Even though his madness is now full-blown, I know that my brother will not harm me. I can subdue him, I'm sure of it. Perhaps this overt sign of his madness is a desperate plea to have it over with at last. If he could spend his days in an asylum where he could see flowers and listen to music . . .

well, I don't know if it is possible, but Catherine, please try to forgive him. He cannot help his madness."

"I'll stay, too, then. We'll subdue him together."

"No, it's not safe for you here. You must believe that, and you must leave now. Later, when it is safe, you can return to claim the island that is rightfully yours, and if you will allow it, I will remain here, too, and we will be cousins, and I hope we will be friends." Natalie smiled softly, a smile of hope, then her beautiful face became focused and solemn. "You must leave, Catherine, *now*. Take the speedboat. It's very easy to handle. Head due north—there's a compass beside the steering wheel—and you will arrive in Nice. Wait here while I get the keys for you. Lock the door behind me and only open it when you know it's me. *Bien?*"

"Oui Natalie, bien. Merci."

She should have waited for Natalie in the living room of her suite, but after throwing the dead bolt lock, Catherine returned to the bedroom and stood before the slashed portrait of her mother.

"Please be alive," she whispered. "Please be alive so that I can tell you I understand what you did, and that I love you."

Catherine gazed at the unseeing sapphire eyes in the portrait, smiling, joyous, hopeful eyes, and when she could no longer see the face because of the blur of her own tears, she knelt on the floor and carefully gathered the red-splattered gems. The red was ink, not blood, she discovered as she wrapped the necklace and earrings in a lace handkerchief and put them in her pocket.

While Catherine waited in the shadowy room that was so like her shadowy suite in Vienna, her thoughts drifted to that night, and to the knife wounds that had been intentionally superficial, not lethal. Why hadn't Alain killed her then? she wondered. What sinister madness had made him need to toy with her, luring her to his kingdom only to charm her into his web of treachery and deceit? She had survived that night in Vienna, because Alain had permitted her to survive. But what if she wasn't so lucky this time? What if, in the next moments a living shadow leapt from the darkness, and the knife sliced deeper, mortally wounding?

If she died here today would there be words of love she should have spoken to those she loved, and hadn't? "Mom, Daddy, I love you," she had said those words over and over in the past year, and she would call her parents again, as soon as she was safe in Nice and tell them again. And if she didn't make it to Nice? Catherine knew that, if she died, there would not be words of love left unspoken to Alexander and Jane. And what about the words of love to Alexa? No, Alexa too knew of her deep love. But, still, how Catherine wanted to speak again with her big sister . . .

She smiled softly as she imagined that future conversation. First she would say, with quiet apology, that it should have been she, not Alexa, who made the almost lethal drive. "Nonsense!" Alexa would exclaim, dismissing Catherine's worry with a loving smile and a graceful wave of her hand. Then, after waiting patiently until she saw that Catherine's worry was indeed vanquished, her emerald eyes would suddenly sparkle and she would announce, "I always *knew* you were a princess, Cat!" To which Catherine herself would reply, very softly, "Yes, Alexa, but have I told you, directly enough, that all I ever wanted to be was your little sister?"

She and Alexa would have that conversation, *please,* but even if she never escaped from L'île, Catherine knew that Alexa knew all the truths about her love.

If she died now, today, there would only be one beloved person to whom the honest words of love had not been spoken.

I must live. I must live so that I can go to him and gaze bravely into the dark blue eyes that filled with such joy at the airport that day and tell him of my love, still, always, forever . . .

Please let me live so I can tell James how much I love him.

"James Sterling?" Alain echoed with surprise when he was informed that James was in the marble foyer awaiting a response to his request to speak with the Prince. "Yes, of course I will see him. Please show him in."

As he waited, Alain was swept with waves of fear and worry. There could only be one reason that James was here: Catherine. Had James come to tell Catherine that he loved her still? And if he did, would she go away with him? *No,* Alain answered in silent defiance. Catherine will not leave me.

515

"Hello, Alain."

"Hello, James."

"I've come to invite Catherine, and you of course, to dine with me and Catherine's mother this evening at the hotel."

"Jane is here? At the hotel? I don't understand."

"Not Jane, Alain . . . Isabelle." James saw surprise, but not confusion, in Alain's dark eyes, and after a moment he continued with quiet rage, "You knew. You bastard."

"Yes, James, I knew," Alain answered with matching quiet, but unlike James's, his voice filled with sadness not anger.

"And you weren't ever going to tell her, were you?"

"I was planning to tell her everything this evening, James."

"What a remarkable coincidence. I don't believe that for one second, of course, but it doesn't matter. I know the truth now, and I will make very certain that Catherine knows it, too."

"You don't know the truth, James."

"Don't I? Why don't I tell you what I know, Alain? I know that you and Catherine are cousins. I know that she is L'île's legitimate monarch. And I know that you are an impostor."

"You are partially right, James, and partially wrong." Alain sighed softly. He knew that he would have to tell James the truth; it was the only possible way he could convince him to leave. "Catherine is L'île's legitimate monarch, and indeed I am an impostor. But I am a far greater pretender than you imagine. Where you are

516

wrong is in your belief that Catherine and I are cousins. We are not. Catherine is Alexandre's daughter, but I am not Jean-Luc's son. I'm not a Castille. I am not related to Catherine at all."

"Who are you?"

"I don't know. I only know the science. My blood type is AB. My mother was type B. which means my father had to be A or AB. Jean-Luc—and Alexandre—were both type O. I'm an impostor prince, James, but there is no pretense in my love for Catherine. I love her with all my heart, and she loves me. I believe she will love me still, and will choose to marry me still, after she has learned all the truths."

Yes, James thought, lovely, generous Catherine will be able to hear your truths and forgive them all.

But there are other truths she needs to hear.

"I don't think you understand, James, about Catherine's ability to love," Alain continued quietly in response to the frown on James's face. "She loved you very deeply once, but you didn't trust her love as I do. You hurt her terribly, far more, I think, than you will ever know."

"I know I hurt her, Alain. I did it in the name of love, but I realize now how foolish that was. I still love her. I still want our love. Catherine doesn't know that, not yet, but after you tell her your truths, I am going to tell her mine."

"So be it," Alain replied softly. "The choice, all the choices, will be Catherine's."

"And I choose Alain," Catherine announced as she walked into the music room. The shortest route from her suite to the cove was along a

517

hallway beyond the music room. She could have passed swiftly and safely, unobserved by Alain, but her stealthy dash had stopped abruptly when she had heard James's voice. She had heard his voice, the sound before the words, and as she approached she had heard the words, *I still love her. I still want our love. Catherine doesn't know that* . . . And now I know, James, and it is what I want, too. But for now I must pretend that our love doesn't matter to me. She repeated softly, speaking to the dark brown eyes of the madman, afraid even to glance at the dark blue ones for fear of revealing her heart, "I choose Alain."

As Catherine walked to Alain, she saw love, not madness, in his eyes. Love, and hope, and a soft, wistful sadness. She wondered at the gentle sadness, and then she realized with a rush of compassion, Alain knows his own madness. It is beyond him, a demon he cannot control, and perhaps, as Natalie suggested, he simply wishes his torment were over. It's almost over, Alain, Catherine promised as she smiled lovingly into his dark eyes. It's almost over.

"I think, Alain, that I need a few moments with James. I would like to explain to him privately about our feelings for each other. Will you wait here while he and I walk to the cove and back?"

"Please don't leave with James, Catherine," Alain whispered with such soft desperation that her heart ached for him.

"Just to the cove and back, Alain."

"There are things I need to tell you, Catherine."

"Yes, I know. I will return very soon to hear them."

"You need to hear them from me, not from James. Catherine, please, let James go now. Meet him later, if you must."

Catherine saw sudden turbulence in Alain's dark brown eyes and feared further provoking his barely controlled madness.

"All right, Alain. I will stay." James will escape now, she thought, and later, after Natalie and I together have helped you, I will join him. "I will stay."

"No, you will go, Catherine." The words, a quiet yet powerful command, came from Natalie. "You and James will take the speedboat and go now."

Natalie stood in the doorway of the music room. In the minutes since giving Catherine the keys to the speedboat, she had changed into a long white satin gown and had adorned her beautiful auburn hair with flowers. She looks like a bride, Catherine thought. She has created a tranquil and soothing vision for Alain.

But like the beautiful portrait in Catherine's suite, the image was confused, and there was unexpected horror mixed in with the tranquil beauty. Because, in her delicate hand, Natalie Castille held a gun. Beauty and violence . . . half-warrior, half-bride.

"James can go now, Natalie," Catherine answered softly. "I will stay with you to help Alain."

"Help me?" Alain asked, taking his worried eyes for a moment from the terrifyingly powerful semi-automatic weapon and looking questioningly to Catherine. "What help do I need, Catherine?"

"I know what you've done, Alain," Catherine replied gently. "Natalie told me everything. It isn't your fault. It is a madness you inherited from Jean-Luc. You love L'île so much. I know, Alain, and I understand."

"What do you know, Catherine?"

"She knows that she is the missing princess," Natalie explained softly.

"I had no idea that you even knew of her existence, Natalie," Alain said quietly, returning his gaze to Natalie and the gun.

"Oh, yes, Alain. Of course I knew. I heard Jean-Luc tell you the story a hundred times."

"Then isn't it wonderful, Natalie, that we have found our cousin?" Alain asked softly as he moved toward her, just a few steps, just enough to put himself between the gun and Catherine. The gun was from Jean-Luc's arsenal, he assumed, hidden by Natalie before he himself had given the command that all weapons be destroyed. What else had Natalie saved from Jean-Luc's reign of terror? More guns? Grenades? *Plastique?*

"Wonderful? Oh, no, Alain. It isn't wonderful at all. L'île is yours. I gave it to you because I knew how you loved it. Catherine can't have L'île, and she can't have you."

"You gave me L'île, Natalie? How?"

"By getting rid of Jean-Luc." Natalie made the announcement with childlike pride, her crazed eyes suddenly innocent and expectant, as if awaiting well-deserved praise for the gift she had given. When no praise came from Alain for the murder of her own father, she explained, using the simple and terrifying logic of her own madness, "I knew that as long as Jean-Luc was alive you would stay away from L'île, and from me. I gave L'île to you, Alain, and I would have given myself, but I knew, since we shared the same father, that you would never touch me. And that was fine, enough!" Natalie's voice aged then, maturing in instants from a disappointed child to a jilted lover, and her eyes flashed as she demanded, "Why couldn't it have been enough for you? Why did you have to fall in love with Monique?"

"Oh, Natalie," Alain whispered softly as he realized that it had been his own blindness to Natalie's madness that had cost the life of the woman he had loved so much. He had been quite blind to Natalie's fatal obsession with him, and he should have been so aware! His own boyhood had been spent witnessing Jean-Luc's obsession with Isabelle. But Natalie had inherited Jean-Luc's cleverness and charm, as well as his madness, and Alain hadn't seen it. "Oh, Natalie."

"Monique had to die, Alain," Natalie said simply, without remorse, but with a slight trace of impatience at his surprise at a death that was so obviously necessary. "Everything was better after that, remember? We were together again, with no intrusions on our privacy."

"I remember," Alain answered quietly as he recalled the immense grief that had kept him on

L'île, a grief that had seemed, for a very long time, refractory even to the island's miraculous healing powers.

"But it didn't last. You got restless. You needed to travel to hear your precious music again, and you even started welcoming visitors into our home." She sighed softly, like a long suffering wife, and her dark eyes narrowed as she scolded gently, "Oh, Alain, you should never have invited the Sterlings to spend Christmas here."

"Oh my God," Alain breathed. He wanted to turn to James, to utter his apology to James's face, but he didn't dare take his eyes from Natalie or turn his back to the finger clutched around the trigger of the lethal weapon. His eyes remained on Natalie—who was smiling triumphantly now as she recalled how successfully she had prevented the Christmas visit of Arthur and Marion Sterling—but he whispered to James, a whisper of grief and guilt, as if he were responsible for Natalie's madness, "I'm so sorry."

"Alain?" Natalie was pleading now, a desperate lover. "I love you. Everything I've done has been for you. Don't you see?"

"Yes, Natalie. I see."

"Then let James and Catherine go. Let them take the speedboat and leave us here, together. Alain, please!"

"All right," Alain agreed. Then, reconsidering almost instantly, he suggested gently, "I have a better idea, *chérie*. Why don't you and I take the boat?"

"Oh. Yes. Why don't we, Alain," she answered softly. "Catherine has the keys."

Alain turned to Catherine and took the keys from her delicate hand. There were words he wanted to say to her, such important words, but it was far too dangerous to speak them aloud, so he sent the silent message of love with his eyes. *I love you, Princess. You must always believe that. Be happy, my precious love.*

He smiled a trembling smile, a forever good-bye to the lovely and yet so bewildered sapphire; and then he looked to James, who had moved closer, ready to shield Catherine, as he himself had in case Natalie's madness suddenly erupted, and he asked, "Will you tell her, please, everything that I told you? It is the truth, James, every word of it, and I want her to know."

"Yes, Alain, I will tell her," James promised quietly.

"Thank you," Alain said softly before leaving them and crossing the room to Natalie. He extended his hands to her as he neared, hoping she would relinquish the lethal weapon, but she only took one of his hands and maintained her expert grasp of the gun. Alain had wondered if he would be able to get the gun and overpower her, but he realized at once that the danger would be too great. It didn't matter. All that mattered was that he get Natalie away from Catherine . . . forever.

Alain and Natalie left through the French doors that opened from the music room into the garden, and in a few moments they were visible beneath the window, walking hand in hand down the white marble path to the cove. As James saw them disappearing in the distance, his worry that Natalie might still harm Catherine subsided, and a new worry took its place. What was happening? It didn't make sense. Surely Alain could not believe they would escape. The speedboat was fast, a powerful state-of-the-art inboard, but still a piece was missing.

And then James knew. The boat was taking Natalie and Alain to a place that had nothing to do with speed . . . a place Natalie had wanted to send Catherine . . . a place where, in her madness, she was quite willing to go, as long as her beloved Alain would be there with her . . . forever.

"Oh my God."

"What is it, James?"

"I have to stop them."

He didn't explain. There wasn't time. He simply moved with graceful speed out the French doors and onto the white marble garden path. Catherine started to follow, but before she reached the French doors there was commotion behind her as a group of heavily armed men, led by Elliot Archer, burst into the music room.

"Elliot! It was Natalie. She—"

"Yes, I know. I just received word that she was in Washington last Wednesday. Where is she?"

"Down there, in the cove. Alain has convinced her to go away with him, but there's something else, something James just realized. He's down there, too."

"There must be a bomb in the boat," Elliot whispered.

"Oh, no!"

"Alain, don't do this!" James yelled when he reached the wharf.

"It is done, James. Let us go. Please."

James saw at once that he had no choice. Natalie still clutched the gun and there was wild fury in her eyes at his intrusion. He stopped but stood his ground as Natalie and Alain boarded the speedboat. Natalie boarded first, moving swiftly and decisively to what James assumed was the lethal ignition switch. She inserted the key and turned it; but the twist of her slender wrist caused a purr not an explosion. The bomb was connected to something else, James realized, just as it had been on the sailboat that had killed his parents. Something set to explode away from port—the throttle, perhaps, a certain lethal speed.

Alain cast off the ropes and looked to Natalie. Her hand was extended to him, a bride to a groom, a graceful invitation to join her in a forever love, and her eyes, crazed now, completely mad, glistened with rapturous anticipation. Alain moved to her with regal dignity, a monarch accepting all blame, even though none was his, quite willing to forfeit his own life to put an end to her madness.

As Alain moved toward Natalie, and the boat moved away from the wharf, James leapt onto the stern. When the boat rocked, signaling that he had boarded, Alain's eyes filled with sad surprise, and Natalie's glared with determined rage. As Alain turned toward James to urge him, or throw him, away from the boat, Natalie's hand grasped the throttle, moving it forward, closer and closer to eternity.

The boat lurched from the sudden acceleration . . . and then it exploded, a burst of fire erupting from the sapphire sea. The red-orange flames reached toward the sky, an orphan sun seeking its parent, and above the flames, like the dark thunderclouds that heralded the appearance of L'île's rainbows, were billowing mountains of ash and smoke.

There were flames and smoke in the azure sky.

And there were rainbows, too, thousands of them, in all the glistening places where the gasoline kissed the sea. The watery rainbows rose and fell with the waves, and they encircled the blazing inferno . . . a sea of rainbows around an island of fire.

Chapter 32

James came up gasping, his starving lungs finding more smoke and fumes than fresh salt air. He surfaced in smoke, not fire, and as his eyes strained to focus through the smoky veil, he saw a vision of white satin—a bride, floating amidst the rainbows and shrouded by the flowers that had adorned her auburn hair. James saw at once that Natalie was dead. And, he thought, like Ophelia, she looked so innocent in death, at peace at last, her madness finally conquered.

James did not see Alain, nor did Alain answer his frantic calls. James heard voices, of course, shouts from the wharf and closer ones, as men swam toward the fiery scene, but he ignored those voices. The only voice he wanted to hear was the voice of the man who had been so willing to give his life to save Catherine. And who *has* given his life, he thought grimly as his repeated calls to Alain were answered only by ominous silence.

Then James saw it, a red much darker than the red of the floating rainbows, a dark, dark red that beaded in small round drops on the surface of slick sheen of the gasoline. *Blood.* His? Natalie's? Or Alain's?

James dove beneath the hot toxic surface into the cool blue depths of the sea. The depths were cool, but they weren't blue. They were red, vividly colored by the blood that flowed freely from the badly wounded body of Alain. James wrapped his arms around Alain's lifeless body and carried it to the surface. The body was lifeless, deathly still, but he felt the frantic pumping of Alain's young healthy heart. The pumping was frantic, the fight for survival desperate and brave; and yet, with each powerful stroke, the hope for survival was critically undermined, because with every valiant heartbeat, Alain lost a little more precious blood into the sea.

This time when James surfaced, there were other swimmers nearby, strong uninjured men who took Alain's wounded body from his grasp and began to transport the Prince swiftly to the wharf. James waved off help for himself—he was quite alive, and Alain might not be much longer.

The men carrying Alain led the processional through the watery rainbows to the wharf. James followed, flanked by two men who swam nearby ready to assist him if he faltered. And behind them, at a somber distance, were the men carrying the white satin body of the Princess.

Elliot had arrived at the palace with a team of agents and had summoned medical backup the moment he realized there might be a bomb on the boat. The royal physician, as well as doctors and nurses from the clinic near the hotel, were waiting on the wharf. All the medical professionals began to attend to Alain the instant he was pulled from the water. But, as it became clear that there was more than enough help, one of the doctors left Alain to meet James when he arrived.

"I'm OK," James assured the doctor quickly, although he was surprised, as he followed the physician's worried gaze, at the extent of his own wounds. Some of his many cuts were quite deep, and there were burns, too. And they hurt, he realized, aware for the first time of the deep searing pain of gasoline and salt on his raw, torn flesh. Still, he repeated, "I'm OK."

"OK, yes, *monsieur*, with proper cleansing and dressing of these wounds. The gasoline will continue to cause damage to the tissues until we wash it away. I would like to take you to the clinic now."

"All right. Thank you. In a moment."

James needed to talk to Catherine. She stood close by, her eyes filled with worry, and Elliot, worried, too, stood beside her. James smiled at the doctor, a smile of gratitude and a promise to return soon, and then walked over to Catherine and Elliot.

"I'm fine," he assured them, too. He looked around briefly, to be certain there was complete privacy for his next words. There was. The activity on the wharf was focused on the frantic efforts to save Alain's life. Even James's doctor had returned to the wall of humanity that surrounded the wounded Prince. Confident that his words would not be overheard, James returned his gaze to the worried blue eyes and whispered softly, "I'm fine, Catherine, but Alain is very badly injured. He needs you."

James saw uncertainty in her eyes, the confusing and conflicting emotions about Alain, whom she loved, but who she believed had so cruelly deceived her.

"Catherine, listen to me. Alain's deception was not what you think. He's not your cousin. He's not related to you at all."

"He's not?"

"No. Alain is not Jean-Luc's son. He was going to tell you everything this evening. He was worried about telling you, but his fear was fear of losing you, not L'île." James stopped, seeing that these new truths merely added to the lovely sapphire confusion. After a moment, he told her a truth she already knew, the most important one, and one that she had once, so angrily, hurled at him. Very quietly, he said, "Alain loves you very much. Catherine?"

"Yes?"

"When Alain realized there was a bomb on the boat, he stopped us from leaving and chose to go himself. He knew that he would die, but he knew, too, that you would be safe. That was all that mattered to him. Do you understand that, Catherine? Do you understand what he did?"

"Yes, James," she answered softly to the man who seemed to have forgotten his own heroism. The moment James realized there was a bomb, he too had made courageous and compassionate choices. He could not stand by and watch an innocent man die. And, she wondered, even though James had once so coldly told her of his wish to fire a bullet into the heart of whoever had murdered his parents, perhaps, after all, he could not even stand by and watch Natalie die. "I understand what you both did."

Her brilliant sapphire eyes—brave and lovely and welcoming—met his, and for a magnificent moment James allowed himself to be lost in the magic. James knew he was lost, and, as always, he had no wish ever to be found, but . . .

"Alain needs you, Catherine," he whispered softly, breaking the magnificent magic spell. "He loves you, and he may be dying, and he needs your love."

"Yes," she answered quietly. Alain loves me, and he may be dying, and he needs my love. Catherine wondered if James heard his own words, and if he remembered that there had once been a time when he was dying too, a death of the heart and the soul, and had refused her love even though he needed it so desperately. She would go to Alain now, of course, and she would be with him for as long as he needed her to be, but the words James had spoken such a short time ago still sang joyously inside her, *I still love her. I still want our love.* But Catherine didn't see that message of love now in the faraway dark blue eyes. Had his loving words only been spoken to lure her away from the madman he had believed Alain to be? Were James's words of love as false as her own *I choose Alain* had been? It didn't matter now, because now she needed to be with Alain, but someday she would find out. She would see James again, *she had to,* because, no matter what, she would bravely keep the wish that she had wished for so desperately as she waited for Natalie to return to the shadowy suite, *Please let me live so I can tell James how much I love him.* I will tell him, she silently promised her loving heart. Then she said very softly to the faraway eyes, "Yes, James, Alain needs me now, and I will go to him."

James watched as Catherine crossed the wharf, and, with only the softest of words, she caused the wall of humanity to part so that she could be near Alain, touching him and whispering words of love. Once Catherine was gone from sight, James joined Elliot, who stood nearby at the edge of the wharf, his eyes fixed on the smoldering sea.

"You were right, Elliot. The motive for my parents' murder was completely personal. Natalie simply killed them because she was annoyed that they were intruding on her Christmas with Alain. And she killed her own parents, and Monique, and she tried to murder Catherine. And do you know what I feel about her death? Nothing. Not a whisper of relief." James paused, collecting his thoughts and emotions, preparing to say more words to Elliot. I even felt a little sad for her, Elliot, isn't that strange? And if I had been able to get the gun from her I would never have turned it on her, *never*. You were so right, Elliot, about the emptiness of revenge. James wanted to make those confessions to Elliot, to his face, but as James looked at him, trying to draw the other man's eyes from the sea, he saw pure emotion on the face of the master spy. "Elliot?"

"I overheard you tell Catherine that Alain is not Jean-Luc's son."

"Oh, Elliot," James breathed softly. That final revelation would have occurred to him, of course, quite soon, once he had any time at all to reflect on the afternoon of astonishing revelations. And now, as he realized, he very gently told Elliot what he knew, "Alain told me that his blood type is AB. Geneviève's was B and Jean-Luc's was O."

"And mine is AB." Elliot's eyes blurred with tears and he whispered emotionally, "He's my son, James. Alain is my son."

He had to be with him! He had to hold his son and tell him of his love for him. Please, *please*, before Alain . . .

But Elliot couldn't kneel beside Alain's wounded body and gently cradle his head as Catherine did. Elliot was in charge, and now there were questions to be answered about transporting Alain off the island. He was alive still, barely, the royal physician informed Elliot. Alain had many wounds and burns, like the nonlethal ones that James had, but he had one wound that could kill him quickly. It was quite simple, a deep knife-like laceration to his thigh, so deep that it severed a large artery through which a great amount of blood had been pumped into the sea. The bleeding was stopped now, by a probably too tight tourniquet, but they feared loosening the bind, even a little, because they knew that the loss of even one more drop of blood might cost Alain his life.

The emergency vascular surgery Alain so critically needed was unavailable on L'île. In moments the decision was made to fly him immediately to Nice. He would be flown in his own jet, accompanied by the necessary medical personnel but no extra passengers; not Catherine, who had spent the last few minutes telling him of her love; and not Elliot, who might never be able to tell his son of his.

Natalie's jet and pilot were in Paris, delivering gems to the Castille boutique, so it was decided that Catherine and Elliot would fly to Nice in one of the many seaplanes used to transport hotel guests from the Côte d'Azur to L'île. Elliot asked Catherine to wait on the wharf while he made the quick trip to the landing strip with the doctors and Alain. It was Elliot's responsibility to see that Alain made it safely off the island, of course. And even though it was impossible for him to whisper his love to Alain, he was able to see the face he had

533

never seen, and as he helped carry the stretcher up the steep path to the palace, Elliot was able to tenderly touch his son's lifeless hand.

Elliot had asked her to remain at the hotel, but the moment she heard the explosion, Isabelle had rushed to the palace, along with almost everyone else on the island, guided by the ominous plume of smoke and fire. She had been in the crowd that had assembled on shore but was kept off the wharf while Alain was there. When Alain was taken away, the crowd followed in somber procession behind their Prince, and Isabelle walked slowly, tremblingly, toward her daughter.

Catherine stood alone at the edge of the wharf, gazing at the sea, awaiting the arrival of the seaplane. There was no reason for her to take her eyes from the sea, no reason to turn at all.

But she felt herself turning, as if drawn by a most powerful magnet. And then there she was . . . the beautiful woman in the portrait, and for a breath-held moment of pain Catherine thought she must surely be a mirage, a wonderful and yet so cruel trick of her mind. But the cruelty—"I fear that Isabelle is dead"—had been Natalie's, spoken simply as a final tormenting sadness for the woman who had stolen Alain from her.

She wasn't a mirage, Catherine realized with wondrous joy. She was alive, and her sapphire eyes were crying and smiling and filled with such hope that the baby she had loved enough to give away would come to her now.

Catherine made the first trembling step, and then Isabelle moved too, and in only a moment they were close enough to touch. With brave and delicate wonder, Isabelle's trembling hands touched Catherine's tear-dampened cheeks, and she smiled the same loving smile that had joyfully caressed her baby girl so very many years before, and then her precious daughter was in her arms again, and Isabelle cradled her gently and whispered softly, "Catherine."

The mother and baby were together again, but Isabelle's baby girl was a grown woman now; and now, for the first time in her life, her beloved daughter spoke to her. And when she did, Catherine spoke in French, the beautiful language in which Isabelle had told her tiny infant over and over and over of her love.

"Maman." And then, because Catherine wanted Isabelle to know everything all at once— that she understood, and that her life *had* been filled with happiness and love, as Isabelle had prayed it would be—she softly whispered the greatest reassurance of all, the same promise of love Isabelle had given her, engraved in gold, *"Je t'aimerai toujours, Maman."*

The vascular surgeons in Nice expertly repaired the severed artery in Alain's leg, and as for the blood he so desperately needed, there were most willing volunteers. A rare and perfect match, the hematologists marvelled when they tested Elliot's blood and found that it was AB, just like the Prince's. Alain could receive any blood type, they knew, since his own AB made him a "universal recipient"; but it was wonderful that some of the new blood circulating in his healing body would be such a perfect match.

Elliot willingly, gratefully, donated his perfectly matched blood, and Isabelle donated, too; and, for the first time in Alain's life there truly was royal blood, Castille blood—Catherine's—flowing in his veins.

His severed artery was repaired, and his blood volume was replenished, but still Alain remained delirious for almost thirty-six hours. The delirium, the doctors explained, was due to a combination of factors—his prolonged shock, his near drowning, the aftereffects of the anesthesia, and the "toxic" effects of the gasoline and sea water that had seeped into his system through his deep open wounds.

Only Catherine was with Alain during his wakeful hours of delirium. She sat with him, softly trying to reassure the wild yet unseeing eyes. What terrifying images does he see? she wondered. Alain was obviously hallucinating, and it was obvious, too, that the distorted images of his delirious mind were quite horrifying; but, at least, when his terror-stricken eyes fell on her, even though there was no recognition, there was neither, for Catherine, any fear.

Elliot stayed away from his son's bedside during Alain's delirious wakefulness. He was a stranger to Alain, after all, and he didn't want his image to confuse Alain, nor to become in his son's hallucinating mind the disturbing image of a monster. But there were times when Alain was sleeping that Elliot was at his bedside, tenderly mopping the brow that became damp as, even in sleep, the images frightened and tormented still.

"Do you think that Geneviève knew Alain was my son, Isabelle?"

The doctors were with Alain, making their frequent rounds on the Prince, and Elliot, Catherine, and Isabelle were alone in the nearby waiting room.

"Oh, no, Elliot, I think not. Her pregnancy was apparent to her so soon after you left L'île that it seemed impossible that the baby could have been yours."

"But Alain was with her when she was killed."

"Yes. I think, as you wondered at the time, that she was trying to take him with her when she escaped. But, Elliot, she may have known only that she could not leave her son with Jean-Luc." She added quietly, "It's a certainty that Jean-Luc never knew the truth."

"No," Elliot agreed softly. "He would not have permitted Alain to live if he had."

Catherine listened in silence to the quiet and emotional conversation between her mother and Alain's father. It was a discussion to which she had nothing to add except her lovely expressions of gentle sympathy, expressions that were so very like Isabelle's.

Catherine had no words to add to Isabelle and Elliot's emotional reminiscence about L'île's long ago past . . . but she had a few very important words to say about L'île's future. And, when their conversation had ended, and the room had fallen silent, she spoke them.

"No one else ever needs to know the truth about Alain."

"Catherine?"

"No one else ever needs to know the truth about Alain, or about me."

They were just a few words, spoken with quiet confidence, but they were monumental words . . . a royal command . . . the first and last royal command Princess Catherine would ever give. The Princess of L'île had spoken, and her face had been solemn and regal as she did. Her beautiful face was regal still, after her quiet proclamation, but now once again there was the soft, lovely, uncertain smile of Catherine Taylor, not the confident princessly smile of Catherine Castille. And then she was a daughter again as she asked Isabelle hopefully, "Would my father have approved, Maman?"

"Oh, yes, my darling." Isabelle gently moved a long strand of black silky hair away from her daughter's beautiful face, a gesture of love between mothers and their babies, even when the precious small faces were fully grown. Catherine didn't pull away from the loving touch, as grown daughters sometimes did. Her sapphire eyes simply filled with joy. After a moment, Isabelle continued softly, "He would most definitely have approved. Because, above all, your father believed in love. He knew very well that the bonds of love are far stronger, and far more important, than the bonds of blood." Isabelle smiled, and as she drew her daughter to her, she whispered,

"Oh, he would have been so very proud of you, Catherine."

"*Bonjour*, Catherine."

"Oh, Alain, you have returned to us," Catherine answered softly. When she had left him at midnight, she had thought that his sleep had seemed deeper and less troubled, and now, seven hours later, his mind at last was clear. "*Bonjour.*"

Catherine kissed him gently on the cheek and then looked very carefully at his handsome face. She saw in the gentle dark eyes she knew so well that Alain was searching, trying to remember. He would, she knew, be completely unaware of everything that had happened after the explosion, but had he also lost some of the memory of the events that had come before? Did Alain, like Alexa, have retrograde amnesia? It would be best if he did, Catherine decided. She could very gently tell him the truth about Natalie, but she could spare him the details of her confessions in the music room, when her mad and fatal obsession for him had been so horrifyingly revealed.

"Alain?"

"I remember James following us to the cove. He jumped onto the boat just as we were leaving. I turned to him, to try to stop him, but it was too late." Alain closed his eyes briefly, as if trying to block out the next image; but it was there, and always would be, whether his eyes were open or closed. "Oh, Catherine, I remember the look on Natalie's face so well. Her eyes were wild and enraged, and yet, at the same time, so full of love for me, and she had a smile of such triumph. She looked like a beautiful little girl whose dream had finally come true." Alain sighed softly and asked quietly, "What happened?"

"Natalie died in the explosion, Alain. She was killed instantly."

Alain nodded. His pale handsome face conveyed sadness and grief; and the solemn recognition, too, that Natalie's death had been a blessing.

"And James?" he asked suddenly.

"James is fine."

"Oh, good. Is he here?"

"No. He has called, of course; to check on you. He returned to Washington late yesterday."

"Did he tell you the truth about me, Catherine?"

"Yes, Alain. He told me that you are not my cousin, and that you had planned to tell me everything that night, and . . ." *And that you love me very much.*

"Catherine . . ."

"I think that all the people who need to know that you are not Jean-Luc's son already know, Alain, and the same is true about the people who know the truth about me."

"What are you saying?"

"That L'île is yours and always will be."

"Oh, no, Catherine."

"Oh, *yes*, Alain." Catherine smiled lovingly at his disbelieving, and yet so hopeful, dark eyes. "You are the Prince and monarch of L'île des Arcs-en-ciel. It is right, Alain, and it is best.

Isabelle says that Alexandre would have very much approved."

Alain gazed at the sapphire eyes he knew so well, and loved so much, and he saw, in the shimmering confident blue, that she had made her generous decision of love and was happy with it.

"Catherine," he whispered softly, emotionally. "Thank you."

"You're most welcome."

Many moments passed before Alain was able to speak again. They spent the moments together, fingers intertwined, eyes tear-misted and loving, smiles gentle and trembling.

Catherine had given him L'île, a treasure of immeasurable value, the second greatest gift she had to give. Alain knew that her greatest gift—herself, her love—belonged to someone else. He had known that the moment James told him of his love, still, for Catherine. And now, when he could finally speak again, he searched for gentle words that would make it very easy for lovely Catherine to say good-bye to him.

"James told you my truths, Catherine, and did he tell you his?"

"No. We haven't spoken since just after the explosion." We haven't spoken since he told me to go to you, because you were dying and needed my love, she thought. And even when he has called the hospital to check on you, his calls have been for Elliot.

"But you heard what he said just before you walked into the music room."

"Yes, but I'm not that certain he meant it."

"Oh, Catherine," Alain assured lovingly, "he

meant it. I saw his eyes when he spoke of his love for you. James loves you very much.''

''Well,'' she answered with a soft uncertain shrug. ''I'm not sure. But, Alain, I need to find out.''

''And you will find that he loves you with all his heart,'' Alain predicted gently. ''How could he not?''

''Oh, Alain, I . . .''

''I understand about your love for James, Catherine. You told me all about it, remember?''

''Yes.'' I told you, Alain, because of your kindness and your warmth and your gentleness, and because . . . ''I love you, Alain.''

''I know that, and I love you, too.'' Alain smiled softly. ''Go now, darling. I will be fine.''

Oh, yes, Alain, you will be fine, Catherine thought as she met his gentle eyes. She saw his sadness at the loss of her love, but she saw, too, such hopefulness. No longer was he the impostor Prince of L'île, and no longer either would his loves be threatened by Natalie's madness. All the storm clouds have vanished, Alain, and there has been the most nourishing rain, and from now on, for you, there will be only the most brilliant rainbows. She smiled softly as she thought about his future happiness, and about the great happiness that would be his very soon . . .

''I will go now, Alain.'' Catherine kissed him gently and then said quietly, ''There is someone waiting outside who wants to see you.''

''Hello, Alain. My name is Elliot Archer.''

''Monsieur Archer,'' Alain replied with polite

surprise. "At last we meet. I have heard of you, of course. I know that it is you who have had me watched for all these years in a relentless search for treachery on L'île."

"Alain . . ."

"I resented the vigil, Monsieur Archer, but now I know that you were right to search."

"I'm not here to talk to you about the treachery on L'île, Alain," Elliot said softly. "I'm here to talk to you about the love."

"The love?" Alain echoed with matching softness as he saw what looked like tears in the dark brown eyes that were so very much like his own.

"Yes. The love. I want to tell you about your mother, Alain, and about your father . . ."

"Maman?" Catherine asked as she looked at the airplane ticket Isabelle had just handed her.

"For this afternoon's Concorde to Washington."

"But I'm going to the château with you to meet Louis-Philippe and his children and grandchildren."

"I think it is far more important for you to go to Washington. Didn't James tell Elliot that he would be leaving very soon to spend the next few months sailing in the Caribbean? You could search the Caribbean for him—and I think that is what you have quietly planned to do—but it seems more sensible to go to him now."

"But we've had so little time together."

"We have our lifetime, Catherine. Now that you are found, my precious love, I will never lose you again," Isabelle promised. "And Louis-

Philippe and I will definitely be in Topeka in February."

"Oh, good. I'm so glad."

"I am, too," Isabelle said, smiling softly as she thought about the joyous family gathering, to which she had been invited, that would happen on Valentine's Day. It wouldn't be a wedding celebration, because Alexa's wedding had already taken place; it would just be a joyous celebration of fathers and mothers and daughters and love. She would try once again, on that visit to Topeka, to thank Jane for loving her precious baby. She had tried a thank-you two days before, when she and Jane had spoken on the phone, but, for both of them, the words had been too quickly flooded by tears. But, Isabelle thought, Jane knew, because, from the very beginning, they had communicated through the silent messages of the heart; and two days ago, those silent messages of love had journeyed quite clearly and quite eloquently back and forth across the ocean. Isabelle gazed at the daughter who had been raised with such love and urged again gently, "We will be in Topeka in February. So, my darling, go to James now. Go to that wonderful man who loves you so very much."

Chapter 33

Inverness Estate, Maryland . . . December 1990

Catherine arrived at Inverness an hour before twilight. Snow fell softly from the pale gray sky, but the winter wind held its breath and the pure white world was very still. As she gazed at the unlighted mansion, a shadowy unsmiling silhouette, she realized that James wouldn't be inside; and she wondered, as she walked swiftly through the barren rose garden and across the lawn to the edge of the cliff above the bay, if he was already gone.

No, she saw with relief when she reached the ledge. *Night Wind* was still there, rocking gently in its moorings, and there were cheery golden lights on inside. James was obviously there, preparing his boat for its long winter sail.

As she looked at the sailboat three flights below, Catherine remembered the only other time she had made the journey down the cliff to the bay. Her mind had sent such urgent warnings on that warm August night. You can't do this! You can get down the stairs but you cannot climb back up.

But then she had gone with James anyway, because she had to.

Just as she had to go to him now.

And now, even though her fit slender body

could so effortlessly ascend the steep brick stairway, her heart told her bravely, You won't need to climb back up. James will want you to stay.

On that warm August night, Catherine Alexandra Taylor had known very little about who she really was. And now, on this snowy winter day, she knew everything, all the truths, and she was so very blessed with such wonderful love.

Catherine knew all the truths now, but there was a most important truth she had learned long ago, on that summer night . . .

When I am with you, James, I am everything I want to be.

James was on the wharf, securing a new rope to a cleat. He wore the scarf she had made for him, the soft and beautiful memory of the moonlit night when they had fallen in love.

James wore the gift of love she had given him a year ago, and Catherine wore the gift he had given her then, too, the brilliant sapphire earrings to be worn for concerts, for kissing . . . and for making love. Catherine wore the magnificent earrings, and she wore even more magnificent symbols of their magical love—her sparkling sapphire eyes, her flushed pink cheeks, and even the hopeful innocence that had been in hiding for so long.

"Catherine," James whispered with quiet joy when he saw her. "You're here."

"Yes," she answered bravely to the dark blue eyes that filled now with such hope, such happiness, and such love.

She had come today to say the words she had promised her heart that she would say. But he spoke first, because there were truths that he, too, had promised his heart he would speak.

"I was so very wrong, my darling. I should never have left our love. I didn't want to, Catherine, but I truly believed that I had to, and that it was best. But it wasn't best," he confessed softly. "At least, my love, it wasn't best for me."

"It wasn't best for me, either, James."

"Oh, Catherine, I'm so sorry I hurt you. I have only and always wanted to love you." His trembling hands touched her cheeks then, and as he cupped her beautiful face' the winter wind blew the softest of kisses, lifting her silky black hair and revealing the sapphire earrings she wore, symbols of love that had been violently stolen and now were found. Just like our magical love, he thought, as he whispered tenderly, "I love you, Catherine. I love you with all my heart."

"Oh, James," she echoed joyfully. "I love you, too."

As James touched his beloved Catherine again, all the gentle voices of his heart began to sing with joy; and as Catherine touched her beloved James again, her delicate fingers learned anew that touching him was a wondrous gift far greater than all her magnificent talent.

They touched, and kissed, and later, on that snowy evening, in their joyous and tender loving, James and Catherine discovered the most beautiful music of all.

IF YOU HAVE ENJOYED READING
THIS LARGE PRINT BOOK AND
YOU WOULD LIKE MORE
INFORMATION ON HOW TO
ORDER A WHEELER LARGE PRINT
BOOK, PLEASE WRITE TO:

WHEELER PUBLISHING, INC.
P.O. BOX 531
ACCORD, MA 02018-0531